1976

To Sister Mary Gerard

from

Joe and Joyce

Selected Stories

THE MACMILLAN COMPANY
NEW YORK · CHICAGO
DALLAS · ATLANTA · SAN FRANCISCO
LONDON · MANILA

IN CANADA
BRETT-MACMILLAN LTD.
GALT, ONTARIO

Selected Stories

MARY LAVIN

The Macmillan Company

NEW YORK 1959

First Printing

Printed in the United States of America

Some of these stories originally appeared in
*The Kenyon Review, Atlantic Monthly, Harper's
Bazaar, The Dublin Magazine,* and in *At Sally
Gap and Other Stories,* published by Little,
Brown and Company. "The Small Bequest" is
reprinted from *Good Housekeeping Magazine,*
copyright 1944 by Hearst Magazines, Inc. The
author and publisher extend their thanks to
these magazines and to Little, Brown and Company for permission to reprint.

Library of Congress catalog card number: 59-6293

Preface

YEARS AGO in the city of Dublin, high over the Liffey there was an old watchmaker. One day when I was a child I went up to his attic, with my father, to see if he would mend a small gold watch. Outside the attic window the sea gulls screamed, and against their screaming, the ticking, even of a hundred watches, was, at first, secret as the beating of the human heart. After a few minutes though, the whirr and tick prevailed over the outer noises and when the old man spoke I could not hear him. So he put out his hand for the watch. It was only then I saw his hands had some kind of ague. They trembled: they shook. And all down the front of his waistcoat and jacket, stains and slops of food showed how badly he was disabled. Surely my treasure was not to be entrusted to those hands? I hesitated, but, decisively, my father took the watch and put it on the work bench. Then, taking the man's hands he directed them downward, till braced by wrists against the edge of the table, they were able to fasten on the watch. Oh but the fixity, the sureness of those fingers when once they had entered the intricate world of their craft.

Is it too fanciful to think that an incident like this, that remains in the mind when so much else is forgotten, had more significance than could be supposed? Would it have echoed in the mind indefinitely if it did not, even at the time, awaken some self-knowledge, or forecast perhaps some event in the future? I know that when it was suggested that I write this preface I thought at once of that incident years ago. And I felt that like that old man, I too had applied myself so singly to the art of fiction that I had maimed, and all but lost, the power to express myself in any other form.

For I have done no book reviewing, I have written no critical essays. I have never kept a journal, nor even a notebook except to put down the isolated words and phrases that shine suddenly in a writer's mind, unrelated to any thought or emotion; single as the stars. Letters? Oh, yes, I write thousands of letters a year I am sure, but these are for the most part so inconsequential, often fantastical, that they are by-products of the imagination and not exercises in lucidity. Ever since I first started to write a story in the middle of writing my Ph.D. thesis on Virginia Woolf—a thesis which I immediately abandoned—I have never, as far as I can recall, with the exception of a few words recently about my farm for a farming journal—I have never written a single paragraph that has not had its source in the imagination.

I do not state this as if I thought it generally commendable. I cannot honestly say if my real work gained or lost by my scrupulosity. I do not know. But *I am* curious about this and all other questions concerning the mystery of imaginative creation. Preoccupations of this kind continually fill my mind. And when nowadays young people write to me or call to see me to talk about my stories I would like to be able to satisfy their rightful curiosity. But only in my stories can I feel certain that I will not want unsaid tomorrow what I say today: only the stories seem to have finality and be immutable.

But how is the unchanging story written? Quite simply I must say that for me the writing of stories is a way of being. And I feel certain that if I were to go back over the incidents of my life, particularly those of childhood, I would see how daily I was being shaped to this end—story writing.

And yet I came late to the craft. Before that first erratic impulse I had absolutely no yearning to write. Indeed I would never have presumed to think I could until I made a sudden sally at it. Once started, though, there was no question of ever reaching an end.

Not that I have ever given much time to putting things down on paper. All my writing life, over twenty years now, the actual writing down of stories has been done in snatches of time filched from other duties, and particularly of late years when I have had to run the farm from which we get our livelihood. It has often been suggested to me that I would make a better livelihood out of writing than out of the farm if I did not neglect one for the other. But to me it has always seemed that this would be impossible. One was life: the other only its echo.

There was a time after I first started to write when I resented having so little time for stories. I used to think, with some bitterness, that if I were to cease writing altogether it would be months, even years, before anyone in my household would notice that this had happened—if they ever did! But now all that resentment has gone from me, and I believe that the things that took up my time, and even used up creative energy that might have gone into writing, have served me well. They imposed a selectivity that I might not otherwise have been strong enough to impose upon my often feverish, overfertile imagination. So if my life has set limits to my writing I am glad of it. I do not get a chance to write more stories than I ought; or put more into them than ought to be there.

But how much is that? I think I begin to know. I even wish that I could break up the two long novels I have published into the few short stories they ought to have been in the first place. For in spite of these two novels, and in spite of the fact that I may write other novels, I feel that it is in the short story that a writer distills the essence of his thought. I believe this because the short story, shape as well as matter, is determined by the writer's own character. Both are one. Short-story writing—for me—is only looking closer than normal into the human heart. The vagaries and contrarieties there to be found have their own integral design.

Because of this conviction that in a true story, form and matter are one, I cannot attach the same importance as the critics to brevity and relevance. It is surely significant that the great short stories of the world have often been studded with irrelevancies. It is to the magical risks that have been taken with the short story that we often owe their most magical embellishments. It is a question whether we really want perfection in this medium as much as we are told that we do in the textbooks. Do we? And if we do, how is it that the early stories of Chekhov can give such pleasure, and the unfinished stories of Katherine Mansfield such satisfaction? Much as we rejoice in the universality of art I think art speaks with its fullest voice when the note of particularity is not lost in that of universality, nor time in that of eternity. Do we really want perfection to such an extent that we can bear all trace of the maker to be lost in his creation? I only ask this question.

There must be many other questions, though, to which I ought to be able to make some answer. There are many things that I have noticed about the habits or compulsions of the creative impulse. It is not possible, or fortunately even desirable, to do so in a short preface, but there is a small observation that might not be out of place. If there was one thing I was not interested in, it was birds. Yet when I had published a number of stories people began to comment on the amount of images I drew from bird life. I saw that this was so with some surprise. Birds abounded in the stories. Numerous as midges they flew about the pages, now flashing a wing, now trilling a note, now dropping a feather. I at once began to be consciously aware of birds and birdsong, and ever since have had therefrom deep pleasure. So too, many of the things about which I wrote in the early years were not then experienced, and yet I think I wrote of them with greater ease and greater intensity than I did later. Intuitive imagination can focus more directly upon the object of its interest than memory or direct observation.

What else is there to say? Have I a good memory? No. I lack almost entirely the power to recreate the past at will. I live too intensely in the moment to lay up a conscious store of observations. Yet details of things I have seen come back to mind when I am writing and fit into the place where they are needed. Does this seem to contradict what I said in the beginning, that the story was all there, form and matter from the start? I do not think so, for shape and size are not the same, and there is artifice needed to reduce or raise a detail to the proportion proper for making it striking or appealing. And it is here that devices of concentration, poetic association and above all implication are sometimes needed. To interpret these devices the reader must be sensitive, alert and above all willing to come forward to take the story into his own mind and heart. Is it not partly his from the moment of its conception? To whom does a story belong; to the writer or to the reader for whom it was written? To whom does the echo belong; to the horn or to the valley?

Mary Lavin

Contents

PREFACE   v

THE WILL   1

CHAMOIS GLOVES   16

ASSIGH   32

POSY   54

THE CEMETERY IN THE DEMESNE   74

THE LITTLE PRINCE   98

MY VOCATION   140

THE SMALL BEQUEST   151

A WOMAN FRIEND   176

BRIGID   192

A WET DAY   201

A HAPPY DEATH   213

The Will

"I couldn't say what I thought while he was here!" said Kate, the eldest of the family, closing the door after the solicitor, who had just read their mother's will to the Conroy family. She ran over to her youngest sister and threw out her hands. "I cannot tell you how shocked I am, Lally. We had no idea that she felt as bitter against you as all that. Had we?" She turned and appealed to the other members of the family who stood around the large red mahogany table, in their stiff black mourning clothes.

"I knew she felt bitter," said Matthew, the eldest of the sons. "We couldn't mention your name without raising a row!"

"She knocked over the lamp, once," said Nonny, the youngest of the unmarried members. "Of late years she always kept a stick beside her on the counterpane of the bed and she tapped with it on the floor when she wanted anything, and then one day someone said something about you, I forget what it is they said, but she caught up the stick and drove it through the air with all her force. The next thing we knew the lamp was reeling off the table! The house would have been burned down about us if the lamp hadn't quenched with the draught of falling through the air!"

"Still even after that we never thought that she'd leave your name out of the parchment altogether. Did we?" Kate corroborated every remark by an appeal to the rest of the group. "We thought she'd leave you something anyway, no matter how small it might be!"

"But I don't mind," said Lally. "Honestly I don't. I wish you

1

didn't feel so bad about it, all of you." She looked around from one to the other beseechingly.

"Why wouldn't we feel bad!" said Matthew. "You're our own sister, after all. She was your mother as well as ours, no matter what happened."

"The only thing I regret," said Lally, "was that I didn't get here before she died." The tears started into her eyes.

"I don't think it would have made any difference whether you got here in time or not before she went. The will was made years ago."

"Oh, I didn't mean anything like that!" said Lally in dismay, and a red blush struggled through the thickened cells of her skin. "I only meant to say that I'd like to have seen her, no matter what, before she went."

The tears streamed down her face then, and they ran freely, for her mind was far away thinking of the days before she left home at all. She made no attempt to dry her eyes. But the tears upset the others, who felt no inclination to cry. Having watched the old lady fade away in a long lingering illness, they had used up their emotional energy in anticipating grief. Their minds were filled now with practical arrangements.

"Don't upset yourself, Lally," said Kate. "Perhaps it all turned out for the best. If she had seen you she might only have flown into one of her rages and died sitting up in the bed from a rush of blood to the forehead, instead of the nice natural death that she did get, lying straight out with her hands folded better than any undertaker could have folded them. Everything happened for the best."

"I don't suppose she mentioned my name, did she? Near the end, I mean?"

"No, the last time she spoke about you was so long ago I couldn't rightly say now when it was. It was one night that she was feeling bad. She hadn't slept well the night before. I was tidying her room for her, plumping up her pillows and one thing and another, and she was looking out of the window. Suddenly she looked at me and asked me how old you were now. It gave me such a start to hear her mention your name after all those years that I couldn't remember what age you were, so I just said the first thing that came into my head."

"What did she say?"

"She said nothing for a while, and then she began to ramble about something under her breath. I couldn't catch the meaning. She used to wander a bit in her mind, now and again, especially if she had lost her sleep the night before."

"Do you think it was me she was talking about under her breath?" said Lally, and her eyes and her open lips and even the half-gesture of her outstretched hands seemed to beg for an answer in the affirmative.

"Oh, I don't know what she was rambling about," said Kate. "I had my mind fixed on getting the bed straightened out so she could lie back at her ease. I wasn't listening to what she was saying. All I remember is that she was saying something about blue feathers. Blue feathers! Her mind was astray for the time being, I suppose."

The tears glistened in Lally's eyes again.

"I had two little blue feathers in my hat the morning I went into her room to tell her I was getting married. I had nothing new to put on me. I was wearing my old green silk costume, and my old green hat, but I bought two little pale blue feathers and pinned them on the front of the hat. I think the feathers upset her more than going against her wishes with the marriage. She kept staring at them all the time I was in the room, and even when she ordered me to get out of her sight it was at the feathers in my hat she was staring and not at me."

"Don't cry, Lally." Kate felt uncomfortable. "Don't cry. It's all over long ago. Don't be going back to the past. What is to be, is to be. I always believe that."

Matthew and Nonny believed that, too. They told her not to cry. They said no good could be done by upsetting yourself.

"I never regretted it!" said Lally. "We had a hard time at the beginning, but I never regretted it."

Kate moved over and began to straighten the red plush curtains as if they had been the sole object of her change in position, but the movement brought her close to her thin brother Matthew where he stood fingering his chin uncertainly. Kate gave him a sharp nudge.

"Say what I told you," she said, speaking rapidly in a low voice.

Matthew cleared his throat. "You have no need for regret as far as we are concerned, Lally," he said, and he looked back at Kate who nodded her head vigorously for him to continue. "We didn't share our poor mother's feeling. Of course we couldn't help thinking that you could have done better for yourself but it's all past mending now, and we want you to know that we will do all in our power for you." He looked again at his sister Kate who nodded her head still more vigorously indicating that the most important thing had still been left unsaid. "We won't see you in want," said Matthew.

When this much had been said, Kate felt that her brother's authority had been deferred to sufficiently, and she broke into the conversation again.

"We won't let it be said by anyone that we'd see you in want, Lally. We talked it all over. We can make an arrangement." She looked across at Matthew again with a glance that seemed to toss the conversation to him as one might toss a ball.

"We were thinking," said Matthew, "that if each one of us was to part with a small sum the total would come to a considerable amount when it was all put together."

But Lally put up her hands again.

"Oh, no, no, no," she said. "I wouldn't want anything that didn't come to me by rights."

"It would only be a small sum from each one," said Nonny placatingly. "No one would feel any pinch."

"No, no, no," said Lally. "I couldn't let you do that. It would be going against her wishes."

"It's late in the day you let the thought of going against her wishes trouble you!" said Kate with an involuntary flash of impatience for which she hurried to atone by the next remark. "Why wouldn't you take it! It's yours as much as ours!"

"You might put it like that, anyhow," said Matthew, "as long as we're not speaking legally."

"No, no, no," said Lally for the third time. "Don't you see? I'd hate taking it and knowing all the time that she didn't intend me to have it. And anyway, you have to think of yourselves." She looked at Kate. "You have your children to educate," she said. "You have this place to keep up, Matthew! And you have no one to look after you at all, Nonny. I won't take a penny from any of you."

"What about your own children?" said Kate. "Are you forgetting them?"

"Oh, they're all right," said Lally. "Things are different in the city. In the city there are plenty of free schools. And I'm doing very well. Every room in the house is full."

There was silence after that for a few minutes, but glances passed between Kate and Nonny. Kate went over to the fire and picked up the poker. She drove it in among the blazing coals and rattled them up with such unusual violence that Matthew looked around at her where she knelt on the red carpet.

"Do you have to be prompted at every word?" said Kate when she got his attention.

Matthew cleared his throat again, and this time, at the sound, Lally turned toward him expectantly.

"There is another thing that we were talking about before you arrived," he said, speaking quickly and nervously. "It would be in the interests of the family, Lally, if you were to give up keeping lodgers." He looked at her quickly to see how she took what he said, and then he stepped back a pace or two like an actor who had said his lines and made way for another person to say his.

While he was speaking Kate had remained kneeling at the grate with the poker in her hand, but when he stopped she made a move to rise quickly. Her stiff new mourning skirt got in her way, however, and the cold and damp at the graveside had brought about an unexpected return of rheumatism, and so as she went to rise up quickly she listed forward with the jerky movement of a camel. It couldn't be certain whether Lally was laughing at Matthew's words, or at the camelish appearance of Kate. Kate, however, was the first to take offense. But she attributed the laughing to Matthew's words.

"I don't see what there is to laugh at, Lally," she said. "It's not a very nice thing for us to feel that our sister is a common landlady in the city. Mother never forgave that! She might have forgiven your marriage in time, but she couldn't forgive you for lowering yourself to keeping lodgers."

"We had to live somehow," said Lally, but she spoke lightly, and as she spoke she was picking off the green flies from the plant on the table.

"I can't say I blame Mother!" said Nonny, breaking into the discussion with a sudden venom. "I don't see why you were so anxious to marry him when it meant keeping lodgers."

"It was the other way round, Nonny," said Lally. "I was willing to keep lodgers because it meant I could marry him."

"Easy now!" said Matthew. "There's no need to quarrel. We must talk this thing over calmly. We'll come to some arrangement. But there's no need in doing everything the one day. Tomorrow is as good as today, and better. Lally must be tired after traveling all the way down and then going on to the funeral without five minutes' rest. We'll talk it over in the daylight tomorrow."

Lally looked back and forth from one face to another as if she was picking the face that looked most lenient before she spoke again. At last she turned back to Matthew.

"I won't be here in the morning," she said hurriedly, as if it was a matter of no consequence. "I am going back tonight. I only came down for the burial. I can't stay any longer."

"Why not?" demanded Kate, and then as if she knew the answer to the question and did not want to hear it upon her sister's lips, she continued to speak hurriedly. "You've got to stay," she said, stamping her foot. "You've got to stay. That's all there is to say about the matter."

"There is nothing to be gained by my staying, anyway," said Lally. "I wouldn't take the money, no matter what was said, tonight or tomorrow!"

Matthew looked at his sisters. They nodded at him.

"There's nothing to be gained by being obstinate, Lally," he said lamely.

"You may think you are behaving unselfishly," said Kate, "but let me tell you it's not a nice thing for my children to feel that their first cousins are going to free schools in the city and mixing with the lowest of the low, and running messages for your dirty lodgers. And as if that isn't bad enough, I suppose you'll be putting them behind the counter in some greengrocers, one of these days!"

Lally said nothing.

"If you kept an hotel, it wouldn't seem so bad," said Matthew looking up suddenly with an animation that betrayed the fact that he was speaking for the first time upon his own initiative. "If you kept an hotel we could make it a limited company. We could all take shares. We could recommend it to the right kind of people. We could stay there ourselves whenever we were in the city." His excitement grew with every word he uttered. He turned from Lally to Kate. "That's not a bad idea. Is it?" He turned back to Lally again. "You'll have to stay the night, now," he said, enthusiastically, showing that he had not believed before that it was worth her while to comply with their wishes.

"I can't stay," said Lally faintly.

"Of course you can." Matthew dismissed her difficulties unheard. "You'll have to stay," he said. "Your room is ready. Isn't it?"

"It's all ready," said Nonny. "I told them to light a fire in it and to put a hot jar in the bed." As an afterthought she explained further. "We were going to fix up a room for you here, but with all the fuss we didn't have time to attend to it, and I thought that the simplest thing to do was to send out word to the Station Hotel that they were to fix up a nice room for you. They have the room all ready. I went out to see it. It's a big airy room with a nice big bed. It has two windows, and it looks out on the ball alley. You'll be more comfortable there than here. Of course, I could put a stretcher into my room if you liked, but I think for your own sake you ought to leave things as I arranged them. You'll get a better night's rest. If you sleep here it may only remind you of things you'd rather forget."

"I'm very grateful to you, Nonny, for all the trouble you took. I'm grateful to all of you. But I can't stay."

"Why?" said someone then, voicing the look in every face.

"I have things to attend to!"

"What things?"

"Different things. You wouldn't understand."

"They can wait."

"No," said Lally. "I must go. There is a woman coming tonight to the room on the landing, and I'll have to be there to help her settle in her furniture."

"Have you got her address?" said Matthew.

"Why?" said Lally.

"You could send her a telegram canceling the arrangement."

"Oh, but that would leave her in a hobble," said Lally.

"What do you care? You'll never see her again. When we start the hotel you'll be getting a different class of person altogether."

"I'll never start an hotel," said Lally. "I won't make any change now. I'd hate to be making a lot of money and Robert gone where he couldn't profit by it. It's too late now. I'm too old now."

She looked down at her thin hands, with the broken fingernails, and the fine web of lines deepened by dirt. And as she did so the others looked at her too. They all looked at her; at this sister that was younger than all of them, and chill descended on them as they read their own decay in hers. They had been better preserved, that was all; hardship had hastened the disintegration of her looks, but the undeniable bending of the bone, the tightening of the skin, and the fading of the eye could not be guarded against. A chill fell on them. A grudge against her gnawed at them.

"I begin to see," said Matthew, "that Mother was right. I begin to see what she meant when she said that you were as obstinate as a tree."

"Did she say that?" said Lally, and her face lit up for a moment with the sunlight of youth, as her mind opened wide in a willful vision of tall trees, leafy, and glossy with light, against a sky as blue as the feathers in a young girl's hat.

Nonny stood up impatiently. "What is the use of talking?" she said. "No one can do anything for an obstinate person. They must be left to go their own way. But no one can say we didn't do our best."

"I'm very grateful," said Lally again.

"Oh, keep your thanks to yourself!" said Nonny. "As Matthew said, we didn't do it for your sake. It's not very nice to have people coming back from the city saying that they met you, and we knowing all the time the old clothes you were likely to be wearing, and your hair all tats and taws, and your face dirty maybe, if all was told!"

"Do you ever look at yourself in a mirror?" said Matthew.

"What came over you that you let your teeth go so far?" said Kate. "They're disgusting to look at." She shivered.

"I'd be ashamed to be seen talking to you," said Nonny.

Through the silent evening air there was a far sound of a train shunting. Through the curtains the signal lights on the railway line could be seen changing from red to green. Even when the elderly maidservant came in with the heavy brass lamp the green light shone through the pane, insistent as a thought.

"What time is it?" said Lally.

"You have plenty of time," said Matthew, his words marking the general acceptance of the fact that she was going.

Tea was hurried in on a tray. A messenger was sent running upstairs to see if Lally's gloves were on the bed in Kate's room.

"Where did you leave them?" someone kept asking every few minutes and going away in the confusion without a satisfactory answer.

"Do you want to have a wash?" Nonny asked. "It will freshen you for the journey. I left a jug of water on the landing."

And once or twice, lowering his voice to a whisper, Matthew leaned across the table and asked her if she was absolutely certain that she was all right for the journey back. Had she a return ticket? Had she loose change for the porters?

But Lally didn't need anything, and when it came nearer to the time of the train, it appeared that she did not even want the car to take her to the station.

"But it's wet!" said Matthew.

"It's as dark as a pit outside," said Kate.

And all of them, even the maidservant who was clearing away the tray, were agreed that it was bad enough for people to know she was going back the very night that her mother was lowered into the clay, without adding to the scandal by giving people a chance to say that her brother Matthew wouldn't drive her to the train in his car, and it pouring rain.

"They'll say we had a difference of opinion over the will," said Nonny, who retained one characteristic at least of youth, its morbid sensitivity.

"What does it matter what they say," said Lally, "as long as we know it isn't true?"

"If everyone took that attitude it would be a queer world," said Matthew.

"There's such a thing as keeping up appearances," said Kate, and she threw a hard glance at Lally's coat. "Is that coat black or is it blue?" she asked suddenly, catching the sleeve of it and pulling it nearer to the lamp.

"It's almost black," said Lally. "It's a very dark blue. I didn't have time to get proper mourning, and the woman next door lent me this. She said you couldn't tell it from black."

Nonny shrugged her shoulders and addressed herself to Matthew. "She's too proud to accept things from her own, but she's not too proud to accept things from strangers."

A train whistle shrilled through the air.

"I must go," said Lally.

She shook hands with them all. She looked up the stairway that the coffin had been carried down that morning. She put her hand on the door. While they were persuading her again to let them take her in the car, she opened the door and ran down the street.

They heard her footsteps on the pavement in the dark, as they had heard them often when she was a young girl running up the town on a message for their mother. And just as in those days, when she threw her coat over her head with the sleeves dangling, and ran out, the door was wide open upon the darkness. Matthew hesitated for a minute, and then he closed the door.

"Why didn't you insist?" said Kate.

"With people like Lally there is no use wasting your breath. They have their own ways of looking at things and nothing will change them. You might as well try to catch a falling leaf as try to find out what's at the back of Lally's mind."

They stood in the cold hallway. Suddenly Kate began to cry awkwardly.

"Why are you crying now?" said Nonny. "You were great at the cemetery. You kept us all from breaking down. Why are you crying now?" Her own voice had thinned and she dug her fingers into Matthew's sleeve.

"It's Lally!" said Kate. "None of you remember her as well as I do. I made her a dress for her first dance. It was white muslin with blue bows all down the front. Her hair was like light." Kate sobbed with thick, hurtful sobs that shook her whole frame and shook Matthew's thin, dried-up body when he put his arm around her.

Lally ran along the dark streets of the country town as she had run along them long ago as a young girl, and hardly remembered to slacken into a walking pace when she came to the patches of yellow lamplight that flooded out from shop windows and the open doors of houses near the square. But the excitement of running now was caused by the beat of blood in her temples and the terrible throbbing of her heart. As a child it had been an excitement of the mind, for then it had seemed that the bright world ringed the town around, and that somewhere outside the darkness lay the mystery of life; one had only to run on, on past the old town gate, on under the dark railway bridge, on a little way out the twisty road, and you would reach the heart of that mystery. Some day she would go.

And one day she went. But there was no mystery now; anywhere. Life was just the same in the town, in the city, and in the twisty countryside. Life was the same in the darkness and the light. It was the same for the spinster and for the draggled mother of a family. You were yourself always, no matter where you went or what you did. You didn't change. Her brothers and sisters were the same as they always were. She herself was the same as she always was, although her teeth were rotted, and a blue feather in her hat now would make her look like an old hag in a pantomime. Nothing you did made any real change in you. You might think beforehand that it would make a great change, but it wouldn't make any change. There was only one thing that could change you, and that was death. And no one knew what that change would be like.

No one knew what death was like, but people made terrible, torturing guesses. Fragments of the old penny catechism she had learned by rote in school came back to her, distorted by a bad memory and a confused emotion. Pictures of flames and screaming souls writhing on gridirons rose before her mind as she ran down the street to the station. The whistle of the train when it screamed in the darkness gave reality to her racing thoughts, and she paused and listened to it for a moment. Then turning rapidly around she ran back a few paces in the way that she had come, and groped along the dark wall that lined the street at this point.

The wet black railings of a gate came in contact with her fingers. This was the gate leading into the residence of the Canon. She banged the gate back against the piers with the fierce determination with which she opened it. She ran up the wet, gravelly drive to the priest's house.

In the dark she could not find the brass knocker and she beat against the panels of the door with her hard hands. The door was thrown open after a minute with a roughness that matched the rough knocking.

"What in the Name of God do you want?" said an elderly woman with an apron that blazed white in the darkness.

"I want to see the Canon!" said Lally.

"He's at his dinner," said the woman, aggressively, and went to close the door.

"I must see him," said Lally, and she stepped into the hallway.

"I can't disturb him at his meals," said the woman, but her anger had softened somewhat at seeing that Lally was a stranger to her. Two emotions cannot exist together and a strong curiosity possessed her at the moment. "What name?" she said.

"Lally Conroy," said Lally, the old associations being so strong that her maiden name came more naturally to her lips than the name she had carried for twenty-four years.

The housekeeper went across the hall and opened a door on the left. She closed it after her, but the lock did not catch and the door slid open again. Lally heard the conversation distinctly, but with indifference, as she sat down on the polished mahogany chair in the hall.

"There's a woman outside who insists on seeing you, Father."

"Who is she?" said the priest, his voice muffled, as if by a serviette wiped across his mouth.

"She gave her name as Conroy," said the woman, "and she has a look of Matthew Conroy, but I never saw her before and she's dressed like a pauper."

The priest's voice was slow and meditative. "I heard that there was another sister," he said, "but there was a sad story about her, I forget what it was." A chair scraped back. "I'll see her," he said. And his feet sounded on the polished floor as he crossed the room toward the hall.

Lally was sitting on the stiff chair with the wooden seat, shielding her face from the heat of the flames that dragged themselves like serpents along the logs in the fireplace.

"Father, I'm in a hurry. I'm going away on this train."

The train had shrilled its whistle once again in the darkness outside.

"I'm sorry to disturb you. I only wanted to ask a question." Her short phrases leaped uncontrollably as the leaping flames in the grate. "I want to know if you will say a Mass for my mother first thing in the morning. My name is Lally Conroy. I'll send you the offering money the minute I get back to the city. I'll post it to-night. Will you do that, Father? Will you?" As if the interview was over she stood up and began to go toward the door, backward, without waiting for an answer, repeating her urgent question, "Will you? Will you do that, Father? First thing in the morning!"

The Canon took out a watch from under the cape of his shiny canonical robes.

"You have six minutes yet," he said. "Sit down. Sit down."

"No, no, no," said Lally. "I mustn't miss the train."

The whistle blew again and the sound seemed to race her thoughts to a gallop.

"I want three Masses to be said," she explained, "but I want the first one to be said at once, tomorrow, first thing in the morning. You'll have the offering money as soon as I get back. I'll post it, tonight."

The Canon looked at the shabby boots and the thick stockings, the rubbed coat with the faded stitching on it.

"There is no need to worry about Masses. She was a good woman," he said. "And I understand that she left a large sum in her will for Masses to be said for her after her death. Three hundred pounds I believe, or thereabouts; a very considerable sum, at any rate. There is no need for worry on that score."

"It's not the same thing to leave money yourself for Masses. It's the Masses that other people have said for you that count." Her excitement leaped like the leaping flames. "I want a Mass said for her with my money! With my money!"

The priest leaned forward with an unusual and ungovernable curiosity.

"Why?" he said.

"I'm afraid," said Lally. "I'm afraid she might suffer. I'm afraid for her soul." The eyes that stared into the flaming heart of the fire were indeed filled with fear, and as a coal fell, revealing a gaping abyss of fire, those eyes filled with absolute horror. The reflection of the flames leaped in them. "She was very bitter," Lally Conroy sobbed for the first time since she had news of her mother's death. "She was very bitter against me all the time, and she died without forgiving me. I'm afraid for her soul." She looked up at the priest. "You'll say them as soon as ever you can, Father?"

"I'll say them," said the priest. "But don't worry about the money. I'll offer them from myself."

"That's not what I want," said Lally, angrily. "I want them to be paid for with my money. That is what will count most; that they are paid for out of my money."

Humbly the priest in his stiff canonical robes, piped with red, accepted the dictates of the draggled woman in front of him.

"I will do as you wish," he said. "Is there anything else troubling you?"

"The train! The train!" said Lally, and she fumbled the catch of the door.

The priest took out his watch again.

"You have just time to catch it," he said, "if you hurry." And he opened the door. Lally ran out into the dark again.

For a moment she felt peace at the thought of what she had done, and running down the wet gravelly drive with the cold rain beating on her flushed face, her mind was filled with practical thoughts about the journey home. But when she got into the hot and stuffy carriage of the train, where there was an odor of dust and of wet soot, the tears began to stream down her face again, and she began to wonder if she had made herself clear to the Canon. She put her head out of the carriage window as the train began to leave the platform and she called out to a porter who stood with a green flag in his hand.

"What time does this train arrive in the city?" she asked, but the porter could not hear her. He put his hand to his ear but just then the train rushed into the darkness under the railway bridge. Lally let the window up and sat back in the seat.

If the train got in before midnight, she thought, she would ring the night bell at the Franciscan Friary and ask for a Mass to be said there and then for her mother's soul. She had heard that Masses were said night and day in the Friary. She tried to remember where she had heard that, and who had told her, but her thoughts were in confusion. She leaned her head back against the cushions as the train roared into the night, and feverishly she added the prices she would get from the tenants in the top rooms and subtracted the amount that would be needed to buy food for herself and the children for the week. She would have a clear two pound ten. She could have ten Masses said at least for that. There might even be money over to light some holy lamps at the Convent of Perpetual Reparation. She tried to comfort herself by these calculations, but as the dark train rushed through the darkness she sat more upright on the red-carpeted seats that smelled of dust and clenched her hands tightly as she thought of the torments of Purgatory. Bright red sparks from the engine flew past the carriage window, and she began to pray with rapid, unformed words that jostled themselves in her mind like sheaves of burning sparks.

Chamois Gloves

It was an important day at the Convent of Our Lady of Perpetual Succour: three postulants were about to take their First Vows.

A beautifully fine day, thank God!

The sunlight glinted on the chapel windows, on the greenhouse roof, and on the windshields of the visitors' cars as they came up the driveway.

One or two cars were already drawn up in front of the chapel, which was a separate building, to the left of the convent, and the tires had made ridges in the loose, clean gravel. It was really too thickly spread, and it rolled about under the feet of the relatives when they stepped out of the cars. No wonder there were no weeds! And there—in case even one small weed should dare to put up its head—was Joe the gardener standing by the yew hedge, with a hoe in his hand. But note he was in his best suit, and he was wearing his hat.

On the other side of the yew hedge, but magnificently unconcerned, two—no—three young nuns were walking rapidly up and down reading their Office. And finally, at an open window in one of the classrooms on the ground floor, the five small girls who were going to be bridesmaids at the ceremony were having their wreaths and veils put straight by a lay teacher.

There were countless guardian angels moving about upon diverse errands too, of course, but being unseen their actions need hardly be related. The principal ones, anyway, were the angels who be-

longed to the young girls about to take their vows, and they were
way up on the top story of the Novitiate at that moment; doubly
out of sight, you might say.

The cars were really beginning to arrive now. Two more were
coming up, and there was the sound of another one changing gear
down at the gates. (The gates were situated at a bad point in the
road; they could not be safely negotiated in top gear.) Ah, here it
was, gathering speed, and causing the gravel to shoot out to either
side of the wheels as if from a peashooter.

In the basement of the convent an old lay sister peered upward
through the window.

Had they all arrived, she wondered? She was the Kitchen Sister—
Sister Ursula—and she was in charge of the luncheon which would
be served after the ceremony. She looked back over her shoulder
at a clock. In exactly fifty minutes more, she calculated, they should
be sitting down to table. But would they?

Tch, tch, she said, as from yet another car, that scattered the
gravel right and left, there descended a whole family, father,
mother, and three small children.

I hope there won't be more than the number, like last year, she
muttered. People had no consideration, no manners, you might
say. Some of them thought children didn't count. But they ought
to be taught a lesson. Children should not be put at the table at
all; they should be put in a classroom and given a glass of milk
and a plate of biscuits. But no, oh, no; nothing would do the parents
but squeeze them in to the table, upsetting everything, especially
the number of knives and forks.

"Here, I have two forks," the father would say; as if the table
was laid wrong!

"Oh, but they don't understand," said the old Sister.

She was the daughter of a small farmer, and it always seemed to
her that the meals at the convent were very grand, and that the
people who were invited to them didn't properly apprehend the
formalities. Where did they see the like before? she would ask. And
if after the meal a grapefruit came back untouched to the kitchen,
or a piece of cutlery was unused, she was very proud. You can't
blame them, she would say to the younger lay sisters. Where did they
see such things before?

On the other hand, Reverend Mother, who came from a well-to-do merchant's family in the Midlands—Reverend Mother was always nervous in case everything was not correct, and on such occasions as now she hovered about the table adjusting the folds of the serviettes, and making minute alterations in the lie of the cutlery. It was a minor, but constant, source of embarrassment to her that they had not got proper grapefruit spoons. She had not quite sufficient confidence to order them, but whenever a young nun's dower included a share of family plate, or when the convent received a bequest in the form of silverware, she eagerly rummaged through it.

"Are there no grapefruit spoons?" she would exclaim, and when there were not, it was manifestly difficult for her to conceal her disappointment, no matter how rare or how valuable were the items.

Sister Ursula knew Reverend Mother's feelings about the spoons, and so, whenever she laid the table for visitors, she always gave the bowls of the teaspoons a squeeze to narrow them.

"They should be pointed, you know," she told the younger lay sisters. "But who'll notice the difference!" Poor Reverend Mother! God gave her wit, some of them won't ever have seen a grapefruit at all!

Today, as she peered upward through the ivy-framed window, she was inclined to think a lot of the cutlery would come back unused. Once professed, she was prepared to accept all the choir nuns as ladies, but some of their relatives . . . she raised her brows so that the band of starched linen across her forehead shifted its place and showed the ridge it had made in her skin.

Ah! There was a familiar car. On the dot, as usual; Father Devaney. She bustled back to the range. Everything would be on time after all; Father Devaney would see to it. Thanks be to God.

The arrival of the priest's car was indeed a signal to all concerned. The young nuns pacing behind the yew hedge closed their breviaries, and walked, not so much quickly, as purposefully, back to the building. The five little communicants were bustled out of sight. Among the guests there was activity also. Some of the menfolk who had stayed sitting in their cars, got out and, pulling up their coats by the back of the collar, as if they were their own footmen, followed their womenfolk. The womenfolk, on the other hand, up to this point confident and chattering, now became ill at ease, and inclined not to know what was to be done. It was always the men who could be relied upon in the end.

"Well, what's keeping us?" they said, and trooped up the steps of the chapel, but they wiped their feet elaborately on the scraper provided, and stepped on the golden parquet as if it were brittle yellow glass.

Yet, in a few minutes, as if the chapel door had been a swallow hole and they had been sucked into it, everyone had disappeared. No longer blocked with people, the open door gave a glimpse of hundreds of candle flames, and let out the first notes of the organ, peremptory; premonitory.

Meanwhile, in the Novitiate, which was also separate from the main building, high up near the copper cupola, viridescent with verdigris, and on top of which, gay as a weathervane, there shone a gilt cross, the three young girls who were about to be received, raised their arms and down over their bodies fell the beautiful white satin gowns they were to wear for their wedding with the Holy of Holies. But although the cubicles were so high up in the roof, nevertheless the lower sashes were covered with a brass grille so that only the pigeons walking about on the cupola could see those beautiful bare arms.

On account of this brass grille, the postulants could not clearly see the cars arriving; they could only hear them as they came up the drive.

That's ours, thought Veronica, the youngest of the postulants. She knew the sound of the engine, and a minute afterward the peculiar noise of the doors slamming. In a little while—the ceremony would be so short really—and the luncheon would not take very long—she would be with the family. A feeling of absolutely delirious happiness passed through her from top to toe. It was too bad Mabel couldn't be there, of course, but even that couldn't spoil the marvelousness of it all. Oh, joy!

But all at once she bit her lip. That was the trouble, you see, she was too happy, far too happy, all the time, yesterday, today, every single day. Since the very first day she entered the Novitiate, she hadn't had one moment of sadness or regret. Surely that wasn't right? Where was the sacrifice if there were no pain of loss, no anguish of indecision?

Take the other postulants, for instance. How many times during the past year had she been awakened in the small hours by a sound of sobbing in one of the other cubicles? It was subdued sobbing, but terrible to hear, all the same, in the darkness. She had never been able to tell whether it was Sister Assumpta or Sister Concepta, but from other indications she felt sure that in both their souls there was some struggle about which she knew nothing at all. And once, at recreation, Sister Concepta had asked her a strange question.

"Do you ever have dreams?" she asked. "Queer ones, I mean?" And when Veronica said she hadn't, Concepta had turned away with a worried expression.

It was shortly after this that Veronica had gone to the trouble of confiding in the Mistress of Novices, or Private Enterprise, as she was called on account of a famous reprimand she had made to a former novice whose zeal she considered excessive. "Do what is asked of you, Sister; no less, and no more. We don't want any private enterprise in piety!"

Private Enterprise had listened for a minute or two, and then grunted.

"So you think God ought to have put more temptations in your way, do you?" she said. "And might I ask what makes you think you'd be able to withstand them? Let me tell you, God knows what He's doing. And if, for some purpose of His own, He occasionally wants some of us poor weak creatures as well as the other kind, well then He has to arrange matters so that there isn't too great a strain put on us."

She spoke so sarcastically that the tears had come into Veronica's eyes, but then, just before she turned aside, the old nun smiled.

"At least, that's the only way I can account for my own perseverance!" she said.

That was Private Enterprise all over. She was always putting people into their place, but somehow at the same time she managed to make them feel glad to be there.

And so, when, out on the landing, Veronica saw the pale faces of

Concepta and Assumpta, even then, at the last minute, she felt an impulse to put her case once more to the older nun.

"Look at their faces," she wanted to say. "Anyone can see what they feel, while I am only—only what?" Scandalized she realized that for the most part she was looking forward to seeing her family: looking beyond the ceremony, as it were, treating it almost as if it were of no great importance at all, this, the Great Day, for which they had been preparing every single day that had preceded it since they came into the convent!

Perhaps after all she had no vocation. In a panic she looked around. Where was Private Enterprise? Ah, there she was, plodding up the stairs. Veronica started forward, but before she could open her mouth, the old nun looked past her at Concepta and frowned.

"You're not going to be sick, are you?" she asked bluntly. "You're very green in the face!

"Wait a minute!" she commanded them all, although just then they heard the faraway sound of the organ that had been a signal for them to start moving down the stairs. "Better be on the safe side," she muttered, and she disappeared into the small pantry on the landing.

When she came out, she had a big enamel basin in her hand.

"I'll bring this down to the sacristy, just in case. I do wish you wouldn't dramatize yourself so much, Sister!" she said irritably.

Humbly Veronica drew back. How glad she was she hadn't said anything!

And then, just before she gave them the signal to start moving, Private Enterprise held them up again for a minute.

"It will be all over in a few minutes," she said reassuringly. "Don't be nervous. Remember that in God's eyes every day of the past year was as important as today. You gave yourself to Him every day. All that's happening today is that you're receiving the outward sign of your union with Him. Don't be nervous. Think of how proud your people will be of you: think of how soon you'll be seeing them."

And so, when she was walking up the aisle of the chapel, actually kneeling at the altar rails, she found herself thinking again of them, she didn't worry. It was a pity that Mabel would not be able to come to the reception, but she would offer up her own disappointment to God and pray that He would bring her safely through things.

And then, as if there was not to be even the smallest shadow on the day, ever such a short time afterward, as Private Enterprise had said—in their black habits now—when they followed her into the parlor—who should she see, first of all, running over to her—but Mabel. Yes—Mabel: running forward ahead of Mother and ahead of Father.

"Why, Mabel—" she cried. "I thought—"

But Mabel only laughed at how puzzled she was, and, all perfume as usual, she kissed her.

"What's this?" cried Father, as he and Mother came up to her, and he pretended to draw back as he was about to kiss her. "I didn't know nuns wore perfume."

Several people in the parlor looked around in surprise.

"Oh, I suppose it's come off Mabel," she cried in alarm, and then they all began to laugh. And indeed, by this time, at both ends of the parlor where each of the other novices was surrounded by her own little groups of friends, there were bursts of laughter like bursts of small artillery fire, until it seemed as if each burst ought by right to be accompanied by a little puff of smoke rising into the air.

And the talk . . . it was easily seen the ceremony had been preceded by the Long Retreat.

"Did you really keep absolute silence for twenty-one days?" cried Mother. "I mean absolute, absolute silence?"

"We can well understand your incredulity, my dear," said Father. "Can't we, girls?"

He was always teasing Mother.

"Oh, indeed!" cried Mother. "You'd wonder why some people were given tongues at all: isn't that so, girls?"

To Veronica, it was just like being at home. She had forgotten, really, how they teased each other, Father and Mother, and how they all talked so much, all together too. Ever so slightly—she couldn't help it—Veronica felt superior to them; even to Father. In the Community Room, at Recreation, the conversation was always happy, but somehow there was a difference. It wasn't so—so scatter-

brain! But realizing this might be spiritual pride, she checked herself quickly.

And anyway, she wanted to hear about Mabel. She still didn't
understand how she was able to be there.

"Don't look so puzzled, darling," cried Mabel herself just then.
"You're an auntie for the past fortnight! I simply couldn't bear to
miss being here and so I got round the old doctor and made him
give me a cocktail!"

Seeing that Veronica didn't understand, Mabel reddened slightly.

"Nursing-home slang, pet," she said. "Don't let it worry you: an
injection to induce me: that's all!"

But she was still a bit red in the face. An awkward silence seemed
to have come over their part of the parlor.

Not that Veronica had really taken in what was said. Only
vaguely did she comprehend that the baby must be born, but a
nervous feeling came into her stomach, and she didn't want to hear
any more details. Just that everything was all right: that was enough.
And there would have been an end to it if Euphemia had not
joined them just then.

Euphemia was their aunt, and she was twenty-seven years now in
the Order, but she considered herself a real woman of the world for
all that. Even the name which she had taken in religion, although
it was used by all the family instead of her name in the world—
which most of them had forgotten—and Mabel and Veronica could
hardly have recalled—was used without a prefix, as easily and
familiarly as if it were a Christian name: a perfect compromise. She
seemed to go in for compromise, Euphemia did. On this occasion she
took Mabel up sharply.

"I must say I'm surprised at you, Mabel. I didn't think you'd go
in for being smart. In God's good time: that was the old-fashioned
way. And the best way in the long run. Things are best left in the
hands of God, my dear, or even of Nature, if you prefer it that way.
It isn't wise to alter the natural order of things. I don't want to
alarm you, but I hope you won't find later on— Well, we'll hope not
in any case. Of course, it's an altogether different story if there are
sound medical grounds for interference—but I take it that was not
so in your case?"

Long ago when she and Mabel were at school, they used to boast about their Aunt Euphemia, because she was so broadminded. You'd never think she was a nun at all. You could say anything to her. And you should hear her talking! That's the kind of nun I'd like to be if I had to be one at all, Mabel used to say.

Well, Veronica didn't want to be that kind. She didn't want to be priggish, but if God ordained that certain things were to be outside her experience, well then she didn't care to know anything about them. And anyway, there were times, in the chapel, when she had seen Euphemia's face across from her in the transept among the choir nuns, when she herself was still a postulant, and it had often seemed to her that there was something unreconciled in Euphemia's face. Was it possible, she had wondered, that for some people there was a struggle to be fought out, anew, every day, even *after* the taking of vows? She looked at Euphemia with new eyes. Was she ever—

But just at that moment, Sister Concepta came and whispered to her. One of Concepta's visitors had been at school with Mabel and she'd like to meet her again.

"Bring her over of course!" cried Mabel, overhearing the whisper, and staring with curiosity across the parlor.

But the friend turned out to be much older than Mabel. She was in the Senior School when Mabel was still in the Lower School. And she was married long before Mabel as could be seen by the size of the big child—four or five years old at least—who was with her, staring up at them all from under an unkempt fringe.

The child stared most of all at Veronica.

"Is *her* hair cut too, Ma?" she demanded.

"Oh, Judy, keep quiet; you are a tiresome child," cried the mother. "How dare you say such things!"

"But you said in the car—"

"Never mind what I said! You know you shouldn't repeat things. You're always being told so. And stop staring. Where are your manners?"

But the child's eyes were riveted on the starched linen band across Veronica's forehead. Everyone felt embarrassed for a minute. Then Father Devaney, who had been talking to Reverend Mother, detached himself and took the child by the arm.

"Well, little girl, what's your name?" he said, and before she had time to say any more he had led her over to where a glass door looked out upon the garden.

There, on a strip of vacant grass, some pigeons were walking decorously up and down.

"Why don't you try and catch one?" he said, and he opened the door.

Judy ran out: the pigeons rose into the air with a flurry.

"Oh, look; so many of them!" cried Veronica's mother. "It's like St. Mark's!"

"Only these are not so tame!" said Euphemia. There she was again! When was *she* in Venice?

"Oh, do look at them," cried Mother again, moving over to the glass door.

Reverend Mother too moved over to the door.

"Sometimes when they are walking up and down, we say they are reading their Office; they look so solemn," she said. She conceived it as part of her duties always to make a mild joke like this on such occasions.

And certainly everyone laughed. Following her lead too, everyone —except Veronica and Father—moved over to the glass door.

Father laid a hand on Veronica's arm.

"Let's stay on this side of the ship to make weight," he said.

Veronica laughed. As a family, analogy was irresistible to them. She knew exactly what he meant. The pigeons had acted upon the company as a floating canister or a bottle will act upon the passengers of a ship, drawing them all to one side to lean over the deck rail, the insignificance of the object that focuses so much attention making explicit a boredom that they would hardly otherwise have realized.

It was getting boring: there was no doubt about it. Much as she loved her own people, Veronica kept thinking of what would happen when the visitors left, and they took their places for the first time in the community.

Meanwhile, her mother, usually restless, had put her head out the french window.

"Couldn't we go out?" she cried, meaning to compliment the garden, but in reality giving the effect of criticizing the parlor.

Reverend Mother's narrow cheeks reddened profusely. Was the

room stuffy? Was she at fault in not having had the glass doors open? She nodded her head vigorously at a young nun, who rushed to unhook the other half of the door.

"Perhaps you'd like to see the garden," said Reverend Mother, speaking generally to the whole company, and stepping out into the air.

As they were leaving the parlor, Father looked back over his shoulder.

"You must have a good greenhouse," he said to Veronica, because, now that it was empty of people, the parlor seemed to be full of ferns, dotted about everywhere in ornamental pots.

Veronica looked back. Even when she was a child, visiting Euphemia, the parlor had always fascinated her, with its strong odor of beeswax, and the stiff unrelaxing arrangement of its furniture. Once it was the only part of the convent she knew, but it hinted at deeper disciplines and coldnesses to be found beyond it.

"It's a lovely room, isn't it?" she said impulsively.

But her mother had come within earshot once more.

"Personally I can't abide pot plants," she said. And then impulsively she looked straight at Veronica. "Aren't you ever lonely for home, darling?" she said bluntly.

It was so easy to see the course her thoughts had taken. She was thinking of the drawing room at home, always filled with masses of cut flowers: simply masses of them.

Veronica didn't want to hurt her, but she just wasn't one bit lonely. It even seemed to her now that cut flowers were out of place anywhere except on the altar. But naturally she wasn't going to say that.

And anyway, at last, perhaps only for a moment, she was alone with Mabel. Something or other engaged the attention of the rest.

"Well, old thing?" said Mabel. "You look marvelous—in your habit, I mean. Of course, you looked divine in"—but Mabel just couldn't bring herself to use the words "wedding gown"—"in the satin gown," she said quickly. "But then who wouldn't cut a dash in that!" She looked critically at her sister. "It takes a good figure to look well in that rig-out," she said, "although it can't be denied that figure or no figure, you look a bit like a penguin, my dear!"

It was an old joke. When they were at school they always called the nuns penguins.

Veronica laughed.

"Do you know, Mabel—" she began, but their mother was calling Mabel.

"Isn't it about time someone made a move to leave?" she said.

"Oh, bother," said Mabel to Veronica. "I wanted to have a word with you— Oh, nothing in particular, just a little chat like long ago, but I dare say I'll get a chance again. Or perhaps I could pop in and see you tomorrow before my train leaves, if that's all right."

Veronica didn't know.

"I'd have to ask permission to have a visitor," she said.

"Good lord!" cried Mabel. "It's plain to be seen I'd never have made a nun."

Euphemia and Father Devaney had joined them by this time.

"God help us, Mabel, if we had to depend on the like of you to fill our convents," said Father Devaney. He was an old friend of Mabel. "In the name of God, what have you on your fingernails?" he asked.

"Oh, go on now, Father. Don't take the good out of that nice sermon you gave this morning. You should have heard it, Vera," she said, "and you too, Euphemia—in case you get too puffed up with vanity—it was all about us poor mothers. It's the poor mothers of this world who deserve their crowns in heaven, I can tell you. Do you know what time the baby woke this morning?"

"It's a bit soon for you to complain about your job, Mabel," said her mother. She had a vague feeling that the topic of the baby's feeds was not quite seemly on this particular occasion. It might be different if he were on a bottle. "Oh, the young women nowadays," she said, and she raised her eyebrows—anything to prevent Mabel from saying something indiscreet—"I don't know what they have to complain about—compared with us, I mean." She sighed. "When I think of what we—my generation, I mean—when I think of what *we* suffered." Suddenly she turned to Father Devaney. "Do you know, Father, these young people are so smart they've put an end to all that! It seems there is some young man—a doctor, of course —who has written a book, and they are all reading it—Mabel never left it out of her hands the whole nine months—and he claims—at least Mabel claims—that having a baby is a pleasure now. Did you ever—"

But suddenly she stopped short. She had jumped into the conversation so hastily to prevent Mabel from going too far, and now what was she saying herself? To make matters worse, she had fallen foul of Mabel.

"It's nothing to joke about, Mother," she said stiffly. "After the first contraction—"

But Father, *dear* Father, came up just then and put his hand firmly on Mabel's shoulder.

"Another time, Mabel dear, another time," he said. "You've had your thunder—this is Veronica's day."

Veronica's day: it was so true. They all looked at her proudly.

"Are you happy about me now, Mother?" said Veronica, impulsively.

"Of course, my dear," said her mother. "It was only that I wanted you to be sure you knew what you were doing." Unaccountably, there was another moment of awkwardness. "I do feel we ought to start going—" she said once more.

And so, very shortly, it was all over: the Great Day.

Once more the cars were crunching the gravel, and there was the sound of doors slamming.

Until the last car disappeared, the three new choir nuns stood at the door, and then turned uncertainly back into the hall. What did they do now?

A mild consternation stirred in them as they saw Private Enterprise, without a glance at them, going down the corridor leading from the chapel to the Novitiate, and passing through that little door—more familiar now than all the doors of home—through which they would pass no more. Like the doors of home, it too was now closed to them.

Veronica glanced at the big clock in the hall. It was only five o'clock.

Suddenly she realized that she was so fatigued she could hardly stand.

Then Reverend Mother approached them.

"Sister Eucharia will tell you your new duties," she said. Then she looked in particular at Veronica. "Why, you look exhausted,

Sister," she said. "I think you had better go to bed tonight, as soon as you've had your tea."

A great feeling of relief came over Veronica. It had been a terrible strain, really, the whole day.

As the other two, Concepta and Assumpta, moved away after Sister Eucharia, Veronica stood for a minute in the empty hall. Then she went down the corridor toward the Refectory. Fatigue had brought a certain dejection, and her shoulders drooped slightly. And could she but have seen it, beside her, the feathered wings of her guardian angel drooped still more. It was all very well for Private Enterprise to take a practical view of things, but with the other guardian angels, bragging and boasting about the sacrifices they had to offer up for their clients, it was a bit hard for Veronica's angel to have absolutely nothing but words to offer on her behalf. Naturally as Veronica enunciated her vows, her angel had flown off with them at once, engraved on a golden scroll, but without even looking at the other two winging their way upward beside her. She felt herself that the golden words had a hollow sound.

Ah, well, the Lord's ways were His own, she thought, and one had to be satisfied. She followed Veronica dutifully down the corridor. Thank goodness they were going to call an end to the Great Day.

Just then, however, a voice called after them.

"Just a minute, Sister," said a voice. It was Reverend Mother again. "I think your sister must have left these behind. Will you be seeing her soon again, or will we post them to her?" In her hand she had a pair of chamois gloves. "Perhaps you could keep them till you see her?" said Reverend Mother.

Veronica took the gloves and bowed to Reverend Mother.

Sister Ursula was not in the Refectory, but the tables were laid, and Veronica sat down and ate some bread and butter, and took a glass of milk from the big jug on the side table. That was enough for her. She wasn't hungry anyway, only tired, deadly tired.

As she passed back along the corridor, she could hear the choir starting the Tantum Ergo. Benediction was nearly over. She went upstairs to the new cubicle in which she had changed out of her white satin dress into her habit. But as she reached the landing, she noticed a small hand basin on one side of the wall, with two taps which meant there was hot water as well as cold. In her hand she still held Mabel's gloves.

Tired and all as she was, it suddenly occurred to her that it would be a nice thing to wash out the gloves and give them back clean. Chamois gloves were so easily soiled. And she and Mabel always made a point of never wearing the same pair twice without being washed.

Impulsively taking off her stiff linen cuffs, and leaving them on the shelf over the hand basin, Veronica ran the hot tap. The steam rose up in a cloud. She made a lather, pulled the gloves on her hands, and plunged them into the water.

Oh, that slimy feel of wet chamois! How well she remembered it. She might almost have been standing in the little wash-up pantry at the top of the house which she and Mabel used all their lives. It used to be a housemaid's pantry in the time of the previous occupiers, but she and Mabel had it for their own.

Very rarely did their mother ever go up there to it, and when she did she closed her eyes in horror at its condition.

"This place is a disgrace. It will have to be done up. I do wish at least you wouldn't get it so littered."

Because Mabel's pots and tubes were all over the place, on the window ledges, and the edges of the cracked hand basin. Yes, there was a big crack across the bottom that got filled with plain dirt. And more than once the down pipe got clogged with hair combings but they managed to free it with a knitting needle.

"Ugh!" cried Mother, when she heard. "And to think you do hygiene at school. Ugh!"

It was pretty disgusting really, compared with the rest of the house that was really so beautifully kept. Mother never tolerated anything that wasn't beautiful.

Yet, she and Mabel spent such a lot of time up there gossiping and exchanging confidences when they were supposed to be brushing their teeth or buffing their nails.

It was there, one afternoon, that she plucked up courage to tell Mabel her plans.

But all at once Veronica couldn't bear to recall any more. Two big tears welled into her eyes and coursed down her face.

Astonished, her guardian angel stared. As far as she knew,

Veronica's mind was filled only with memories of cracked sanitary ware, steamy walls, and a litter of quite unsightly broken combs and misused tubes of toothpaste.

No matter! The tears were there, real tears, one, two, three. All the little angel's fatigue was dispelled in an instant. She was as fresh as a daisy once more. The other angels had got ahead of her, of course, but better late than never, and cupping two tears in her hand, she sped for Heaven.

As for Veronica, she soon dried her eyes, and rinsing the gloves she took them into her cell to hang up and dry. In a few minutes she was asleep.

But over her head, high above roof and cupola, loud, loud, loud, could she but hear it, the bells of Heaven were ringing out her sacrifice.

Assigh

ONLY once in all the years did he say anything about it, and that was a few days before he died. He was lying so still she thought he was asleep, but he was staring at the rags on her leg.

"Does it trouble you much?" he said. Just that, but her fear of him flared up as fierce as on the day he struck her, and ill though he was, and helpless—dying—she wanted to lie to him; to say it didn't trouble her at all: to exonerate him.

But the saturated rags wrapped round her leg would show up the lie.

"Only a bit, Father," she said cautiously, "not much."

"It was the brass of the buckle that did it," he said, as if it were only yesterday. It was a sort of apology. She knew that at once. But not for his action. Never for that! Only for its unfortunate outcome. "There must have been verdigris on the buckle," he said. "And verdigris is poison! If your mother was alive she'd have put something on it to kill the poison."

He must have turned to look at her again, but she was looking out of the window herself and she didn't notice. He rapped on the table by his bed.

"Did you know verdigris was poison?" he cried, and he rapped again on the table. "You didn't know it!" he cried accusingly. "Well, you know it now!"

And then, as unexpectedly as he opened them, he closed his eyes again, and she realized that whatever need made him break the silence of twenty years had now been fully satisfied.

He was asleep almost at once, in one of the heavy, unnatural sleeps that came down so often upon him. They would soon close in upon his consciousness altogether. She looked at him. He couldn't last much longer. It would be over then, the long imprisonment of their lives with him. She took no pleasure in the thought, but it passed frequently through her mind. To put it away she looked out at the fields.

Closed in by summer, the fields were deeper and lonelier than ever, and the laneway out to the road was narrowed by over-hanging briars. Away in a far field down by the river, her brother Tom was scything weeds. He was cutting away with an easy rhythmical movement, but as she watched he stopped to put a new edge on the blade, and when he reached down for the whetstone she was startled to see how stiff he was, and awkward. Why, the man on the bed was suppler than him! A feeling of pity for his dried and wasted years assailed her, but suddenly her leg throbbed again. It may have been that her father's words had wakened the pain, for it was so bad it might have been, again, the moment it happened, when he came upon her suddenly in the churchyard, from behind the vaulted yew trees, and before all the other stragglers—and there were plenty of them—raised the head collar in the air and swung it over her head. Sparkling like a star in the day sky the buckle held her eyes for an instant, and then it darkened down upon her.

She fell with the pain. And as she fell, she saw Jake take to his heels across the slabstones. But her father didn't give him a glance. "Get up!" he said to her. "Get up!" and, as if she was a beast that had fallen, he struck her again to rise her. Not that he was a man that ever ill-treated a beast. For that matter, neither was he a man that had ever objected, before that, to her having a word now and then with a man. You might say he used to give her a sort of coarse encouragement.

"You'd better watch your step in that jacket, my girl," he'd say sometimes when she was going out for a walk of an evening, even when she was too young to know what he meant. She used to feel there was a queer meaning in his words but she didn't want to un-cover it. She'd run out of the door, laughing. Sometimes he used to bring her into the town on the eve of a fair, and buy her dresses that made the neighbors click their tongues.

"It's easily seen you have no mother, you poor child." That was said to her more than once when he decked her out as if it was Sunday, on a plain ordinary day of the week. She couldn't play in the kind of dresses he got her. Maybe that was how she got the habit of standing about, drawing looks on herself, like the looks she got from over the wall in the school yard that divided the boys from the girls, and later on, the bolder looks from their own work-men; particularly Jake. It was behind her father's back for the most part that she got those looks, but he knew about them all the same, and he never seemed to mind. She even used to think he put some construction of his own on them; that they were a measure of something in his mind.

In her own mind, that was all they were, a measure: a measure of her attraction. Obscurely she knew, even then, that nature made use of small affinities to prepare the heart for the fatal, the im-mortal affinity of love.

And so, when there was a sound of wheels rattling over the cobbles of the yard one day, a week before she was seventeen, and a spanking back-to-back trap drove up to the yard door, she was drawn to the doorway by something more compelling than mere curiosity.

"The name is Mellors—Tod Mellors," said the owner, jumping down and going to meet her father who came out of the cowshed at the sound of the wheels. She was left standing at the yard door. But he had seen her. And if she knew in that instant what she had been waiting for—although it was only a short wait—there was a look in his eyes that made her feel that he too had come to the end of some kind of waiting. In his case, though, it had been a longer wait, he being a mature man, owning a big farm of his own.

Because he announced outright that he had just bought the farm next to them.

"The two divisions," he said proudly, "and it's the best of land, but it was overstocked at the back end of the year, and I'm thinking I'll be short of hay. I'm told you have a field of second-crop meadow for sale on foot."

"It's for sale all right," said her father slowly, "but I was thinking of making it up myself." His shrewd eyes were trying to sum up the stranger, but afterward she knew it was for other reasons than she thought at the time. He had paired them up in his mind in that first moment.

Of course, it was all only looks. But in the silent fields, living close with the mute beasts, there was perhaps more meaning to be got out of looks and glances than there was for people in the towns. She used to think sometimes that for people like them, her and her father and Tod—words only ran alongside looks—as the song of the stream runs alongside the meaningful ripples. But there were times when words had their full potency too, and never more than when men were making a deal.

"Will you give me the first refusal of it one way or another?" said Tod Mellors that day.

"Do you want to have a deal here and now?" said her father.

"That depends on what you're asking for it," said Mr. Mellors.

"How much is it worth?" said her father.

They moved across the yard toward where a gate led into the meadow. Her father leaned back against the gate, facing away from it, for he knew every blade of grass that was in it. But Tod Mellors leaned forward, looking deep into the grasses that swelled like a sea, and were as green as the sea, with not a blotch of blossom marring it, from mearing to mearing, but only darker clots of green where the cow pads had coarsened the growth. And standing to one side of him, she could see how he coveted the grass with his eyes, and how his mind coveted the skill that had brought a crop like it out of their light gravelly land. But above all, she saw how his eyes took pleasure in its moisture and richness.

Then the bargaining began again involuntarily.

"Well, what is it worth?" said her father.

"Do you mean to me, or to you?"

"What's the differ?" said her father, surprised.

"Oh, there's a big difference," said Mr. Mellors. "And what's more, I'd say you were a man that sets a steep value on anything you have to offer."

Her father laughed. And seeing her beside him, he flung out an arm and put it round her waist, like he might have done perhaps with her mother when they were early-married.

"I can afford to ask a nice price," he said. "I never put anything on the market that I'm ashamed to stand behind!"

Mr. Mellors looked for a minute into her father's eyes, and then he looked into hers, and again she felt the fated weight of the moment, like when he first rode into the yard, and she knew that it wasn't altogether the meadow grass they were talking about, either of them. Although it was no longer the olden times, when such things were commonplace, but her own day, when such things were laughed at and mocked, they were for all that making a match for her there and then: both of them.

And she wanted it that way! She wanted it. And her heart was so filled with joy that when just then, high up in the blue sky over their heads, out of sight, a lark began to trill, it seemed as if it was the voice of her heart singing out for all to hear. She looked at Tod Mellors. And he looked at her.

"Well, I'm not a man that's ashamed to pay a good price for a thing if it's true to its worth," he said. "But there's no hurry, I suppose." He nodded at the grass. "It can go a while longer, wouldn't you say?"

"Oh, a good while longer," said her father. He was glad he could be prodigal with something. "You can take your time. You'll have the first refusal anyway, I promise you that!"

They shook hands then, and the clasp of their hands was so strong it dipped them forward and downward as if they were two middle-sized men for a moment, instead of the tall men they both were. Tod Mellors straightened up.

"Goodbye, sir," he said to her father. "Goodbye, Miss!" he said to her. No more. The next minute he was spanking down the road. And standing in the yard, for as long as they could hear the sound of the mare's feet, they could see the tip of his whip over the road hedge.

"Well, that's that!" said her father. He was in great spirits. "I told you that was the best bit of meadow in the countryside," he said to Jake, who was coming against them as they moved back into the middle of the yard.

"Did he make a deal?" said Jake.

"No," said her father, "but I put out a feeler and I'm well satisfied."

When her father bent and went into the cowshed, Jake looked

at her queerly.

"What did you think of the fine Mr. Mellors? He'll be looking for more than the meadow before long, I'd say!"

"I don't know what you mean," she said coldly.

"Oh, not you!" said Jake sarcastically.

She walked away from him, toward the meadow gate, and she stood for a minute looking over the gate where they had all stood together. And she remembered the covetous look in Mr. Mellors' eyes. Her own eyes seemed to see the beauty of the land for the first time. Was I blind before? she thought wonderingly. Then she followed her father into the cowshed.

"Well, girl?" he said gaily, when she went up to him in the dimness that was slatted with light from the loosely jointed boards.

They never got on as well together as in the few weeks that followed, and even Tom didn't seem to rub him the wrong way as much as usual.

"What has him in such good form these days?" said Tom to her one evening.

"I don't know," she said. But she lied. "Why don't you take heart, while he's in good humor, and tell him about you and Flossie?" she cried quickly.

For cautious and all as Tom was, she knew Flossie Sauran and he were meeting more than an odd time; on Sundays, and in the evenings. If her father knew it he'd flay him. He gave him no encouragement at all. She didn't know why he made this difference between them, unless it was that he was able to identify something of himself again in her that wasn't in Tom. It might have been her impudence! He had plenty of impudence himself in his young days, especially for women. A cattle dealer in the town was talking to her one day, and he said he knew her when she was only a sparkle in her father's eyes. Her father laughed.

"And she has the same sparkle in *her* eye, I can tell you!" he said, meaningfully.

But there was no sparkle in Tom's eye. Still, she couldn't see why he was so covert about his meetings with Flossie.

"He can't kill you!" she said. "Tell him, why don't you! He might think more of you for it."

But it terrified him to talk about it.

"Take care would he hear you!" he said, and he looked over his shoulder, although their father was out in the fields, counting the cattle.

"He'll have to know sometime," she said, but she said it lightly, because, already, she was letting her mind run ahead. When she was married, she thought, she'd have some authority over their father, and she'd talk straight to him about Tom. She'd have Flossie to the house too, and have them all meet naturally. And Tod would put in a word for them.

For Tod Mellors had bought the meadows, and called a few times to bargain about the aftergrass.

"He means business," cried her father, making no disguise now about his meaning, and pulling her hair with an affectionate gesture. "Aftergrass indeed! No beast could want for aftergrass that had the sweet pickings his can get any day down between the flaggers in his own river field. If he takes our aftergrass, there's more in his mind than he's declared!"

As if she didn't know that. The old collie in the yard knew it! He had given up barking at Tod, and he a cross dog that barked at many people that passed the place every day of their lives.

But she would have liked if Tod Mellors showed his hand more plainly, or showed it to her instead of only to her father. She couldn't settle her mind to anything. She hung about the yard most of the day, or stood at the door to listen if there might be a trap coming up the road, with the tip of a whip showing over the hedge. And even when he didn't pass, it was good to stand looking out over the fields. How sweet must be the moment when feelings roused by such beauty were shared with another soul! She was impatient, though, for that moment of sharing to come. And it was slow in coming.

For one thing Tod never came to the place unless he had business with her father. She would have begun to think there was nothing between them and that it was all only her own imaginings, if it weren't for Jake. She was able to draw confidence from his impudent looks. Since Mellors had appeared on the scene, Jake had got bolder. He felt he was playing safe. More than ever their flirting was no more than a whiling away of the long summer evenings.

But her father suddenly seemed to take a different view of things, and several times she and Jake met at the pump in the yard, or when he came to the door of the kitchen to get the pig feed or the hot mash, she saw her father staring at them. But she feared her father then, no more than she feared the covert advances of the laboring man, for she felt wiser and more knowing than either of them. For all the fears the farmers had of their daughters mixing with the laboring classes, and those below them, it was nothing to the fear the fellows themselves had of getting into a situation that would make trouble between them and the men that gave them their hire. Oh, she knew Jake! She knew him better than her father knew him.

And that day in the churchyard, if her father only knew it, it was talking about Mellors they were! Jake was going on about him, and teasing her.

She was coming out from the service, and going through the churchyard, down the grass path to the stile that led into their own fields, when she saw Jake standing to one side of the path, under one of the old yew trees that vaulted it. He was probably going back to the yard to rinse the milk cans, a job that was often left till after the service on Sunday; and when he saw her he waited for her.

"I suppose you'll be going home by the other path soon," he said, and he nodded back toward the main path that led out to the road. And she knew Tod must have been going out that way because she had seen him in the church. He left before she did, and although she hurried out quickly afterward, she couldn't see him anywhere. Or at least she couldn't see him without stopping and looking around, so she was glad to come upon Jake. He gave her an excuse for lingering for a minute or two longer, and while she was talking to him she could look back casually over her shoulder. She wouldn't care then if he saw her. It might even provoke him to a bit of life. Because Jake might be only a workman, but he was a fine man, and young blood didn't make the same distinctions as old blood!

Jake wasn't one for hanging back, though. He wanted to get back to the yard and get his work done. He was going to a football match after his dinner.

"Are you coming home?" he said.

"What's the hurry?" she said, stealing a backward look as she spoke. Tod was still in the churchyard all right. He was standing at the gate talking to an old woman from a cottage near him, who did a bit of baking and washing for him. He was facing her way, but she couldn't be sure if he saw her. "What's the hurry?" she repeated absently. But Jake gave her sleeve a pull, and his voice was rough.

"I know what's in your mind," he said. "And you're not going to make a teaser out of me!"

She turned back to laugh at him, but when she saw the look in his eyes she felt ill at ease and restless. If only she could bring that look into the eyes of the other one!

It was at that moment her father came over the stile.

Her first feeling when she saw him was only a simple surprise. He ought to have been far away in the upland pasture putting a head collar on the mare, to bring her down to the home fields. What brought him back? And what brought him this way?

The next minute he raised the head collar.

"Don't!" she screamed, when she realized why he swung the strap in the air, and she saw the buckle glittering in the air. "We were only talking, Father," she screamed.

For one instant it seemed that the glittering buckle was stayed in the air, and she saw, too, by his eyes that her father did, perhaps, in that moment, believe her. But she knew him well; and she knew that her innocence wouldn't save her. He had caught a glimpse of her from the fields, by the yew tree, talking to someone, and he thought it was Tod Mellors. Then when he came up on them and saw it was not him, but Jake, he was disappointed, and it was for his disappointment she would suffer.

To this day she wasn't sure if he missed or not with that first lash at her. She fell down on the grass, but that could have been cowering as much as anything else, cowering before the blow and the temper in his eyes.

"Father, Father! Do you want to make a show of me before everyone?" she cried.

It was the wrong thing to say. He threw a glance beyond her to where the few people that were still about the churchyard had drawn together astonished, not knowing what to do or say. And among them, rooted to the ground with astonishment, was Tod.

And then, before he lifted the head collar again, she cowered again, covering her face and chest. Oh, she knew him so well! He would strike her now for sure. He was in the wrong, but it was she who put him in the wrong, and he'd strike her for it. Mortified at what he had done, and unable to undo it, he would do it again, putting himself altogether beyond the comprehension of gapers and gossipers.

It was the second blow that did the harm. It fell on her leg and it tore open the skin. Yet, even then, at the time she didn't feel any bitterness. If anything, it was pity for him that she felt, pity for the damage he had done through her to his own secret vanities and ambitions. But then, none of them, neither her father, nor herself, nor Tod, nor any one could know the cut was going to fester the way it did, and fail to heal.

In the days that followed, he must have been looking at it covertly though, times that she didn't know, because about a week afterward—the next Sunday it must have been—when she was getting ready to go out, he shouted at her.

"Take off that stocking!" he said. "Do you want the dye to get into the cut and destroy you altogether?"

It meant she had to stay at home, but she wasn't sorry that day. But after a few weeks, tied to the house all the time, it was a different matter. And one evening, about a month later, it was such a lovely evening she decided to take a walk even if it was only a little limp of a one.

He was in the yard when she opened the door. He looked at her.

"A person would think you'd want to hide your shame, instead of going out to show it off!"

The tears rushed into her eyes. How could he speak to her like that: him that did it? How could he? But she had a lot to learn. She didn't know then all the years that lay ahead when it would have been a relief if he sneered at her instead of the terrible silence that came down on the house in respect to her infirmity. Not only her father and Tom, but not one in the whole parish ever spoke of it directly to her. Only Tod. He always asked about it, right from the start.

The first night, the night it happened, he came straight up to the house, to ask how she was. Her father was out, and Tom and she were in the kitchen.

"It's Mellors," said Tom. "You'd better not let him see you," he said to her. But she limped to the door.

"How are you?" he said, as soon as he caught sight of her, and his eyes went at once to the rags she had tied around her leg. It was an old sheet she had torn up and wound around it.

"You saw what happened?" she said.

"I only saw him strike you. I didn't see why he did it."

"You saw all there was to see!" she flashed. "I was only talking to Jake Hewett."

He looked unbelievingly at her.

"He'd hardly strike you for that!" he said, and his voice was harsh. But she hardly bothered to clear herself any more because such a feeling of joy went through her at that harsh note in his voice.

I know now that he cares, she thought.

"Don't you believe me?" she asked.

"I don't know," he said. "I don't know!" And he turned and went away, without once looking at Tom, who was standing there like a fool, while it was all going on.

"I thought he wanted to see Father," said Tom.

"Did you!" she cried, and she laughed at him. "That's all you know!"

And if it weren't for the aching pain of the cut she'd have thought it was all for luck what happened. It could be the cause of bringing things to a head. And she went back to the kitchen and rolled down her stocking and looked at the leg. Maybe it might be a good thing to stoup it again, she thought, because she felt it would want to heal quickly if she was to follow up whatever advantage she had gained by it. It would surely be better in a few days.

But the pus formed in it again and again, no matter how often she stouped it. No matter what she did, no scab stuck to it long enough for it to dry.

At last one day about six months after it happened, when her father and Tom were at the three-day fair of Ballinasloe, she got herself taken to the dispensary in the town. Even then, she didn't put much stock on what the doctor told her.

"Is an ulcer a bad thing, Tom?" she asked cautiously, the morning they came back, when they were alone together for a minute in the kitchen.

He was sharpening the scythe up against the kitchen table, and drawing the whetstone slowly along the blade, as if it was to get music out of it he was doing it.

"In a beast, is it?" he asked absently.

"Man or beast," she said weakly.

"They say it's bad," he said. "Why?"

"Oh, don't mind!" she said dejectedly.

Tod knew all about ulcers though.

"Is that leg no better?" he said one day irritably, when he met her in the town. "Would it be ulcerating?" he said. "Did you see a doctor about it? Ulcers get incurable if they're neglected at the start."

His voice was cruel, but she knew what made it cruel, and she wouldn't have it any other way.

"You believe me now, Tod, don't you?" she said softly. "It was only because he was a workingman that my father was annoyed with me for talking to him, and—"

"I know," he said sharply, interrupting her. "I believe you." But there was a look on his face that made her heart go slow. It was a look she had seen once on Tom's face when they were children. He had a new watch that their father gave him for his Confirmation, and they were playing in the fields when suddenly his face got white.

"My watch is lost!" he said.

All afternoon they looked for it in the fine fringe of the meadow, and in the strong high grass of the headland. And then, just as they were going to go home, she heard him draw a breath like a cry.

"What's the matter?" she asked, running over to him, where he was standing on a plank that ran across one of the ditches, and served for a rough bridge.

"I've found it!" he said, but she thought he was going daft, because instead of looking pleased he looked—well, he had the look on his face that Tod had—

The watch was on the bottom of the ditch, under a foot of water.

"But you've found it!" she said.

"I wish I didn't," he said.

That's the way Tod feels about me, she thought. He wishes he didn't believe me! Now that I'm useless to him. It would have made it easier for him.

Because she knew by then herself that the leg was never going to be better. It didn't come against her too much: she could work about the house and the inner yard; she could churn and bake, but she'd be no use at all for calf rearing and pig feeding, and the heavy jobs of a farmer's wife.

A fierce resentment went through her. That was the country for you! If they lived in the town it would have been different. In the country, all that men thought about was breeding a family, and getting as much work out of a woman as a beast. But then she remembered the first day Tod drove across the cobbles, when their eyes met; and she knew she was doing him an injustice, or a bit of an injustice anyway. He wanted a bit of romance in his life too. But he wasn't prepared to have it at the cost of everything else.

He came less and less often to the house. Sometimes he didn't call for months, and he always had a strict purpose when he called. Now, though, instead of being glad to see him, her father found it hard to be civil to him. She didn't even see him in church, because although for a long while she used to sit behind him but on the other side of the aisle, so she could glance at him slantways without being seen, he must have felt her eyes upon him, for he took to sitting at the back of the church. And he went out quickly and drove away. He had given up the trap. He was one of the first in the countryside to have a motor. The motor seemed to take him out of her life still further. She hated that motor. She knew too that it would keep him eligible a long time yet for the young girls growing up around them, in spite of his aging appearance and his solitary ways.

He was aging fast; she could see that on the rare occasions she met him. And her heart was stabbed with sadness for them both. But he never married! In this thought her heart exulted, and in its implications. Standing at the window or the door sometimes still, she was unable to stem the little false feelings of hope that stirred in her, above all in summertime, the time she first met him. Then,

when the fields were rich and flowing, the hedges flecked with blossom, and the scent of the clover sweetened every breath in the air,
she used to argue with herself in her heart.

It ought to be enough, she thought, the beauty and the peace of
it all. But it wasn't enough. It seemed impossible to think it was not
meant to be shared.

Her leg had become a lot less troublesome after a number of
years, and sometimes she looked around her in the church, and it
seemed to her that the forced rest she had got from having to mind
it, had left her, in the end, a younger-looking woman than the
women that had been girls with her, and that were married, and
worn out with childbearing and work.

Even Tod remarked on it one day in the town.

"You're looking well," he said, and although it was a mild enough
remark, she knew it meant she was looking well indeed.

"I'm feeling well!" she said. And she laughed. "I was thinking
in church only the other Sunday that I'm wearing better than a
lot of my neighbors."

It was a flash of her old boldness, a boldness that had gone utterly
from her spirit much less her tongue. But Tod turned aside abruptly.

"They had their strength when they needed it," he said. Somehow
she didn't feel humiliated or hurt. He did care! she thought, and it
came into her mind that if she really knew—for certain—not just
by hints and insinuations, but in words—that he had loved her then,
and that that was why he never married—and never would—
she'd be satisfied. He'd be hers in a kind of way then.

It wouldn't satisfy some people, but it would satisfy her—or she
thought it would. But if she did know it for certain would she
be able to keep it a secret, she wondered? Wouldn't it only be like
her dreams and imaginings over again if she didn't tell it to someone: just one person. And who would she tell? Flossie Sauren was
the only one who might understand.

Poor Flossie! She and Tom had never married either, so although
she and Flossie didn't meet often she felt there was a bond between
them. Not that she had much sympathy with Flossie. It seemed to
her that whereas she and Tod had been kept apart by inmost, un-
knowable causes hidden in the human heart—Tom and Flossie
were unmarried because they hadn't any spirit.

There was one evening she tried to goad Tom into doing something about it. It was once more the eve of the three-day Fair in Ballinasloe, and for the first time in their lives their father was not going to it. Tom was going on his own.

"He mustn't be feeling well if he's not going. Will you manage by yourself, Tom?" she asked nervously. He would be buying springers; a knacky job.

But he didn't answer, and she saw by him how stupid she had been. He was glad to be going alone. He looked younger and livelier than he'd done for a long time, and he was excited: he was almost queerly excited.

"You'd think you were going to a wedding," she said.

She didn't often make jokes, but she ought to have been cured for ever by the look he gave her.

"What made you say that?" he said, and he stopped up in the middle of blacking his shoes and stared at her.

"Don't look at me like that!" she said. "I was only thinking how well you looked. And anyway, I don't see what harm it was! By rights it ought to be a wedding—your own!" And she ran over to him. "Oh, Tom, I'm not standing in your way, am I? You know what I mean! If you're waiting for me to be gone, and the place to be clear for you to take in your wife, then you'll never marry, because I'll never be gone. It's not my fault though, you know that, don't you, Tom? But I wouldn't be in anyone's way. You can tell that to Flossie. I'd be good to her: I would. I promise you!"

He was blacking the other shoe by this time, but he left down the blacking brush and took his foot down off the chair and pointed toward the yard where their father could be heard clattering about the cobbles.

"What life would she have in the house with him?"

It was true.

"Here, let me do those shoes for you," she said, in a fit of compassion.

"They're done now."

They were shining like laurel leaves. She couldn't help exclaiming.

"Aren't they very light shoes for wearing to the fair?"

He was so touchy, though, she could have bitten out her tongue for noticing them.

"I want something besides hobnail boots to wear in the evenings in the lodging-house parlor, don't I?" he said.

"That's right, Tom," she said weakly, thinking that when their father went with him, it was very little he saw of the parlor, but was sent off to bed like a gossoon, to be up at the first screech of daylight.

He'd be a new man if he was left on his own, she thought. And where she would have felt guilty thinking of the gain to herself if anything happened to their father, it seemed different altogether to think of the gain it would be to Tom.

How long will it be till he gets the place? she wondered. But it seemed that their lives must go on, day after day, as it had always done, until it was less of a duration than a kind of immediate successiveness: a kind of eternity.

Ah, well, he'll enjoy the fair, she thought, and she watched him go next morning in the dawn with a little excited feeling. Maybe he'd have things to tell her when he came back. She tried to imagine the lodging-house parlor.

Would there be any young women there, playing the piano to amuse the farmers and the dealers? It would be hard on poor Flossie if he put his eye on one of them, but somehow she couldn't think of him making advances to any young woman, but only sitting down, pleased with being away from home, and proud of his shoes, shining like the laurels. She was longing for him to come home, and tell them all about it anyway.

Her father too was looking forward to him coming home. The fair seemed to gain in importance for him by his being unable to go to it. He never quit reading the account in the paper of the weights of the beasts, and the prices they made.

"I ought to have gone," he said, "no matter how I felt. He'll buy backward springers; that's what he'll do. He has no experience."

Tom didn't buy backward springers though. He bought none at all.

"They were going too dear," he said, and she thought he said it lamely.

"You didn't buy any beast at all?" she echoed.

She was nearly speechless with surprise.

Their father wasn't speechless though; far from it.

"Four days' food and lodgings and nothing to show for it," he shouted. "God damn it, what kind of a fool are you?" He looked as if he might strike him. Then he sat down heavily on the chair behind him.

"Are you all right, Father?" she cried. "Tom! Tom! There's something the matter with him! Quick!—hold him."

It was a stroke.

She forgot about Tom and Flossie for many a long day after that. For seven years he never left the bed. She thought about Tom and Flossie now and then, but she never liked to mention it again. The matter was linked in her mind with her unfortunate joking the night before the fair. And when, after years, she ventured to mention it he cut her short.

"I've had enough of that!" he said crossly.

She felt he too was reminded of the night of the fair, and he didn't want to be. But later, he spoke of that night himself.

"I feel I killed him!" he said.

"Nonsense," she said. "And he's far from dead anyway," she added.

But he wasn't so far from it. The next day was the day she caught him looking at her leg, and that was the day he asked about it.

The next day he was dead.

As she stood beside the bed, after the priest had gone, and she was waiting for the undertaker, she found herself pondering on the changes that would come. Already the house was filling with people. One by one the neighbors had congregated. It was almost like the way, one by one, cattle are drawn over to a part of the field where something unusual has happened, like a tree falling, or even one of themselves getting lame and unable to rise.

At first the voices were subdued, but as the house filled up, and as the neighboring women saw small tasks to be done, and set about doing them, there was a lively air about the house that it had not had for years; if it ever had.

It was like a breaking of ice. And like, sometimes, when the ice of winter is breaking, and the growth of spring has already started underneath it, she felt within her a great expectancy. Expectancy of what? She didn't know, but she did wonder if Tod would come to the funeral.

He didn't. He stayed away. He was the only one for miles around that wasn't seen at the house or in the cemetery.

"A nice neighbor, that fellow!" said Tom, when all was over and they were alone on the day of the burial.

"He never forgave Father," she said.

Tom stood up abruptly. He was still in his best clothes, but he was restless, and didn't have much fancy for sitting talking. Above all, he didn't seem to fancy the turn the talk had taken.

"I think I'll change my clothes," he said.

She knew what that meant. He was going out with the old scythe to cut weeds. He's married to that old scythe, she thought, partly bitter, and partly amused. And a few minutes later, when she heard steps in the yard, she thought it was him coming back for something: the whetstone, or the can of grease.

But it was Tod.

"You didn't come to the funeral," she said, for the sake of saying something. She didn't ask him in, but stood up and went toward him, and they both stepped out into the yard.

"I never forgave him," he said.

They were the words she had used only a moment before to Tom.

"For what he did to me?" she asked carefully.

He looked straight at her face.

"—and to me," he said deliberately.

Like a lark in the sky—like when she was young—her heart sang out for joy. But under a hedge of the field in front of them, a corn-crake made himself heard with a harsh sound, not like a song at all, more like the sound of the clappers at Tenebrae.

"He came between us: he spoiled everything for us."

It was true, she thought. At last, after all the years it was said. Not in the words of youth, not in the way she would once have wanted to hear it—but in his own way, in the only way it could be said now perhaps—he had said it. She looked at him with gentleness and pity.

He saw the look in her eyes, and he took a step nearer to her, but suddenly she moved back. She had condemned him long ago for not thinking love was enough, and for thinking only of breeding and rearing up a family. But now, when the days of her own fertility were over, she saw things in another light. Her heart was still filled with the old feelings she knew now so well, the feelings of hope and premonition, but she realized, at last, that it wasn't from Tod any more that she looked for their fulfillment. It was too late.

In the intensity of this realization she could think of nothing else for a moment. Then her mind seized urgently upon her brother. Tom! He was younger than her, and Flossie was years younger. She made a rapid calculation, for practical reasons, of Flossie's age. There was time yet surely for them to be fruitful in their marriage.

I must talk to him, she thought, but it was no longer a vague romantic notion that animated her mind. It was not their satisfaction either that she looked for from their union. It isn't ourselves that matter any more, she thought, Tod or I: or even Tom or Flossie. It's those that come after us.

Looking past Tod, she filled her eyes with the beauty of the sight beyond him, the field he had once bid for, that was again heavy with meadow. Oh, to stand leaning over that gate with a crowd of youngsters around her—or even one small creature, gripping her hand— Oh, the joy of it!

Impatient suddenly, she put out her hand to Tod.

"Thank you for coming up," she said, and she shook his hand. He looked as if he were going to say something else, but she gathered her coat closer around her. "I must see Tom," she said. "I was on my way down to him when you came." He had to stand aside to let her pass, and when she walked quickly away, he had nothing to do but to go back out to where he had left the car on the road. Once she looked back at him, but he didn't see her. She was taking her leave of him at last in that backward glance. Then she hurried down to the river.

They must get married at once, she thought. They mustn't wait at all; not even in decency to the dead.

"Tom! Tom!" she called to him, as she drew nearer. Already she had forgotten about Tod Mellors. He was unimportant to her at last.

"Oh, Tom, I couldn't stay in the house," she cried, as she reached him. "I had to come down to you. I know you hated me saying it the last time, but it's different now, isn't it?" She hesitated, but only for a minute, "—about you and Flossie, I mean?"

He had stopped scything when she first called, but when he took in the words, he assumed the stiffness of a stranger. Then, deliberately, and without answering her, he began to pull the scythe heavily through the reeds again.

She tried to take his silence for attentiveness.

"You'll have to wait a little while, I know that," she said apologetically, "but we could have everything planned." Her excitement rushed back and overwhelmed her. She didn't notice the pronouns she had used. "You could talk it over with Flossie, and we could begin to get things ready without anybody knowing, and if you told her that I was in the know then she could come up here, and we could both be getting the house ready. We could—"

Tom stopped scything again, but he took up the whetstone.

"Well, Tom?" she cried.

He drew the whetstone across the blade.

"Take it easy," he said then. "Take it easy, will you!"

"Oh, but Tom! How can you say that? After all the years that have been wasted. Time is so precious for you now—for both of you."

But her eagerness seemed to annoy him.

"Take it easy, for God's sake, will you?" he said again. "I suppose I'll have to make a few changes now. Death always brings some changes anyway. But there's no hurry. There is *no hurry* I tell you," he repeated, and this time he said it so positively and meaningfully that she felt there was more to him than she had ever known.

"I know it wouldn't be the same as long ago," she said less confidently, "but surely it would be—"

"—better than nothing. Is that what you mean?" he said bitterly. He was so bitter she began to get frightened.

"No," she cried, all the same, "that's not what I mean. But wouldn't you like to have a family growing up around you? Wouldn't any man?"

He pondered that for a minute or two and her hopes rose, but he looked her in the face with a strange expression.

"I'll have no family," he said shortly. "I can tell you that now."

"How do you know?" she cried. "You never can tell. I—"

He put out his hand and caught her by the arm, and his fingers pressed her like a vise.

"How do I know! How does any man know? My father thought I was a gom; I accepted that," he said, "but I didn't know you took me for one too. I may have been afraid of him, afraid to face up to him openly, but that didn't say I let him own me body and soul. When I said we'd have no family, I knew what I was saying. Don't look so stupid! You know what I mean!"

But as her mind tried to follow him, he sneered at her.

"Oh, it's not what you think now!" he said. "It was all respectable and as it ought to be; or as near as we could make it like what it ought to be. We're properly married and all that, but it's not the cause for rejoicing that you seem to think it: not now anyway."

They were standing near an old thorn tree, and she sank back against it weakly. She was utterly confounded by what he had said. Looking at her he felt bad: he could not see what injury he could have done her, but he wanted to make amends.

"I was going to tell you a couple of times, but I thought it was safer—for your own sake too—not to know anything about it. And then as the years went by—"

She looked up quickly. "Years? How many years?"

"Oh, I don't know," he said indifferently, but then he made an effort. "It was before Father got ill—it must be seven years ago, or eight maybe. As a matter of fact I thought you had got wind of it. It was the night I was supposed to be going to Ballinasloe to the fair." Suddenly he put his hand up to his forehead in a mild distress. "You remember, I didn't buy the springers—and he flew into a rage—it brought on the first stroke he got—I used to think for a long time that it was my fault he got it. Because I wasn't at the fair at all. That was the time we got married; we went up to Dublin."

The fair: the thin shoes he was polishing for the lodging-house parlor! She thought him odd that night: she remembered it well. So that was what he was up to that night. He hadn't gone to the fair at all! She looked at him. She never thought he would have had it in him.

And at the surprise on her face, he felt a momentary flash of the liveliness and spirit that had led to his one solitary escapade. But it died away at the thought of the long, unproductive years, ushered in by that brief bravado.

"Well, that's the way things are," he said tiredly and dejectedly.

"You see what I mean when I say there's no hurry. There'll be changes all right, I know that—but I don't know what changes they'll be yet—I doubt if Flossie will want to come to live here, being so used to living near the road—it's lonely here you know. I might go and live in their place because there's some talk of her sister going to live in Dublin. That might work out all right. Their place is small, but we'll have no use for a big place." He looked at her suddenly. "There's you to consider, of course," he said. "It'd be very lonely here for you on your own. But as I said, there's no hurry. And now, will you leave me alone for God's sake and let me get on with the scything. You know it's the only bit of pleasure I get."

There was no choice for her but to turn and make her way back to the house. Evening was coming down quickly, and the western sky glowed with so fierce a light that as the homing rooks flew across the path of the setting sun, they were made for a moment as transparent as glass birds.

At the door of the house she stood and looked back. The light of day had not yet faded, but a few stars had made their way through the heavens. Their beauty stabbed her through and through. She used to want to share that beauty, first with Tod, and then, in a last hysterical longing, she wanted to share it with anyone —anyone—even the unborn. But now there would be no one to share it with ever. Why did she have this terrible need? We try to make it a part of our life, she thought, and sure what are we all only but a part of it.

She looked back toward the river field. It was almost too dark to see Tom, or for him to see what he was doing, but he was still swinging the scythe expertly from side to side, slicing through the reeds and the wild grasses, with a gesture so true and natural it might have been a branch swaying back and forth in the wind.

Posy

"DANIEL, I think you'd better come into the shop."

Hannah came to the door of the storeroom where he was on his knees unpacking a crate of china. He shook his head. Hannah was no use in the shop. Leaning on the crate, he got to his feet quickly enough, because in spite of his sixty years he was not much troubled by rheumatism. As a matter of fact, both Kate and Hannah considered that he was very well preserved. The word was apt: the sap was gone out of him.

"I'm coming: stop calling me," he muttered irritably, as he heard Hannah coming to the door again. Another few minutes and he would have had the crate unpacked. He hated stopping a thing in the middle. But the real mistake was starting it at all when Kate was out.

He ought to have waited until she came back. She couldn't be very long: she only went down the town for a few minutes because it was the day of the Assizes, and she always took a great pleasure in seeing the strangers round the courthouse, particularly the solicitors and the barristers. She always had a great respect for the professional class. So had Hannah, for that matter. They were always the same, even when they were girls, thinking they ought all to make wonderful matches—him included. Well—they didn't; and that was that!

Daniel gave a quick shake to each skinny leg to get rid of the sawdust that stuck to him, before he opened the door of the shop. Then he stepped forward.

54

Standing in the middle of the shop, and leaning upon a silver-headed cane, was an elegantly dressed young man. In particular, Daniel noted his chamois gloves, and with some surprise he decided that he must be a solicitor from Dublin.

In spite of his surprise, however, Daniel's manner was easy and affable.

"Good afternoon, sir," he said.

The stranger, too, was easy and affable.

"Good evening, Mr. Dogget," he said. "You have a very fine shop here"—he looked around—"and carry a very fine stock, I see." He looked back at Daniel and smiled. "But I'm afraid there's not much profit from the commodity I want."

Such humility was unusual in a customer. Daniel was just about to assume a lordly attitude of indifference to profit, large or small, when the young man leaned over the counter.

"All I want," he said, "is a bit of information."

The unexpected word fell imperfectly upon Daniel's ears, but all the same he felt vaguely uneasy.

Apparently, however, the feeling was completely unjustified. The young man was merely inquiring about people who used to live in the town. He had made inquiries elsewhere, without success, and had at last been recommended to come to him: Daniel.

"Oh, certainly, certainly," said Daniel, as soon as he understood. "I'll be glad to give you any help I can. What was the name of this family?"

"Well, as a matter of fact," said the young man, "the people I have in mind are long gone out of these parts altogether. All I want to see is the cottage where they used to live, or the remains of it, because even the cottage, I think, must have tumbled down long ago." He paused for a moment. "The name," he said, "was Mallows."

Was there an involuntary sparkle of interest in the dull eyes of the shopkeeper? The young man thought so, but he could not be certain. And when the old fellow replied his voice was even.

"I knew people of that name all right," he said. "There was a big family of them."

"Yes, that would be right," said the young man.

There was a slight pause.

"Were you interested in one of them in particular?" said Daniel.

This time it seemed as if there was a bit of an edge in his voice.

"Yes," said the stranger. "I was particularly interested in one of them. Her name was Mary: Mary Mallows."

"Oh!" Quite clearly Daniel had expected to hear another name. The young man felt a sense of anticlimax.

"Did you know her?" he asked, but he felt the flatness of the question.

But Daniel, however, was very polite.

"Well, I can't say that I did," he murmured. "I suppose she was one of the Mallows of Meadow Lane, but I don't seem to recollect a Mary among them."

"Meadow Lane!" exclaimed the stranger. "Yes, that would be right. Mary Mallows of Meadow Lane: I often said it was like the title of a song."

"It must be the same Mallows so," said Daniel, drawn into the topic in spite of himself. "I thought I knew them all, but I don't recollect a Mary among them. No, I don't recollect a Mary." He shook his head. "Of course there was a very big family of them. She may have been one of the ones that were before my time. Still, I ought to have heard something about her. Let me see. There was Ellen; she was the oldest I think. She was like the mother of them all. Their poor mother was worn to a shadow after bringing the lot of them into the world. Ellen got the job of bringing them up. Then there were two sons that went to America, and there was another son named Roger that died. No, I'm wrong there, Roger went to Australia. It was Bartlet that died. And another poor girl named Bessie. She was drowned in the river when she was only a young girl at school. Then there was Judy. She was in service with cousins of mine, but she isn't with them any more. She saved up a bit of money, I believe, and bought a shop. They say she's a wealthy woman now. Then there was Tod, and I don't know what became of him; he was a bit wild. And there was Bridget. She was in service with a bank clerk that used to be in this town, and when he was made manager down in the south he took her with him. That's the lot of them, I think." For the briefest possible moment the old bachelor's voice halted. "Except one," he said then hastily. "It wouldn't be her you mean?" But before there was time for a reply he answered his own question. "Anyway, her name wasn't Mary," he said, and his jaws set firmly upon the matter.

The young man felt himself possessed by an obstinate interest in this other girl.

"What was her name?" he asked.

This time, however, Daniel was decidedly irritable. It took every ounce of his respect for the professional classes to enable him to conceal his irascibility.

"Oh, she was of no account," he said briskly. "She used to work here for us." He paused for a moment. "She used to scrub the floors," he said vindictively.

At once the younger man was alive to that vindictive undertone. He fixed his eye on Daniel.

"Her name?" he said quietly.

Daniel's thin, characterless face trembled slightly from the strain of an unaccustomed obstinacy.

"We used to call her Posy," he said then suddenly, and the trembling in his face became all at once painful to watch.

"Posy!" The stranger was taken aback at the strangely intimate pet name.

"Yes, Posy," said the old bachelor. "At least that was what we began to call her here, and the name stuck to her. It sort of suited her," he said sheepishly. "As a matter of fact it was me that first called her Posy," he added, still more sheepishly.

Posy! All at once, as if a faded flower pressed in a book should suddenly swell with sap again, and breathe again, and quiver again with life, the pet name of Posy was no sooner uttered upon the air than it brought back so potent a memory of the young Mallows girl, that some softening of the heart seemed to take place in the old bachelor.

"When she first came to work for us I didn't know what she was called," he said. "There was always one of the young Mallows in service with us. Before Posy there were several others of them. I forget their names. I think we had Judy at one time. And poor Bessie that was drowned was often sent up after school to run messages or carry slops. There was always one of them about the place. I never took much notice of them. They were all alike as far as I could see, strealy and dirty most of the time; meek as milk when you met them in the passages, and as saucy as monkeys when you'd meet them in

the streets at night. God help you if you had the misfortune to take
a short cut through Meadow Lane. It was torture to pass those cottages in the dark. Half a dozen of those Mallows would be sitting in
the dark in the doorway, and they'd whistle and catcall at you.
And the giggling! I used to say they had cats' eyes that could see
in the dark, but you couldn't see them, and it made you feel kind
of foolish, you know, because the next day you wouldn't know but
that the very one that was serving up your meals to you was the one
that was boldest and sauciest in the dark the night before. I declare
I never knew them apart—until I took heed of Posy. I called them
by the first name that came to me. They'd answer to any name.
Judy would do for the lot of them! Or Bessie. And my mother, God
rest her, never called any of them anything but Young Mallows.
As I told you, it was I gave Posy her name. I don't know what
she was called at the font. But after a while everyone in the town
called her Posy. Even when her hair grew again she was still called
Posy, although I used to think afterward that it didn't suit her so
well then. And she didn't like it either, when she got older.

" 'How can I be dignified with a name like that?' she used to say
to me.

" 'Why don't you change it?' I used to say.

" 'A lot of good that would do in a mean little town like this.
I'll never get rid of it till I get myself out of here.'

"Sometimes she used to work herself up about it.

" 'It is your fault,' she said one day. 'It was you began it.'

"I only laughed at her.

" 'It wasn't my fault that you got ringworm, was it?' I said, and
that made her twice as angry. She hated any mention of that time.
You see, it was shortly after she came to work for us that she got
it. My mother was alive at the time, and I remember well the day it
all started.

" 'That young Mallows has a dirty head,' she said. 'I do believe
she has ringworm! That's the worst of these Mallows. They're great
workers, but there's no knowing what filth they'll bring into a house.
I'll have to send her down to the Dispensary and have her examined.'
And my mother was right. It was ringworm. The next thing I knew
she was sent off about her business, and that evening my sisters came
home with the news that her head was shaved. They were out for a

walk, it seemed, when they saw her, and they thought they'd never get home quick enough to tell my mother. They were on their way home when just as they were getting near the town they thought they heard someone crying under the hedge by the side of the road. Hannah wanted to go on. She said it was nothing, but Kate went over and looked across the hedge and there, stretched out on the grass, was young Mallows, with her head shaved to the bone, and she was crying so hard she didn't even hear them when they burst out laughing. She must have been ashamed to go home through the streets. I suppose she got over the wall at the back of the Dispensary and crossed the fields to where they found her. She was waiting till it got dark before she went home, she said, when they climbed through the hedge and asked her what was wrong with her. 'And get your death of cold? You'll do nothing of the kind!' said Kate. 'You'll get up this minute and go straight home, daylight or no daylight. A lot of attention you'll get, anyway; a little slut like you!' "

Daniel's face took on a shamefaced look as he said the last words. It could even have been that they slipped from his lips accidentally.

"They were always very hard on her," he said, "but to give them their due I think there were a lot of cattle in the field where she was lying and they were all gathered round her, breathing on her and smelling her, and my sisters were afraid she'd come to harm, I suppose. They were always acting for the best, no matter what anyone said. I always recognized that. Anyway, they made the girl go home in front of them. Afterward they told Mother all about it. They said it was the funniest thing they ever saw in their lives. She was like a calf being driven along the road. She kept right in the middle of it and they had to keep poking her in the back every other minute to keep her moving, but just as they got to the top of Meadow Lane what did she do but throw up her skirt over her head like a shawl and make a dash for the cottage as if there was a pack of beagles after her. They thought they'd die; Hannah and Kate. There they stood at the top of the lane watching her making down it, and the best part of it all was the cut of her petticoat behind! It was as black as soot. They nearly died laughing. Hannah was the worst. Kate had to call to her mind that there were other people in the street. That sobered her, because they were always very concerned with keeping up our position. Our mother was inclined to be more practical. And she didn't think their story was so funny at all. She was wondering what we'd do without the girl. It might take a long time to get rid of ringworm.

"But as a matter of fact it didn't take long at all. It was attended to in time. My mother made inquiries at the Dispensary, and they said it would be all right to take her back in a week or two, and that she was well disinfected. But it was only then the real fun began. It appeared that the young one wouldn't come back because of her shaved head. She was ashamed of her life to let anyone see it. She wouldn't come back no matter what was said or done. My mother went down to the cottage to her, and still she wouldn't come back. Then my sisters went down, but she wouldn't even come out into the lane to speak to them."

Daniel looked up at his listener suddenly.

"Do you know, I think she was more ashamed of me than of anyone!" he said, "although I never took any notice of her at all in those days, but all the same I think it was me she had in her mind, because it was after I met her in the lane one evening by chance that she came back.

"It was a summer evening about a month after she left our place, and I was coming home from a walk on the shores of the lake, that was my usual walking place, and as dusk was beginning to gather I thought I'd take a short cut up through Meadow Lane, but first of all I glanced up it to make sure the young Mallows weren't playing outside their cottage, but the lane seemed to be empty. Then, just as I was about a third of the way up the length of it, and safely past the Mallows cottage, all of a sudden I got a start, because, right in front of me, I saw a head rise over the wall. I hardly got time to catch a glimpse of it when it bobbed down again, but it was one of the Mallows, anyway, I was certain of that much. For a minute my heart nearly stopped. I thought the whole lot of them were inside the wall and that they were lying in wait for me, because you've no idea how wild they were. They wouldn't stop at anything. They'd throw a bucket of water over you as quick as they'd wink, all the more especially if they saw, as on that occasion, that a person had his best suit of clothes on him; and they of a light color into the bargain.

"I suppose when I thought they were all there I should have

put my pride in my pocket and made a run for it, but something made me stop.

" 'Is that you, Tod?' I cried, and I ran over to the wall, but knowing at the same time that he'd be gone if he was the only one in it.

"He wasn't gone, though. There he was crouching under the wall and his head pressed so close against the stones that he didn't see me when I leaned over the top and looked down at him.

"And then, all at once, I remembered the way my sisters had found the young one after they had shaved her head at the Dispensary, and I suppose that, and the fact that this creature under the wall, in spite of its cropped head, seemed to me even in the bad light, to be wearing some sort of skirt made me give an exclamation. It wasn't Tod at all. It was his sister; the young one that had her hair shaved. But if it had been shaved to the roots it must have grown quickly because all over her whole head there was a mass of the tightest little golden curls you ever saw in your life. The very minute I recognized who it was I looked down at her again, without her seeing me, because her little round head was pressed in tight to the stones, and the first thing that came into my mind was that she was like a little posy. And before I had time to think of myself I opened my mouth and said it aloud.

" 'Posy!' I said, just the one word. 'Posy.'

"Well, I never forgot, from that day to this, the start she gave. At the sound of the voice, she threw back her head in fright, and when she saw me she sprang to her feet. For a minute I thought she was going to dash away, but this time I think her temper got the better of her shame, and curiosity got the better of her again, because with one foot raised to run away, she turned back suddenly and her eyes were flashing.

" 'What was that name you called me?' she said, and she looked so surprised I couldn't help laughing. I suppose she thought it was some bad name I called her, although there could hardly be any names like that unfamiliar to anyone who lived in Meadow Lane!

"I laughed again. But I didn't laugh long.

" 'How dare you laugh at me?' she cried. 'You may think you're smart, Mr. Daniel Dogget, but let me tell you that I won't be called names by you or anybody else, whether I am a servant or not!' "

There had been such spirit in that young voice long ago that the dried-up yellow face of the old bachelor took on some animation as he tried to imitate it. Then his muscles relaxed again.

"Do you know what I did?" he said. "I just stepped back a bit for safety, and I looked her in the eyes.

" 'Wait a minute,' I cried, and stooping down I gathered up a few cowslips and wild orchids that were growing round about there, and I dragged out a few ferns from a crack in the wall. 'Just a minute and I'll soon show you what I mean by a posy,' I said, and I broke off the stems and gathered the heads of the flowers together. 'There's a posy for you now,' I said, and I looked up at her, because while I was picking the flowers she had ventured to stand up again and lean over the wall. She looked more of a posy than ever. I hadn't noticed it before, but she had a lovely face, round and sweet, with soft eyes, although there could be a flash in them when she liked: I learned that afterward. But this day she was gentle enough. For another minute she leaned over the wall, looking at me, and then suddenly she laughed and slipped down out of sight, and I could hear her, still laughing, as she ran across the field on the other side of it."

Daniel paused, almost as if he still listened to those light footsteps through the moist evening grasses. Then his voice quickened.

"Next morning when I went in to breakfast after taking down the shutters of the shop, there she was, without a word, washing the delph in the kitchen. It gave me a surprise to see her, I can tell you. There had been no mention of her coming back. In fact, I don't believe my sisters knew she was in the house at all; they hadn't come downstairs. I got such a surprise I called out.

" 'Who's that?' I cried, although of course it was only an exclamation, as you couldn't mistake the girl, with her headful of little tight curls like a boy. But if she knew it was an exclamation she didn't pretend. Instead she looked over her shoulder and smiled with a wicked little smile.

" 'It's Posy!' she said.

"Well, that was the beginning of it. And I doubt if anyone in the town ever called her again by her Christian name! Like myself, they probably forgot it!" he added jauntily.

But as he looked up at the other man he suddenly gave a little gasp.

"You don't think—?" he cried.

The young man nodded his head.

"I do," he said quietly. "Posy Mallows and Mary Mallows were one and the same person."

The two men stared at each other. Why, the young man wondered, had the girl lived so vividly in the old fellow's mind? And why, thought Daniel, was this stranger so interested in his story of Posy Mallows. Had she gone into service with his mother? It was extraordinary how those Mallows had all got themselves into good families. And Posy was clean enough to get work in the best of houses, in spite of all his sisters used to say about her, although even he himself used to think she'd never make a real servant: there was something too impudent in her nature. But she could have changed. Was she still alive? he wondered.

For a minute they continued to stare at each other, each with a question in his eyes. It was a question as to which of them would give way first.

I'll have to ask him outright, thought the younger man, but just then Daniel, who was facing the window, gave a start.

Coming down the street toward the house was Miss Kate Dogget.

Daniel uttered a small, elderly exclamation of vexation.

"What is the matter?" asked the young man in surprise.

But Daniel hardly trusted himself to speak. He felt that he had been put at a disadvantage. If Kate came in while they were talking about the Mallows there would be no knowing what she might say. One mention of Posy and she'd be sure to make some bitter remark that would let everything out. Those lawyers had their ears well washed!

"I'm afraid I must ask you to excuse me, sir," he said, hurriedly and awkwardly. "I see my sister coming down the street, and I had some things to attend to in her absence. If you still want to see where Posy lived, you can find the place easily without any help." He caught the young man by the arm and urged him toward the door. "Just take the first turn on your left after you pass the gable of this house," he said.

Was the old fellow daft? The young man couldn't help raising his eyebrows. Waves of humiliation swept over Daniel.

"You know what women are!" he said desperately. Kate was so near now they could hear her heels on the pavement. "I'd just as soon my sister wouldn't know what we were talking about. I have reasons!" he cried, and it seemed to himself that this last was such an outburst of confidence that his face flamed. But although there was a glint in his eye, the young man contrived to look obtuse.

"You see," gasped poor Daniel, "there was talk at the time!"

"Talk?" said the young man then.

"About Posy," said Daniel quickly. "And me," he added.

It was out: the small dried-up secret.

"Mary Mallows and you!" It looked for a minute as if the young man was going to burst out laughing, but seeing the way the old fellow's face had begun to twitch he put another countenance upon his surprise. "A man of your position!" he said quickly, and at his words, an extraordinary change came over Daniel.

"I see you are an understanding man," said Daniel, "—more so than most!" And suddenly becoming as agile as a cat, he slipped out again from behind the counter. "Would you like to hear more about it?" he asked, at the same time catching the young man by the sleeve.

The young man glanced at his watch.

"I'd like to see the cottage in Meadow Lane," he said, "if it's still standing." He wasn't so interested after all in Daniel's dried-up romance.

"It's not," said Daniel hurriedly, "but you could see where it used to be. And I could show you where I first saw Posy when she bobbed her head over the wall!" He was beside himself with excitement.

"Very well," said the young man, and he turned in the direction of the door. But Daniel shot out his arm.

"Not that way!" he shouted. "This way, sir!" he cried, as he flung open a door at the back of the shop. The door led into the yard, at the far end of which a large gate stood open showing the green and yellow fields beyond the town. "If you cross the yard and go out that gate you'll find yourself at the top of Meadow Lane," said Daniel, pointing with his anemic hand. "I'll try and get out as quickly as I can and I'll follow you." The next moment the door shut upon the young man's heels.

Outside in the yard there was still a false brightness because of the white lime upon the walls, but when the young man stepped

into the lane beyond the gateway he saw how the day had declined.
Between the narrow walls to either side of him, the rutted ground
was indistinct, and the wayside grass so dark that a solitary cow
that grazed it remained unseen until it raised its head against the
rosied horizon.

The lane was not long. Even in the failing light he could see
to the far end of it where a humped bridge went over a small river
and brought one a few yards farther only to abandon one to the
open fields. And as for the cottages, there were not more than a
dozen of them. He ought to be able to find what he was looking for
without waiting for Daniel. He had had enough of the old fellow.
He hurried forward down the lane. And sure enough, in the middle of the flickering chain of lights from the little windows along
the lane, his eye was caught by a dark gap, where the bright chain
was broken and no light shone. His eyes went quickly from this
dark gap to the end of the lane. There was no other break in the
line of little lighted dwellings.

So that was it! The young man moved forward slowly, and in a
few paces he had come to the place where the Mallows cottage had
stood, but of which nothing now remained but the gables, and a
portion of one outer wall in which a window frame without glass
gave a cheerless view of the desolation within. The little cottage had
been thatched, but the roof had long fallen down and rotting remnants of it filled the empty cavity that had once been the hearth-
stone.

The young man leaned against the derelict mud wall and looked
over the sill of the window at the rotting thatch and nettles. Soon,
however, even this desolation was hidden from him and there was
nothing at all to be seen except a mass of dark shadows. But still
he stood there silent in the darkness; a prey to the sadness and
loneliness of the place. And after a few minutes his ears became
more sensitive and he began to listen, although he did not exactly
know what it was he expected to hear. Was it only the sounds that
are heard in all lonely places, the sound of the cricket and the frog,
and the thin piping of the bat? Or did he think to hear in fancy the
voice of the young servant-girl, Posy Mallows? Whatever it was that
with closed eyes the young man thought to hear, however, it was certainly not the voice of Daniel who rose up beside him suddenly like a

shadow on a wall.

"It all worked out as nicely as possible," said Daniel, breaking at once into his burden. "I was hoping Kate hadn't seen you," he said, "but it was all for the best that she did. 'Who was that?' she said, her eye clapped on the yard door as soon as she stepped inside the other door. There was nothing for it but to tell her. 'What did he want?' she said again. So I had to tell her; not about Posy, of course, but about Meadow Lane. 'He had business in Meadow Lane,' I said, 'and he was inquiring the way to it.'

"I thought she'd never believe that. I thought she'd ask what the like of you would be doing in a place like Meadow Lane, but she was too anxious to get a dig at me to notice anything. She never loses a chance of that: a chance of giving me a dig.

" 'And if that was the case,' she said, taking off her hat and going right behind the counter at once, 'do you mean to stand here and tell me you let him make his way down that dirty lane by himself at this time of the evening'—this was where she gave me the dig— 'you that knows it so well?' You see, she never loses an opportunity of throwing it in my face about long ago. Indeed, she often made insinuating remarks at the time, and in front of Posy too!"

Here the younger man stirred slightly in the dark.

"How did Posy take them?" he asked quietly.

"Oh, she never said anything to Kate," said Kate's brother. "She didn't want to be sent home, I suppose. I didn't know it at the time, but I suppose she was saving the money to go away. It was to me she used to say anything she had to say. She'd say anything to me! 'Are you a man at all?' she said to me one day, 'or how can you listen to talk like that if all you say about me is true?' " Daniel laughed sheepishly. "I used to say an odd thing about her hair or her eyes: girls like that kind of thing, you know. But sometimes she wouldn't listen to anything.

" 'Why don't you face up to them?' she used to say, because Hannah was as bad as Kate in her own way. 'Why don't you tell them to mind their own business?' I used to be in mortal dread they'd hear her, because this would all be said back of a door or in the passageway, or maybe out in the storeroom, but the house wasn't so big you could get much privacy anywhere in it.

" 'What if they do hear me?' she used to say, and she would

drag her arm away from me. 'It would give them a proper fright. I suppose they'd nearly go mad. They'd be sure and certain you were caught, and that I'd be walking in here to take the keys out of their hands.' 'Maybe you will be doing that some day,' I said, because she was the kind of girl you'd find yourself saying things to without altogether meaning them, you know. But wasn't I very foolhardy in those days? You see, I didn't understand. I remember the way the sweat broke out on me when Kate said the Mallows could have taken every penny we had from us if Posy brought a Breach of Promise action against me and repeated things like that in the Court: not that Posy would ever have taken a mean advantage of me—she wasn't that kind. In fact, if things had been otherwise I don't suppose I would ever have done better, but considering our position in the town, of course it was out of the question from the start. Even Posy could see that.

" 'Before you think of buying a ring for any girl you'd better buy a couple of railway tickets,' she said another day, 'because no girl will ever go into a house with those two old sisters of yours.' I used to laugh when she went on like that. She used to look her best when she was giving out about Kate or Hannah. I think she never forgot the day they drove her down the street with her head shaved.

" 'What would you think,' said I, 'if I went down to the station this minute and got two tickets to Dublin for the mail train tonight? What would you think of that?'

"Posy only laughed.

" 'I'd think it was a miracle, that's what I'd think.'

" 'Does that mean you'd come?' I said.

" 'It does not,' she said. 'If ever I leave this town I don't want a millstone round my neck. No thanks. I'll buy my own ticket, but I won't have to buy it if your sisters catch you here behind the door with me! They'll buy it for me!' And that was true, you know. I don't know how they got wise to it but they began to think I was in danger. They were older than me, you know, and they knew the world better.

" 'You're so soft,' they used to say to me, 'that Posy Mallows could twist you round her little finger.' "

In the darkness the younger man stirred again. It was an impatient movement.

"If she wanted to do it!" he said impulsively. "From what you say, it seems to me that she had other plans."

"—Than me, you mean?"

"Yes."

"—Because of all the talk she had about leaving the town?"

"Exactly!"

"That was what I thought too! But that's where my sisters were wiser than me. 'That's only to lead you on, Daniel,' they said, and I declare they were right, because every time she mentioned leaving the town a queer sinking feeling used to come over me, and I used to think how quiet and lonely the house would be if she wasn't moving about it, humming, or singing under her breath. There is no doubt about it but my sisters were right. A few more remarks about going away and I'd have begun to lose my head. There is no knowing what I mightn't have brought on myself, but as I say my sisters had great insight into things. Women understand things better than men, I suppose. Anyway, when all was said and done I had to admit they were right. When it was all over and she was gone I saw the situation better. My head was clearer, anyway, than when she was around the place, because no matter what my sisters said about her, she had a way with her; Posy. You wouldn't want to be long near her, if you know what I mean. And my sisters knew that, and they knew another thing too! They knew enough not to let me know their plans until everything was all settled. You see I didn't know they had said anything to Posy at all. I didn't even know she was going away. She was working up to the very last minute. I suppose that was part of the bargain Kate made with her. And if I didn't have to go down to see the stationmaster about a crate of china that was damaged on delivery, I might not even have seen her to say goodbye. I thought badly of that for a long time. And I thought badly of what Posy must have thought of me, although she wasn't one to hide her mind and she didn't say much in the few minutes I was talking to her.

"You see, I had just come out of the goods-yard, after making my complaints, when I happened to glance at the train drawn up alongside the platform, ready to depart. I only glanced at it carelessly, you know the way one does these things—I suppose the lighted windows of the compartments drew my attention when I was walking along the dark platform, and the platform in this town is darker and more dismal than most places, I think; but that's beside the point. Anyway, to make a long story short, as I was glancing carelessly from one compartment to another, suddenly I got a kind of start at the familiar look of a young girl in one of the carriages, although her back was to the window, and she was reaching up to settle her baggage on the rack. And then I saw that her coat was familiar too; it was just like the blue coat Kate used to wear, although it looked a lot different from what it would look like on Kate, and round the neck of it this girl had tied a bright red scarf, the like of which you'd never see on Kate. Kate always held red to be a color of no class. But anyway, I was just thinking that the red scarf was like a thing Posy would wear, when all of a sudden it came over me with a clap that the girl was Posy. But how could it be Posy? I thought. And then at that moment the girl turned round, and not only was there no mistake about its being Posy, but she looked out, and in spite of the dark of the platform the next thing I knew she had seen me—do you remember people always said the Mallows had cats' eyes; they could see in the dark.

" 'Hello! Is that you?' she said.

" 'Posy?' I cried. 'What is the meaning of this?' And I tried to open the door of the carriage but the train was on the point of pulling out of the station; in fact, I could hardly hear my own voice with the noise of the whistle and the steam hissing, and then, even while I was dragging at the handle of the door the train began to move.

" 'Mind yourself!' cried Posy.

" 'Wait a minute!' I shouted, so taken by surprise that I didn't know what I was saying.

"Posy only laughed. 'Sorry,' she said, 'but I'm not the engine driver.'

"She was like that: saucy and impudent to the last. The train began to move. I ran along the platform with it.

" 'Where are you going?' I shouted. 'When are you coming back?'

"But Posy only laughed again.

" 'Wait and see,' she said, but just at the last minute, as I came to the end of the platform and couldn't go any farther with the train, she seemed to change her mind about something.

"'Goodbye, Daniel,' she said. She had never presumed on my Christian name before, so I knew she had something important to say. I put up my hand to my ear to catch it, although the way the wind was blowing back the sparks from the engine and the clouds of steam and smoke I suppose I would have heard her, anyway; if indeed everyone on the platform didn't hear it as well as me. 'Goodbye, Daniel,' she said. 'You owe a lot to your sister Kate.'"

Daniel's voice cracked under the unusual strain of so much talk and excitement.

"It was true for her too," he said then, more quietly. "There is no knowing what foolishness I might have got into if Kate hadn't taken things in hand. Young men are very inflammable. It's not till they get old they get sense. As sure as anything I would have thrown discretion to the winds and run away with her."

All at once in the distance a train sounded, shunting at the junction beyond the town.

Sudden compunction smote Daniel.

"But what am I thinking about?" he cried, "talking away about myself like this and never thinking about you, sir. I suppose you have to catch the mail train?"

"The train Posy took?" said the stranger, and he seemed to have regained his spirits.

"Yes," said Daniel absently. He had recalled with misgiving and alarm that Kate had told him to be sure to bring the young man back for a cup of tea before he left the town. She would have it all ready, he knew. She'd have a fire in the upstairs drawing room, and she'd have taken out the best china and linen. But there wouldn't be time for that now. How would he face her at all? It would be another occasion for cutting remarks. "My sister will be annoyed with me," he said. "She was expecting you to come back for a cup of tea."

"Oh, thank you very much," said the young man, "but I must be getting down to the station." They had come to the top of Meadow Lane and were abreast of the gable of Daniel's shop. Just as Daniel thought, there was a lamp lighting in the upstairs parlor. "There's just one other thing I'd like to ask," said the stranger, "if you don't think me impertinent?"

"What is it?" said Daniel.

"Did you never have any regrets?"

Daniel stopped for a moment.

"Well," he said reluctantly, "nature is nature, and a man would want to be made of sawdust not to have an odd feeling in that direction, if you know what I mean?"

The young man nodded.

"But on the whole," said the other, "I knew it was all for the best."

"Still, I understand you never married?"

Daniel made an impatient gesture.

"Oh, that had nothing to do with it!" he exclaimed. "I had plenty of chances to marry. In fact, to this day there are people trying to make matches for me. Not that I'd have anything to do with them or their matches." A flash of real irascibility came into his voice. "You wouldn't want to be very long in this town to see that there isn't another town in Ireland to beat it for plain-looking women!"

The young man nodded sympathetically.

"All the same," he said, "I should imagine there would be things you'd regret. For instance, you might have your family growing up beside you now."

"If I married Posy, you mean?" said Daniel.

"Well, that wasn't exactly what I meant," murmured the young man.

"But, don't you see that was the whole trouble," said Daniel. "That was what my sisters brought home to me.

" 'It's all very well for you,' they said. 'You can lower yourself if you like, but how would you like to have people throwing it in the face of your children that their mother was a chit of a servant-girl from the back lanes of the town?' That was what they were looking into all the time, that and the disgrace to themselves, of course, but mainly that. And I came to understand it, of course, after a while. I'm surprised that you don't understand it, sir; a man of your position."

The young man, however, seemed to have grown stiffer in the

last few minutes. "I certainly owe a great deal to my mother," he said, "she was a woman in a thousand." But his manner as he said it was withdrawn and cold.

Daniel felt a chill descend on him. Was it for this he had broken the silence of years; to be misunderstood?

"Wait a minute," he said. "Put it another way. Put it like this. Where would you be, young man, if your father had lost his head over some uneducated slip of a girl from a back street? You never considered that, did you? No! and neither did I—but my sister Kate did!"

They moved a few steps forward. The light from the upstairs parlor fell across the street in a long oblong.

"Well, it's a good thing you feel grateful to her," said the young man, and then as Kate's shadow at that moment fell across the glass, suddenly he put up his hand and doffed his hat. "As a matter of fact I have cause to be grateful to her myself." And with this inexplicable remark he glanced at his watch and put out his hand. "I mustn't miss my train," he said, and he turned quickly and went down the dark street.

For a few minutes Daniel stood listening to his footsteps in the stillness. And not until they were out of earshot, and not indeed until the shrill whistle of the Dublin train pierced the blackness, did he recall that he had fed the stranger's curiosity, but not his own.

Who was the strange young man, and what was the source of his interest in Posy? He did not know—and, fainthearted, he did not want to know with any degree of precision. He knew enough for his needs. The stranger had borne testimony to the fact that his secret hope, for so long cherished, had indeed come true and that Posy's bold venture had been crowned with success. She had been justified of her saucy contempt for Kate, and for Hannah—and for him. She had envisaged more in life than they in their cowardice and caution had ever dared to envisage.

And as he stooped to go through the wooden wicket of the big gate leading back into the yard, instead of feeling sad he felt curiously elated. He like Hannah and Kate had to live out the rest of his life in the dungeon of obscurity and petty provincial existence, but he had not held Posy down, he had let her fly away.

And if he never saw the upper sunlit air, nor ever now would see it, by the thrust of her flight he had guessed that somewhere the sun shone.

And now he need no longer guess! He knew.

The Cemetery in the Demesne

"HE MAKES me sick," said the carter's sister-in-law. "He never stops talking. I don't know how you stick it, in the same room with him at night. He doesn't shut his mouth for five minutes. I can hear him down through the boards in the floor. I'd go mad listening to him if I didn't put my head under the bedclothes."

"I wouldn't mind you!" said the carter's wife, testily. "You're odd! You're queer! You'd want him to sew up his mouth, and never say a word." She flicked the crumbs from the table with a sweep of her elbow. "As for me," she said, "I like listening to him. He has something to say about everything."

"You don't need to tell me that," said her sister. "I never knew such a bag of wind."

"Let me tell you this then," said the carter's wife. "It's not a bad thing at all, to be able to talk at your ease on any subject. He's never lost for a word, no matter what he's talking about. And what is more, he can talk to any and everyone. The highest and the lowest are all one to him."

"You don't need to tell me that either," said her sister. "I know it well. A bag of meal would be as good as a wife to that man, any day, if it had ears on it to listen to his old talk and his old stories."

"I don't think words like that come well from you, Sissie," said the carter's wife, "while you're depending on him for every bit you eat, and for the roof over your head if it comes to that."

"Don't worry," said Sissie. "I pay well for everything I get by listening to him talking, every evening, till my eyes are dropping out of my head with sleep."

"No one asks you to stay up!"

"Don't I tell you I can't sleep in my bed at night with the sound of his voice coming down through the floor. How would it be, do you suppose, if I was inside in my room, listening to him out here, with nothing but this little bit of a partition between me and him?" She gave a thump to the partition of plywood that cut the room in two.

"You can't hear what he's saying, can you?" said his wife, uneasily.

"I don't try! I put my head under the blankets, and, even then, it's like as if he was shouting in my ear!"

"I hope they don't hear him next door?" said his wife. "The walls are very thin. I must warn him." She tapped on the wall at the other side of the room, and it gave a hollow response.

"He won't take much notice of your warning, if I know him rightly," said his sister-in-law. "The bigger the audience, the more he likes it. He'd stay up till morning if he thought the neighbors could hear him."

There was a sound of feet on the floor overhead. A door opened and steps sounded on the stairs.

"Don't let him hear you criticizing him," said his wife, taking down the teapot from the dresser and shoving it into her sister's hand, while she herself took up a loaf of bread and began to slice it down rapidly with a long knife, that she wiped from time to time on her skirt, to free its jagged edge from the crumbs that clogged it.

"Are my boots polished?" asked the carter, as he took them up from the side of the range. "There's nothing like real leather for taking a decent shine," he said, turning amicably to his sister-in-law. "Most of the shoes they sell in the shops today are made out of some kind of cardboard. They're not putting real leather into the cheaper class of shoe nowadays. You can hardly tell the difference in the shop, but the first time you try to polish them you can tell the difference at once. The imitation leather won't take the shine." He sat down and began to put on the boots. "Of course, if you know where to go, and who you're dealing with, you can be sure of getting the worth of your money. I always get my boots at one particular shop. I never go anywhere else. The man I deal with knows that there is no use giving me anything but the purest of leather. And look at the difference!" He held up his left leg with his hand, and showed the boot, tightly laced on it. "Look at this!" he said, lifting the other foot, with the other boot on it, the laces streaming back on the floor. "Anyone with an eye in his head could see that that was real leather." He bent down to lace the second boot, but before he had drawn the laces through the first eyelet, he looked up again. "What in the world would we do without leather?" he asked. "Did either of you women ever stop to think of all the uses leather is put to in this world? Did you ever stop to think about that?"

"Do you know the time it is?" said his wife, shortly, and she avoided looking at her sister Sissie, because she knew that Sissie was sneering at them both. She knew it by the very way the other woman went over to the back of the kitchen door and took down her brother-in-law's coat, and held it out for him to get into it. The carter thrust his hands into the sleeves and went over to the table where his wife was pouring the tea into a Thermos flask and wrapping up the slices of bread in a piece of brown paper.

"I tell the fellows down at the sheds that I have two wives to look after me, instead of one," he said. And, while he stuffed the flask and the brown paper parcel into his side pocket, he laughed at his little joke, and repeated parts of it. "That's right. I have two wives instead of one," he said, and going out the door he waved his hand over his head at the two unsmiling women who went back to the table, and sat down, and began to pour out fresh tea into their stale cups, on top of the cold dregs of the breakfast tea.

As the carter went along to the garaging sheds he took out a piece of paper on which his directions for the day had been written the previous night by the foreman. He was directed to take the three-ton truck with a full load of gravel, and deliver it at a graveyard in the other end of the county. The directions were typed on office paper, but the foreman had written something on the back, with a short stub of pencil that wrote indistinctly. As far as the carter could make out it said that the graveyard was inside the walls of a gentleman's demesne.

That's a queer place for a graveyard, he thought to himself, as he reached the sheds, and found that the other trucks had drawn out. He was the last. The truck was loaded and ready. He started up, and pulled out of the shed. The day was gray, and what thin sunlight there was kept failing and disappearing as clouds blew over the sky. He thought about the long journey ahead, and he thought about the two women he had left in the house behind him. They'll have another cup of tea after I'm gone, he thought; and they'll sit there talking till it's time to bring the children to school. He envied their freedom and gripped the steering wheel tighter, and stared at the blue tar road in front of him. He hated to think of the miles of flat Midland country that lay between him and his destination. And he hated the return journey over the same flat roads. Women have an easy time, he thought, going about the house at their ease all day, and chatting with the tradesmen and messengers that come to the door. Not that he minded working—he gripped the wheel tighter—it was up to men to work and keep their women in comfort. Woman is the weaker sex. He wondered where he had heard that saying. It was a very true saying.

But as the day crept on, and the truck traveled over the flat blue road, the carter began to feel that he might have had a better job than the one he had. It was no life for an able-bodied man, he thought, going along, mile after mile, all by yourself without a sinner to talk to, and doing nothing but keeping the truck in the middle of the road. It wasn't natural. No man should work alone, out of earshot of his fellow men. Man should work with man. It was a poor thing after all to spend the best part of your day with your mouth shut.

The carter had to do the journey inside a certain scheduled time, but it was lax enough to allow for short stops along the way. Once or twice he looked with envy at a crowd of mechanics at a garage door, when he flashed by a filling station, but his truck was overhauled every night, and oiled, and filled with petrol, and there was never any occasion to stop at a garage. However, as he came near to a small town, about middle way in the journey, he began to notice that there was a knocking noise in the region of the engine. He was debating with himself whether it was worth bothering about or not when he came to a filling station with four bright red petrol tanks outside the door in a row. A big red-faced man stood at the door, with his hands in his pockets. There's no harm in having it seen to, the carter thought. It doesn't pay to take risks.

"It doesn't pay to take risks," he said to the red-faced man when one of the mechanics had examined the engine and found that there was nothing the matter except a loose nut that could be tightened in a second.

"You're quite right," said the garage proprietor. "If there were more people like yourself there would be less accidents."

"It's a risky job, driving a truck night and day," said the carter. "You never can tell when some fool will come round a corner on the wrong side of the road and send you into Eternity."

"That's right," said the red-faced man. "And you could meet your death on a straight piece of a road, as quick as on a bend. A skid could send you flying over the ditch to your death."

"If a tire blew out while you were traveling against time, where were you?" said the carter.

"If it comes to that," said the garage proprietor, "life is all risk. You could drive that truck for forty years and in the end you could be killed by a slate falling off your own roof."

"That's a fact," said the carter. "I heard of a man who was a steeplejack and he met his end by eating sardines that were tainted from being too long in the tin."

"There you are!" said the garageman, "life is one long risk."

"I knew another man," said the carter, "and he was sitting by his own hearth when the leg of his trousers caught fire and he was burned to death, with his wife and children looking at him and not able to do anything for him."

The garageman threw up his hand in horror.

"You must hear queer things," he said, "in your journeys back and forth across the country. I often envy the lorries, when I see them flashing past here, at all times of the day and night. I think it's hard on a man to have to stay all day in the one spot."

"We see Life, all right," said the carter, and he patted the red enamel sides of the truck. There were two ways of looking at everything, he thought. "Of course," he said, turning back to the other man, "it isn't everyone that would profit by his experiences the way I do."

"I suppose not," said the man.

"There are men," said the carter, "who have the same job as I have and I meet them off and on in the course of my job, and they haven't as much to say as a mule. You'd think they were never outside their own back doors. Would you believe that?"

"I would," said the garageman. "I would. Indeed I would," and he moved over to the edge of the path as another car drew up at the curb.

"I'll be on my way," said the carter, and he swung up into the seat of his truck and, waving his hand, he let out the brake. He felt like singing. There was nothing like a bit of company. There was nothing like passing the time of day with another human being. Ditches and hedges streamed by on either side, and their greenery brought him gladness, although he kept his eyes on the blue road, and only glanced away from it to look at the battered signposts.

The demesne was only a quarter of a mile away now. The hedges and ditches were rich and deep from the dampness that remained under the trees, even in sunlight. He drove slowly, and ventured to look around him at the country. Sissie and the wife would be glad to hear the layout of the land. They'd be anxious to know if the place was well kept up, in the vicinity of the demesne. Women set great store by little things like that.

The demesne was on his left when he went around the next corner. The gate was high, and there were spikes along the top of it. He blew the horn for the gatekeeper and then he sat and looked around him. The trees were the best he ever saw. They spread out over the road. There was one tree and the branches of it stretched right across the roof of the gate lodge. He looked at the door of the lodge which was wide open, expecting to see someone run out to open the gate, but the doorway remained empty, although he could see the throbbing flames of the fire in the grate. He blew the horn again. Still no one came. At last he alighted from the truck and began to push back the heavy wings of the gate. They were no sooner pushed open than they began to swing slowly back again. He was looking around for a stone with which to keep them open when a woman ran out of the house, pushing her hair back with her hand as she ran. She caught the left wing of the gate and flung it back without looking at him and without saying a word.

"Did you hear me blowing the horn?" said the carter, looking at her before he went back to the truck.

"I did," said the woman.

"It's a wonder you didn't come out sooner," said the carter. "Every minute that I'm delayed counts against me on my pay sheet. I have to do this journey in scheduled time. Do you know that?"

The woman was unlikely to offer an apology. The carter knew this and he spoke more to himself than to her. Suddenly, however, she pushed her hand through her hair again and gave the only apology that can be expected from certain natures; an explanation.

"I have a sick child inside there," she said, beckoning at the open door with her head. "I sit looking at him and I don't remember rightly where I am. I don't think to get as much as a cup of tea for myself. You could be talking to me, and I wouldn't think to answer you. You could be shouting in my ear, and I wouldn't think to raise my head and look at you. Isn't that a terrible thing?"

"What is the matter with the child?" said the carter.

"I don't know," said the woman. "Nobody knows. It just lies looking up at me, and doesn't ask to move. I'm afraid it's done for!" She spoke with that calm and curious acceptance of misfortune that is found only among peasants, and which passes among those who do not understand them, for callousness and indifference.

"Did you get the doctor?" said the carter, with the city man's urgency to act, to do something, to throw up some bulwark between him and an impending doom.

"I got the district nurse to look at him," said the woman. "The doctor wouldn't come out all this way from the town just to look at a child no bigger than a cabbage."

"What did the nurse say? Did she do anything for the child?"

"She looked at him. She took him up and she looked at him, but she said there was nothing she could do. She said I'd better start getting him ready for the road."

"Is she a capable woman?" said the carter, taking off his cap and scratching his head in perplexity.

The woman looked at him without comprehension. After a minute or two she remembered that he had said something about the nurse.

"The nurse is every bit as good as the doctor," she said. "It's the opinion of many people around these parts that she's better than the doctor. There are people around these parts who would sooner see the nurse called in to them than the doctor, any day. And there are other people that would sooner get a bottle from the vet than from either the nurse or the doctor!"

"How old is the child?" said the carter.

"Would you like to see him?" said the woman.

"I'll just bring the truck inside the demesne," said the man, and he ran out the gate.

When he came back the woman had gone in, and he looked at the lodge as he went over to the door. It was single-storied, but it was as high as a two-storied house. The walls were made of stone, and the windows were mullioned. There was a crest over the high pointed arch of the door but it had been obscured by green cushions of lichen, as well as by Time, which had altered the spelling of many of the words. The lodge had been built at the same time as the main house, and it had been decorated in keeping with it, and not in keeping with the furniture and possessions of the people who would inhabit it.

He stood at the dark doorway.

"Come in," said the woman.

The room was dark. The few chairs and tables, the black steel box, and the chest of drawers that made up the entire furniture of the room had the temporary and even incongruous look that is given to a grand gilded reception room when it is filled with cheap cane chairs for a public meeting. The mullioned windows that looked so well from without, let in so little, and so frail a light, that at first the carter thought that there were no windows at all in the room, and he moved toward the shadowy light of the fire, expecting to find the child in a cradle before it. But the child was in a corner of the room, directly under the thin pointed window, and its pallor was made greater by the elongated shafts of white light that fell across its face.

"How do you think he looks?" said the woman, staring down at the cold wax doll in the cradle.

The carter thought at first that the child was already dead, but at the sound of the voices it opened its eyes and looked up with a straight stare that excluded the mother and the stranger alike, and which had yet some definite object on which it focused with all the intensity of which it was capable. The eyes were dark, and unlike the eyes of a child.

"Do you ever lift it up?" said the carter.

"Oh, yes," said the woman, stooping down and lifting the child up at once and dandling it halfheartedly for a few minutes, but as the heavy head fell from side to side on the weak neck she dandled it still less eagerly and wrapped her arms around it closer.

"It's as light as a feather," she said, then, with a faint flash of pride in her voice. She tossed the child up and down again as she said this, in her pride at being able to claim at least one superlative quality for it. "It's the lightest child I ever came across for its age," she said.

The carter held out his arms.

"Would it come to me?" he said.

The woman wiped the child's face with a corner of her dress, and laid it into the carter's arms.

"Is it this child?" she said. "This child would go to anyone." And now her voice was strengthened with still more confidence and pride. "He's not a bit shy. He wouldn't act strange with anyone. Isn't that a great thing? I hate children that cry and make a fuss the minute a stranger looks at them. This is the bravest child I ever saw. I've seen a great many children in my time, and I never saw a child that could equal this one in making up to strangers. It never struggles. It never cries. It's not the least bit afraid. The greatest stranger that ever was could take up this child and he wouldn't pass the least remarks on him no more than if it was his father. There's a child in a house down the road from here, the third house from the crossroads—you'll pass it on your way out, I'll point it out to you, you can see it through the trees—and in that house, as I was saying, there is a child that's two weeks older than this one, and as strong as a young bull, and yet, with all that, it wouldn't let a stranger touch it without struggling and raising the roof with screams. If you want to look at it you have to stand behind the cot, because the very first minute it catches sight of a strange face it begins to bang its fists on the rails of the cot, and kick off the blankets and scream till it's as red as a turkey cock. Isn't that a horrid disposition for a child? What way will it grow up, I wonder, when it's ugly tempered like that, and it only a young child? That's what I say to my husband. Do you know, I hate going over near that house. Would you believe that? And I'll tell you another thing. When I have to go over there I'm always glad to get back to this little creature that's as good as gold, and never cries, or kicks, or stirs from one side to another from the time you lay him down till you pick him up. He's afraid of nothing. The other day there was a wasp walking over his face and he never took the least notice of it, but just lay there looking up at me till I chased it away. He's a remarkable child. That has to be admitted. The day and the night are all one to him. He'll lie as quiet in the darkest room as he will out under the brightest sun that ever shone. He's afraid of nothing, and he's afraid of no one." She leaned over and wiped the child's mouth again, with the corner of her dress, as he lay in the carter's arms.

"See!" she said. "No matter what you do to him he doesn't cry. He has a lovely disposition. He wouldn't be afraid in a graveyard, as the saying is." She pushed the thin hair back from the frail white temple where the veins showed as if under glass. "He's a little angel," she said.

"It's the best that are taken," said the carter, and he put the child back in her arms.

"He might get over it yet," said the woman dully, as she took the child and rocked it from side to side, as one might soothe and comfort a frightened or disturbed child.

"He might," said the carter. "I have heard of cases where children worse than that got better, and were as good as ever they were."

"I heard of cases like that myself," said the woman. "I heard of children that were as good as boxed up for the clay, when they took a change for the better and never looked back once at the way they were going!"

"I can believe that," said the carter. "Children that begin weakly are often the strongest at the finish. Many a bad start had a good end." As he said this he made his way reluctantly toward the door. "I'd better be getting on with my work," he said. "I have a load of gravel to deliver."

"Are you delivering it at the big house?" said the woman, coming after him to the door.

"No," said the carter. "I understand there is a cemetery here?"

The woman nodded her head.

"I have instructions to deposit the gravel at the gate," said the carter. "It appears they are going to put a new path across it from one end to the other."

"It's about time they thought of doing something to that cemetery," said the woman. "It's a disgrace to the parish. Just because it's inside the walls of a gentleman's demesne the public never think to pull up a weed out of it, much less lay down a decent path for the funerals to travel over on a wet day."

"It's a queer place for a cemetery, isn't it?" said the carter.

"There's hardly ever anyone put down in it now," said the woman. "There's a new cemetery on the other side of the village. Once in a great while some old woman that has outlasted her time is brought in here to be put down with the rest of her family. But there's not many left now to go down there. When they put down one old woman that lives beyond at the crossroads, and another old one that lives in the next parish, but who belongs here by rights, they'll close up that graveyard altogether, and no one will ever go near it. That's my opinion. The weeds will eat into the stones."

"How far up the drive is it?"

"It's one-third of the way up the drive. You'll have to watch out for the pathway with both your eyes, because it's all grown over with nettles and dandelions, and the bushes touch the ground."

"It must be an awkward place to get into?" said the carter, as he started the engine of the truck.

"It's an awkward place to be put down in," said the woman, coming over to the side of the truck. "If the river is flooded the open grave gets filled up with water, and they have to put the coffin down into the water. The people have to stand back, it goes in with such a splash. Sometimes the chief mourners don't like to stand back in case it would look like slighting the dead. They stand where they are, and the coffin is pushed over the edge. The diggers run back from the splashes, but the mourners stand where they are and get it all over them. Your heart would break just to look at the poor creatures, coming out this gate on their way home after it's all over, and their good mourning clothes, that came straight out of the shop, all covered with dirty big splashes, and their shoes sopping wet."

She rocked the child to and fro as she spoke, and the carter nodded and let in the clutch. She stood back a few paces as the truck began to move, and she looked at the child to see what it made of the noise and the bright red enamel of the truck. It was staring straight in front of it and it was impossible to tell what it saw and what it did not see.

"You're a little angel," said the mother, rocking it again as she went into the house.

The carter went slowly up the drive. This must be the path, he thought, as he came to a slight thinning in the shrubs along the drive. He got out and pushed aside the laurels. There was a gap there all right, and there was the remains of a path, but it was grown all over with grass and nettles and great clusters of dockweed. He went up the pathway a few yards and came to a slight rise in the ground. In the distance he could see the slow river, clogged with reeds and stifled with the overhanging branches of ash trees. Down in a hollow near the river, he could see the irregular grassy mounds of the graveyard. There were rough stones strewn about, moss-covered and lichen-eaten. There were five or six headstones tottering this way and that, like human figures scattered suddenly and indiscriminately by a great gust of wind.

"I'll go in and have a look at the place," he said to himself, and he broke his way still farther through the laurel, but the strange, damp odors of the underwood began to assail him at once; the pungency of the dock leaves at their prime, the stench of the decaying elder flowers, the rotten smell of ancient beech leaves lying on wet clay. He stood irresolute. Then there was a stir in the wet leaves near his feet, and two gleaming jet eyes were fixed on him for an instant and were gone, as a small living creature dragged itself away through the weeds.

"A rabbit!" said the carter. But he knew it was a rat. "I'd better unload the truck first," he said, and he went back to the driveway.

It didn't take long to unloose the tailboard of the truck, and let the gravel rattle out in a heap on the grass, but when it was fastened again, and the chains secured, the carter took out his watch and looked at it. "It's getting late," he said, "I'd better not delay. I'll probably be down here again sometime," and he backed the car into the laurels to turn it. The low branches of the trees, and the branches of the laurel slapped the sides of the car, and the back wheel caught in a rut between the drive and the grass bank, but at last the truck was turned, and he started back to the gateway.

The gate had been closed. The carter had to blow the horn again. This time the woman came running out so fast that he thought that the child must have taken a turn for the better. She grabbed the iron gates with both hands and swung them back against the stone piers with such great energy that they trembled for a time with the impact.

"Is the child any better?" said the carter.

"No," said the woman, "but I had some good news. The postboy has just been here and he left me a letter from my mother."

The carter shut off the engine and leaned out to hear better.

"My mother told me to wrap the child up in some warm clothes and take it down to the priest and ask him to read a gospel over it! She said the priest would make a lot of excuses, but that he couldn't refuse. She said I wasn't to listen to any excuses or arguments, and I was not to go away until he read the gospel. And anyone that has a gospel read over him will get better and be as well as ever he was!"

She pushed her hair off her tanned face and the carter was surprised at the fine white texture of the skin on her forehead where the thick hair had lain. After the damp and lonely graveyard, with its rotten smells and foul weeds, he was anxious to linger in the warmth of this woman's company. Slight as it was, he clung to the small human relationship that she represented. He was grateful to this stranger who intruded her intimate talk upon the unnatural loneliness of the countryside. Above all she gave him what he wanted most of all, a chance to break his own silence. He stepped down from the truck.

"I have heard of such a thing as a gospel being read over a person," he said, "but it is a very unusual thing. I thought it was more usual to touch the sick person with a relic. Have you got a relic?"

"No," said the woman.

"Has anyone in the village got one?"

"I never heard tell of one."

"That's too bad," said the carter, "because it would be more suitable than getting a gospel read. Getting a gospel read is a very serious step to take, specially in the case of so young a child."

"I suppose so," said the woman dully.

"The priests don't like being asked to do it, you know."

"But they can't refuse!" A timid defiance brightened her cheeks.

"They can't refuse," said the carter, "but that is why they don't like being asked to do it. They want the people to realize what a serious step it is. Don't you see?"

The woman did not see.

"I think they ought to be glad of a chance to use their influence to cure people." The carter said nothing for a few minutes as he pondered these words.

"I suppose they can't cure everyone," he said at last, "or there would be no sick people in the world at all."

"Wouldn't that be a good thing?" said the woman simply.

For a moment the carter was taken aback. Then he looked at the woman with a stern expression on his face.

"If there were no sick people there would be no dead people, and if there were no dead people it would be a queer world."

"Why?" said the woman.

The carter was about to show annoyance, but on second thoughts he controlled himself and showed only a small trace of exasperation, by the slow way he spaced every word.

"The world would get overcrowded," he said. "There would be people being born all the time, and none of them dying. Oh, it wouldn't do at all. It wouldn't do at all." He looked very sternly at the woman.

"That's true," she said. "I never thought of it that way." Then suddenly she put her head to one side. "Did you hear a cry?" she said, turning back to the doorway.

The carter followed her. They went into the dark lodge. The child was all right. He seemed to be sleeping.

"Poor little mite," said the mother. "Isn't it terrible to see it lying there not able to say what's wrong with it?"

"God knows," said the carter, "but it might be all for the best if it was taken."

"That's what I say to myself, over and over again, when I'm going about the house, doing my work."

"The world is full of wickedness," said the carter.

"I can believe that," said the woman.

"A man in my position sees Life, you know," said the carter.

"Yes, to be sure," said the woman.

"And do you know, there were many times that I thought to myself that it might be no harm not to be born at all! Life is harder on a man than it is on a woman. I'm always telling that to my wife. Women know nothing at all about the evils of the world. They know nothing about its wickedness."

"I often heard my husband say the same thing."

"I have no doubt of that," said the carter, "but of course in my job a man sees more of Life in one day than most men see in a lifetime. In my job you see Life, and you see it at its worst." He looked down at the child. "Yes indeed," he said. "It might be the best thing that ever happened to this helpless little creature, if he was taken now, before he has time to find out the suffering and evil of the world."

"The poor little mite," said the woman. She leaned in across the cot and took down a letter from the windowsill. "Here's the letter I got from my mother," she said, and in the instant of taking up the letter and looking at it she forgot all they had said in the last few minutes. "I wonder what the priest would say to me if I only just asked him if he'd consider it was wrong to read a gospel over this poor mite?"

The carter sat down on the edge of a chair. "No man can be expected to know exactly what another man will say," he said, "you know that yourself, ma'am, as well as I do, but just the same I'd venture to give it as my opinion that the priest would say the same thing that I have just said to you myself. It's a very serious step."

"But he couldn't refuse?" said the woman again. "My mother said he couldn't refuse!"

"He couldn't refuse. That's true. But it's my opinion that he'd advise you to leave well enough alone!"

The carter uttered the last four words in such a low and ominous tone of voice that the woman, who had been abstractedly reading the letter again, looked up with a fright.

"What do you mean by that?" she asked.

"He might try to warn you of the cost!"

"The cost? But the priest wouldn't take any money!"

"I didn't mean money."

The woman did not understand.

"Wouldn't I give anything to save the poor mite," she said, but she looked uneasy.

The carter shook his head.

"You may say that now," he said, "but how do you know that you will always feel the same way?"

"I don't know what you're talking about," said the woman.

"Well," said the carter, "it seems to me that I heard tell it wasn't lucky to have a gospel read over anyone. Those that are to go, are to go, and that is all there is to it. It's my opinion that if there is any interference in their going, either by relics or the reading of gospels, some shadow is sure to fall on the family as a consequence."

"I never heard that," said the woman slowly, considering his words. Then she looked up swiftly. "What shadow could fall on us?" she asked, and then she thrust her own words aside. "And what if one did fall on us? Could it be worse than losing the child?" She pondered for another instant, this time over her own words. "Wouldn't I gladly suffer anything," she said, "rather than have that poor helpless child taken away without having a taste of life?"

The carter grew more engrossed in the conversation.

"You might be ready to suffer anything," he said, "but who knows where the cross might fall!" To emphasize his words he threw out his hand and pointed toward the cot. "Who knows but that it might not be the child itself that would suffer in afteryears. It might even live to regret the day that it was made to prolong its unwilling life in this vale of tears!"

The mother looked at him with her fierce eyes, and then she turned them on the cot. With an urgent gesture then she caught up the child and held it close to her. It made no sound, but the carter saw that it had opened its strange dark eyes and was staring at him.

"Now that I bring the subject to my mind," he said, "I seem to remember hearing a story about a woman that had a gospel read over a young child one time, and from the minute the priest walked out the door (and I believe he was very upset, with the sweat rolling off him, they said), the child looked up and began to take a turn for the better. It never once looked back. It got stronger every day, and brighter in the cheeks, and freer in the limbs, till it was the grandest child you could ask to see."

The carter looked critically at the pale child before him while he described the other child, as if he was prompted in his words by the great comparison between them, and as his eyes fell on the pale floss of hair on the child in front of him, he broke off in the middle of another sentence to say that the child he was speaking about had a great head of black curls.

"I forgot another thing," he said. "That child had the grandest head of black curls you ever saw on a human being and it never changed in spite of all he went through afterward, and even on the day that they carried him in and laid him on the dirty counter of the public house, his hair was the most remarkable thing about him. The people that were staring in through the splits in the blinds were all agreed that he had the most beautiful head of hair they ever saw. 'Isn't it a shocking tragedy,' they said to one another, 'and look at the lovely head of hair he had.' "

"What happened to him?" said the woman, pressing the child so tightly against her bosom that it seemed to make a faint sound of protest, and there was a trickle of moisture from its mouth.

"I was telling the end before the beginning," said the man, "my wife is always complaining that that is a great habit with me! Well, I've spoiled the story now, I suppose, but you can piece it together for yourself. The child lived, and grew to be a fine limb of a boy, too fine, you might say, because he seemed to be thriving at the expense of the rest of the family. From the day he recovered there was a shadow of misfortune over every one of them. First a sheep died . . ."

"I wouldn't mind a sheep," said the woman impulsively.

"Oh, they didn't mind the sheep either," said the carter. "As a matter of fact I don't think they connected it with the reading of the gospel at all. Even when another sheep died they didn't connect the two things. And even when the cow was found dead in the ditch, they didn't connect it with the gospel, although by this time the people all around the countryside were beginning to whisper and gossip about them. But after the cow died things got worse every day. In fact, misfortunes began to fall on that family as fast as the leaves fall off the trees, until one day, without giving them time to save as much as a plate off the dresser, the house took fire and went up in flames like a barrel of oil. It was burned to a cinder before their very eyes!"

"God between us and all harm!" said the woman. Then a spark of defiance lit in her eye. "I suppose it was a thatched house?" She looked up at the high ceiling over them. "I hate this lodge," she said. "I wouldn't care if it burned down this very minute. It's as damp as a vault. On a wet day the water streams down the walls just as if there was someone up on the roof pouring it down through the slates, but there's no danger of it taking fire. That's one good thing about it!" Defiance was now gleaming brightly in her face.

The carter felt an obscure resentment.

"Misfortune comes in different forms," he said sharply. "To everyone according to his needs, you might say."

"What happened the young lad in the end?"

The carter stared through the doorway at the bright trees outside.

"There's no use cataloguing the misfortune that came on the poor creatures," he said, "and on the children that weren't even born at the time that the gospel was read in the house, but it was the young fellow himself that got the worst fate of all."

"What happened him?"

"Well, ma'am, you know as well as I do, that there are some things that can happen a young man that are too terrible to be told among decent people? Isn't that the case? Well, it was the case with this young man anyway, and you saw the end he got, stabbed in the back in a drunken brawl and laid out on the counter of a public house for a coroner's inquest."

"God help us all," said the woman, and she laid the child back in the cot again. "It's a wonder my mother didn't warn me about the bad luck that might come of the cure," she said.

"There are some people," said the carter, "and they can't look ahead. Sufficient for the day is their motto. Let tomorrow take care of itself is their motto."

"My mother is an old woman," said the lodgekeeper's wife, with a trace of apology in her voice.

"Old people have strange notions," said the carter, relenting somewhat.

"They put a lot of faith in prayers and relics," said the woman, disparagingly.

"Oh, prayer is all right," said the carter hastily. "I have nothing against prayer. I never go to bed myself without kneeling down for five minutes beside my bed, if it's only counting the flies on the wall I am, but I don't care to have anything to do with relics and gospels. Relics and gospels are unnatural, that's the way I look on it. I'm a great believer in Nature. Trust in Nature I always say, and she won't fail you."

"The nurse said something like that too," said the woman. "She said you'd never know the minute the child would take a change for the better."

"What did I tell you?" said the man, and he stood up. "Trust Nature. Don't be talked into anything unnatural. That's my advice, but please yourself, of course. Please yourself." He went over to the door and stepped outside. Still he was reluctant to go. "I suppose you couldn't tell me the meaning of this inscription over the door?" he said, looking upward.

"I heard what it meant one time, but I forget it," said the woman. "If my husband was here he could tell you. He got a scholar to figure it out and write it down for him."

"I suppose a scholar would only have to stand out a bit from it and he could rhyme off the meaning without any trouble, as clear as if he was reading from a newspaper? Isn't learning a great thing? The people nowadays don't pay as much attention as they should to the value of learning. The old people knew what could be accomplished by learning. The old people . . ."

The woman raised her head, and held it to one side again.

"Did you hear a noise?" she said. "I think I heard the child cry?" She went back into the house.

"I'd better be on my way," said the carter, and he got into the truck and drove out the gate.

He alighted again outside the gate and got down and closed the heavy wings and fastened the padlock by putting his arm through the bars. The woman was still inside the house.

"God help us all," said the carter as he drove away, and he thought how interested his wife and Sissie would be, when he went home that night, and took off his boots, and related all that had happened.

He went faster as he thought of the pleasures of his own fireside.

The trees and hedges cast dark shadows. Day was failing. High in the leafy summits of the trees, among the pale green leaves, the last gold birds of sunlight fluttered their vanishing wings. The carter kept his eyes on the road. And all the way along he was planning the words that he would use when he told the day's story to the two women at home, and, as he thought about it, the day's events fell into place and formed a picture, where the still white child and the damp graveyard, and the furtive rat and the rainy funerals, and the fierce blue eyes of the lodgekeeper's wife had each a prominent position.

All the way along the darkening road, and all the time while he was walking back from the sheds, after putting up the truck, the carter thought about the child, and the rats, and the water-logged graves, and he began to set more value on life than he had ever set on it before. Life is a great thing, he said to himself. There's no avoiding death, but there's no use in taking needless risks. Not that I hold with reading gospels over people, he said, or trying to prolong life beyond its normal course.

At the door of his own house the carter paused and rested for a few minutes. He felt more tired than he had ever felt, and yet he had often made longer journeys. He didn't feel much like talking when he went in and hung up his coat on the peg inside the door.

"How did you get on today?" said his wife.

"All right."

"Anything strange?"

"No."

"Did you meet anyone interesting?"

"No."

"You don't seem to be in very good humor?"

"I'm all right," said the carter.

When he had eaten his supper, he sat down by the fire.

"I'm trying to remember something," he said. "I'm trying to remember the name of that woman you told me about one time, who had a gospel read over her son and who never had a day's luck afterward. What was her name?"

"I don't know who you're talking about," said his wife.

"Of course you do. It was you that told me the story in the first place. Some woman that you knew long ago had a gospel read over a child and the child got better, but the family had one misfortune after another until in the end the boy himself was stabbed in the back when he was only twenty years old."

"I never told you any such thing. I never heard of anyone that had a gospel read over a child."

"You're a stupid woman," said the carter. "You must remember it. First the sheep died, and then the cow died, and in the end the boy himself died. Don't you remember he was laid out on the counter of a public house?"

"I never told you a story like that. Maybe Sissie told it to you. Did you, Sissie?"

"I did not," said Sissie flatly. "I don't know what you're talking about. What does it mean, getting a gospel read over a person? I never heard of it being done." She looked at her sister.

"It was never done where we came from," said the carter's wife.

"Where did I hear it so," said the carter, "if I didn't hear it from one or other of you women?"

"Maybe you heard it down at the sheds from one of the other men?" his wife suggested.

"I often told you before," said the carter crossly, "that those fellows haven't got a word to throw to a dog."

"Maybe you read it in a book," said his sister-in-law, looking back viciously at his wife, as she went out of the room, because she was always saying that it would be an ease to them all if the carter could be persuaded to read at night when he came home. It would keep him quiet and take the edge off him. He'd sit still and not be going from one room to another, all the time, never shutting his mouth.

"She knows I never read a book," said the carter indignantly.

"Maybe you made it up," said his wife, giggling, and she pulled a lock of his hair playfully.

"Leave me alone," said the carter, roughly, pulling away from her. "And for God's sake stop talking nonsense. How could I make up a long story like that, if there wasn't some truth in it? If that's your idea of a joke I don't like it," he said. "I often heard that women had queer ideas! I'm going to bed!"

"What ails him?" said Sissie, coming into the room.

"I don't know," said the carter's wife. "He kicked off his boots and wouldn't say a word to me. He's gone to bed." The tears ran down her cheeks. "He didn't even say good night to me!"

"That's nothing to cry about," said Sissie. "We'll have a bit of peace. We can get something done." She stood looking around the room, as if she had never been in it before. Then she ran over to the cupboard in the corner and threw back the flaps of the door. "We can play draughts," she said, and began to take down the black-and-white checkerboards and the counters that were as new and glossy as the day they were bought, ten years before.

Her sister dried her eyes in the sleeve of her blouse.

"I'll have the black counters," she said, "if you have no objection."

"No objection at all," said Sissie, and she began to lay them out, whistling as she did so, and beating time to the whistling by tapping her feet against the rung of the chair.

Her sister blew her nose, and roughened her cheeks with the palms of her hands where they had been streaked with her tears. Then she looked at Sissie.

"You look real pretty tonight, Sissie," she said. "I never saw you with such a good color."

"I never felt better," said Sissie. "Where will you sit; in the armchair or on this chair?"

"Any chair at all."

"I think you'd be more comfortable in the armchair," said Sissie. "I'll give you the first move."

"I almost forget how to play," said the carter's wife, and she moved the corner counter.

"It doesn't look as if you had forgotten," said Sissie, making a countermove. "Your move!" she called then, impersonally, and continued to call it out gaily, as the pattern of the counters altered on the board with the course of the play, and the clock ticked loudly, and the fire made faint sounds, and a big bluebottle that had been closed into the room when the window was shut flew here and there with a complaining drone, and hit off the white porcelain lampshade with a sharp sound every few minutes.

The last thing that the carter thought about that night was the woman with the white forehead and the dying child. He wondered if the child was dead, and when he went to sleep he dreamed of an open grave filled with water, and when he looked at the mud-splashed mourners he saw they were rats dressed up as humans and they looked at him with the same still stare as the dying child. He woke up and leaned out of bed, with his elbow supported on a chest of drawers. There was a sound of rain falling in heavy drops on the tin roof of a shed. He shivered and looked around the room to see if there were extra blankets, and drew one over himself.

Next morning his wife shook him by the shoulder.

"Here's your tea," she said.

He sat up in bed and took the cup in his hand.

"Is it raining?"

"No," said his wife.

"I'm glad of that much itself," said the carter, preparing to get up.

"I don't see what difference it makes to you whether it's raining or shining," said his wife. "You're under cover all day long. I have to leave the children to school and call for them again in the afternoon. Last Wednesday it poured all day and I was sopping wet. I came home and changed my clothes, and just when they were dried it was time to go out again and bring the children home."

"Is my breakfast ready?" said the carter. "I can't dress and talk at the same time."

His wife looked at him and bit her lip.

"What's wrong with you this morning?" said Sissie, when she saw her coming downstairs drying her eyes.

"He cut me short," said the carter's wife. "He said he couldn't dress and talk at the same time."

"It's the first obstacle that was ever put to his tongue if that's the case," said Sissie. "Stop your crying and have some sense. If I know him he'll make up for his silence when he comes down. He'll be talking with his mouth full and spitting crumbs all over the table-cloth."

"You're very unkind, Sissie," said his wife. "That only happened on one occasion when he was excited over something."

"Once is enough!" said Sissie. "Ugh!"

"Don't let him hear you criticizing him!" said his wife as his foot sounded on the stairs.

"Are my boots polished?" said the carter, coming into the room.

He put them on. "Is my lunch ready?" he said, and he took up the parcel of bread and butter.

"Where are you going today?" said his wife.

"How do I know until I go down to the yard and get my directions? Don't ask foolish questions!" said the carter. "Women are always asking foolish questions. I never knew a woman yet that was happy with her mouth shut! It's talk, talk, talk, all the time. Why don't you shut up once in a while!"

He went out and banged the door. The sun was getting warmer and the sky was as blue as a woman's eye. The carter looked upward and whistled as he went along, but after a few minutes he saw that there was a soft white mist rising up from the moist earth under his feet.

The women stood at the window looking after him.

"What is he kicking the ground for?" said Sissie, as they saw him give a kick to the clay on the path.

"There's something wrong with him," said his wife.

Three evenings later his sister-in-law was polishing his boots by the range while his wife was putting up the draught board and closing the doors of the cupboard.

"He didn't have two words to throw to a dog tonight," she said. "It gave me the creeps to see him sitting there saying nothing before he went to bed."

"He hardly opened his mouth six times since in the last week," said his wife. "And I hate to see him going off to his bed at nine o'clock; a man that liked to stay talking till the daylight came in the window."

"I don't hear him talking at night," said Sissie.

"He's asleep when I go upstairs," said his wife. "Or he lets on to be."

"There's something wrong with him all right," said Sissie, "there's something on his mind."

The wife sat down on the edge of a chair, grateful for a chance to talk about the situation.

"Yes," she said, "yes," and she pondered the possibility in silence, looking down at the floor. Then she looked up again. "Or maybe it's something he ate?" she said.

The Little Prince

~~~~~~~~~~~~

I

ABOUT four o'clock in the afternoon, while she was upstairs giving her father his medicine, she thought she heard her brother's voice in the shop below her. She hurried down. But he wasn't in the shop. There was no one there but Daniel.

"I thought I heard Tom's voice," she said. "Did I?"

Reluctant to betray him, Daniel could only nod his head miserably.

"So he broke his promise!" she cried. "What did he say? Who was with him?"

Apparently, however, it was the same old story. Her brother Tom had been doing the good-fellow again, as usual, walking into the shop, and up to the counter, with a crowd of good-for-nothing companions, and calling for drinks all round as if he were a customer! If the business came into his hands, he'd make short work of the profits, at this rate.

"Oh, how can he be such a fool!" she cried, and the impetuosity of her cry seemed to imply that there was a time when better might have been expected of him. But it was not a time for sentiment. She had to concern herself with the practicalities of the situation. "I'll have to speak to him," she said decisively. "It's plain to be seen that he has become a regular toper."

But as she uttered it, she knew that the word "toper" was neither just nor suitable to her brother Tom. His faults were not such as could be described by any word that connoted age or decay; they were still the faults of youth, and were it not that she and Daniel would be involved in his downfall, she might have been prepared to find something appealing in his reckless prodigality. But as things stood, he could not be allowed to go on.

"Something must be done at once, Daniel," she said. "I didn't get a chance to tell you earlier in the day, but the doctor's report on Father was not so good this morning. He said that we could not expect him to last much longer." She paused. "And you know what that means!" she said significantly.

Daniel knew.

"All I wish is that I could do it for you, Bedelia," he said, "but I explained my position to you and—"

"Oh, that's all right!" she said impatiently.

She fully understood his position. If her brother failed to see things in the proper light, it would not do for him to have a wrong impression about Daniel, particularly when, like everyone else in the family, he was unaware, as yet, that there was anything between herself and Daniel. It might be different if Daniel were already his brother-in-law. Although, even then, it would probably be more delicate for her to handle the situation in her own way. Not indeed that she felt it to be a very difficult situation! There was no real harm in Tom. He would be the last in the world, she felt sure, to wish to harm anyone, much less his own sister and her future husband. He might not—he could not—be made to mend his ways, but he could be made to see how his way and theirs ran counter to each other, and how advisable it was that, if he must pursue his folly, he pursue it in some other clime.

"He will listen to me, I know he will!" she said, triumphantly. "I tell you I know him inside and out. I can read him like a book. Didn't I tell you that he would never be able to keep his promise? Didn't I tell you it would be a waste of time to put him to a test?"

For it had been in deference to Daniel's scruples that Tom had been given a last chance. It had been a mistake though as Daniel must now see. It had only postponed an unpleasantness that would otherwise be over and done with by this time.

"I won't let this night pass without making my mind plain to him," she said. "I'll bring him out here, when the shop is shut, where we won't be interrupted—while the rest of you are at supper would be a good time, wouldn't it?"

"There he is now!" she cried, as at that moment, beyond the green baize door that led from the shop into the dwelling part of the premises, they heard his voice raised in horseplay with his younger sisters.

Bedelia glanced at the clock.

"Don't you think you could start to put up the shutters?" she said, and as he set about doing as she suggested, she watched him irritably. She was eager to be rid of him, and to advance upon her designs.

Yet, when a few minutes later he was gone, and she stood alone in the darkness, she did not immediately move, but, involuntarily in the gloom, her eyes turned toward where upon the wall behind the cash desk, there hung an illustrated calendar from one of the numerous shipping companies for which her father had been an agent. On the yellowed and flyblown print her eyes had rested daily since she was a child, and as clear as by day she could, in the darkness, make out the great liner afloat on its cerulean ocean. Tom would not be the first black sheep to be sent across that ocean. Far away though that new world might be, to be reached only by crossing the vast Atlantic, what other remedy was there for a spendthrift like him: who had no sense of what was due to his family? Many a young man like him went out in disgrace to come home a different man altogether; a man to be respected: a well-to-do man with a fur lining in his topcoat, his teeth stopped with gold, and the means to hire motor cars and drive his relatives about the countryside. Might not Tom make good there too? It did not seem likely, but it was at least possible.

Abruptly cutting short her meditations, Bedelia went through the baize door into the small parlor behind the shop. Supper had already started. Liddy was pouring out the tea, and Alice was cutting the bread. Tom himself had started to eat, and his mouth was full when he looked up in answer to his name.

"I want to talk to you," said Bedelia. "Yes, now!" she said relentlessly, when he protested that he was hungry, but she felt bad when he put his saucer over the cup of tea that Liddy had just poured out for him, as if he thought he'd be back in a minute.

"What's up?" he said, following her out of the room. "Hey, what's the idea of coming out here?" he cried, as she opened the door and stepped into the shuttered darkness of the shop.

"I don't want to be interrupted in what I have to say," she said shortly, and she held the door open for him, as she would for a child.

"But I say! It's pitch dark in here," he protested, making his way awkwardly between the numerous display cases disposed about the center of the floor.

Bedelia, on the other hand, made her way unerringly, and as she heard him stumbling against one thing after another, it was with difficulty that she restrained herself from commenting on his unfamiliarity with his surroundings.

"In here," she said, when they reached the other end of the shop, where, behind the bar, there was a small room set aside for the use of customers desiring privacy, and commonly called the snug. Here too the small window giving on to the backyard was shuttered for the night, but unlike the plain wooden shutters on the front windows, in the center panel of the snuggery shutter, someone in a flight of fancy had cut a vent in the shape of a heart. And through this little heart-shaped vent there came sufficient light for Bedelia's purpose. When she turned around she could see her brother's face.

It was a surprisingly clear face, and she had to admit as she looked into it that it was fresh and undissipated.

But that will not last long, she told herself, and at once she broached her subject.

"Well, Tom! I suppose you know why I want to talk to you?"

To her annoyance, however, he did not seem to be listening to her. Instead, he had lifted up an old cracked jardiniere of yellow glaze that stood upon a rickety bamboo table, and into which had been rammed a large misfitting flowerpot, containing a single wretched stalk of geranium.

"Are you listening to me?" she demanded, because he seemed to be absorbed in looking at the wretched plant in the pot.

Still he didn't answer, but lifted the flowerpot out of its holder and held it up to his nose, passing the dried-up stalk under his nostrils as if it were a sweetly smelling bloom of summer. She began to feel that he might be making a fool of her.

"Perhaps you think I am not aware of your having broken your promise?" she snapped. "I heard that you and your friends were here all afternoon!"

She had the satisfaction of making him look up quickly.

"You don't miss much, do you?" he said. "I suppose the faithful Daniel gave you a full report of my conduct?"

"It's none of your business where I got my information," she snapped, trying hard not to lose her temper at this stage.

"On the contrary, it is very much my business, dear sister, because, you see, it happens that you were misinformed!"

She was taken aback, but only for an instant.

"Are you accusing Daniel of telling lies?"

"I am accusing no one," said Tom, with the quiet of someone that has something in reserve. She began to feel uneasy. "I have my faults, Bedelia, but I do not break my promises."

That was true: as a small boy he had always been truthful, but was it not said that drink broke down a person's character? She looked fixedly at him.

"Which of you am I to believe?" she said.

"Why not believe me, Bedelia?" he said simply, and then, abruptly, he lifted up the flowerpot out of the jardiniere. "Do you smell anything?" he demanded, and he pushed it forward almost into her face.

Instinctively she recoiled, but not before she had smelled a sour, acrid odor that arose from the cracked clay.

"It smells like whisky?" she said, surprised.

Tom laughed.

"There's nothing wrong with your nose, Bedelia," he said gaily. He was restored to his usual easy manner. "Now do you believe I kept my promise? It's true that I was here with my friends this afternoon, and I filled up my glass every time I filled up theirs, but I didn't drink a drop! Not a drop! When no one was looking I poured the stuff into this," he brandished the flowerpot again. "It looked as if it needed watering too," he said. "Not that it looks anything better now." Lightheartedly he laughed. Lightheadedly, Bedelia thought.

She was aware of a bitter feeling of disappointment. Her plans were set at naught. There was no immediate justification now for the suggestion she had been about to make to him.

Or was there? Suddenly she saw a loophole in the situation.

"I suppose you think you were very smart?" she cried. "I suppose you think I ought to be tickled to death to hear how clever you were. Well, I'm not. See!"

She didn't look at him, but she sensed that he was disconcerted, and it gave her confidence.

"I do believe I'd think more of you if you drank the stuff!" she snapped. "You must be an out-and-out fool to pour away good whisky like that. Don't you realize it was money you were pouring away. Money!" She almost screamed the last word. "Well, isn't it true?" she said defensively, because she was frightened for a minute at the look upon his face.

He lowered the jardiniere.

"I thought you'd be so pleased, Bedelia," he said.

She bit her lip.

As a little fellow he used to say that to her, and it always won her heart, but now she forced herself to believe that he was only trying to make things difficult for her.

"I'm afraid, Tom, that you are one of those people who have to be protected—from themselves, I mean," she added quickly, as she saw him raise his eyebrows. "It was a fatal thing for a person of your character to be put in the position in which you were put by Father's illness. I was never one to beat about the bush, and I may as well tell you that when I called you out here I thought you had broken your promise, and I was determined there was only one thing for you, and that was to get right away from this town altogether, from the bad company you've been keeping, idlers and spongers, who knew they had only to rub you down with a few soft words, and they were sure to have their bellies filled with whisky. No, don't interrupt me! I know there are some of them that have not been as ready to soak you as the others, and have even lent you money, and that kind of thing, but believe me, they knew they didn't stand to lose on you. A young man with your prospects! Your friends would be your worst enemies! Well! That's what I was going to say to you, but after what you've just told me I am beginning to think that your very worst enemy is yourself. Pouring good whisky in a flowerpot! You must be a real fool!"

He was looking down at the floor while she was speaking.

"I suppose you are right, Bedelia," he said quietly. "But what's the remedy?" he asked. "I take it that since you had a remedy in the first case, you will be able to provide one in this case also. Indeed, the remedy may be the same in both cases?"

Was he being impertinent? Only for the delicacy of the situation, and the need for handling it carefully, she would have lost her temper.

"This town is not the place for you," she said, coldly. "If you were to go away—for a time anyway—make a fresh start as it were—"

But he interrupted her.

"So the remedy in either case is the same!" he said, and he laughed. "That's a good one, you know. It reminds me of a joke I heard the other day. Would you like to hear it?"

Bedelia wasn't in the mood for jokes, but when he had a good yarn to tell there was no stopping Tom.

"It's a good story, Bedelia. Don't look so sour," he said. "Wait till you hear it. There was a little fellow one time, and he was married to a big bully of a woman, who hardly tolerated him about the place at all, except perhaps on pay nights. She had to give the poor devil his meals, of course, but I believe she never sat at the table with him, but just slapped them down in front of him, without a word, and all the time he was eating she'd go about the kitchen, banging away with the sweeping brush, or whatever she happened to have in her hands, and taking no more notice of him than if he were a dog.

"Well, one day, anyway, when he came home to his tea, she slapped down his cup and plate in front of him as usual, and threw a few cuts of bread on the plate, and poured out a cup of tea from an old brown pot that was stewing at the back of the range, maybe for a few hours. It was a big brute of a teapot, with a big awkward spout on it, and the tea used to belch out of it as if it was choked with something, as was probably the case.

"Anyway, this day when she had splashed out a cup of tea for him and given the milk jug a shove in his direction, she went back to her work as usual. But although she wasn't taking any notice of him, after a bit she got a feeling there was something wrong. Maybe she didn't hear him stirring the spoon around in the cup, or else she didn't hear him sucking the tea off his mustache—the way he used to do—but anyway, she threw a look at him, and sure enough, he hadn't touched the tea. And after a few minutes when she looked again the cup was still before him full to the brim.

" 'Well?' she said, stopping her work, and putting her hands on her hips. 'What's the matter with you? Why don't you drink your tea?'

"The poor little fellow: he got as red as a lobster, and he looked up at her apologetically.

" 'There's a mouse in it, Maggie,' he said.

"I suppose she got a bit of a start at that, because you must admit it wasn't a thing a woman would expect to happen. And so, after giving him a glare like as if it was his fault in some way, she stepped across and looked into the cup. And sure enough, floating on the top of the tea was a dead mouse: it must have got into the old teapot while it was standing at the back of the range—and come down the spout—maybe it was that was clogging it all the time! Well, there it was, anyway.

" 'Hmm!' said she, and she took up the cup and carried it over to the sink, and taking up a spoon she fished out the mouse and threw him into the swill bucket.

" 'There!' said she then, putting back the cup of tea again on the saucer in front of him, and, taking up the sweeping brush, she went banging away at her work again.

"But, like the last time, it wasn't long until she began to feel that he was still sitting in front of the cup without touching it, and she looked back at him. Right enough, he hadn't touched the tea, but was just sitting in front of it. The very sight of him drove her into a rage.

" 'Well, what's the matter with you now?' she demanded. And she raised her eyes to heaven. 'I declare to God I don't know what kind of a man you are: you won't drink your tea with the mouse, and you won't drink it without the mouse!' "

It was a good story. Or so Tom had thought when he first heard it, and even now as he came to the end of it, he was inclined to laugh again. But at sight of Bedelia's face, his own face sobered. He made no attempt to bring home to her the application of his parable.

Instead, as if he took a bitter pride in doing what was expected of him, he drew himself up.

"When do you want me to go?" he asked. "Oh, yes, and at the

same time, it might be convenient for you to tell me where you want me to go?"

Bedelia's face twitched at the last question. It touched at the nerve center of her whole plan, but she didn't flinch from answering him.

"America!" she said, flatly. But she almost broke down when she saw the look of disbelief, and then, worse still, belief, dawn in his eyes. "It's the obvious place," she murmured. "A new country, a fresh start—"

But he put up his hand and waved away her words.

"Oh, yes! Yes! Let's take all that for granted, my dear sister," he said. "I know that you think me singularly uninterested in the business, but I have occasionally flicked over the pages of the shipping catalogues, and I know all the patter about the brave new world. We can take it as said. Let us get down to more practical matters." He looked down at his waistcoat, on which there was a speck or two of clay from the flowerpot, and he brushed it off. "What a good job I have this suit in such good condition! It will be just the thing for the voyage: save buying a new one, and all that!"

It was impossible to tell whether or not he was serious. But she gave him the benefit of thinking he was joking.

"Anyone would think you were going in the morning," she said.

"And am I not?" he said.

So this was to be his attitude, to make it seem as if she was driving him out of here.

"You know very well that there are a lot of arrangements to be made. We'll have to come to some sort of agreement."

"Arrangements? Agreement?"

"You'll be entitled to your share of the business, of course," she said coldly.

"Oh, yes. Well, run up and tell the old man I'll take it now!" he said. "How is he this evening, by the way?" he asked suddenly, in a different tone of voice. "I haven't been up to see him all day."

"Oh, he's all right," said Bedelia impatiently, "but you know right well he doesn't know anything about all this! I'm not speaking of the present; I'm speaking of the time when—"

"Oh, I see. I'm glad the old man isn't a party to it. You're talking about when he's out of the way." He looked up at the ceiling over their heads. "Poor Father!" he said, irrelevantly, and she didn't like his tone.

"Quite naturally there will be a lot of changes to be made when that time arrives," she said stiffly.

"Oh, naturally!" he repeated dryly, but it seemed to Bedelia that he was beginning to see things reasonably.

"As Daniel said—" she began.

"Oh, so Daniel is in this too?" he said.

Bedelia bit her lip. She had made a slip there, but it was no time for prevarication.

"You may as well know that Daniel and I are going to be married," she said curtly.

"Good God!"

She had certainly given him a jolt this time, she saw with some satisfaction, but he controlled himself quickly.

"I suppose you mean afterward," he said, jerking his finger upward toward the ceiling, and it was impossible not to feel there was something caustic in the question, but the next moment he shot out his hand. "Oh, well! The best of luck to both of you," he said. "Sorry I won't be here for the wedding."

"Oh, but that's what I'm trying to explain," she said. "There's no need for you to go away until afterward either! All we want, Daniel and I, is to know where we stand! And then, too, there are the financial arrangements to be made!"

But Tom was not listening to her. He had raised his head, and although it might be an absurd fancy, she felt that, in imagination, he was already far away from her, standing perhaps upon the deck of an outgoing Atlantic liner, such as was pictured in the shipping calendars, breathing in the deep sea breezes that she supposed must for ever blow on the wild Atlantic. Then suddenly he came back to earth; to land: to the little dark snuggery.

"You and Daniel have everything nicely arranged for yourselves, I must say," he said, and he smiled, this time, oh, yes, absolutely— she could be sure of it—absolutely without malice. "But I don't think that I'll be able to fit in with all your arrangements. If I have to go at all, I'll go at once."

"But what about Father? How can we explain to him?"

He smiled again.

"I have no doubt you'll be able to find some satisfactory way of doing that too," he said.

"But your share of the business?" she cried. "I'll have to make some arrangement about your share of the property. And how can we do that without telling Father. Can't you see our hands are tied at the moment?"

Tom did not seem to see any great difficulty in the situation. He looked around him.

"Have you got a pen?" he asked. "I'll make over my share to you and Daniel. How will that be? Won't that straighten out everything? It will be a little wedding present from me, or if you like to put it another way, it will be a little farewell present!"

But Bedelia had her pride to safeguard, or better perhaps it would be more correct to say she had Daniel's pride to safeguard.

"Daniel would never agree to that," she said stiffly. "I'll have to speak to him about the matter. I dare say we will be able to come to some temporary agreement, and afterward we'll get a solicitor to draw up a proper settlement, and we'll send your money to you every year." Just then, however, another aspect of the situation struck her. "That's another thing," she cried. "We'll have to settle what part of the country you'll go to at first. In the ordinary way, people usually go to some part where there are other people from home, but in your case I thought—"

"Oh, that's right, a fresh start for me! I see your point, my dear sister, but I think you can leave me to settle that matter for myself. And now?" He glanced at the door. But Bedelia was not satisfied to end the interview so abruptly.

"As soon as you get there, you'll be writing to us, of course," she said.

In the dusky light of the snug, he moved, so that for the first time his face was out of the patch of light from the shutter.

"Very well, we'll leave it at that," he said. "As soon as you know my address—my permanent address that is to say," he added, "you can write to me."

She thought for a moment there was a curious expression on his face, but the next moment he spoke so normally that she decided she must have been mistaken.

"And now," he said, "if you don't mind, Bedelia, I'll go back to my supper."

After he had gone, Bedelia felt so tired that she leaned back against the wall of the snuggery, out of the shaft of light that had, all during their colloquy, fallen intermittently, in broken lines, upon her brother's face, but which now fell upon the opposite wall, unbroken in its outline, a little patch of golden light, in the shape of a heart.

II

"You'd think he'd write us a line at this time, wouldn't you?" said Bedelia to Daniel, who was now her husband, as they came out of the church after the first anniversary Mass for her father, one month from the day he died.

Although it was a year and seven months since Tom Grimes had left for America, and although they had not heard from him once in all that time, it was impossible to think that on this occasion at least they would not hear from him.

Up to this, his silence could have been put down to carelessness, but now it seemed as if it must have another cause. Nor could they console themselves that he had not heard the news, because in addition to requesting the American papers to please copy the announcement of the death, they had sent him two cablegrams in care of Mary Conaty, a former servant of Bedelia's mother, who had emigrated to Boston many years before, and who, in a recent letter to her sister at home, reported having met Tom Grimes in the street, not once, but on two or three occasions. He had promised to visit her, and although he had not done so up to the time of her last letter, it might reasonably be assumed that she had been able to communicate to him the sad information in the cablegrams.

So certain were they that they would hear from him that Daniel had anticipated the event by including his name in the newspapers among those from whom messages of sympathy had been received, although afterward he had been a bit scrupulous about the matter. Bedelia, however, only scoffed at such scruples.

"I would have included his name in any case, even if I knew

we were not going to hear from him. We could not let people think that he had dropped out of our existence!"

Daniel sighed. He was afraid that was what Tom Grimes had done.

Bedelia, however, was not at all reconciled to such an idea.

"He'll write yet. We'll get a letter out of the blue one of these days," she maintained.

Meanwhile, pending their getting hold of his address, conscientiously every month Daniel set aside a percentage of the profits, and this money was lodged in the account which he had opened in Tom's name the day after his father-in-law died.

"He can't want money very badly, that's one thing certain," said Bedelia caustically, at the end of the second year, when they were making up the books, and she saw the amount that had accrued to her brother's credit.

"I don't know about that," said Daniel. "He was deep, that fellow."

Just what he meant by this, however, Bedelia did not wait to find out.

"Oh, depend upon it, we'll hear from him when he needs it," she cried.

But in this estimate of human nature, she was basing her judgment upon the generality of men, not upon the particular individual in question. And although he did not altogether agree with her, Daniel conscientiously lodged the money every month. You never could tell!

And so he was not altogether taken off his feet one morning when, regardless of who was in the shop, Bedelia, an excited flush on her face, came to the green baize door and beckoned him to her. When he saw that she held a letter in her hand, he jumped at once to the conclusion that it was from the outlier.

But it was not from Tom Grimes. It was from Mary Conaty. She wrote to say that she had met Tom again, and had a long chat with him. She knew they were worried about him at home, and had written to tell them there was no need for concern.

"He is perfectly well, and seems to be prospering," said Bedelia, quoting from the letter, an excited flush on her face. "Wasn't it good of her to write?" she cried. "And to take so much trouble to describe the whole thing. She was walking down Tremont Street—that must be a street in Boston—and who did she see looking into a shop window but our Tom! Can you imagine it, Daniel, such a coincidence!"

Although he was disappointed, having thought the letter was from Tom himself, Daniel did not want to dampen Bedelia's enthusiasm, and so he tried to appear as pleased as she was.

"So we've traced him at last," he said. "Well, tell me everything. How is he? What is he doing?" He put out his hand for the letter.

But some reticence seemed to come over Bedelia, and, appearing not to see his outstretched hand, she moved away.

"Oh, I'll give it to you later," she said. "I didn't read the letter properly yet; I only glanced through it."

Her evasiveness was not lost on him, and momentarily she saddened him. Before they were married, before her father died, there seemed to be a greater bond between them than there had ever been since; he used to think then it was the bond of affection, but now he sometimes thought it had been only a bond of connivance.

It was not until he went in for his dinner at midday that he heard any more about Tom Grimes, and even then he noticed the oblique way he was told about him.

"About that letter I got this morning, Daniel," she said. "I think it would be just as well if we didn't mention it to anyone, for the present, anyway. After all, it's very backhand information, not much better than gossip really, and for all we know, Mary Conaty might be misinformed about some of the things she said about him." She paused here, and looking into her face, Daniel knew that she had at last made up her mind to impart to him whatever it was she had found unpalatable in the letter. "It's quite possible that she may have been mistaken about his employment, for instance," she said, going slowly and carefully, as if, between each word and the next, she was trying to take a sounding of his reaction.

What a born conniver she was, he thought, with mixed emotions. She could not really think that she had told him what her brother was doing. But if it made things any easier for her, he was prepared to play her game, and he made no protest.

"It hardly seems possible that he would have taken a job as a waiter, does it?" she said.

"A waiter!"

In spite of his determination to play up to her, Daniel couldn't keep back the exclamation of incredulity, but he regretted his indiscretion when he saw her wince.

"Of course, it must take some time to get a footing in a strange country," she said quickly. "And I always heard that they look at things differently in America. Over there people take all kinds of employment, and no one thinks any the worse of them. It's not like here! It seems to be a very classy hotel too—" Here she dived her hand into her pocket and took out the envelope of Mary Conaty's letter on which she had transcribed the name of the hotel. "The Parker House it's called," she said, as if this ought to impress him. "Mary Conaty spoke as if it was a great achievement to get into the Parker House!"

It was a difficult moment for Daniel, who wanted at one and the same time to be kind, and to be truthful.

"I suppose to a person of Mary Conaty's origins a waiter's job would seem a superior position, but I'm afraid there's no denying it's a comedown for your brother, Bedelia."

Instantly Bedelia flared up.

"Oh, but it isn't only Mary Conaty who thinks it, but the Westropps—you know they are the people for whom she's working over there—you must often have heard the name—she mentions them in all her letters—they told Mary Conaty that it was very hard for a young man to get a job in the Parker House. It seems Mary told them about him, because she knew they used to be in and out of there, and they asked her to describe him, and when she did they remembered him at once. They had already picked him out, I suppose, as different from the others. Anyway, they told her she could be proud of him. They said he was like a little prince!"

But as she repeated those words of the unknown Westropps, Bedelia's voice suddenly faltered.

"What's the matter, Bedelia?" cried Daniel.

"Oh, nothing, nothing," she said. "It's only that I just remembered something that people used to say about him long ago too, when he was a little fellow—I often told you about it—when Mother began to ail, I used to have to mind him, and I used to dress him up in a little velvet suit with a white lace collar, and people were always stopping me in the street to look at him, and admire him, and that's what they used to say—that he was like a little prince. I had forgotten it until this minute."

To his astonishment, she took out a handkerchief, and pressed it to her eyes.

"Oh, come now!" he said, and he put his arm around her shoulder. "This is not the time to cry! On the contrary. Now we know where we are! We have something to grasp. We have his address for the first time. We don't have to depend any more upon roundabout methods of getting in touch with him. Who can be sure if he ever got any of those other messages? But now we can write to him direct. A letter addressed to the Parker House will get him: you'll see!"

He was so confident that Bedelia put away the handkerchief.

But the letter which was that day dispatched to the Parker House Hotel came back unopened, with a note on the back from the management to say that Tom Grimes had left their employment without leaving any address: they were unaware of his present whereabouts.

"Now what will we do?" cried Bedelia, as she stared at the returned letter.

It was a bit of a blow, all right, although Daniel was determined not to take it too seriously.

"Never mind," he said. "We'll get in touch with him again before long."

But it was to be twenty-seven years from the day that Daniel made that singularly unprophetic remark, before they again got news of the little prince. Not that he was ever out of their minds for long, in all those years. For one thing, they had a constant reminder of him every month when they lodged the money against his name in the bank, although their reactions were not identical, and Daniel's indeed was not even stable. It had changed out of all recognition with the passage of the years.

At first he had been concerned only with his own honesty and integrity in lodging the money so scrupulously, and in the beginning also it had pleased him to see it slowly accumulate. Every month as he completed the transaction at the bank, he made the same remark to the cashier.

"Well," he said complacently, "it's there for him if ever he comes looking for it."

And as he went homeward, he reflected, with a certain amount of pride, on the way a comparatively small amount of money increases when it is left untouched, and computed at compound interest. They wouldn't feel until it had grown into quite a considerable amount.

But somehow, as the money accumulated, Daniel's attitude began to change. Scruples that might have been supposed to have decreased with the years, were discovered to have increased instead, like shadows, to gigantic proportions. And where it had not seemed a great matter for a man to stand out of a small share in a small business, the true nature of the man's loss now seemed to be making itself apparent to all—or at least to all but the one most concerned: Tom himself!

"I don't suppose he has any idea of how much it has amounted to by now," he said once or twice to Bedelia.

And he began to vary his remark at the bank.

"He'll get a surprise, I bet, if he ever turns up and finds what's here for him!"

And then, as the years began to be measured in decades, and there was still no news of the wanderer, Daniel began to perceive a diminishing ratio between the way the sum was growing in proportion to the years at Tom's disposal for the enjoyment of it, until at last a time arrived when he used to wonder sadly what use would it be to him at all—even if he turned up that very day. A great feeling of pity for Tom then took possession of him, and it even threatened to spread its gloom over himself.

For things had not prospered, as they had augured in the old days when Matthias Grimes was alive, and he himself was a raw shopboy, greatly in awe of the premises in which he humbly served his humble role.

Sadly now he used to look around the little shop and wonder how he had ever thought it was a big and flourishing business, for particularly in the twilight hour, before the lamps were lit, it sometimes seemed to be only a small box of a place, and it was hard to credit that one-third of the profits from it had been able to accrue to a sum as large as that which stood in Tom Grimes's name in the bank. Daniel himself and Bedelia had nothing like it to show for their profits. Why, it was unlikely that the whole business, premises, stock, and goodwill, would be worth half as much as that sum in the bank. And although he had always been considered good at figures, his mind was confused by what seemed a mathematical fallacy. How had it come about that the part was greater than the whole? He and Bedelia had done their best.

What had happened to make their achievement fall so short of their ambition? Or was it that their ambitions had been distorted, and out of proportion to what it was possible to attain?

Was it perhaps always a little box of a shop, and his feelings about it, long ago, no more than the illusions of a penniless shopboy?

But what immense illusions they must have been to make him desire it so much: to covet it, you might say, and to make it seem such an important thing that Tom Grimes be prevented from squandering it!

And as he lingered in the shop at night until later and later, it sometimes crossed his mind to wonder what might have become of him if Tom Grimes had proved obdurate, and failed to part with his birthright? But he did not ponder it deeply, because it was unlikely that his life would have been very violently altered. He might have left the employment of Grimes & Son, but only to go behind the counter of some similar concern, probably in the same town, for although it now appeared to him that there was nothing very noble or exalting in life as he had led it, he knew that this philosophic knowledge had only come to him as the fruit of age and experience, and that there had been nothing within himself in his youth to engender it. He had taken the only way that was open to him at the time.

There was just one thing that consoled him, and that was the thought of little kindnesses now and then he had been able to do for people, by which he meant the credit that he occasionally extended to the poor wretched creatures who came to him, shamefaced, without money to pay for the food they needed. If he had continued all his life to be a paid shop assistant, he would never have had the power to do these little kindnesses. So, down in the shop at night, long after closing time, thinking of some of those poor people whom he had befriended, he would at last be able to rouse his spirits sufficiently to end his gloomy meditations, and blow out his candle and fumble up to bed.

Bedelia's attitude was altogether different. Even at the beginning it had seemed to her that it was not necessary to have given Tom so large a share in the profits. After all, he was putting nothing into the business, a factor which she felt ought to have been taken into consideration when calculating the percentage due to him. And so, right from the start, it had galled her slightly every month to see Daniel put on his hat and go up the street to the bank.

During the first years when she could see that the business was doing fairly well, she did her best to stifle her misgivings, although when Daniel showed her the ledger at the beginning of one new year, it came as a bit of a shock to her to realize how large a proportion had been drawn for household expenses, but it was a still greater shock to realize how much of the profits had to be reinvested in stock.

"Shouldn't Tom contribute something toward stock?" she demanded.

But she accepted Daniel's argument that it would only complicate the bookkeeping, because she was getting heartily sick of the way his head was eternally stuck in the ledgers. She shrugged her shoulders. After all, he must know what he was doing, she thought, recalling his competence in her father's time.

But there were times when the ability he had shown in those days seemed to her to have been only the ability of a servant. Why else had they not prospered and advanced? It was not that he lacked industry, but sometimes when she watched him sprinkling sawdust on the floor, putting up or taking down the shutters, it occurred to her that it was not the business he loved, but the shop itself, the tangible thing upon which he could lavish his care and attention.

There was indeed only one matter in which he had not hesitated to take the initiative of a proprietor, and that was with regard to giving credit, but before this worrying thought, Bedelia brought herself up short, for at the time she was expecting their first and only child, and the doctor had expressly warned her against annoying herself in any way. And so, during that year, and the following years, when her son was small, she did her best to keep her thoughts engaged on domestic matters.

At the end of a few years, however, she began again to experience a curiosity about the state of the business, and it was then, upon being shown the ledgers once more, that her misgivings grew into resentment. For the shop recently had had to be painted, inside and out, and the cost of this work made a large cut in their profit.

Rapidly she glanced at the end of the book where a column of figures recorded the payments lodged in her brother's name.

"So he's to go scot free this time too," she said angrily, and she swung around to Daniel. "I wouldn't mind if he needed it," she cried.

For it was her rooted conviction that her brother had done well for himself in America, and that that was the reason that he never bothered to claim his share.

"He would probably laugh at the thought of it now," she said. "It would be a mere nothing to him! Americans have an altogether different scale of value from us, whereas—"

She looked discontentedly around the shop. Since it was painted, somehow it looked less prosperous than before, and on the brightly painted shelves the newly arranged stock looked smaller than it used to look, she thought. Or was it only her fancy?

On an impulse, she went out to the storeroom at the back of the premises and looked around her. Surely there used to be a bigger reserve of stock in this store?

She came back, determined to demand an explanation from Daniel, but when she came back into the shop he was deep in the ledgers once more, and seeing him thus occupied, the explanation occurred to her. It was not possible to have money laid out in two directions at the same time, and there was, as she knew, a considerable amount outstanding in credit.

It was a matter upon which they had had hot words on several occasions. When her father was alive, the business was conducted entirely upon a cash basis. Indeed, listening to Daniel in those days, it had been her impression that it was largely due to him that this policy was so inflexible.

"I'm sorry," she used to hear him murmur humbly, "but I'm not in a position to give credit upon my own responsibility."

Sitting behind the counter at the other side of the shop, taking care not to be seen, she had applauded this tactful handling of a difficult situation. For such she took it to be: it never occurred to her that he was speaking no more than the simple truth, and that no sooner would he be in full command than he would begin to give credit on all sides.

At first it had only been to an odd person, now and then. She would find an entry in the ledger, and when she questioned him as to the advisability of trusting the person, he would only shake his head.

"But they were in a very bad way, Bedelia. If no one gave them credit they would starve."

"But why did they have to come to us?" she would cry. "Why couldn't they go somewhere else?"

To which he would reply with infuriating calm.

"I believe they'll pay us back if they are ever in a position to do so."

"If?" She was hardly able to contain herself with irritation.

And soon the ledgers were bursting with debts. With so much money tied up, how could she expect the stock to be replenished, as it used to be in former days?

Perhaps, as Daniel said, it would all be repaid in time, but meanwhile, where was money to be found for advancing their progress?

At such times it was very trying to think of Daniel's attitude with regard to Tom's money, lying idle and useless in the bank. If it had even been lodged in their names, it wouldn't have been so bad, but nothing would satisfy Daniel but to lodge it in her brother's own name.

"We could have made temporary use of it," she complained bitterly one day.

That they were unable to do so seemed but another proof of the way Daniel's conscientiousness had set limits to their advancement.

But Daniel was adamant.

"It's safer never to meddle with things belonging to other people!"

"Belonging to other people!"

She could only echo his words indignantly, because indeed she was coming more and more each month to regard the landlocked money as theirs, which they were only prevented from making use of by reason of an irritating technicality.

"It is my belief he intended us to keep his share," she said one day. "Don't you remember he wanted to give it to us as a wedding present? And when I would not take it, and insisted we would send it to him as soon as he sent his address, all he said was that we would leave it at that! Well! I didn't pay much heed to him at the time, but I remember distinctly now that he looked at me with a peculiar expression, and although I didn't understand it at the time, it looks as if he never intended to send the address. In other words, that was only his way of telling us to keep the money."

And it seemed quite possible that this might have been the case. To Daniel, such behavior might have been compatible with Tom's character as then, and since, he had often tried to read it. But such an interpretation on his part could have no bearing upon their present circumstances.

"What you say may be true, my dear," he said, a trifle dryly, "but I'm afraid your words wouldn't cut any ice with the bank manager. You made a mistake not to get him to make a written statement."

As if this might still be possible, Bedelia sighed.

"Oh, if only we could get in touch with him," she cried.

Their discussions all boiled down to that wish in the end, with just one difference, that where Daniel wished to do so with some hope of benefiting the absent one, Bedelia did so in hope of gain for themselves. Each thinking his own thoughts, they stood staring at the floor. Then Daniel took up his pen.

"Ah, well—who knows! One of these days we may hear from him out of the blue!"

He had said it so often it had ceased to have any meaning other than that it had come to be regarded by both of them as a terminal phrase for a painful conversation.

On this occasion, however, Bedelia sneered openly at him.

"How often have we heard that? Do you know what I think? Well, I'll tell you. It's my belief he's dead."

Shocked at her bluntness, Daniel looked up.

"He may have been dead for years," she cried. "After all, it's a queer thing Mary Conaty never ran into him again! It's a queer thing no one ever met him or heard of him. Oh, to think of that money lying there idle when it could have been so much use to us!"

Daniel looked at her. Had she no feeling at all to be able to speak so callously?

It was different for him; there was no blood tie: for him it was a matter of business.

"If he was dead the money would be ours," he said, "unless he married, or had children," he added suddenly, a new aspect of the situation dawning on him.

On this point, however, Bedelia confidently reassured him that her brother was not married.

"You'd find that he'd have made his claim on us if that was the case," she said. "Whatever notions he might have had himself, you'd find his wife wouldn't be long about helping him to get rid of them. No matter how much money he'd have made on the other side of the ocean, you'd find she'd grudge leaving us the few pounds on this side of it. Oh, I think you may take it that he never married."

Since his experience of the female mind was confined entirely to his contact with her own, Daniel was inclined to believe that she might be correct in her reasoning.

"In that case the money would be ours all right, as the next of kin," he said.

But Bedelia looked contemptuously at him.

"What good is it to us whether he's dead or not when we can't know it for certain!"

Daniel, however, had oddments of knowledge stored away in his slow mind.

"And there might perhaps be some means by which we could get control of it. I think there is such a thing as obtaining a court order to presume death," he said, unexpectedly.

"Where did you hear that?" she exclaimed, incredulously, but there was a gleam of interest in her eyes.

Not that she intended to seek the assistance of the law as yet. It was indeed as if there were two compartments in her mind. In one compartment she was not only able to tolerate, but even to welcome, the idea that Tom was long gone to his reward; but in the other she steadfastly refused to believe such a thing. The habit of years was not altogether to be broken like that.

How many times in the years that were past had she started at the sound of a voice in the shop, and thought it was the voice of her brother? And in the days that followed Daniel's suggestion that they get an order to presume him dead, a kind of guilty nervousness made her start violently at the sound of every strange voice.

"We'll wait another while before we take any step," she said.

In the meantime, Daniel suggested they might write to Mary Conaty again.

Bedelia wrote that night.

It was four months, however, before a reply came to their letter, and it was not from Mary Conaty.

"She's dead: poor Mary Conaty is dead, Daniel," said Bedelia, scanning the first page.

"Well, that puts the lid on it," said Daniel, somewhat coarsely for him.

"No, wait a minute," cried Bedelia, her eyes running on over the next page, and then leaping to the name at the end. "This is from her daughter Biddy, and Biddy says—" She looked back to the beginning. "Isn't that good of her—that she's going to look him up for us. And what do you suppose? She was with her mother that day long ago when Mary met him outside the Parker House Hotel! Isn't that extraordinary! Of course, she was only a child at the time, but she says she remembers him well—he was really very striking-looking, Daniel—he had a kind of presence about him, I always thought. Anyway, he must have been remarkable in some way for a child to remember him like that! I dare say he made a deep impression on her when she's so anxious to be a help to us in the matter, although I dare say she's doing it for her mother's sake too; she knew how devoted Mary Conaty was to our family. I must write at once and thank her for her offer."

Then there began a frantic correspondence between Bedelia and Biddy Conaty, letters going off regularly, at set intervals, like cannon balls from Bedelia's end, without even waiting for the reply volley.

Daniel was inclined to be skeptical of this young girl succeeding where her mother had failed, but he had to admit her efficiency. For in the second letter, Biddy told them how, having taken into consideration that Tom Grimes might well be dead, she had looked up the records right back to the last time he was positively known to have been alive. That was a remarkably thorough piece of work for a young girl to execute, thought Daniel. And furthermore, not having found any record of the demise of such a person, she quite properly concluded that there was a good chance of his being still alive. But, she added—and this Daniel thought very astute—he must be an old man now, and very likely incapacitated, and so her next proposal was to make inquiries at all the large state hospitals, and homes for incurables, that took in elderly patients of his kind.

"My poor brother," said Bedelia, as they came to this part of the letter, and she tried hard to feel compassion, but all she really felt was a renewed exhilaration in the chase. "Isn't she wonderful, Daniel?" she cried, as letter after letter fell into the letter box, now asking for details, now giving rise to little hopes, and now to little fears.

"What a nice girl she must be," said Bedelia. "When this is all over, we ought to invite her over for a summer: she has people outside the town belonging to her mother, of course, but she doesn't seem the kind of girl who would enjoy being in the heart of the country, with no conveniences—we must ask her to stay with us!"

"She's a great girl all right," Daniel agreed. "She'll find him yet!" he said.

"She will: she will!" said Bedelia.

All the same, it came as something of a shock when the letter arrived in which Biddy Conaty purported to have indeed done that very thing that they predicted so lightheartedly; to have found Tom Grimes.

"Oh, Daniel!" cried Bedelia. "What do you think? Biddy Conaty's found Tom Grimes!"

And even though he was shocked himself, Daniel couldn't help noticing the way she used her brother's surname, as if he were a stranger.

"He's ill," she went on, excitedly. "She found him in a hospice for the dying."

She spoke as if she felt nothing, but at this, Daniel was not surprised, because he himself felt nothing but a tendency to tremble at the legs.

"Was she talking to him? What did he say?" he asked at last.

"Oh, she hasn't been to see him yet," said Bedelia. "She just dashed off a letter to let us know she was on his track—the home is in a place called Norwood. She's only been in touch with the officials through the post, and by telephone." Suddenly struck by some new aspect of the affair, she stopped short. "We'll have to compensate her for all this postage and telephoning, I suppose," she said. "We can't let her be at a loss on our account—let's hope there won't be too much of it."

Daniel, however, brushed this aside.

"Oh, don't worry, we'll see about that," he said, although it crossed his mind that it might not be such a small matter at all, and, once found, there might be no end to the expenses which Tom Grimes would cause them to incur. There was always his own money upon which to draw, but there might be a lot of red tape before they could lay hands on it, and in the meantime ready money might have to be found, but there was no good in bothering Bedelia about it at this point.

"It's a pity she didn't wait to write until after she'd seen him," he said.

"Well, Daniel, I must say I think that's the most ungrateful thing I ever heard—the poor girl thought she'd never get the news away quick enough to me. Not that I can expect you to understand my appreciation of that. After all, he's not your brother!"

And here she pulled out her handkerchief.

"My only brother!" she sobbed. "And to think he's dangerously ill in a home for incurables—that means dying, I suppose. Dying!"

Daniel, however, remained cold and unmoved.

"A man named Tom Grimes is dying," he said soberly. "It's not at all impossible that it may be your brother, but neither is it impossible that it is an altogether different person who happens to have the same name."

So astonished was Bedelia, that she could only gape at him dumbly, and a look that bordered on imbecility came over her face.

"Oh, I dare say it's him all right," he said hastily, "and I was wrong to criticize the girl. I must say she handled the whole thing most satisfactorily!"

Yes. Biddy Conaty had behaved very satisfactorily, and in the next few weeks she continued to do so: it was the facts which she disclosed which turned out to be unsatisfactory.

Her next letter revealed a most extraordinary state of affairs:

My dear friends,

I went out to Norwood last Saturday, as I wrote you I intended. I found that, as the authorities had informed me, there was a patient there who went by the name of Thomas Grimes. They were not able to give me much information about him, as he was a casualty case that had been brought in by the ambulance from a lodginghouse in a poor quarter of the town. It appears he had collapsed from exhaustion, the poor old man.

As she read it, Bedelia bit her lip at these words, but went on:

He was in a bad state of debility, but was able to give his name, which was the same as that he had given to the lodginghouse keeper, who called to inquire for him some days later. When the authorities interviewed this woman, however, she was unable to give them any useful information about him, as he had only just moved in the night before his collapse. This person, whom I will endeavor to go to see myself, evidently knew nothing at all about him. She only called at the hospital in case she would be implicated in any charges of neglect, as he was very thin and undernourished looking. She wanted to hand over his luggage.

I thought there might be something to identify him among the luggage, but the authorities had evidently thought the same, and gone through everything, with no success. There was only a few personal effects, in fact, nothing but a woolen sweater, showing signs of wear, a small roll of red flannel with two safety pins fastened in it, a razor and a shaving brush, a spare pair of boots, and a railway timetable. The contents of his pockets were of no importance from the point of view of identification.

At this point, there had evidently been a break in the writing of the letter, which when it was taken up again, was in ink of a different color, and ran as follows:

Since I began this letter, I had several interruptions, and I am sure you are asking yourself why I do not hurry and tell you if I saw this man, and what I thought of him.

Well, I'm afraid my visit wasn't as satisfactory as I hoped. The poor old man tried to be as cooperative as possible, but it was true for the authorities that he was in a very low state and failing rapidly. The nurse said he was perfectly normal mentally when it was a question of obeying instructions about medicine and the like, but he seemed totally unable to comprehend who I was, and why I had come to see him. Naturally I couldn't ask him too many questions all at once, but I gradually managed to introduce a few names into my conversation to see if they were familiar to him. I mentioned my mother first, and then I mentioned your name, taking the liberty of referring to you by your Christian name, and then gradually I began to talk about Ireland. I think it was when I mentioned "the old country," as my mother always called it, that his face seemed to alter in expression, but then, of course, it's very hard to judge with old people like that, and the nurse said it might be only a twitch, because he was twitching badly when he was brought in to them.

I do think myself, though, that his face did alter, and so the next day I said something—I forget just what, but it was something about the old days that I remembered my mother telling me—and then he definitely gave a sign of recognition. At least, he put up his hands to his face like a child. I think he must have felt bad or something. I felt sorry for him anyway, and what is more, I felt absolutely certain at that moment that he was your brother.

Well, I'm afraid this letter is not very satisfactory for you, but I can only hope you will believe me when I assure you that I did my best. I will call to see him again, of course, and I left my address with the hospital authorities, who will notify me if there is any change in his condition. Perhaps if he gets stronger, I will be able to question him a bit about his earlier life.

Hoping you are all well, and that you will excuse this very long letter, but I felt certain you would want as many details as I could give you. I wish I had more.

Yours truly,
Biddy Conaty

PS. It has just occurred to me that you will wonder that I have said nothing about whether or not I recognized him, having already said that I had met him when I was a child. But I am sure you will understand that the years would have made a great change, to say nothing of sickness and poverty. Then, too, I always think people look altogether different from themselves when they are in bed, particularly in hospital. After all, I was very young too at the time I was supposed to have met him, and I daresay in the interval I could have mixed him up in my mind with someone else.

B. C.

"Did you ever know such nonsense?" Bedelia cried in the same breath that she read the last line. "I think she must be a bit stupid after all. Either that, or else she never met him at all. I don't care what she says about age or anything else: if she ever laid eyes on Tom Grimes she ought to be able to recognize him again unless she's a fool." She flicked back the letter with an exasperated look on her face. "Couldn't she tell us whether he was the same build as our Tom? Had he the same features? Was he Irish at all!" But it was too exasperating to contemplate.

"And now where are we?" she cried.

And indeed, it seemed an extraordinarily trying situation in which to have been placed. Even Daniel thought they were in a pickle.

"We'd better send her some money, anyway," he said at last.

For one thing was clear, that if this man was Tom Grimes, he had not become the millionaire that Bedelia had so often fancied him.

"We'd better send this girl some money, and tell her to see that he has whatever he wants."

"But supposing it's not Tom at all?" cried Bedelia.

Daniel shook his head.

"I don't think we'll be under much expense one way or another," he said. "Or not for long, anyway," and he put out his hand and took the letter.

"I don't know so much about that," said Bedelia. "The girl said something about going to see him again when he got stronger."

"If—not when—he got stronger," Daniel amended. "And some-how I don't think he will," he added.

"You don't mean to say you think he'll die, and leave us in this ridiculous situation of not knowing for certain whether it is him or not?"

It was as if all the years, with their varying degrees of suspense, had been pressed into one unbearable moment.

"Oh, how can that girl be so stupid!" she exclaimed. She wrung her hands. "To think that it all could be settled in an instant if I could as much as get one glance at him!"

It was only an exclamation—only an expression of irritation and annoyance, but in it was the seed of an idea that had only to be released to begin to stir with life.

"You wouldn't think of going over there, Bedelia?" said Daniel.

"Are you out of your mind? Is it me—at my age?" cried Bedelia, for it seemed, at that moment, a preposterous idea.

Yet it was only five days later, Daniel, as agent, having been able to expedite matters with the shipping company, that he and Bedelia set out for Belfast, to board the S.S. *Samaria* bound for Boston Harbor.

It was a bad crossing. The fog in which they set out from Belfast did not lift the whole way across, and the foghorn sounded continuously. It nearly drove Bedelia mad, as for the first four days of the voyage she stayed down in her cabin, deadly sick.

Daniel got on a bit better. He got his sea legs after a day or so, and he was able to engage in such mild dissipation as shuffleboard, and guessing how many knots they traveled each day. He also kept a sharp watch out for porpoises, and he took a great interest in passing ships, particularly at night. Once he believed he saw a disturbance in the water, which might have been a whale. He also made a few friends, but he did not speak about them to Bedelia: it would only annoy her.

On the fourth day, Bedelia came up on deck, weak and watery-looking in the face.

It was characteristic that her first and only encounter was with an angular woman in deep black, whose husband had died in the course of their first trip home to England in forty years, and she was now bringing him back to America for burial. He was in the hold.

Up to meeting Bedelia, this woman had spoken to no one in the course of the voyage. But she made fast friends with Bedelia, and they were constantly to be seen promenading round the deck in dismal discourse. After a day or two, Daniel began to feel that the slight revulsion that the other passengers felt for the bereaved woman had extended to include Bedelia also.

Indeed, as he stood in the bar one afternoon, where although he was a teetotaler, he spent a lot of his time, the bulletin board being there, on which the results of the various competitions were posted, an Englishman whom he had not met before jerked his glass in the direction of the two women, who could be seen slowly pacing past the doorway.

"Rum thing to think of that chap down in the hold, isn't it?" he said. "Should think it would have been a better job to have put him down on the spot, not tote the poor devil about like this!"

For a moment, both men had a gloomy vision of the coffin down in the hold, stoutly propped no doubt, and corded down, but within which they visualized the dead man, like a shuttle, rattled backward and forward with each uneasy movement of the water.

Both together they laughed awkwardly.

"Bet my old woman wouldn't go to all that trouble," he said then, but the warmth of his voice implied such good-humored relationship that Daniel immediately conjured up a picture of a large woman, red in the face, her big bosom always lolloping up and down with laughter.

As if he read his thoughts, the Englishman pointed out again to where the two women in black, having made a round of the deck, were starting off upon a second round.

"I must say she looks a cold fish to me," he said. "I bet she has some shrewd motive for taking the poor stiff back to the States. Look at the face of her: I can't stand a conniving woman!"

It was with a start Daniel realized that the other had mistaken Bedelia for the owner of the corpse. Too awkward, too embarrassed, to put things right, he mumbled an excuse, and went out of the saloon. But he couldn't put out of his mind the derisive description of Bedelia.

Poor Bedelia! She was at her worst all during the trip, he thought.

Sinking down on a deck chair, he tried to compose his mind enough to make out his forecast of the ship's speed for the day, when through the porthole he caught sight of her. The other woman had evidently gone below, and Bedelia was waiting for her. He was struck by how poorly she looked, the harsh salt winds were blowing her thin hair back from her face, as the years had blown back the skin from the bone. He began to think that perhaps he had neglected her.

"Oh, there you are, Bedelia," he cried, hurrying out to her. "There is going to be a ship's concert tonight," he said. "I was thinking we might stay up for it?"

Bedelia looked at him with scandalized eyes.

"I'm afraid I cannot forget the object of our trip as easily as you, Daniel," she said. And turning aside, she began again to pace the deck with mournful steps.

Looking after her, Daniel reflected that in a certain sense her words were true: he had enjoyed the voyage, very much indeed, but he could not see that to do so was in any way culpable. Of course, Tom Grimes was only a brother-in-law to him, but all the same, it was forty years since Bedelia herself had seen him, and it seemed a bit much to think her feelings could still be so quick.

If, however, Daniel had enjoyed himself mildly on the voyage, when they arrived on the other side he was no whit less lost and strange than she.

To begin with, they had never heard such a din in their lives. As they drove away from the dockside, sirens were screaming, and just as they supposed they were getting away from the babel of dockland, their taxi shot into a street above which an overhead electric trolley ran by, with a noise so deafening that they sat dumbly side by side in their taxi, and waited with desperation for the real character of the city to manifest itself to them.

But as Biddy Conaty had chosen their hotel for them solely on the merits of its nearness to the hospital, which was situated in a poor quarter, in a few minutes they found themselves drawing up in a street little better than any of those through which they had driven, and they began to think the whole city clamorous with noise.

And then, just before their taxi stopped on the other side of the street, where a short alley led off the main thoroughfare, they saw that a crowd had gathered.

"Oh, was there an accident?" cried Bedelia, hesitating to get out of the car.

But Daniel hurried her out, and up the steps of the hotel. On the top step, however, she stopped and looked across the street, and having now a full view over the heads of the crowd, she could see clearly what was going on: could see, yes, but understand? No.

Bewildered, she pressed against Daniel, for through a hole in what seemed to be an ordinary white sheet, that had been sketchily erected on a wooden frame, a black head protruded, and just as she was looking, a man in the crowd took up something—she couldn't see what, a stone or a turnip it looked like, big and round anyway —and aiming straight, it seemed, at that sweating black face, missed it by only an inch.

"Oh, my God, what are they doing?" she cried, feeling sick and faint.

Confused remnants of things she had heard about lynchings and mob law flashed through her mind, and she put up her hands to her face, and now, quickly, one after another, half a dozen men were raising their arms and flinging missives straight at that pilloried head.

"Oh, what is it, Daniel?" she cried again.

"Come away," was all Daniel was able to say, but neither of them could move a limb.

And then, out between her fingers, she saw the round object flying through the air again, and this time, smack, with a nauseating sound, it landed right on the Negro's face, and burst open, splashing everything around, the sweating face, and all the sheet, with a soft pulpy mess.

Her heart turned to stone. For a moment she thought it was the living fleshy face of the victim that had burst into pulp; then she realized it was the missile itself, some kind of grotesque, unnatural-looking gourd, with which she was unfamiliar.

And the Negro, unable to wipe away the mess about his eyes and mouth, was shaking his head to free himself in splatters of the nauseating mess, but as he did so, she could see his great mouth opening in a laugh, while a showman in a white coat proceeded to make ostentatious payment to the successful shier, and the crowd roared with applause.

In a disgust and contempt almost greater than her original horror, Bedelia turned into the hotel, Daniel following her, shaking his head. He felt it was unfortunate that she should have witnessed such a thing at such a time.

But the episode was in one way providential, for it intensified her impression that America was a queer place, where anything could happen, and unconsciously prepared her, in some little way, at least, for what was to come.

It had been arranged that Biddy Conaty would meet them at the hotel, and so as they went into the vestibule, they were prepared when the young woman who had been seated there got to her feet and came toward them. They were not so prepared for her agitation.

"Oh, I'm so glad you got here at last," she cried, and a painful flush spread over her pretty face.

He's dead! thought Bedelia, and she said so.

"Yes, the night before last," said the young woman, almost indifferently, and then she rushed ahead with the rest of her story, as if the death was a mere detail, a thing of small importance, beside the rest of what she had to tell them. She didn't even give Bedelia time to recover from what, after all, she ought to have considered a shock. She seemed to be thinking only of herself for some reason or another. She was actually trembling, and hardly able to speak coherently.

"You must forgive me," she cried, "but the most awful thing has happened—I didn't tell you in my letters—it didn't seem important then, but I realize now that perhaps I ought to have mentioned it. You see, as well as me, there was a man who used to go to see your brother—I keep calling him that, no matter what. He was a very well-off man, a farmer from the Middle West who came to live on the east coast, and one day, I don't know how exactly, he happened to find out about your brother being in hospital, and he came to see him, because it seems Tom—as he called him—used to work for him years ago, and he had a great regard for him. I must say I thought he was a very generous man: he brought him fruit and magazines and all kinds of things, and told the nurses not to stint him in anything, but just send the bill to him. I didn't say anything, because of course your brother could easily have been in the Middle West all those years that no one knew where he was, and after all, if he worked as a waiter, he could just as well have been a farm laborer—"

At this point, involuntarily, after all the years that had intervened, Daniel suddenly recollected his own remark that Mary Conaty might think it a grand thing to be a waiter. Well, her daughter had come along a bit in her ideas, it seemed! Then he brought his mind back to Biddy. Her agitation was increasing.

"Well, as I say, I didn't pay much attention to this man. Really, I didn't see any harm in him being kind to your brother, and I don't believe you would either, if you were in my place, but last night things took on a different aspect, as it were. When I went down to the hospital, this man was there again, and he was making arrangements for the burial! So of course I had to tell him that I was instructed to do that, and that as a matter of fact you were on your way over to this country, and would probably be here in time for the funeral—" She turned from Daniel to Bedelia, both of whom nodded, as if acknowledging the veracity of her statement.

"Well, what did he say to that?" said Daniel.

"Oh, well, there's no use in giving you every word," said Biddy delicately, but as Daniel seemed to frown, she overcame her scruples about their feelings.

"Well, what he said was, 'Who the hell are they?' I'm afraid I misjudged him at the beginning, you see, he is really a bit coarse, and certainly very headstrong. I explained, at once, of course, and then he said something that took the ground from under my feet. He said that as far as he knew, Tom Grimes was never in Ireland in his life—that he had given him to understand that he was born in America—out there in the Middle West as a matter of fact. 'Oh, but that couldn't be!' I said, and I began to tell him all I knew about your brother"—she faltered—"about our Tom Grimes, I mean," she said. "But he only laughed. I don't think that was very nice of him, do you? And he said he knew Tom Grimes for thirty years, and he never once heard him mention the Old Country."

But Bedelia could listen to no more.

"Do you mean to say you've brought us all the way across the Atlantic on a wild-goose chase?" she cried. In spite of Biddy's fine appearance, Bedelia remembered that her mother had once been their servant. "I must say—" she began.

But the events through which Biddy had passed within the last few hours had, however, transported her to a state of excitement that made her impervious to Bedelia's anger. Indeed, she brushed it aside like a thing of nothing.

"Oh, you don't understand," she said impatiently. "It's much worse than you think! I wasn't able to communicate with you all the week while you were on sea, but in the last few days before he died, I mean, although there was nothing positive to go upon, I got a feeling—only a feeling, of course, but you know how absolutely reliable feelings can be? Well, as I say, I got a feeling that the man from the Middle West mightn't know everything. He said he never heard the poor old fellow mention the Old Country. Well, he could have had his reasons for that, couldn't he? It might have been a matter of pride with him not to let people know he'd got down to being a common workman. He might even have had some idea in his mind about not wanting to shame you and your family —you'd never know. And then, there was another thing that I didn't think of until just now! I was judging him by my mother, and other people I'd met from Ireland, who were ever and always talking about the old sod—but of course they lived in the country —why wouldn't they be always talking about it, and thinking about the hawthorn bushes and the cuckoo and the corncrake, the bogs and the little boreens. But your brother only lived in a town; isn't that all? There wouldn't be anything much to remember, would there?"

Involuntarily it flashed into Daniel's mind that it was Bedelia this time who had made a miscalculation about the second genera- tion of Conatys, when she spoke of how much she would appreciate staying with them instead of with her mother's people in the country.

"Well, as I was saying, I began to have those feelings that per- haps I wasn't so wrong about the poor old fellow after all, and then, the very last time that I saw him before he died, although he was a lot weaker, of course, and couldn't talk at all, I was al- most absolutely certain that he was your brother." She shrugged her shoulders. "It was only a feeling, of course, but as I say—"

But Bedelia was a woman too. She knew those feelings.

"I know!" she cried.

Biddy was completely exonerated, she was reinstated to her former position of confidant and ally. Bedelia gripped her by the arm.

"Do you mean this man is an imposter?" she cried. "Do you mean he's trying to prove a claim on our Tom?"

Feverishly two spots blazed in her cheeks, and she turned around to Daniel.

"Oh, what a mercy we came over!" she cried. "All I suffered on that awful ship, in that stuffy cabin, with the foghorn going all the time, was not for nothing. It was Providence: an Act of God. This man found out about the money, I suppose," she cried feverishly, "and he thinks he'll get hold of it. That's it. He thinks that if he can make out a good case he—"

Daniel, however, was steady.

"Calm yourself, my dear, I beg of you," he said. "Don't you see that if this man found out about the money—which is very unlikely, I must say—and if he had designs upon it, which is also unlikely, since Biddy here says he is a very wealthy man—but if such a thing were possible, don't you see that he's going the wrong way about advancing his interest? Indeed, he is doing quite the contrary. It is our Tom who owns the money. His Tom Grimes couldn't possibly have any claim to it. No, my dear, I'm afraid we're up against something harder for us to understand."

"But why—" began Bedelia.

Daniel shrugged his shoulders, and even Biddy seemed unable to supply a reason.

"He says he only wants to do right by a faithful servant," she said, but in looking at Bedelia's plain but respectable attire, she blushed a little at having used the word "servant." Some of her excitement was ebbing. A little nervously, she went on. "He's bought a plot in the cemetery, and he's ordered a lovely coffin, and he says—"

But before she said anything about the memorial monument, the sample picture of which she had seen, she recollected something, and dived into her purse, and somewhat shamefacedly drew out a little roll of notes. "This is the money you cabled to me for

the funeral expenses," she said. Clearly she hadn't been a match for
the man from the Middle West. "Oh, I hope you don't think I was
in any way to blame," she said, and not only did she look very,
very inexperienced, but it was quite plain to be seen that at that
moment she was very sorry she had got involved in the affair in
the first place.

"I don't see that it really matters, one way or another," she added,
rallying somewhat, "so long as he's dead," she said, flatly, defiantly.
"And the monument this man is putting up is really beautiful—he
showed me a picture of it in the mortician's catalogue—you really
couldn't have chosen anything better—he certainly didn't spare
expense."

She implied that it, alone, cost more than all the money they had
sent.

"And he has arranged to have several Masses said for him
too," she added, after a minute. "It was I suggested that to him.
You see, there was a medal around the old man's neck. I didn't
know about it when I wrote to you the first time. I was only told
about it after he was dead: the nurse asked me what she should do
with it. I said to leave it on him, of course, but I didn't think any
more about it till I was back in my apartment. Then all of a sudden
it seemed to me that the medal was a proof he was our man. But
when I got in touch with Mr. Coulter—that's the farmer's name—he
said it didn't signify anything. He said he never knew an Irishman
who didn't have a medal pinned on to him somewhere. He said if a
Paddy ever got drunk, or got knocked down, the first thing you'd
find when you opened his shirt was a medal." She shrugged her
shoulders.

"You see, I did my best," she said, "but he put me down every
time."

Then, realizing perhaps that the responsibility, that had rested
so heavily upon her, was hers no longer, she brightened.

"But now that you're here," she cried, "he may listen to you! I
told him you were arriving today." She looked guiltily at the clock.
"I said we'd go straight to the hospital the minute you got here!"

Solicitously Daniel put an arm around Bedelia.

"Do you feel able for it, Bedelia?" he asked.

But of course there could only be one answer to that question for

Bedelia. Everything hung upon her evidence.

She stood up.

"It will all be settled in a few minutes," said Daniel, soothingly. He did so dislike melodrama. "I think these people will hardly gainsay the word of the man's own sister."

And by these people he meant the hospital authorities, as well as the man from the Middle West. Only one thing troubled him, and as they went out through the hotel door, he whispered to Biddy.

"Oh, no! There's no need to worry about that," said Biddy. "They gave me their word that they wouldn't close the lid until you got a chance to see him."

That was very satisfactory. The porter hailed a taxi, and Daniel placed the two ladies in it. He sat beside Bedelia, but naturally, it was not to be expected that she would feel like talking. She turned her face to the window. Daniel, who felt under an obligation to be civil to Biddy, inclined his ear in her direction.

"They were very decent about the whole thing, because of course hospitals hate anything irregular like that," prattled Biddy. "As a matter of fact, they thought I was awfully silly to take exception to this other man's offer. So long as he was getting a Catholic burial, they didn't see why I should make a fuss."

In spite of the solemnity of the occasion, she giggled.

"They thought I ought to be glad he was getting such a fine funeral at someone else's expense."

Seeing Daniel's face, however, she sobered again.

"They said that there would be an awful delay if the question of identity was raised, and it wasn't as if there was anything really at stake. I suppose you can't blame them for not wanting a fuss, but all the same, I do think they were playing on me a bit, on account of my being young, and a woman, and all that—" She looked at Daniel for confirmation, and Daniel had to agree.

"They changed their attitude, I can tell you, when they heard you were on the way over here. That's when they agreed to hold over the funeral for a few hours."

They were nearing the hospital. Bedelia, who had listened, as in a dream, to the prattle of the girl, was looking out of the window of the taxicab, outside which on the crowded sidewalks an immense number of people seemed to be coursing up and down the streets.

Among them, here and there, on more than one occasion, it seemed to her that she saw young men that bore a strange resemblance to Tom, though not one was as fine a man as he.

He had been so handsome: it was part of his undoing, she supposed. Had his good looks worn well, she wondered, in the years that had passed since they had last stood face to face?

I must be prepared for a great change in him, she told herself, but the meaning of the words did not really penetrate to her mind, and she kept seeing him as she had last seen him, young, and gay, and mocking, and the words that had been used to describe him on so many significant occasions came again into her mind: a little prince. And slowly, tears welled into her eyes, and spilled down her cheeks.

For the first time since she was a child, there was no connivance in Bedelia's heart. All considerations of money had faded from her mind. It was as if an angel of light had come and sat down beside her in the dark cab, illuminating everything with a blinding radiance.

Daniel, who looked at her covertly, saw a great change in her face, but he did not know what to say or do. As for the light that shone for her, so blindingly beautiful, he was as unregarding of it as of the light of day. For in it, like millions of other simple men and women, unwittingly he had lived out all his life. He only hoped she was not going to break down now that they were nearly at the hospital. Awkwardly he patted her knee.

"You're not sorry we came?" he asked, and he was surprised at the vehemence of her answer.

"Oh, no, I'm glad—so glad, Daniel," she said.

And it was true. Her heart was filled with love for her brother— her little brother that she had cared for like a mother when he was a child—her gay, reckless brother, whose charm had been so great a danger to him that she had to take a hand in his destiny and send him away—her brother, who at one word from her, had severed all ties of home and family, and come away to this alien land!

For years past she had thought never to look upon his face again, and now it had come about that she was, after all, to gaze upon it. In death, no less than life, compared with never seeing it again, to see that face would be a sorrow so exquisite as to be almost a joy.

For it was him—of that her heart was certain.

The taxi stopped.

"We're there!" said Biddy.

"This way, Bedelia!" said Daniel, as they went up the steps.

"This way, please!" said a nurse, as they went down a long white corridor.

"Now!" exclaimed Daniel involuntarily, as the nurse opened the door of the room where the corpse was waiting for them.

Now!

It was forty years since Bedelia had last seen the wasted form that, heavy now as stone, lay uncovered before her. It was forty years since she had last seen that face—if she had ever seen it? But had she? Before its implications of poverty and illness, she took refuge in a sudden doubt.

Could it be possible that those other people were right, and that it wasn't her brother at all? Surely no one could change so much, even in so long a time; even in death?

That nose! Tom never had that tightened drawn look about the nose. The hair, although it was white, was stiff and strong like Tom's hair used to be. But wasn't Tom taller?

Desperately her eyes fastened on detail after detail.

And then a voice—no, several voices, began pressing upon her.

"Well?" they said, Daniel, and Biddy, and someone else at whom she did not bother to look.

"Well?" she seemed to say to herself.

She looked again into the dead man's face. But if it was her brother, something had sundered them, something had severed the bonds of blood, and she knew him not. And if it was I who was lying there, she thought, he would not know me. It signified nothing that they might once have sprung from the same womb. Now, in this fateful moment, they were strangers.

Bewildered, she turned to Daniel.

"I don't know," she whimpered. "I can't say—I—"

She felt them all staring at her, and a nasal voice, now near, now far, like a voice heard under the first influence of an anesthetic, kept saying the same thing over and over again.

"It ain't natural: it just ain't natural!"

And then, loud in her ears, as she was being led out of the room, she heard a woman begin to cry and scream hysterically, and only confusedly did she comprehend that she herself was the woman who was behaving so unseemingly.

Outside in the street, the cab still waited, and she stumbled into it eagerly. For was it not here that the angel had come and sat by her side, shedding all about him the radiance of love? And might she not feel again, as she felt then, for now, too, as then, all connivance dead, she laid her heart open to him. But it was too old and cracked a vessel to hold any emotion at all, however precious, however small a drop.

There was no angel sitting in the cab. It was stuffy and close, and smelled strongly of feet.

My Vocation

I'M NOT married yet, but I'm still in hopes. And judging by the way my hopes are itching, I'd say I was never cut out to be a nun in the first place. Anyway, I was only thirteen when I got the Call, and I think if we were living out here in Crumlin at the time, in the new houses that the Government gave us, I'd never have got it at all, because we hardly ever see nuns out here, somehow, and a person wouldn't take so much notice of them out here anyway. It's so airy you know, and they blow along in their big white bonnets and a person wouldn't take any more notice of them than the seagulls that blow in from the sea. And then, too, you'd never get near enough to them out here to get the smell of them.

It was the smell of them I used to love in the Dorset Street days, when they'd stop us in the street to talk to us, when we'd be playing hopscotch on the path. I used to push up as close to them as possible and take great big sniffs of them. But that was nothing to when they came up to the room to see Mother. You'd get it terribly strong then.

"What smell are you talking about?" said my father one day when I was going on about them after they went. "That's no way to talk about people in Religious Orders," he said. "There's no smell at all off the like of them."

That was right, of course, and I saw where I was wrong. It was the no-smell that I used to get, but there were so many smells fighting for place in Dorset Street, fried onions, and garbage, and

the smell of old rags, that a person with no smell at all stood out a
mile from everybody else. Anyone with an eye in their head could
see that I didn't mean any disrespect. It vexed me shockingly to
have my father think such a thing. I told him so, too, straight out.

"And if you want to know," I finished up, "I'm going to be a
nun myself when I get big."

But my father only roared laughing.

"Do you hear that?" he said, turning to Mother. "Isn't that a good
one? She'll be joining the same order as you, I'm thinking." And
he roared out laughing again: a very common laugh I thought,
even though he was my father.

And he was nothing to my brother Paudeen.

"We'll be all right if it isn't the Order of Mary Magdalen that one
joins," he said.

What do you make of that for commonness? Is it any wonder I
wanted to get away from the lot of them?

He was always at me, that fellow, saying I was cheapening myself, and telling Ma on me if he saw me as much as lift my eye to a
fellow passing me in the street.

"She's mad for boys, that one," he used to say. And it wasn't true
at all. It wasn't my fault if the boys were always after me, was it?
And even if I felt a bit sparky now and then, wasn't that the kind
that always became nuns? I never saw a plain-looking one, did you?
I never did. Not in those days, I mean. The ones that used to come
visiting us in Dorset Street were all gorgeous-looking, with pale
faces and not a rotten tooth in their heads. They were twice as good-
looking as the Tiller Girls in the Gaiety. And on Holy Thursday,
when we were doing the Seven Churches, and we used to cross over
the Liffey to the south side to make up the number, I used to go into
the Convent of the Reparation just to look at the nuns. You see
them inside in a kind of little golden cage, back of the altar in their
white habits with blue sashes and their big silver beads dangling
down by their side. They were like angels: honest to God. You'd be
sure of it if you didn't happen to hear them give an odd cough now
and again, or a sneeze.

It was in there with them I'd like to be, but Sis—she's my girl
friend—she told me they were all ladies, titled ladies too, some of
them, and I'd have to be a lay sister. I wasn't having any of that,

thank you. I could have gone away to domestic service any day if that was only all the ambition I had. It would have broken my mother's heart to see me scrubbing floors and the like. She never sank that low, although there were fourteen of them in the family, and only eleven of us. She was never anything less than a wards' maid in the Mater Hospital, and they're sort of nurses, if you like, and when she met my father she was after getting an offer of a great job as a barmaid in Geary's of Parnell Street. She'd never have held with me being a lay sister.

"I don't hold with there being any such thing as lay sisters at all," she said. "They're not allowed a hot jar in their beds, I believe, and they have to sit at the back of the chapel with no red plush on their kneeler. If you ask me, it's a queer thing to see the Church making distinctions."

She had a great regard for the Orders that had no lay sisters at all, like the Little Sisters of the Poor, and the Visiting Sisters.

"Oh, they're the grand women!" she said.

You'd think then, wouldn't you, that she'd be glad when I decided to join them. But she was as much against me as any of them.

"Is it you?" she cried. "You'd want to get the impudent look taken off your face if that's the case!" she said, tightly.

I suppose it was the opposition that nearly drove me mad. It made me dead set on going ahead with the thing.

You see, they never went against me in any of the things I was going to be before that. The time I said I was going to be a Tiller Girl in the Gaiety, you should have seen the way they went on: all of them. They were dead keen on the idea.

"Are you tall enough though—that's the thing?" said Paudeen.

And the tears came into my mother's eyes.

"That's what I always wanted to be when I was a girl," she said, and she dried her eyes and turned to my father. "Do you think there is anyone you could ask to use his influence?" she said. Because she was always sure and certain that influence was the only thing that would get you any job.

But it wasn't influence in the Tiller Girls: it was legs. And I knew that, and my legs were never my strong point, so I gave up that idea.

Then there was the time I thought I'd like to be a waitress, even though I wasn't a blonde.

But you should see the way they went on then too.

"A packet of henna would soon settle the hair question," said Paudeen. And Mother was only worried about my morals.

True they were doubtful that I'd get any of these jobs, but they didn't raise any obstacles, and they didn't laugh at me like they did in this case.

"And what will I do for money," said my father, "when they come looking for your dowry? If you haven't an education you have to have money going into those convents."

But I turned a dead ear to him.

"The Lord will provide," I said. "If it's His will for me to be a nun He'll find a way out of all difficulties," I said grandly, and in a voice I imagined to be as near as I could make it to the ladylike voices of the Visiting Sisters.

But I hadn't much hope of getting into the Visiting Sisters. To begin with, they always seemed to take it for granted I'd get married.

"I hope you're a good girl," they used to say to me, and you'd know by the way they said it what they meant. "Boys may like a fast girl when it comes to having a good time, but it's the modest girl they pick when it comes to choosing a wife," they said. And such-like things. They were always harping on the one string. Sure they'd never get over it if I told them what I had in mind. I'd never have the face to tell them!

And then one day what did I see but an advertisement in the paper.

"Wanted, Postulants," it said, in big letters, and then underneath in small letters, there was the address of the Reverend Mother you were to apply to, and in smaller letters still, at the very bottom, were the words that made me sit up and take notice, "No Dowry," they said.

"That's me," said I, and there and then I up and wrote off to them, without as much as saying a word to anyone only Sis.

Poor Sis: you should have seen how bad she took it.

"I can't believe it," she said, over and over again, and she threw her arms around me and burst out crying. She was always a good sort, Sis.

Every time she looked at me she burst out crying. And I must say that was more like the way I expected people to take me. But as a matter of fact Sis started the ball rolling, and it wasn't long after that everyone began to feel bad, because you see, the next thing that happened was a telegram arrived from the Reverend Mother in answer to my letter.

"It can't be for you," said my mother, as she ripped it open. "Who'd be sending you a telegram?"

And I didn't know who could have sent it either until I read the signature. It was Sister Mary Alacoque.

That was the name of the nun in the paper.

"It's for me all right," I said then. "I wrote to her," I said and I felt a bit awkward.

My mother grabbed back the telegram.

"Glory be to God," she said, but I don't think she meant it as a prayer. "Do you see what it says: calling to see you this afternoon, Deo Gratias? What on earth is the meaning of all this?"

"Well!" I said defiantly, "when I told you I was going to be a nun you wouldn't believe me. Maybe you'll believe it when I'm out among the savages!" I added. Because it was a missionary order: that's why they didn't care about the dowry. People are always leaving money in their wills to the Foreign Missions, and you don't need to be too highly educated to teach savages, I suppose.

"Glory be to God," said my mother again. And then she turned on me. "Get up out of that and we'll try and put some sort of front on things before they get here: there'll be two of them, I'll swear: nuns never go out alone. Hurry up, will you?"

Never in your life did you see anyone carry on like my mother did that day. For the few hours that remained of the morning she must have worked like a lunatic, running mad around the room, shoving things under the bed, and ramming home the drawers of the chest, and sweeping things off the seats of the chairs.

"They'll want to see a chair they can sit on, anyway," she said. "And I suppose we'll have to offer them a bite to eat."

"Oh, a cup of tea," said my father.

But my mother had very grand ideas at times.

"Oh, I always heard you should give monks or nuns a good meal," she said. "They can eat things out in the world that they can't eat in the convent. As long as you don't ask them. Don't say will you or won't you! Just set it in front of them—that's what I always heard."

I will say this for my mother, she has a sense of occasion, because we never heard any of this lore when the Visiting Sisters called, or even the Begging Sisters, although you'd think they could do with a square meal by the look of them sometimes.

But no: there was never before seen such a fuss as she made on this occasion.

"Run out to Mrs. Mullins in the front room and ask her for the lend of her brass fender," she cried, giving me a push out the door. "And see if poor Mr. Duffy is home from work—he'll be good enough to let us have a chair, I'm sure, the poor soul, the one with the plush seat," she cried, coming out to the landing after me, and calling across the well of the stairs.

As I disappeared into Mrs. Mullins' I could see her standing in the doorway as if she was trying to make up her mind about something. And sure enough, when I came out lugging the fender with me, she ran across and took it from me.

"Run down to the return room, like a good child," she said, "and ask old Mrs. Dooley for her tablecloth—the one with the lace edging she got from America." And as I showed some reluctance, she caught my arm. "You might give her a wee hint of what's going on. Won't everyone know it as soon as the nuns arrive, and it'll give her the satisfaction of having the news ahead of everyone else."

But it would be hard to say who had the news first because I was only at the foot of the steps leading to the return room when I could hear doors opening in every direction on our own landing, and the next minute you'd swear they were playing a new kind of postman's knock, in which each one carried a piece of furniture round with him, by the way our friends and neighbors were rushing back and forth across the landing; old Ma Dunne with her cuckoo clock, and young Mrs. McBride, that shouldn't be carrying heavy things at all, with our old wicker chair that she was going to exchange for the time with a new one of her own. And I believe she wanted to get her piano rolled in to us too, only there wasn't time!

That was the great thing about Dorset Street: you could meet any and all occasions, you had so many friends at your back. And you could get anything you wanted, all in a few minutes, without anyone outside the landing being any the wiser.

My mother often said it was like one big happy family, that landing—including the return room, of course.

The only thing was everyone wanted to have a look at the room.

We'll never get shut of them before the nuns arrive, I thought.

"Isn't this the great news entirely," said old Mrs. Dooley, making
her way up the stairs as soon as I told her. And she rushed up to my
mother and kissed her. "Not but that you deserve it," she said. "I
never knew a priest or a nun yet that hadn't a good mother behind
them!" And then Mrs. McBride coming out, she drew her into it.
"Isn't that so, Mrs. McBride?" she cried. "I suppose you heard the
news?"

"I did indeed," said Mrs. McBride. "Not that I was surprised," she
said, but I think she only wanted to let on she was greater with us
than she was, because as Sis could tell you, there was nothing of
the Holy Molly about me—far from it.

What old Mr. Duffy said was more like what you'd expect.

"Well, doesn't that beat all!" he cried, hearing the news as he
came up the last step of the stairs. "Ah, well, I always heard it's the
biggest divils that make the best saints, and now I can believe it!"

He was a terribly nice old man.

"And is it the Foreign Missions?" he asked, calling me to one side,
"because if that's the case I want you to know you can send me raffle
tickets for every draw you hold, and I'll sell the lot for you and get
the stubs back in good time, with the money along with it in postal
orders. And what's more—" he was going on, when Mrs. Mullins
let out a scream.

"You didn't tell me it was the Missions," she cried. "Oh, God help
you, you poor child!" And she threw up her hands. "How will any
of us be saved at all at all with the like of you going to the ends of
the earth where you'll never see a living soul only blacks till the day
you die! Oh, glory be to God. And to think we never knew who
we had in our midst!"

In some ways it was what I expected, but in another way I'd have
liked if they didn't all look at me in such a pitying way.

And old Mrs. Dooley put the lid on it.

"A saint—that's what you are, child," she cried, and she caught
my hand and pulled me down close to her—she was a low butt of

a little woman. "They tell me it's out to the poor lepers you're going?"

That was the first I heard about lepers, I can tell you. And I partly guessed the poor old thing had picked it up wrong, but all the same I put a knot in my handkerchief to remind me to ask where I was going.

And I may as well admit straight out, that I wasn't having anything to do with any lepers. I hadn't thought of backing out of the thing entirely at that time, but I was backing out of it if it was to be lepers!

The thought of the lepers gave me the creeps, I suppose. Did you ever get the feeling when a thing was mentioned that you *had* it? Well, that was the way I felt. I kept going over to the basin behind the screen (Mrs. McBride's) and washing my hands every minute, and as for spitting out, my throat was raw by the time I heard the cab at the door.

"Here they come," cried my father, raising his hand like the starter at the dog track.

"Out of this, all of you," cried Mrs. Mullins, rushing out and giving an example to everyone.

"Holy God!" said my mother, but I don't think that was meant to be a prayer either.

But she had nothing to be uneasy about: the room was gorgeous.

That was another thing: I thought they'd be delighted with the room. We never did it up any way special for the Visiting Sisters, but they were always saying how nice we kept it: maybe that was only to encourage my mother, but all the same it was very nice of them. But when the two Recruiting Officers arrived (it was my father called them that after they went), they didn't seem to notice the room at all in spite of what we'd done to it.

And do you know what I heard one of them say to the other?

"It seems clean, anyway," she said. Now I didn't like that "seems." And what did she mean by the "anyway" I'd like to know?

It sort of put me off from the start—would you believe that? That, and the look of them. They weren't a bit like the Visiting Sisters —or even the Begging Sisters; who all had lovely figures—like statues. One of them was thin all right, but I didn't like the look of her all the same. She didn't look thin in an ordinary way; she looked worn away, if you know what I mean? And the other one was fat. She was so fat I was afraid if she fell on the stairs she'd start to roll like a ball.

She was the boss: the fat one.

And do you know one of the first things she asked me? You'd never guess. I don't even like to mention it. She caught a hold of my hair.

"I hope you keep it nice and clean," she said.

What do you think of that? I was glad my mother didn't hear her. My mother forgets herself entirely if she's mad about anything. She didn't hear it, though. But I began to think to myself that they must have met some very low-class girls if they had to ask *that* question. And wasn't that what you'd think?

Then the worn-looking one said a queer thing, not to me, but to the other nun.

"She seems strong, anyway," she said. And there again I don't think she meant my health. I couldn't help putting her remark alongside the way she was so worn-looking, and I began to think I'd got myself into a nice pickle.

But I was prepared to go through with it all the same. That's me: I have great determination although you mightn't believe it. Sis often says I'd have been well able for the savages if I'd gone on with the thing.

But I didn't.

I missed it by a hair's breadth, though. I won't tell you all the interview, but at the end of it anyway they gave me the name of the convent where I was to go for Probation, and they told me the day to go, and they gave me a list of the clothes I was to get.

"Will you be able to pay for them?" they said, turning to my father. They hadn't taken much notice of him up to that.

I couldn't help admiring the way he answered.

"Well, I managed to pay for plenty of style for her up to now," he said, "and seeing that this mourning outfit is to be the last I'll be asked to pay for, I think I'll manage it all right. Why?"

I admired the "why?"

"Oh, we have to be ready for all eventualities," said the fat one.

Sis and I nearly died laughing afterward thinking of those words.

But I hardly noticed them at the time, because I was on my way out the door to order a cab. They had asked me to get one and they had given me so many instructions that I was nearly daft.

They didn't want a flighty horse, and they didn't want a cab that was too high up off the ground, and I was to pick a cabby that looked respectable.

Now at this time, although there were still cabs to be hired, you didn't have an almighty great choice, and I knew I had my work cut out for me to meet all their requirements.

But I seemed to be dead in luck in more ways than one, because when I went to the cab stand there, among the shiny black cabs, with big black horses that rolled their eyes at me, there was one old cab and it was all battered and green-moldy. The cabby too looked about as moldy as the cab. And as for the horse—well, wouldn't anyone think that he'd be moldy too? But as a matter of fact the horse wasn't moldy in any way. Indeed, it was due to the way he bucketed it about that the old cab was so racked-looking: it was newer than the others I believe, and as for the cabby, I believe it was the horse had him so bad-looking. That horse had the heart scalded in him.

But it was only afterward I heard all this. I thought I'd done great work, and I went up and got the nuns, and put them into it and off they went, with the thin one waving to me.

It was while I was still waving that I saw the horse starting his capers.

My first thought was to run, but I thought I'd have to face them again, so I didn't do that. Instead, I ran after the cab and shouted to the driver to stop.

Perhaps that was what did the damage. Maybe I drove the horse clean mad altogether, because the next thing he reared up and let his hind legs fly. There was a dreadful crash and a sound of splintering, and the next thing I knew the bottom of the cab came down on the road with a clatter. I suppose it had got such abuse from that animal from time to time it was on the point of giving way all the time.

It was a miracle for them they weren't let down on the road— the two nuns. It was a miracle for me too in another way because if they did I'd have to go and pick them up and I'd surely be drawn deeper into the whole thing.

But that wasn't what happened. Off went the horse, as mad as ever down the street, rearing and leaping, but the nuns must have got a bit of a warning and held on to the sides, because the next thing I saw, along with the set of four feet under the horse, was four more feet showing out under the body of the cab, and running for dear life.

Honest to God, I started to laugh. Wasn't that awful? They could have been killed, and I knew it, although as a matter of fact some-one caught hold of the old cab before it got to Parnell Street and they were taken out of it and put into another cab. But once I started to laugh I couldn't stop, and in a way—if you can under-stand such a thing—I laughed away my vocation. Wasn't that awful?

Not but that I have a great regard for nuns even to this day, al-though, mind you, I sometimes think the nuns that are going now-adays are not the same as the nuns that were going in our Dorset Street days. I saw a terribly plain-looking one the other day in Cabra Avenue. But all the same, they're grand women! I'm going to make a point of sending all my kids to school with the nuns any-way, when I have them. But of course it takes a fellow with a bit of money to educate his kids nowadays. A girl has to have an eye to the future, as I always tell Sis—she's my girl friend, you remember.

Well, we're going out to Dollymount this afternoon, Sis and me, and you'd never know who we'd pick up. So long for the present!

The Small Bequest

IT WAS generally understood that when Miss Tate died she would leave a small bequest to her companion, Miss Blodgett. There had never been any direct statement of the old lady's intention in the matter, but it was felt by all their friends to be an understood thing. Meanwhile, of course, Miss Blodgett was getting an excellent salary, most of which she should have been able to put aside, for not only was her keep provided but, as well as sharing the necessaries of life with Miss Tate, she had full enjoyment of all the luxuries that the Tate family were continually bestowing upon the old lady: the sweets, the fruits, the books, the papers. For Miss Tate, at eighty, was able only to appreciate the kind thought of the giver, the bodily appreciation of the gifts fell entirely to Miss Blodgett. As she herself often remarked, Miss Blodgett was just like one of the family. And indeed it was as such she was always treated.

The Tates felt themselves greatly in Miss Blodgett's debt for her tireless devotion to Miss Adeline Tate. It was now twenty-seven years since Miss Blodgett had moved into the elegant house in Rattigan Rowe, with her big wicker suitcase and her iron trunk. They didn't know what Miss Adeline Tate would have done without her. Lord Robert, Miss Tate's oldest nephew, expressed the feelings of the whole family one evening after a visit to Rattigan Rowe.

"What a good job it is," said Lord Robert, "that Miss Blodgett is only sixty. She's fairly sure of outlasting Aunt Adeline."

There had been a large family gathering in Rattigan Rowe that afternoon, and some of the family were dining that night with Lord Robert. They all agreed with their host except Honoria Tate, his first cousin, who, being a lady barrister, felt compelled to point out that in that case instead of Miss Tate they would have Miss Blodgett on their hands.

"Oh, not at all!" said Lord Robert impatiently. "Aunt Adeline will see that Miss Blodgett is well taken care of after her death."

"How?" asked Lucy Tate, Lord Robert's youngest daughter.

"Don't be silly, Lucy dear," said her father. "You know it is understood that Aunt Adeline will make a substantial mention of Miss Blodgett in her will."

"Oh, of course!" murmured Lucy, abashed and blushing. "I forgot! The bequest!" For she recalled at once that she had often heard her aunts and uncles mention Miss Blodgett's small bequest. "Dear Aunt Adeline!" she murmured.

Miss Tate was not Lucy's aunt at all, of course. Miss Tate was her grandaunt, but like all the younger members of the family she had grown into the habit of calling the old lady by the name she heard on the lips of her elders. Miss Tate was Aunt Adeline to all of them. Even Lady Elizabeth's children, who were her great-grandnephews, never called her anything else.

It was quite disconcerting at times to hear some of the extremely young members of the family calling the old lady by such a familiar name. But then it was even more disconcerting to hear Miss Blodgett calling all the family by their familiar names, although perhaps it was natural enough for her to do so, considering that she knew them all since they were in their cradles, and had dandled most of them on her knee with as much affection, and a great deal more energy than Miss Tate had ever done. Sometimes, indeed, it seemed as if Emma Blodgett had never noticed that they had grown up, and in some cases, even grown old. Lord Robert was always Robbie to Miss Blodgett. The caustic Honoria was still Honey. And I never heard her call Lady Elizabeth Tate-Conyers anything else but Bessie.

The Tates were an old family, that went back for eleven recorded generations of plain but prosperous people, who had, however, linked themselves all along the way with the best stock in the country. The root was a plain and sturdy natural growth, but successful grafting had resulted in the frequent breaking out of blossom. The family had rarely failed in any decade to show a famous belle, a great soldier, or a poet.

And so, when Miss Tate's nephews, nieces, grandnephews, grand-nieces, and great-grandnephews came to pay their respects to her on a Sunday afternoon, the drawing room in Rattigan Rowe was filled with a gallant company, of which the old lady might well be proud.

And Miss Tate was extremely proud of them all. So, too, was Miss Blodgett. Although, here again, when one saw Miss Blodgett famil-iarly chaffing with judges and peers, and scolding a bishop for hav-ing snuff on his cuff, it was a little surprising to recollect that she had originally joined the Tate household in a humble capacity.

The only trace that still remained to indicate Miss Blodgett's original position in the family was that Miss Blodgett herself was never called by her Christian name. Miss Tate was the only one who called her Emma. The others delicately shrank from doing so in case it might seem to be taking advantage of her dependence. They felt it better to emphasize the difference between her and Hetty. Hetty was Miss Tate's old maidservant who had been with the family for fifty years. Hetty was another treasure, but of course she was only a plain servant.

The first day I moved in to the house next door to Miss Tate in Rattigan Rowe I found two visiting cards lying in the empty letter box. On one neat glossy card was engraved the name of Miss Adeline Tate. On the other card, which was equally neat, equally white, if perhaps a little thinner, a little less glossy, there was printed the name of Emma Blodgett in pen and ink.

That afternoon I saw Miss Tate in her garden. It was some few days before I saw Miss Blodgett.

As a matter of fact, I was at first under the mistaken impression that I had seen both Miss Tate and Miss Blodgett, for there had been two old ladies in the garden, and the two old ladies in the garden had been dressed remarkably alike. They both wore long blue silk gowns, weighted at the hem with rows and rows of heavy braid, and tightly clipped bodices. They both wore wide and delightfully dilapidated blue straw hats, wreathed, or overpowered you might say, with large floppy silk flowers shaded from deep rose to pale pink, which the bees, that clouded around them like a nimbus, must have mistaken for real blooms. It is true that one of the old ladies was extremely elegant, and that the other was distinctly shabby, her silk gown having indeed innumerable patches and darns, but nevertheless I think my mistake was pardonable. I might perhaps have guessed that the old heiress would give away her worn gowns to her servant, but how on earth could I have known that Miss Tate's fanatical affection for animals, birds, insects, and even slugs, was so great that on no account would she allow old Hetty to come out into the garden in either her cap or her apron in case their stiff white glare might startle her beloved pets, who wandered about the garden with as much composure as the ladies; the pet dogs, the tabby cats, and the countless tame pigeons. Within doors, with the blue gown hidden under her old-fashioned capacious aprons I would never have mistaken poor old Hetty for Miss Blodgett. Indeed, no two people could have been more dissimilar, although as a matter of fact Hetty and Miss Tate were not too unalike at all. Both were small and frail, but at the same time agile and keen. And in Hetty's face, as well as in Miss Tate's face, where the flesh had thinned away with the years, the bone was seen to be fine and well chiseled. Miss Tate's face had, of course, the more delicate outline.

It was a pity that Miss Tate had never married. It was a pity she should have thought fit to discontinue the work of eleven generations, for there could be no doubt, I think, that this charming old figurine was the result of careful selection and breeding. And yet, it was surprising to see how a generation or two of poverty and privation could accelerate the pace of this bone refinement, because there was undoubtedly something attractive and endearing in old Hetty's clear and angular face. Still, no matter what is said, it was stupid of me to have mistaken her for Miss Blodgett. And when I saw Miss Blodgett go down the steps into the garden a few days later, it was immediately clear that Hetty was no more than a servant.

"Hetty," called out Miss Blodgett, "I forgot my sunshade. Run into the house and get it for me."

And when Hetty, who had been putting some seedlings into the ground for Miss Tate, stood up to do the message, she lowered her eyes deferentially while Miss Blodgett sailed past.

There could be no mistake this time. This could be no other than Miss Blodgett. When she got to the end of the garden I was amused to see Emma Blodgett wag her finger at Miss Tate.

"Not so much bending!" she cried. "Not so much bending!" And drawing up a garden seat, she called Hetty, who had returned with the sunshade, to send her into the potting shed for an iron footrest. "The grass is so damp in a garden," she said, as she settled herself plumply down to watch Miss Tate and Hetty continue their work with the seedlings.

Miss Blodgett was a big woman. She had a soft, warm, friendly face; a very nice person, one would say unhesitatingly, but rather dull, perhaps even stupid. She was only about sixty; much younger than Miss Tate, much younger even than Hetty, but less active. Her round plump face was perpetually flushed. She had a mass of gray hair, strong, straight and unruly. Her figure was stout too, and she had a surprisingly matronly bosom for a spinster of her years.

Miss Blodgett wore blue also. As a matter of fact, she, too, was dressed somewhat similarly to Miss Tate, and yet there was some very great difference which even I, from my study window, could see but could not at once define. First I thought it was a matter of length, for although, like Miss Tate, Miss Blodgett wore her skirts longer than was fashionable, they were not as long as Miss Tate's. Whatever impulse made her disregard fashion had not been as strong as the old lady's, and was probably only imitation of her, for where Miss Tate's long blue silk hemline hung down to hide her ankles, Miss Blodgett's stopped short a cowardly inch or two up from the ground, and revealed a pair of plump ankles with a tendency to swell, and possibly some other weakness as well, because Miss Blodgett wore thick blue woolen stockings even at this, the hottest time of the year. It was impossible to tell what kind of stockings Miss Tate wore; no one ever saw Miss Tate's little ankles. But to go back to Miss Blodgett's dress again, as I said, I thought at first it differed only in length from Miss Tate's blue gown. Then I thought I detected a slight difference in the shade. Still later I decided it was a matter of age, but I soon dismissed that idea because Hetty's gown, although so tattered and shabby, was in other respects exactly like Miss Tate's new gown. It was not, however, until the first day I went to take tea with the ladies that I discovered the difference between the three blue gowns. It was simply this: that Miss Blodgett's gown did not rustle! You know what that meant. It was blue. It was silky. It was cut to much the same pattern as the gown Miss Tate wore. But it didn't rustle. In other words, it was not quite the same quality. It was not the genuine real thing. And of course Miss Blodgett did not realize this at all.

"Look at Miss Tate," she said to me one day after we had become familiar over many cups of tea in their house and in mine. "Look at Miss Tate! She pays twice what I pay for the material in her gowns, and mine is just exactly the same. No one could tell the difference. But the shopkeepers impose on Miss Tate. They know she has plenty of money. They don't impose on me! I'm well able for them!" And having triumphantly said this, Miss Blodgett begged me to have more cake, and as she went over to the table, I heard the slight creaking sound of the artificial silk fabric; while at the next moment Miss Tate delicately rustled across the room to me. And indeed, as my ear caught that rustle, which was as faint as a sigh, at the same time, in the far corner of the room where Hetty was pouring out tea, I caught another rustle that was fainter still. And if the rustle in Miss Tate's gown was like a sigh, the rustle that came from under Hetty's voluminous white apron was like the echo of a sigh.

I became very friendly with the ladies in the house next door, but long before I met them I had become extraordinarily familiar with the sight of Hetty and Miss Tate in the garden.

The gardens of the houses in Rattigan Rowe were large and secluded for city gardens. They were separated from each other by solid high walls of beautifully cut granite, on which stonecrop and red valerian flowered freely. But from the upper windows of the houses the gardens were not so secluded, and from my study at the back of the house in the second story I could see into every nook and cranny of my neighbor's gardens. The best comment I can make upon Miss Tate's garden is that from the first day I looked down into it I never bothered to look into the other gardens in the Rowe. They, like my own, were plain city gardens, with a plot of grass at the top and a few apple trees at the end. But Miss Tate's garden—well, I was hardly a day in Rattigan Rowe when I realized I would have to change my study to the front of the house if I was ever to do any work. It was the most distracting garden I had ever seen.

In the first place, it was almost entirely given over to the old lady's pets, and everywhere on the small plot of lawn near the house, upon the grass and upon the green metal seats, and even raised on specially constructed standards, there were bowls of water of all shapes and sizes, wide and narrow, deep and shallow, to facilitate the different needs of bird and beast and butterfly. And although to either side of the grass plot there were small flower beds, in them there bloomed only a few of those fragrant old flowers that were fashionable when Miss Tate was a girl; muskroses, heliotrope, lavender, and clove carnations, and a few other flowers of unpretentious aspect, whose names I did not know, but which I afterward found out were grown specially for the bees and the butterflies. There were no vegetables, unless you count a giant clump of catmint in the corner under my window which was grown specially for the tabby cats.

This grass plot with its border of flowers was, however, only one small fraction of the garden. The rest of it was planted all over with small flowering trees in which the birds and bees kept up a continual orchestration, the bees and pigeons supplying the low bass undertones, the blackbirds and thrushes breaking the hum with high trebles. These flowering trees, although they were fully matured, were of such a nature that, although as old as Miss Tate, they were, like her, frail and delicate even in their age. And in comparison with the plain old trees in the public park beyond the lane at the back of our gardens, they looked like mere branches stuck into the ground and tied all over with paper flowers, some pink, some yellow, some blue.

Viewed from my study window, indeed, the whole of Miss Tate's garden looked as unreal, but as entrancing as the miniature gardens that children used to construct long ago in shallow saucers, Japanese gardens which, when they were made, tantalized them with a longing to be small enough to wander within them.

Watching Miss Tate and Hetty wandering in their dreamy unreal garden, under the small flower-trees, I was often tantalized myself with a desire to throw down my books and join them under those bloom-laden branches that seemed to be continually shedding either petals or fragrance—or fragments of bird song.

It was at night, however, that Miss Tate's garden was most tantalizingly beautiful. Then, the moon shone down in misty brightness over it, leaving the dark depths undisturbed and mysterious as the cold sea, but washing the tops of the small trees with light, and striking gleams from the glossy leaves as gleams are struck from the pointed wave. And in the middle of this misty moonlit sea the small white-painted glasshouse with its pointed roof seemed to float through the night like a silver barque of romance.

If ever a house were the harbor of happiness, it should surely be the house looking over that blossom-tossed garden. Yet, the first day I ever set foot in it, I felt there was something wrong. There was some uneasiness in the house. There was some slight strain between Miss Tate and Miss Blodgett. But what it could be was impossible to imagine, for seldom had two people more to give each other. On the one hand Miss Tate gave Miss Blodgett not only a home, but a beautiful home, not only a salary but a bountiful one. And lastly, although not least, there was this understanding about the small bequest. Miss Blodgett, on the other hand, was a perfect companion for Miss Tate. She not only ran the house, and supervised Hetty, but she had, it appeared, no friends or relatives at all of her own, and so even such time as she was supposed to have free for her own purposes, was lavished also on Miss Tate, and occupied in doing errands and messages for her in town. In short, Miss Tate gave Miss Blodgett a share in everything she possessed and made no distinction whatsoever between them, and Miss Blodgett, although she could only give Miss Tate her time and her interest and her care, gave them without stint and kept back not one morsel for herself.

Yet, as I say, I felt there was something uneasy in their relationship. I felt it instinctively on the first day I took tea with the ladies, but I could not name it nor trace it to any cause. And when I became an habitual visitor in the house next door, still never a visit passed, however happily and pleasantly, without my getting at some time or another a feeling that all was not well. At some time or another I would see a little arrow in Miss Tate's blue eyes, and something sharp would shoot through the air.

At first I merely felt the vibration it left in the air. But then one day I actually saw it flash out; a little silver arrow of dissatisfaction. I saw it flash out, yes, but I was no wiser afterward. I still could see no cause for the old lady's sharpness, and when, afterward, I pieced together the conversation of that visit, a more innocuous conversation could not be imagined. There wasn't a single remark in it that could have rasped anyone's nerves as far as I could see. And Miss Blodgett who was picking up some dropped stitches had contributed to it only by smiles and nods or at most, I am almost sure, a single remark. Yet it was at Miss Blodgett that the arrow had been aimed.

There was only one grandniece to tea that day: Honoria's eldest girl, Martha, one of the quietest of the family, a bit dull you might even say. Whenever Martha was there the conversation was always somewhat slow. The two ladies knitted, and the talk never ventured much beyond worsted and yarn. It is hard to recall an insipid conversation. But I took pains to recall every word in order to see why that little silver arrow had been sped from the bow.

Tea was over and Hetty was clearing it away.

"That's pretty wool, Aunt Adeline," said Martha, looking at the candy pink wool that Miss Tate was knitting.

"You saw it the last time you were here," said Miss Tate.

"Did I? Are you sure, Aunt Adeline? I thought you were knitting something with blue wool the last time."

"It's two years since I knitted anything in blue wool," said Miss Tate. "The last thing I knitted in blue wool was a scarf for your brother Edward."

"Oh, but this was only the other day, Aunt Adeline," said poor Martha, "and it wasn't a scarf for Edward, it was a shawl for Miriam's child."

Miss Tate looked up, and so did Miss Blodgett.

"This is the shawl," the two ladies said, speaking at the same time, and then Miss Tate said that she had been working at it for the last six weeks. "I'll never make a shawl again," she said; "it's so tiresome."

Poor Martha put out her hand and drew over a corner of the pink knitted shawl.

"Such an intricate pattern!" she said. "You have wonderful patience, Aunt Adeline."

At this point, I remember it all exactly, Miss Tate dropped a stitch, and while she was trying to take it up she did not catch Martha's last remark.

"What did you say, Martha, dear?" she said, when the stitch was safe on the needle again.

"I said you have wonderful patience, Aunt Adeline," said poor Martha the second time.

But Aunt Adeline did not hear it the second time either. Now Aunt Adeline was not deaf, but she was decidedly nervous in case she might get deaf, and, always, if she failed to catch something that was said for any reason whatever, whether it was due to a noise in the room or an indistinctness on the part of the person who spoke, or, as in this case, because she just wasn't listening, she was always flurried, and it usually resulted in the remark having to be repeated several times after that before she caught it. It was nervousness, nothing else. I often noticed that on such occasions Miss Blodgett was invaluable, either repeating what had been said calmly and clearly, or better still diverting Miss Tate's attention to something else so that she forgot that she had missed hearing something. But on this occasion when Miss Blodgett came to the rescue, in my ignorance I thought it was her interference that annoyed Miss Tate, for it was right after Miss Blodgett spoke that I saw the arrow.

"Martha said you have wonderful patience, Aunt Adeline," said Miss Blodgett kindly, and she was just putting out her hand to fix a cushion that had slipped out of place on Miss Tate's chair when Miss Tate let loose the arrow.

"All old people are patient!" snapped Miss Tate. "But the Tates were never patient before ninety."

Poor Martha blushed. But it was not at Martha the arrow was aimed. It was at Miss Blodgett. I saw it. I saw it go out, aimed straight for Miss Blodgett's heart. But somehow it missed its aim. Miss Blodgett sat knitting as placidly as ever, smiling, and nodding her head in rhythm with the clicking knitting needles. Perhaps the arrow hit and splintered against the large cameo brooch that rose and fell on her big bosom. I don't know. Martha, however, was upset. She was not quick enough to see the arrow, but she was not dull enough to be unaware that something was amiss. She thought, poor girl, that she was at fault, that she had said something to offend Miss Tate. Her eyes filled with tears.

Miss Tate saw the tears. She understood at once what had happened. I saw her give an angry look at Miss Blodgett's cameo brooch and then she turned around with a gracious smile to Martha.

"Come and we will go into the garden, Martha my dear," she said. "Give me your arm. I must get a rose for my favorite grand-niece." The old lady was her gracious, sweet self again. Over me, too, she shed her graciousness. "Will you come with us," she asked, turning toward me, "and I'll get one for you too." But at the door the old lady paused. "Martha is like all the Tates," she said, "she loves flowers." And then, turning around again sharply she nodded at Miss Blodgett, who had gone over to the window and was sitting with her back to it. "Miss Blodgett wouldn't know a cauliflower from a rose," she said, and in an instant another little arrow went through the air.

But Miss Blodgett smiled. Miss Blodgett did not feel any prick this time, either. Before she turned around to answer I saw that her dress was fastened up the back with a little row of white pearl buttons. I was not near enough to see if one of them was scratched or broken, but I think it could hardly have been otherwise.

Miss Blodgett smiled when she turned around.

"I don't mind gardens," she said complacently, "but there are so many unpleasant things in a garden, bees and wasps, and ants and slugs. I'm quite satisfied to sit here at the window and get the sun through the glass." And smiling benignly, she went on with her knitting.

Miss Tate took Martha's arm and my arm, and we went out gossiping lightly, Miss Tate making an unusual fuss over Martha all the time, picking her the best and most beautiful roses, and several times asking me if I saw any likeness between them.

She was determined to be charming. She insisted on giving me a bouquet too, and as she pressed the bunch of red roses into my hand I felt that this charming old lady may have known that I saw that arrow speeding through the air, and wanted to divert my mind from what I had seen. In fact, when I was leaving, she kept me standing at the small green gate at the end of the garden telling me how good Miss Blodgett was to her, and how much she was indebted to her dear companion.

"She has a kind heart," said Miss Tate. "Not like the Tates. The Tates all have a bitter streak in them." She smiled at me then, and she smiled at Martha. But Martha protested.

"Oh, Aunt Adeline! you're very naughty! Such a thing to say about us!" said poor Martha, who was destined to be again the cause of trouble.

For just then Miss Blodgett came to the steps leading down to the garden and, overhearing Martha's remark, she smiled at her with her wide benevolent smile.

"Did I hear you say Aunt Adeline was naughty, Martha?" she asked, and before she said another word, there in the brilliant sunny air, with the birds singing and the bees humming from flower to flower, Miss Tate let fly a third and dreadfully sharp little arrow.

What was the meaning of it at all? I hugged my roses tightly, said goodbye, and went into my own garden greatly perplexed.

After that I saw the arrow several times, but only when I was near at hand.

At other times I would sit in my window and look down at Miss Tate and Hetty in the garden and think how gentle and sweet Miss Tate looked. And even when Miss Blodgett came out, and the two old ladies took tea together under the trees, there seemed to be tranquillity, and they presented a charming picture of peace and happiness and sweetness. They would sip tea, the two of them, and Miss Tate would perhaps call Hetty and pour out a cup of tea for her, and insist on the old servant drinking it there and then, standing beside them at the tea table with perhaps one of the lap dogs she had been combing caught up under her arm, or a bundle of weeds that she was going to burn at the bottom of the plot. On those occasions I saw no arrows.

Yet as surely as I went to tea with the old ladies a little slender arrow would pierce the air, and make straight for Miss Blodgett's heart.

I pondered a great deal over the whole thing. At first I thought there was some deep and serious reason for Miss Tate's antagonism to Emma Blodgett. Then a small incident occurred to make me veer around to quite the opposite opinion, and decide that it was something very trivial that was getting on the old lady's nerves, and that it was another case of the Princess and the Pea.

I had not called on the ladies for some days and this afternoon I went to the green garden gate and pushed it open to pay them a short visit. They were going to take tea in the garden, and Hetty had just laid the tray on the wicker garden table. When I walked across the grass the old ladies were pulling their chairs over to the table, and Miss Blodgett relieved Miss Tate of a large catalogue at which they had both been looking. She threw it down on the grass underneath the table.

"Hetty, another cup!" said Miss Blodgett, and Miss Tate put one of the tabby cats down from his chair and invited me to take his place. Then as Hetty brought out the other cup and turned to go back into the house, Miss Tate called her again.

"Hetty," she said, "I want you to put on your hat and coat and go down to the hospital to ask how Mr. Robbie's baby is getting on today."

"Is the baby sick?" I cried. "In hospital, did you say?"

Lord Robert's son and namesake young Robbie had recently married, and there had been great excitement at the birth of his first son, Lord Robert's grandson, and another great-grandnephew for Miss Adeline Tate. I felt very bad at hearing it was not doing well.

"The doctor says he won't live," said Miss Tate, when I begged her again to tell me what was the matter with it. "There's something the matter with its spine," she said. "It was weakly from the start."

"Oh, dear," I said, and I looked at them both. Miss Blodgett sighed sadly.

I felt uncomfortable.

"Perhaps if I hadn't come you would be going to the hospital to see it?" I said, rising from my chair. "Please don't let me intrude. I only called for a minute. I'll call again another day."

But the two old ladies excelled each other in assuring me that I must on no account leave them. Miss Blodgett rose to press me down into my chair again, while Miss Tate insisted over and over again that a few minutes before I appeared they were planning to send Hetty out with a note asking me to call.

"Because we just got a present of some rose geranium jelly that we want you to sample with us," said Miss Tate. "Sit down! Sit down!" And they began to pour out three cups of tea and take the cover from the geranium jelly that its fragrance might tempt me to stay.

I stayed, but I was uneasy waiting for Hetty to come back. She was a long time away. In fact, she did not come back until I was going. I was letting myself out by the front door when I met Hetty in the hall.

I looked inquiringly at her.

"Is it better?" I asked eagerly.

Hetty was calm.

"No," she said, "but it was a good job I went up there. It's dead," and with a remarkable compromise between deference and impatience, she prepared to pass me. "I must tell Miss Tate," she said.

I was confused. I tried to detain her. Surely she was not going to rush out and tell them the news bluntly, like that?

"Hetty, wait," I cried. "Are you going to tell them at once?"

Hetty looked surprised.

"What else would I do?" she asked.

"Don't you think if you waited a little while, and broke it gently to them?" I stumbled with my words. Had Hetty no sense? Couldn't she see what I meant? "If you said it was worse, and then later on you could say it wasn't expected to live and then perhaps they might be prepared for the shock and you could tell them the truth?"

But Hetty stared at me. "What about the wreath?" she asked.

"The wreath?" I repeated.

"Yes," said Hetty. "Miss Tate will want to order it at once. She'll want time to decide on what flowers to have put in it. She'd be most annoyed if she wasn't told in time." Hetty looked at me, and then, taking into consideration that I was after all a comparative stranger, she paused to give me an impatient explanation. "Miss Tate always sends a magnificent wreath to any funeral inside the family," she said.

And with this Hetty hurried away. I stood uncertainly looking after her. I saw her run down the steps into the garden. I saw her go across the grass and I saw the ladies look up expectantly. I saw Hetty say something to them and make an energetic gesture.

I waited. In spite of what Hetty said, I felt I might be needed. And I was on the point of turning around and going back to the garden, anyway, when I saw the two ladies rise excitedly to their feet. And in the soft summer air Miss Tate's voice carried in to me distinctly.

"The wreath!" she said. "Quick! Where is the catalogue?" and they hastily pushed aside the tea table and picked up the catalogue from the grass; the catalogue that they had been scanning when I went in. It was a florists' catalogue, and even at such a distance I could see the illustrations of wreaths and artificial bouquets, flowering crosses, and glass-domed immortelles. "Give it to me," said Miss Tate, putting on her glasses and stretching out her hand.

"Wait a minute," said Miss Blodgett, withholding it. "We marked a pretty one, don't you remember?"

I didn't wait to hear any more. I could see why it had not occurred to Hetty to break the news to them. The old ladies had long since passed into that time of life when they were no longer capable of feeling the great emotions; like children their joys and sorrows were as real as other people's, but they were inspired by smaller things.

I stood looking out at them in their sunny garden for a few minutes longer, and as I did the thought occurred to me that whatever discord there was between them sprang from something trivial and small. I decided to put it out of my mind, and not to let it bother me further.

This, however, it was impossible to do for long. I never went into the house next door without feeling the familiar quiver in the air. The room might be filled with nieces and nephews. The talk might be gay and general and happy. But at some time or another, I would see the little arrow in Miss Tate's eye. And at the most unexpected moment she would let it fly. Perhaps one of the young people would call something to her across the room, and Miss Tate, talking to another member of the family, would not hear.

"Aunt Adeline!" the young thing would call out again; and then Miss Blodgett would step in.

"Aunt Adeline! Aunt Adeline! Lucy is calling you."

Miss Tate would look up. She never failed to hear Miss Blodgett. And inexplicably then, she would let fly the little arrow.

"I hear! I hear!" Miss Tate would say. "It's nothing important, I suppose!" and she would glance very fiercely at Miss Blodgett. But to the young thing who had called her she would cross the room courteously and, sitting down beside her, she would listen to all she had to say.

This, as a matter of fact, was a common scene, but one day when the drawing room was crowded with a great many of the Tates, and their husbands and wives and betrotheds, there was a slight difference in the scene, although it began in the same way, and it was Lucy who called out to her grandaunt and Miss Blodgett who drew Miss Tate's attention to her. But this day, Miss Tate, who had been sitting beside me, stood up, and I positively trembled. I felt that she was going to let loose a whole quiverful of arrows, so fierce did a strange light shine in her eye.

"Aunt Adeline! Lucy is calling you."

That was all Miss Blodgett said; but Miss Tate shot a fierce glance at her and turned around to Lucy, almost as crossly.

"I can't come now, my dear," she said, and she turned to indicate me, as I sat behind her on the sofa. "I just promised our neighbor here that I would show her the family photographs."

I felt more uneasy than ever. This was the first I had heard of the promise. I saw, too, that Lucy was crestfallen at the snub. But Miss Tate was inexorable. She moved over to the mantelpiece on which there were set out anything from twenty to thirty photographs in silver and filigree frames, showing a bewildering array of old ladies and young, of bearded men and men so young they were like girls. There were small girls in frilly dresses and little boys in velvet suits and little boys in sailor suits. There were brides without number, in silks and lace. There were at least six men in uniform. There was Lord Robert in his wig, Lucy in a ball dress, Honoria in her college gown—but simpler to say who was absent than who was present in this crowded silver gallery on the mantelpiece. Miss Tate beckoned me to follow her and took up the frame nearest to hand.

"This was my mother," she said, pushing the silver frame into my hand, but I had hardly time to glance at it when it was snatched away and another pushed into my hand. "That was a granduncle," she said, and she nodded back at the young people. "He would be the children's great-great-granduncle." She snatched back the great-granduncle. "This is a nephew," she said. "He was killed playing polo."

And then, one after another, she rammed the silver frames into my hands, and snatched them away again almost as quickly, so that I had hardly time to do more than glimpse the merest details of them. At first I strove to keep pace with her; tried to exclaim that the old ladies were charming, the young officers handsome, and the soldiers fearless and brave. But as she rammed the cold frames into my hands and snatched them away again I became aware that behind this plan of showing me the photographs there was some hidden motive.

At last she had come to the end of them.

"Well?" she said in a loud voice, and I saw her look all around the room. She wanted everyone to hear.

"Well?" she said, "what do you think of that for a family?"

"They all have remarkably fine faces," I said, awkwardly. It was true, but I felt embarrassed saying it out aloud.

"But didn't you notice anything?" asked Miss Tate. And then I knew that it was not my comment she wanted but an opportunity to make one of her own. "Didn't you notice how strong the likeness is all down the line?" She turned back and took down the great-granduncle again. "The Tates all had aquiline noses," she said. "All the dead Tates had them; all the living Tates have them." I looked around nervously, and true enough, although I had not paid much attention to it before, there were a large number of noses in the room, all of an aquiline shape. Miss Tate had snatched up another frame. "Look at Great-Uncle Samuel's nose!" She snatched up another. "Look at this nose. Look at that nose!" and then, leaving down the last frame so carelessly, the young man in uniform who was looking out from it over his aquiline nose, fell flat on his face on the marble slab, Miss Tate held up her little head. "Look at my nose!" she said triumphantly. Then in still a louder clearer voice, that had by now caught the attention of the whole room, the old lady repeated her first statement. "Yes, the Tates all have aquiline noses," she said. "And the men are all tall, and the women are all small. And"—here Miss Tate drew a deep breath—"we were always noted for our ankles." The old lady turned around swiftly to Lucy. "Look at Lucy," she said. "Pull up your skirt, Lucy, and show your ankles." She turned around. "Look at Martha!" she said. "Martha, why do you wear such dark stockings? It's a shame. Dark stockings are all right for people with clumsy feet." And then, to my astonishment, Miss Tate's little hand swooped downward and lifted the hem of her own blue gown. "In my day," she said, "we might as well have had no legs at all, but I have the Tate ankles, too. Noses and ankles: that's how you can always tell the Tates!"

And then, as she said this, Miss Tate turned around deliberately and looked at Miss Blodgett, and distinctly, as on the other occasions, I saw it flash out, the little glance of hatred. And where did it fly? It flew straight for the spot where Miss Blodgett sat smiling complacently upon all the company, and it was aimed, of all places, at a point just below the hemline of the blue gown of imitation silk where Emma's fat ankles were complacently crossed one over the other in their thick, ribbed, woolen stockings.

And all at once I understood.

And I think that Lucy, who was a sensitive girl, might have understood too, for she gave an embarrassed laugh.

"I'm afraid you're as vain as a young girl, Aunt Adeline!" she said.

But Miss Blodgett did not betray the slightest upset. As a matter of fact, she laughed heartily.

"That's good! Did you hear what Lucy said?" she cried, poking Miss Tate with the end of her knitting needle. "You're as vain as a girl, Aunt Adeline."

Aunt Adeline!

There they were, the simple words that had occurred in all the simple sentences I had analyzed so unsuccessfully in my effort to find out what was poisoning Miss Tate against Miss Blodgett.

Aunt Adeline. Aunt Adeline. I recalled at once how these words had occurred on every occasion just before the venomed arrow was let fly from the bow. Everything that Miss Tate possessed in the world was at the disposal of Miss Blodgett, except one thing—the family blood. Miss Blodgett had no drop of it and without it, and without the Tate nose and the Tate ankles, she was guilty of a grievous lapse every time she called Miss Tate by the family name reserved for the use of the Lucys and Robbies.

I felt an instant pang of apprehension in my heart. I recalled the gossip I had heard about the small bequest. What if Miss Blodgett should jeopardize her chance of it? What if she should forfeit it?

I positively trembled. Why, Miss Blodgett was so much a part of the family that most of her salary, lavish as it was, went in buying worsted for the bonnets and shawls she was continually knitting for the Tate progeny and in small but frequent purchases of confetti and ribbons and good-luck tokens for the numerous Tate brides. Why! I thought in panic, what a lot of money she must have spent if it was on nothing more than wreaths for the Tate corpses. Why! Miss Blodgett could hardly have saved a penny. She would be absolutely dependent on that small bequest.

Really, I felt so bad I took my leave shortly afterward. And all that week the affair preyed on my mind. I began to dread going into that house. For every time that Miss Blodgett addressed Miss Tate as Aunt Adeline, I felt my heart freeze. Every time she said it I felt the small bequest was more and more in jeopardy.

And so when at the end of the summer and I about to leave for the South of England as was my custom, I felt a certain relief as I went out to say goodbye to the ladies. They came to the door to wave me out of sight. They seemed sorry to part with me. Miss Blodgett had tears in her eyes. As I went down the steps from the hall door she linked her arm in Miss Tate's arm and called out after me.

"Aunt Adeline will miss you? Won't you, Aunt Adeline?"

Those were her last words to me before I set out. I didn't dare turn round. I simply could not bear to see that little silver arrow.

The following spring when I came back the house next door was boarded up for sale. A few forlorn pigeons hovered uncertainly on the eave shoot. A stray cat or two slunk in and out between the railings. They were not the regular pets belonging to the house, but it was clear they had had claims on its hospitality and could not realize their claims had ceased.

Miss Tate was dead.

There was no sign whatever of Miss Blodgett.

About a week after my return, however, one day as I was walking into town I took a short cut through those dreary intermediary streets that lie between the business section and the residential areas like Rattigan Rowe, but which have not yet degenerated into slums. Here fine old houses that had once been fashionable residences stood forlorn, bereft of their elegant curtains and their gay window-boxes; their elaborate brass knockers painted to save labor. The particular street through which I passed had been saved from complete degeneration by reason of the fact that several of the houses had been turned into offices and sets of service flats, and the few that had remained in private hands had been retained by their owners at the cost of turning them into respectable boardinghouses.

And coming down the steps of one of the most precarious and ramshackle of these boardinghouses, who should I see but Emma Blodgett.

Dear Miss Blodgett! How glad I was to see her! I waved to her, and hurried across the street with both hands outstretched. But even before I reached the other side I saw with a sinking of the heart that, although only a few short months had passed since I had last seen her, Miss Blodgett was decidedly shabbier in her appearance. Her clothes were as clean and neat as ever; but she no longer had that sheltered look that all Miss Tate's household had had last summer, from Miss Tate down even to the fat cats and the fat pigeons. Indeed, Miss Blodgett, at that moment, reminded me of the poor perplexed pigeons that I had seen clinging to the eaves in Rattigan Rowe.

But of course I did not pretend to notice any change, although I felt dreadfully upset about the poor thing, and feared that my worst forebodings about the bequest had been true. And yet somehow it did not seem like Miss Tate, dead or alive, to break her promise. I found it hard to see how she could have omitted Miss Blodgett's name from her testament when it was, as it were, an understood thing that it would be included.

"Dear Miss Blodgett!" I cried, and I sympathized with her for the loss of Miss Tate. And yet I felt a necessity to be guarded in my condolences. "So poor Miss Tate has left her garden," I said, and I watched Miss Blodgett carefully as I said it.

But Emma Blodgett's eyes filled with tears.

"Yes," she said. "Poor Aunt Adeline!" and then she took out a small handkerchief, that was not, alas, as spotlessly laundered as it might have been last year, but which, from the border of real lace that ran delicately around its hem, I saw was undoubtedly one of the small treasures that Miss Blodgett had amassed in her years at Rattigan Rowe. "Yes," she said, and she blew her nose, and there was no mistaking her sorrow.

I felt very much better. I felt I had been unjust to the memory of Miss Tate. Miss Blodgett's shabby appearance was due no doubt to the fact that she now had to be more prudent. She was living her own life now, and not the life of an heiress. And wasn't she justified in her prudence? Wasn't thrift a virtue when you were poor? And when you had no home, but had to pay for every morsel you eat, and for the roof over your head, could you afford to be too prodigal with your money?

And then, all those years when there had been talk and gossip about the bequest that Miss Tate was expected to leave her companion, had it not always been particularly stated that it would be a small bequest? Why—another aspect of the situation struck me. Goodness knows how small it might not have been! It might have been a mere nothing; a paltry sum. Then a worse thought struck me! Perhaps it had not been money at all. How often have old ladies and gentlemen of eighty or ninety set such a value on small personal possessions that they have carelessly disposed of their impersonal millions at the advice of lawyer or vicar, to lavish all their attention on the disposal of some worthless little trinket, a lock of hair, or an old Bible, because on it they had, in those last sad hours of abnegation, set more value than upon all their millions; some worthless object in which they felt they had distilled the essence of a life, and which they were loathest to leave behind them, but which unfortunately was of no more value than a stone, and was, like a stone alas, negotiable into nothing.

I looked hurriedly at Miss Blodgett, who was indeed weeping copiously now, as between sobs she described Miss Tate's last hours to me.

"I was with her to the last breath," she said, and here she sobbed again. "I held her hand all the time. She clutched my fingers till the very end."

At this point Miss Blodgett put out her hand and clasped mine in illustration of that last touching scene, but as she did so she was recalled swiftly from the bedside of her dead friend as her eye, and mine, caught sight of a large hole in the finger of her glove. Miss Blodgett hurriedly withdrew her hand.

"Oh," she cried, "I must have caught my glove in something. It seems to be torn."

But the tear was not a new one. It had a jagged and frayed edge that told its own story. And irresistibly my eye traveled to Miss Blodgett's other hand. In the other glove there was a second and indeed a slightly larger hole, and out through it came another finger, which, alas, was not as immaculate as one would have expected. The fingernail was indeed decidedly grimy, and showed that Miss Blodgett's landlady evidently allowed her paying guest the privilege of doing out her own room, and blacking her own fire grate.

I looked away hurriedly. But you know how it is? The eye is a most unruly member. Do what I might it would rove back irresistibly to the hole in Miss Blodgett's glove, and where my eye went, irresistibly it seemed Miss Blodgett's blue eye followed.

At last it came to a point where I must either go away or one of us must make some remark. We must lay the ghost of that torn glove that hovered between us interrupting our conversation, making us awkward and ill at ease. Miss Blodgett laid it.

"Poor Miss Tate," she said suddenly, and she held out her hand frankly and displayed not only the torn tips of the gloves but the fact that the palms of both gloves were worn so thin that her pink flesh showed through them. "Poor Miss Tate. How distressed she would be if she saw me looking so shabby!"

I didn't quite know what to say, but remembering that Emma Blodgett was so friendless and isolated, with no one perhaps in the whole world to take an interest in her, I felt that I could venture a step further without any danger of being thought vulgarly curious.

"I hope her death has not caused too great a change in your circumstances," I said, and then feeling that I had not handled the situation very well I ran on impulsively. "I mean, I always understood that Miss Tate intended to arrange matters so that you should never want for anything after her death." I hurried my words. "You know!" I cried. "The small bequest!"

I spoke hurriedly with my eyes on the ground. I was afraid to look up. But Miss Blodgett had dissolved into tears again, and lo! again they were tears of love, and affection.

"Poor Aunt Adeline!" she said. "A small bequest! That was so like her, to underestimate every impulse of her dear, kind heart." She looked at me a little sternly. "You wouldn't call a thousand pounds a small bequest, would you?" she asked.

I was astonished; astonished. I had never thought about how much Miss Tate was likely to leave her companion, but I must admit I had hardly expected it to be more than a few hundreds.

"Oh, Miss Blodgett," I said, putting out my hand again and taking hers, "I congratulate you!" But what, I wondered, was the mystery of the broken gloves?

Miss Blodgett withdrew her hand quickly.

"Congratulate me?" she asked. "Sympathize with me, you mean. There's nothing to congratulate me about. You see, I didn't get the money. And what is more, it looks as if I'm never going to get it."

"What?" I was bewildered; up one minute and down the next. Surely none of the noble and wealthy Tates were going to contest this reasonable if generous bequest? Considering how much they must have shared among themselves, the size of this bequest, if its size had surprised them, should have added to the family pride in its own magnanimity. "Surely they're not going to contest the will?" I cried.

"Oh, dear no," cried Miss Blodgett. "They feel worse than I do. In fact, Lord Robert is doing all in his power for me. He insisted on my getting the best solicitor I could get, and Miss Lucy Tate couldn't be surpassed for her kindness. They are all, all so kind, and so upset on my account. The Tates are like that you know! They are the kindest people in the world. They think of me as one of themselves." She sighed. "And poor Aunt Adeline!" she said. "She was the kindest of them all. Indeed, I can only hope she is not looking down now and seeing all the trouble she caused, without realizing it, out of the goodness of her heart. For you see," said Miss Blodgett, and she looked up at me earnestly, "it was because she was trying to be too kind to me that I lost the legacy."

I didn't pretend to understand.

"Well, you know," said Miss Blodgett, "you know the way she always considered me one of the family. You know how she liked me to call her Aunt Adeline, just as if I was related to her in blood? You know all that, don't you? You could see it for yourself?"

Miss Blodgett looked at me earnestly with her big obtuse face and her big stupid eyes filled with love and affection. I felt a great uneasiness gather again in my heart.

I didn't answer, but there was no need, for Miss Blodgett went on.

"Well!" she said. "Poor Miss Tate, when she drew up her will, put in a few words as a last message to me. I suppose she wanted to let me see my place in her affections. She wanted to let me see how

she considered me so close to her. And so," here poor Miss Blodgett
forgot for a moment about Miss Tate as she was recalled to the
dreadful weeks that had passed, spent mostly in a solicitor's office,
being questioned and browbeaten, and for a moment she broke
down and her poor lower lip fell open, and a tear, that was not for
Miss Adeline Tate, but for poor Emma Blodgett, stole down her fat
red cheek. "And so," she said, "in the will, Miss Tate designated me
as her fond niece Emma. 'And to my fond niece, Emma,' she said, 'I
hereby leave and bequeath the sum of one thousand pounds.' " Miss
Blodgett spluttered. "A . . . A . . . A thousand pounds! And to
think that I'll never touch a penny of it." She suddenly tucked her
handkerchief into her sleeve again, and looked up at the clock on a
church tower showing between the high offices. The little gold wrist
watch she used to wear was not on her arm. "I am on my way down
to the solicitor now," she said. "I have to go down every other day.
They're doing their best for me. Lord Robert is most upset. And
Miss Lucy. Indeed, they all are extremely kind. But as for myself, I
haven't much hope. You see, it would have been all right if poor
Miss Tate had not tried to show me that last mark of affection. It
would have been all right if she had left the money to Miss Emma
Blodgett. That was what the solicitor said. 'You are Emma Blodgett,'
he said. 'But who is this fond niece Emma?' There is no such person.
There are fifty-four nieces, counting grandnieces and two great-
grandnieces; but none of them is called Emma! It is perfectly clear,
of course, to everyone that it was me that was meant. But"—Miss
Blodgett's lips trembled again—"but what good is that to me?" She
put out her hand. "I must be going," she said. "Those solicitors are
very exact. They don't like to be kept waiting, although, indeed,
they think nothing of keeping others waiting. I'm often kept waiting
an hour up there, and at the end I sometimes have to go away
without seeing him, if an urgent call comes on the telephone and he
has to go down to the courts. But his typist is very nice. She always
gets me a chair." For an instant she brightened as she held my hand.
"Do you know what I discovered the other day?" she said. "The
typist is a niece of Hetty's. You remember Hetty? Hetty was always
very careful with her money, you know, and she educated all her
brother's children. They all have good jobs. This girl in the solicitor's office is a very well-educated girl. She's very civil. And she's al-

ways very sorry for me if I have to go away without seeing the solicitor. 'Don't worry, Emma,' she says, 'everything will be all right!' She's a very exceptional girl. Her name is Miss Hynes. Hetty's name was Hynes, you know."

I had almost forgotten to ask about Hetty.

"And how is Hetty?" I asked.

"Oh, Hetty is all right," said Miss Blodgett. "She's gone to live with her brother. They're glad to have her, of course; she has a nice nest egg saved. And then, of course, Miss Tate left her a nice little sum too."

"And Hetty got it all right?" I asked.

Miss Blodgett's big, stupid blue eyes were turned on me in swift surprise.

"Why, of course!" she said. "Why wouldn't she get it? It was left to Hester Hynes. That was Hetty's right name. Hetty was nothing to Miss Tate! Miss Tate had no special feelings for Hetty. She just mentioned her name as a matter of course." Miss Blodgett had risen again for a moment to the height of the old days. Her bosom swelled. Her eye gleamed. "Hetty was only a servant!" she said. "She was nothing to Aunt Adeline!

"Well, I must be going, my dear," said Miss Blodgett. "Sometimes, you know, I get tired of going up to the solicitor's, but I say to myself that Miss Tate will never rest in her grave until I have made the last possible effort to rectify her mistake." She put out her hand. "Goodbye, my dear!" she said. "Thank you for your sympathy. I'll let you know how things turn out."

She turned away then, and I saw that the tears had gathered again in her eyes. I heard her mutter something to herself as I stood looking after the blue dress, and the ample ankles in the blue woolen socks. I couldn't be sure, but I think what I heard was a sigh and an exclamation.

"Poor Aunt Adeline! Poor Aunt Adeline!"

A Woman Friend

AFTERWARD, when the investigations were over and he walked out of the boardroom everything might have been the same as before—only for Bina. As a matter of fact, the whole thing passed off well. It hadn't been anything like the ordeal that he had envisaged on that awful night when the boy died, and he knocked up Bina in the small hours. No blame had been attached to him at all. The charge of negligence was dismissed after the first five minutes. The boy would have died in any case. Possibly there was some bungling in the diagnosis, but that was not altogether his fault; the boy was sent up as an appendectomy from the county infirmary. And could he be sure that he would have made a new diagnosis if they succeeded in reaching him with that urgent summons in the middle of the night?

Why now it almost seemed like a stroke of luck that he was not available when they phoned him, whereas at the time it seemed so disastrous. That, of course, was because of the way the staff behaved; and then there was the unfortunate encounter he had with the boy's mother as he was running up the steps in the early hours of the morning—when the boy was dead. That had unnerved him more than anything.

It was probably that which caused him to behave so ridiculously in Baggot Street, although there was undoubtedly something in what Bina said about his being overworked. If he hadn't been under such a strain already, he wouldn't have paid any heed to the poor wretched woman.

He ought to have had more confidence in his reputation. If anything, it was higher after the investigation. There was so much stress laid on his attentiveness; his late visits to the wards, his interest in the aftercare of his patients.

Admittedly there had been an awkward moment when he was asked why he was not available to answer the phone after saying that he was going back to his rooms. They had phoned repeatedly. But at that point, seeing that opinion was generally favorable to him, he took a chance, he had a brainwave really, and asked if it was certain they were connected to the right number; there had been some technical flaw in the hospital switchboard that week, and he just recalled that fact at the right moment. There could have been some confusion in the porter's office? Had that occurred to anyone? It seemed all the more likely since they succeeded in reaching him in the early hours of the morning. Wasn't that odd? And then, seeing that he had scored a point, he followed up with a counter allegation against the hospital.

"Did it not occur to anyone in the hospital to send a messenger over to my rooms? After all, Fitzwilliam Square is not a hundred miles away! It would only have been a matter of seconds—"

The lawyer for the next of kin interrupted him just there.

"And would they have found you in your rooms, Dr. Anderson, if they had done as you suggest?"

That was the climax of the investigation. There was a hush of suspense. The attorney may have thought himself exceptionally sharp. As a matter of fact the man had played right into his hands.

"Unquestionably." That was his answer.

"Yes or no, Doctor, if you please."

"Yes."

"You understand that you are on oath, Doctor?"

"Certainly—I mean yes."

But his first answer had filled the bill to a greater nicety because unquestionably they would have found him; without going up to the doorway at all they would probably have noticed his car outside the door, and if they went up to the door and got no answer they would surely have wondered at the car being outside, and taken a look into it. And all the subsequent bother for everyone would have been avoided.

Well, no matter; the boy would not have been saved. That was the main point. When that was made evident there was less stress laid on his failure to answer the phone.

Integrity counted for something after all. And he had no scruples. It is quite possible that they would have believed him if he told the absolute truth, but that night—or early morning, rather—when he went to pieces so completely in Baggot Street, it seemed fantastic to expect them to believe that he had fallen asleep in the car.

It was all very well for Bina to say it was the most natural thing in the world, but then Bina was Bina.

"It was only to be expected!" she said. "I was often afraid you'd fall asleep at the wheel going home from here some night."

He had often been afraid of that himself, and when he got into the car that night in particular he was deadly tired. It was a wonder he reached Fitzwilliam; it wouldn't have surprised him in the least if he woke up and found that he hadn't started the car at all but that he was still outside the little hotel.

It was in Baggot Street, of course, that he got the habit of dropping off to sleep regardless of the company. It was there that it first happened, anyway, not when he was a student, needless to say, but years afterward on one of his rare visits—all too rare, indeed—when he called back, as he had promised, to see how they were getting along, Bina and her mother. As a matter of fact it must have been a good few years later, because it wasn't until after she got the second stroke that Mrs. Cussen became bedridden. After the first stroke she still managed to get downstairs to the basement for a few hours at night after Bina got finished with the work. But she wasn't downstairs the night he fell asleep. Bina was alone. She was getting him a cup of tea before he went back to his rooms in Fitzwilliam. She was standing in front of him with the teapot in her hand waiting for the kettle to come to the boil on the bars of the little black grate, and he was leaning back in the battered old armchair, looking at her, when, quite suddenly, he fell asleep. It was only for a few minutes; a few seconds. He woke with a jerk. But when he opened his eyes Bina had made the tea, and in the series of small actions that led from lifting the kettle to replacing the lid on the teapot he had missed a whole sequence in the middle. He had been as soundly asleep as if he were stretched in his bed.

But Bina had noticed nothing. Didn't that prove there was no affectation about it? Not that night, anyway, and perhaps not at any of the other times either, although he could not help being aware that his little weakness was beginning to be something of a legend in the hospital. And once or twice when he dropped off in the staff room he could see, when he opened his eyes again, that he had only added to his renown. It was as if everyone realized that nature had to establish a proper balance for such as him, who exerted himself above the ordinary—abused himself, you might say, continually, for the sake of others. Yes: everyone understood. Indeed, paradoxically it seemed that his reputation gained more luster from his little idiosyncrasy than from anything else in his career since the day he was awarded the Medical Society's gold medal! But there was no question of his having any regard for the figure he cut in Bina's eyes when he dropped off in Baggot Street; because somehow or another he was always genuinely dog-tired the nights he called at Baggot Street. Perhaps indeed that was why he felt like dropping in there. It was so homely. And then again it was always pretty late when he got there. He never seemed to get around to calling early in the evening. And anyway, he knew the run of the little hotel; it fitted in with Bina's routine as well as with his own, to leave it till after ten o'clock to call. At ten o'clock the little hotel stopped ticking. The maids went to bed; the hot bottles were filled and put up in the rooms, and Bina was able to go downstairs to her little sitting room. It was in the basement: for privacy, Bina said. She managed to keep the residents out of it too—in all the years he was staying in the place he had never once set foot in it—the stairs that led down to it were steep, narrow, dark, and were blocked midway down by a green baize door beyond which only the most accustomed foot could descend in safety. And that was by day. At night, when the light could only be switched on from below, the stairs was a black hole, and the privacy of the little sitting room was secure. And after eleven, when Bina made her last ascent to put the chain on the hall door, and turn out the hall light, the little room might as well have been a cave tunneled under a mountain. But it was a cozy little cave. At either side of the fire there was a big battered armchair, and when the two women sank into them they had things nicely arranged so that they didn't have to get up again until they got up for good.

Everything was to hand. They had a little tin kettle—specially small to fit on the bars of the narrow little parlor grate—so they could heat the water for their own hot bottles, or make a cup of tea for themselves if they felt like it. They even—and this always made him smile—they even had an old gray woolen sock hanging on the knob of the tongs to catch hold of the handle of the kettle. It was a man's sock, too, he noticed one night, with amusement. It might even be an old sock of his own after all this time. He left a lot of odds and ends behind him when he was shifting to Fitzwilliam because it wasn't as if it was an ordinary lodgings: he knew they would treasure everything belonging to him. And he could pick them up at any time. He'd be dropping in to see them very often. In fact, he'd promised. He knew it would mean a lot to them.

It had been a bit of a break for him leaving the little hotel. But he couldn't afford to let the grass grow under his feet. It wasn't as if he was buying a practice. The Pierce Malone medal, alone, gave him the right to set up in Fitzwilliam, but he had to put up his plate straight away before he was back-numbered. He did: he set up without any delay, in the thick of the established men; the usual thing, reception room and consulting room on the ground floor, with accommodation in another part of the house; not exactly homely, not exactly comfortable, but he had a good eye for what was right in such things. His rooms were just the same as those of any other specialist in the city; and just as cheerless. But he didn't mind. They were as he envisaged them, when he was a student, taking note of the rooms of the big specialists. There was a coldness that characterized those men, and everything belonging to them, their manner, their voices, their hands, and, above all, their austere rooms that were never more than moderately heated. He used to think there was an air of touch-me-not about their furniture, with its high cold gloss. He knew so well from his student days the feeling of shame that came over one when a ring of mist spread suddenly under one's hands, and then as suddenly contracted again almost as if the highly polished wood shrank repulsed from the contact.

Well! he had the same cold mahogany now in his own reception room, but it did not mist or shrink from his hands because they were no longer hot and moist. They were acclimatized now to the cool atmosphere of professional life.

Anyway, he was very seldom in his rooms for long. And as for sitting down! As he said to Bina one night, he hardly ever sat down in an armchair except when he dropped into Baggot Street to see her.

It was true. When did he get a chance to sit down? He was in the operating theater from nine to eleven every morning, and after that he had his clinics. The rest of the morning was spent in the wards and a good part of the early afternoon as well. From three to six he saw private patients, and then the night visits began. He had only himself to blame for the night visits, because in the beginning of his career—whether from ambition, or from conscientiousness he could not now say, although he was inclined to be a bit scrupulous in his early days—he had formed a habit of paying a late visit to the hospital before he went to bed every night.

They were a mistake in a way, those late rounds, although there was no doubt that they helped to establish a reputation for him. But they imposed an unnecessary strain upon him as well, and in the end the staff became so accustomed to having him drop in around midnight that they began to count on his coming, and decisions that should have been the province of the matron or the house surgeon— or even of the nurses in many cases—were deferred instead to him. It really meant, in the long run, that everyone shifted his or her responsibility on to his shoulders, day and night. And the worst feature of it was that, as time went on, they lost sight of the fact that this nightly attendance was voluntary. It would seem like neglect of duty if he failed to put in his appearance.

But he didn't mind. It was all part of the price he had been prepared to pay from the start.

Per ardua ad astra. He hadn't forgotten his motto when he got to the top like some of the other fellows that qualified with him. It wasn't enough to get to the top, you had to stay there, and as far as he could make out, to stay there meant ruling out comfort for good.

How many of his contemporaries had fallen back into mediocrity for the sake of some bodily comfort! It was usually marriage, of course.

Almost without exception his contemporaries had made indifferent marriages. They never seemed to have considered suitability a necessary ingredient of matrimony. And what had determined their choice? As far as he could see, it was nothing more than propinquity; they had almost all married nurses, or else their first receptionist or their first secretary. It was really very noticeable that the wives of the specialists were so different from the wives of general practitioners. He used to think they must be a special breed, and wondered where they were to be met, but when he made a few inquiries he was surprised at the origin of some of them. As a matter of fact, Mandeville's wife came from a small hotel, just like Bina. But it was at some seaside resort, Kilkee or Tramore, and that made a difference, he supposed. Because you couldn't imagine Bina ever turning into a Mrs. Mandeville. Not that he was criticizing Bina. On the contrary: he always had the highest opinion of her. He often wondered that she never married. He felt that she ought to have made a good marriage too, with someone who could give her a comfortable home. Bina was used to comfort. But she never made any effort to have friends, men or women. She was very unambitious. He used to think she might marry one of the middle-aged men staying in the hotel, specially after she began to get on a bit in years.

It was mostly men who stayed in the little hotel. And although Mrs. Cussen didn't like keeping permanent boarders—nor Bina either—it came to almost the same thing in the end because the same people kept coming there month after month. It was only because he got the soft side of Mrs. Cussen one night that he himself was taken in there. They never kept students, and never under any circumstances did they keep medicals. But once he got into the place he knew he was in clover, and he was determined to stay there.

They didn't know he was a medical at first. As a matter of fact he got around Mrs. Cussen to let him stay before he told them. He got around her with a pitiful account about all the digs he had tried, and about the place in Grantham Street where he had to stuff his sock in the broken window, and put the rug off the floor on his bed at night. She was a motherly soul, and he touched her heart. She agreed to take him for a few weeks. But she soon saw that he wasn't the usual run of student; that he was quiet and ambitious, and she admired him for it. She was shrewd too: she probably saw that he meant to get to the top of the ladder, and once she began to take an interest in him he was all right. Indeed, if it weren't for the

way she and Bina minded him all those years he'd hardly have done
so well.

Poor Mrs. Cussen, she couldn't have minded him better if he
were her own son. And Bina never let a night pass without bringing
him up a cup of hot milk before he went to bed.

He'd want to be very ungrateful before he'd forget that to them.

And he hadn't altogether forgotten, although he hadn't gone back
to see them often enough after he went to Fitzwilliam. They were
so glad always to see him, though, whenever he did find time to call.
Yes, it was really pathetic the welcome he got from Bina, the first
night he went back.

"It's not you!" she cried, looking at him as if she could not believe
her eyes. "Come on downstairs," she cried, and she brought him
right down to the basement, right into their little private room.

He remembered it all so well, the way she went down the stairs
sideways like a crab in order that he would have more light to pick
his steps, or so he thought at the time. It may just have been that
she didn't want to miss a minute of him. She couldn't take her eyes
off him.

"You've put on weight," she said. "And I like your new suit."

It gave him such a homely feeling.

And it warmed his heart the way she called down to her mother
when they got as far as the baize door.

"It's Dr. Lew, Mother!" she cried.

That was another thing. Right from the moment he qualified they
stopped calling him Lew, and began to call him Dr. Lew. As a matter of fact their entire attitude toward him changed subtly after he
moved to Fitzwilliam. And mind you, he appreciated it. It helped
him to realize his own importance. And it wasn't as if they were any
the less friendly or kind toward him. It was just that they knew the
difference between intimacy and familiarity, particularly Bina. Now
and again Mrs. Cussen used to be a little bit free with him, but he
never minded.

"You're working too hard," she said one night. "You're not the
young dog you were when you were here, you know."

He thought that was a bit overfamiliar, but he knew it was
motherliness that made her say it. And she was as proud of him as
if he was her own son. She admitted it.

"It isn't because you're a big pot that we're proud of you, you know," she said one night. "We're proud of you because of all the good you do for the poor; isn't that right, Bina?"

He used to laugh.

"Is she codding me, Bina?" he used to ask, to hide his gratification.

But Bina was twice as proud of him.

"You don't know all the things we hear about you," she used to say.

It was Bina who stuck his picture up on the mantelpiece, and when he remarked it she wasn't a bit put out.

"Indeed, it's about time you gave us a proper photograph," she said, "and not have us put up with that old stickyback we found in your room after you were gone."

Bina had no sense of propriety. He often noticed that. When her mother got the stroke and wasn't able to come downstairs any more, she still brought him down to the little room in the basement, and it never seemed to cross her mind that it was any way peculiar to be alone with him like that until all hours, as they were so many nights.

That was just like her, of course; unselfconscious, or if you liked to put it another way: unambitious.

It was curious all the same that she never thought of him in any other light than that of an old friend. Of course, that was the light in which he saw himself too, but once or twice when he was sitting in the little room with her, it had crossed his mind that it wouldn't be too bad at all if, instead of getting up and going out into the cold, to his cheerless rooms, he could sit there opposite her until it was time to stand up for good.

The thought didn't excite him, of course, but then he never thought of it as anything that could still happen but only as something that might have happened.

There they would be sitting, married, or single, in just the same way, with him yawning every other few minutes, and Bina accusing him of working too hard.

She never minded whether he talked to her or not. He could just sit there in front of her like a pig with his legs stretched out, not saying a word if he didn't want. She never made any demands on him: not even the smallest.

How then had the picture altered so quickly; in a few minutes, you might say, on the night that boy died? That was what he simply could not understand. That was why he kept going over and over it again and again.

Of course, he was very upset that night. That was what drove him to Baggot Street. And then Bina looked so different, so altogether different from other times, that may have acted upon him. For one thing she was in her nightdress, and for another she was without her glasses.

She had heard his knock and come down herself to the door. It was like her to come down. The maids would have been afraid, thinking it was some drunk who had come to the wrong door. But Bina never hesitated. She threw open the door.

"My God, Lew, what is the matter?" she cried.

"Let me in," he said, roughly. "I'll tell you then."

He wanted to get in off the street, the vacant dawn-lit street that had accentuated the unreality of his situation. But to his astonishment she hesitated for a minute.

"I'm not dressed," she said.

Then, under his withering look she held back the door for him. Did she think he was fool enough to be affected by the sight of a woman in her nightdress?

"I don't think it's the first time I saw you in this elegant garment," he said, cuttingly, because even in his trouble he had taken in the stained and faded condition of the old woolen dressing gown she had bundled about her. But curiously enough, although he was so sharp about it he didn't really mind the dirty old dressing gown. It reminded him of when he was staying in the place; made it seem more natural for him to have come back there in his trouble.

But his nerves were all on edge.

"For God's sake don't keep clutching it round you like that; you're not naked under it, are you?" he said. He knew she was far from being naked. Under the woolen thing, as far as he could make out, she had some preposterous garment. Could it be flannelette? He didn't think there were still women who wore such garments. It was like what his mother used to wear—God be good to her—when she came in to him in the middle of the night if he wakened in a nightmare. He knew just how it would feel, warm and moist. He knew just the way it would smell, stuffy and sweet. Oh, with what relief he used to bury his head in the stuffy flannelette folds.

For a moment he had an almost overpowering longing to bury his face in Bina's bosom. But at that point he was still in full command of himself; he knew he couldn't do that. And in any case all he wanted was just to be with her, someone he knew; someone who was not a stranger.

"Oh, Bina," he said, and he covered his face with his hands. "I'm in such trouble." But they were still standing in the hallway, and he felt uncomfortable. He glanced up the wide well of the staircase. If there was anyone else awake in the house his voice would easily carry up to them. "Come on downstairs," he said, and he motioned toward the basement steps. But Bina held back. For a minute he thought that she was looking at him queerly. Perhaps she thought he had taken a drink because she wasn't wearing her glasses. As a matter of fact he had never before seen her without them, although he used to wonder what she would be like without them, and he remembered thinking, once, that if she got married her husband would see her without them; it would be one of their first intimacies, and he felt in some way sorry for her as if over and above the pitiful exposure of her sex she would be submitted to an additional indignity. But here she was now blinking at him. He was wrong, though, in thinking that she had any doubts about his sobriety, because she had only delayed to run into the dining room and snatch up a glass and a decanter.

He had to stop her from pouring it out.

"No—please," he cried, impatiently. "No; they might smell it off my breath."

It wasn't until then that she realized there was something seriously wrong. The extraordinary thing was that she jumped at once to the conclusion it was the boy.

"Is it that boy you were telling me about last night; the one that was brought in just as you were leaving?"

He nodded. He couldn't help being touched by her interest, because he hardly remembered telling her anything at all about the case, but he must have made some reference to having an appendectomy for the morning.

"Is he dead?" she asked quietly.

He nodded. She said nothing for a moment or two.

"My poor Lew," she said then, and he almost burst into tears.

That was what you might call a friend: he was touched beyond words. She was so loyal to him; she didn't wait to hear what had happened; she was on his side. It was so different from the hostile attitude at the hospital.

"Surely you're not blaming yourself, Lew?" she cried. "You know you often told me that there is no such thing as an unsuccessful operation—that the damage is done long before the case comes on to the table!"

He couldn't help being a bit edgy. Couldn't she give him a chance to tell her what had happened?

"You've got it wrong," he said abruptly. "I didn't have time to operate."

But she wasn't one to waver.

"Do you mean they didn't get you in time? Why that was criminal negligence!"

He winced. "It wasn't their fault," he said impatiently. "They tried to get me on the phone repeatedly. Can't you let me tell you, Bina, and not keep interrupting me?"

But she wasn't listening. Her face was actually white.

"You were sick, Lew?" she cried, and she made a start forward almost as if she were going to put out her arms to him, but she stopped short of it.

"No, no, there was nothing the matter with me," he said, "at least not in the ordinary sense of the word." He paused and took a breath. "I was asleep, Bina—outside the house—in the car!" Even telling *her* wasn't easy; how could he tell the Board: it sounded so foolish. "If I was in the house I'd have heard the phone, but I fell asleep at the wheel. I must have closed my eyes for a minute when I got to the curb, and the next thing I knew it was morning— morning!—and the telephone was ringing; but it was only to tell me he was almost gone!"

At the thought of the way he felt when he woke up cramped and frozen, and staggered into the house to take up the receiver and hear the consequences of his lapse, he gave a violent shudder.

She seemed to be shocked at last into giving a thought to the dead.

But her thoughts quickly returned to him.

"But it wasn't your fault, Lew. Think of the hundreds of lives you've saved. Think of that!"

She still didn't seem to understand the full seriousness of the situation.

"You don't seem to realize: there'll be an inquiry," he said sharply.

"Do you mean you'll be blamed?" she said, and she looked so bewildered as to appear actually stupid. There was something in what she said all the same. "How could they possibly blame you? If it was anyone's fault it was the fault of the hospital—yes, I mean it—you're grossly overworked down there—you know it—I told you so a hundred times, I'm not only saying it now, you've heard me yourself—I'm always saying it. So was poor Mother. I used to say to her, 'I hope they're grateful, that's all—' "

She was so vehement he stared at her in surprise. It was true what she said; he was overworked. Many a time he had to acknowledge it when they were all three sitting around the fire in the little basement room, so cozy, so warm.

Oh, they were so happy; those evenings. Would such evenings ever come again?

"You don't understand at all, Bina!" he cried. "This could be the end of me. A man in my position has so many enemies; people are so jealous, you know nothing about it; they're only watching for you to make a false step and they come down on you."

It was true, and as he said it, involuntarily as a wave of nausea the longing came on him again to press his head into the soft moist flannelette bosom. But Bina's practicality was like cold water.

"What kind of talk is that?" she said. "I'm surprised at you. Have you no confidence? I must say that I think you ought to have a little more confidence in the hospital too, if it goes to that!"

He couldn't help admiring her. She built him up.

"Inquiry indeed!" she cried. "I'll tell you what there ought to be: an inquiry into when you last had a holiday! I'm surprised at you, Lew. You'll be ashamed of yourself when you think things over. You'll find there will be no inquiry at all, or if there is, it will all blow over in no time."

She was so matter-of-fact. Just then she stepped out into the hall, and looked up the well of the stairs.

"I thought I heard someone stirring. It's getting on for seven. The maids will be getting up. It wouldn't do for you to be seen here. And anyway, you're not shaved," she said. "Are you going back to the hospital? Because if you are I think you ought to go back to Fitzwilliam first and have a wash. You look a bit the worse for wear. Take a look at yourself," and she nodded at the little diamond of mirror stuck over the hall stand.

He looked bad. There was no doubt about it. It sobered him to think that he had to go out into the street in that condition. But he had to go.

"I'd better get back, I suppose," he said.

"That's the spirit," said Bina, and she opened the hall door.

It was later than he thought.

Instantly, when the door was opened, his reluctance to go out vanished. In fact, he felt eager all at once to get away. There was a stuffy night odor in the little hotel, and out in the street the air was fresh, untouched. He felt stifled every minute he remained within. But he could not rush out abruptly. After all he had wakened her up out of her sleep; it was too late now for her to go back to bed. She would be on her feet all day. She was fagged looking even now, he saw with compunction—of course she was not as young as she used to be. Suddenly he wanted desperately to be kind: to show his gratitude. She had done so much for him in the bad half-hour that had passed. Perhaps she was right in thinking everything would be all right; he was inclined to see things in a different light already, but there was no doubt things looked bad to him when he came knocking at her door. Only for her—well, he didn't like to think of what would have happened to him only for Bina. She helped him to live through the worst hours of his whole life.

"You're a good friend, Bina," he cried, from his heart.

She was pleased. He could see she was pleased, but it wasn't enough.

"I wish there was something I could do for you, Bina."

He must let her see how he felt. He meant what he said too. "Isn't there anything I could do for you?" he pleaded.

But what needs had she that he could satisfy?

"Take care of yourself, Lew," she said quietly. "That's the best thing you could do for me."

It was inexpressibly touching. He was bowed with humility before such unselfishness.

"I will," he said simply.

You had to be simple with a person like Bina. He stepped out into the air. Then he turned and put out his hand. She took it.

"When this is all over, Lew, I hope you'll take a good holiday."

It was something positive that she was asking him. He owed it to her to treat it seriously.

"I'll do that, Bina," he said. "I promise. When this thing blows over I'll take a good holiday."

It was quite an idea; he needed a rest.

"I'll do that," he repeated emphatically, "not just a few days either, but a decent holiday. I might take a few months and do a trip over to the Continent." He looked over the rooftops in the direction of the coast. "This would be just the time of year for it," he said. He took a deep breath. He felt better every second that passed. It was hard to think that he had been so rattled. He hoped they had not seen in the hospital that he was rattled. If so, the sooner he got back there the better, to let them see him in his new frame of mind. "Well, Bina—thanks again!" He went down two steps.

"You won't forget the holiday?"

"I won't forget," he said. He was standing on the pavement. Desperately now he wanted to get away. "But you'll see me again before then." Surely she didn't think that he would be as casual as all that?

And yet it was just what he'd be likely to do to her, unless—

Unless: just as he was about to step briskly away from the doors this word pulled him up short. Supposing he was too confident; supposing things went badly with him. He'd be back to her soon enough then. He told her she was a good friend. She was more than that: she was the only friend he had.

If things went against him at the inquiry and he had to pack his bags, he'd have to have someone to go with him wherever he went. He'd never be able to start all over again without someone to help him. He'd never build up a practice again in a new place: alone.

But Bina was closing the door.

"Bina!"

He felt if that door closed he would be all alone in the whole world. He ran up the steps.

"Will you be here all day, Bina?" he cried.

Bina looked frightened.

"I suppose so," she said.

She looked back over her shoulder. The maids would be coming downstairs any minute.

"Why?" she asked, but absently.

"I might be back," he said. He didn't feel safe in leaving it at that. He'd have to go the whole hog. "Wait a minute, Bina. Don't go. I want to ask you something. Will you come with me—on the holiday, I mean?"

It gave him some satisfaction to see how stupefied she looked. He hadn't been walked into it, anyway; it was his own doing. It was the last thing in the world that Bina expected of him. It was all his own doing.

"Will you marry me, Bina? No matter what happens: no matter how things go with me?"

It was the only thing he could do. You couldn't ask any woman to wait and see how things went: even a person like Bina.

The only pity was that there had never been any question of things going badly. If he had kept his head he would have known that everything would be all right. It was only a little cloud that blew up in a clear sky and after a few days it had blown over. And now everything would be the same as ever—only for Bina. Not that he was altogether sorry. And he badly needed a holiday.

Brigid

THE rain came sifting through the air, and settled like a bloom on the fields. But under the trees it fell between the leaves in single heavy drops; noisily, like cabbage water running through the large holes of a colander.

The house was in the middle of the trees.

"Listen to that rain!" said the woman to her husband. "Will it never stop?"

"What harm is a sup of rain?" said the man.

"That's you all over again," she said. "What harm is anything, as long as it doesn't affect yourself?"

"How do you mean, when it doesn't affect me? Look at my feet. They're sopping; and look at my hat, it's soused." He took it off, and shook the rain off it on to the spitting bars of the fire grate.

"Quit that," said the woman. "Can't you see you're raising ashes?"

"What harm is the ashes doing?"

"I'll show you what harm," she said, taking down a dish of cabbage and potato from the shelf over the fire, "there's your dinner destroyed with them." The yellow cabbage was slightly sprayed with ash.

"Ashes are healthy, I often heard it said. Put it here!" and he sat down at the table, taking up his knife and fork, and indicating where the plate was to be put by patting the table with the handles of the cutlery. "Is there no bit of meat?" he asked, prodding the potato critically.

"There's plenty in the town, I suppose."

"In the town? And why didn't somebody go to the town, might I ask?"

"Who was there to go? You know as well as I do there's no one here to be traipsing in and out every time there's something wanted from the town."

"I suppose one of our fine daughters would think it the end of the world if she was asked to go for a bit of a message? Let me tell you they'd get men for themselves quicker if they were seen doing a bit of work once in a while."

"Who said anything about getting men for them?" said their mother. "They're time enough getting married."

"Is that the way?" said Owen. "Mind you now, anyone would think that you were anxious to get them off your hands with the way every penny that comes into the house goes on bits of silks and ribbons for them."

"I'm not going to let them be without their bit of fun just because you have other uses for your money than spending it on your own children!"

"What other uses have I? Do I smoke? Do I drink? Do I play cards?"

"You know what I mean."

"I suppose I do." The man was silent. He left down his fork. "I suppose you're hinting at poor Brigid again?" he said. "But I told you forty times, if she was put into a home she'd be just as much of an expense to us as she is above in the little house there." He pointed out of the window with his fork.

"I see there's no use in talking about it," said the woman, "but all I can say is God help the girls, and you, their own father, putting a drag on them so that no man will have anything to do with them after hearing about Brigid."

"What do you mean by that? This is something new. I thought it was only the bit of bread and tea she got that you grudged the poor thing. This is something new. What is this?"

"You oughtn't to need to be told, a man like you that saw the world, a man that was in England and London, a man that traveled like you did."

"I don't know what you're talking about." He took up his hat and felt it to see if the side he had placed near the fire was dry. He turned the other side toward the fire. "What are you trying to say?" he said. "Speak plain!"

"Is any man going to marry a girl when he hears her own aunt is a poor half-witted creature, soft in the head, and living in a poke of a hut, doing nothing all day but sitting looking into the fire?"

"What has that got to do with anybody but the poor creature herself? Isn't it her own trouble?"

"Men don't like marrying into a family that has the like of her in it."

"Is that so? I didn't notice that you were put out much by marrying me, and you knew all about poor Brigid. You used to bring her bunches of primroses, and I remember you pulling the flowers off your hat one day and giving them to her when she started crying over nothing. You used to say she was a harmless poor thing. You used to say you'd look after her."

"And didn't I? Nobody can say I didn't look after her. Didn't I do my best to have her taken into a Home where she'd get proper care? You can't deny that."

"I'm not denying anything. You never gave me peace or ease since the day we were married. But I wouldn't give in. I wouldn't give in, and what is more I won't give in now, either. I won't let it be said that I had hand or part in letting my own sister be put away."

"But it's for her own good . . ." said the woman, and this time her voice was softer and she went over and turned the wet hat again on the fender. "It's nearly dry," she said, and then she went back to the table and took up the plate from which he had eaten and began to wash it in a basin of water that was at the other end of the table. "It's for her own good. I'm surprised you can't see that; you, a sensible man, with two grown-up daughters. You'll be sorry one of these days when she's found dead in the chair—the Lord between us and all harm—or when she falls in the fire and gets scorched to death—God preserve us from the like! I was reading, only the other day, in a paper that came round something from the shop, that there was a case like that up in the Midlands."

"I don't want to hear about it," said the man, shuffling his feet.

"This hat is dry, I think," he said, and he put it on his head and stood up.

"That's the way you always go on," said the woman. "You don't want to listen to anything unpleasant. You don't want to listen to anything that's right. You don't want to listen because you know what I'm saying is true and you know you'd have no answer to put against what I'd say!"

"You make me tired," said the man; "it's always the one story in this house. Why don't you get something else to talk about for a change?"

The woman ran to the door and blocked his way out.

"Is that the last you have to say?" she said, "you won't give in?"

"I won't give in. Poor Brigid. Didn't my mother make me promise her that I'd never have hand or part in putting the poor creature away? 'Leave her alone,' my mother used to say, 'she's doing no harm to anyone.' "

"She's doing harm to our daughters," said the woman, "and you know that. Don't you?" She caught his coat and stared at him. "You know the way Matty Monaghan gave up Rosie after dancing with her all night at the dance in the Town Hall last year. Why did he do that, do you suppose? It's little you know about it at all! You don't see Mamie crying her eyes out some nights after coming in from a walk with the girls and hearing little bits of talk from this one and that one, and putting two and two together, and finding out for herself the talk that goes on among the young men about girls and the kind of homes they come from!"

"There'd be a lot more talk if the poor creature was put away. Let me tell you that, if you don't know it for yourself! It's one thing to have a poor creature, doing no one any harm, living quiet, all by herself, up at the end of a boreen where seldom or never anyone gets a chance of seeing her, and it's another thing altogether to have her taken away in a car and everyone running to the window to see the car pass and talking about her and telling stories from one to another till it would be no time at all they'd be letting on she was twice as bad as she is, and the stories about her would be getting so swollen that none of us could go down the streets without being stared at as if we were all queer!"

"You won't give in?" said his wife once more.

"I won't give in."

"Poor Mamie. Poor Rosie," said their mother, and she put the plates up on the dresser.

Owen shuffled his feet. "If you didn't let it be seen so plain that you wanted to get them off, they might have a better chance. I don't know what they want getting married for in any case. They'd be better off to be interested in the place, and raise a few hens, and make a bit of money for themselves, so that they could be independent and look people up and down and outstare the boldest!"

"It's little you know about anything, that's all I have to say," said the woman.

Owen moved to the door.

"Where are you going now?" said the woman.

"There's no use in my telling you and drawing down another stream of abuse on myself, when I mention the poor creature's name."

The woman sighed and then stood up and walked over to a press in the corner.

"If that's where you're going you might as well take over these clean sheets." She took down a pair of sheets from where they were airing on the shelf over the fire. "You can't say but that I look after her, no matter what," she said.

"If you remembered her the way I do," said the man, "when she was only a little bit of a child, and I was growing up and going to school, you'd know what it feels like to hear talk about putting her in a home. She used to have lovely hair. It was like the flossy heads of the dandelions when they are gone past their best. No one knew she was going to be a bit soft until she was toddling around and beginning to talk, and even then they thought she was only slow; that she'd grow out of it."

"I know how you feel," said the woman. "I could cry sometimes myself when I think of her. But she'd be so happy in a home! We could visit her any time we wanted. We could hire a car and drive over there, all of us, on a fine Sunday now and again. It would be some place to go. And it wouldn't cost no more than it costs to keep her as it is."

She didn't know whether he heard the end of the sentence because

he was gone down the path, and was cutting across through the
field, with the ash plant in his hand.

"He was cutting across the field with the ash plant in his hand,
when I was coming up the road," said Rosie, when she came in to
her supper, and her mother asked her if she had seen her father out
in the yard.

"He was going to your Aunt Brigid then," said her mother. "Did
you not see him after that?"

"That was three hours ago," said Mamie. "He wouldn't be over
there all this time." Mamie was sitting down taking her supper.

"The tea is spoiled," said their mother. "I may spill it out.
There'll have to be a fresh pot of tea made when he comes in."

"I suppose he's mending a chair or a table for Aunt Brigid," said
Rosie. "He wouldn't be just sitting over there all this time."

"You wouldn't know what he'd be doing," said the mother, and
the girls looked at each other. They knew then that there had been
words between their father and mother while they were out.

"Maybe one of you ought to run over and see what's keeping
him?" said their mother.

"Oh, let him alone. If he wants to stay over there, let him stay.
He'll have to be home soon to put in the calves anyway. It's nearly
dark."

It was quite dark, and the calves were still out. It was beginning
to rain, and the girls had gone out again to a dance, when Owen's
wife went across the field herself, and up the boreen to the hut
where the poor soft creature lived all alone.

How can she sit there in the dark? thought Owen's wife, when
she didn't see a light in the window, but as she got nearer she saw
there was a faint light from the flames of the fire on the hearth.
She felt sure that Owen wasn't there. He wouldn't be there without
lighting a lamp, or a bit of a candle! There was no need to go in.
She was going to turn back from the middle of the yard, but it
seemed an unnatural thing not to call to the door and see if the poor
creature was all right.

She was the same as ever, sitting by the fire with a silly smile, and
not looking up till she was called three or four times.

"Brigid, did you see Owen?"

Brigid looked up. "Owen is a queer man," she said, and that was all the answer she gave.

"So he was here! What time did he leave?"

Brigid grumbled something.

"What are you saying?" said Owen's wife.

"He wouldn't go home," said Brigid. "I told him it was time to go home for his tea, but he wouldn't answer me. 'Go home,' I said, but he wouldn't say anything."

"When he did go, at last, what time was it? Did you notice?"

Brigid was difficult sometimes. Was she going to be difficult now?

"He wouldn't speak to me," said Brigid, suddenly.

Suddenly Owen's wife saw his ash plant lying on the table.

"Is he still here?" she said, sharply, and she glanced back at the door. "Is he out in the yard? I didn't see him! I didn't hear him!"

"He wouldn't speak to me," said Brigid again.

The other woman couldn't see her in the dark. The fire was flickering too irregularly to see by its light.

"But where is he? Is he in the yard? Is there anything the matter with him?" She ran to the door and she called out into the dark, but there was no answer. She stood there trying to think, and then she heard Brigid talking to herself again, but she didn't trouble to listen. She might as well go home. Wherever he was, he wasn't here. "If he comes back, tell him I was here looking for him," she said. "I'll go home through the other field."

Brigid said something then, that made her turn sharply and look at her.

"What did you say?" she said.

"Tell him yourself," said Brigid, and then she seemed to be talking to herself again.

Owen's wife looked at her. She was worse than she ever was before. Brigid was leaning down in the dark before the fire.

"Why don't you talk?" she was saying. "Why don't you talk?"

Urgently, Owen's wife began to pull out the old settle bed that was in front of the fire without knowing why she did it, but she could feel the blood beating in her ears and behind her eyes.

"He fell down there and he wouldn't get up!" said Brigid. "I told him to get up. I told him that his head was getting scorched. But he wouldn't listen to me. He wouldn't get up. He wouldn't do any-thing."

Owen's wife closed her eyes. She was all of a sudden afraid to look. But when she opened her eyes and looked down, Owen's eyes stared up at her, wide open, from where he lay on his back on the floor.

"Owen!" she screamed . . . and she tried to pull him up.

His shoulders were stiff and heavy. She caught his hands. They were stiff and cold. Was he dead? She felt his face. But his face was so hot, she couldn't put her hand on it. If he was dead he'd be cold. She wanted to scream and scream and to run out of the house, but first she tried to drag him as far as she could from the ashy hearth. Then suddenly feeling the living eyes watching her from behind, and seeing the dead eyes staring up at her from the blistered red face, she sprang upright, knocking over a chair, and ran out of the house, and ran down the boreen.

Her screams brought people running out from their doors, the light streaming out each side of them. She couldn't speak, but she pointed up the hill.

It was dark down at the pump. And she could hear the feet running in the way she had pointed. Then they had reached the cottage, and there were no more feet, but great talk and shouting. She sat down on the side of the pump, but there was a smell of burning in the air, and when she saw that it came from her own hands she wanted to scream again. There was burnt hair stuck to her hands. Desperately she bent forward and began to wash them in the water, while all the time a pain gathered in her heart, not yet the pain of loss, but the pain of having failed; failed in some terrible way.

I failed him always, she thought, from the start. I never loved him like he loved me; not even then, long ago, the time I took the flowers off my hat. It wasn't for Brigid, like he thought. I was only making myself out to be what he thought I was—what he thought I was. I didn't know enough about loving to change myself for love. I didn't even know enough about it to keep him loving me, either. He had to give it in the end, to Brigid.

He gave it all to Brigid; to a poor daft thing that didn't know enough to pull him up, or call someone, when he fell down in a stroke. If it was anyone else was with him, he might have had a chance.

Oh, how had it happened? How could love be wasted, and go to loss like that?

It was like the way the tossy balls of cowslips that they used to make as children were forgotten and left behind in the fields, till they were trodden into the muck by the cattle and sheep.

Suddenly she thought of the heavy feet of the neighbors tramping the boards of the cottage up in the fields behind her, and rising up almost swifter than her thoughts, she suddenly ran back to them.

"Oh, you poor woman," said someone near the door, seeing her thrust past the children at the threshold.

They began to make way for her to where, on the settle bed, they had laid her husband. But she tried instead to part her own way through them to the door of the room off the kitchen.

"It's Brigid I'm thinking about," she said.

They knew her mind better than she credited them, because one of them plucked her sleeve.

"Something will have to be done about her now."

"It will that," she said, decisively, and her voice was as true as a bell. "It'll leave a mark on her, poor thing. And the worst of it was to have to leave him lying there and not be able to stir him."

She went over to the door of the room.

"That's what I want to tell you," she said, looking around her defiantly, falsifying their meaning. "She'll need proper minding. To think she hadn't the strength to run for help, or pull him back a bit from the heat. Where is she? Where are you, Brigid?"

Then she saw her, sitting on the side of the bed, in the other room.

"Get your hat and coat, Brigid," she said crossly. "You're coming home with me."

A Wet Day

"How is your lettuce, ma'am?" asked the old parish priest. "I hear it's been bad everywhere this year." He paused and blew his nose loudly, and then he looked around him. "Slugs!" he said then, very sternly, and went on a few paces after my aunt. We hadn't room to walk abreast on the narrow garden path. We went in single file; the three of us. After a minute the old man turned around and looked back at me.

"Slugs," he said again, and only the fact that he put the word in the plural kept me from feeling that this sturdy and blunt old man was calling me names.

"Our lettuce is very good this year," said my aunt, as all three of us somewhat unconsciously turned down toward the sodden path that led to the kitchen garden, and she took a firm grip of my arm although it meant that both of us got our legs wet by the border grasses. Father Gogarty distrusted students and my aunt probably linked me in case I might take offense at some remark of his, although it is scarcely likely that this would have happened. My aunt was always nervous when the local clergy called because we had had a couple of brisk arguments, she and I, about one thing and another, and she was beginning to realize that in my estimate of a man's worth I did not allow credit for round collars and tussore. I met some fine men who were in clerical clothes, but my respect for them had nothing to do with their dress. My aunt, however, had no use for anything I said on certain subjects. She banged the door

201

against all my arguments. Sometimes she went as far as saying that she doubted the wisdom of my parents in sending me to the University at all. It was there that I got my ideas, she said; ideas she distrusted. When she wasn't too angry to listen, she kept interrupting so much that she couldn't hear half what I said. Cheap anti-clericalism was the phrase she used most often to batter a way through my remarks. But as a matter of fact I believe that secretly she enjoyed these encounters that we had, and that they gave her a feeling of satisfaction as if she were Fighting for the Faith. I could understand, of course, that she wouldn't care to have outsiders over-hear my views. And she lived in terror of my offending the local clergy.

That was why she linked me so close as we went into the kitchen garden. She wanted to keep me near her so that she could squeeze my arm, and nudge me, and, in general, keep a guide over my conversation and demeanor.

We walked along the garden path.

Just inside the kitchen garden was a large, ramshackle fuchsia bush that hung out, heavy with raindrops, over the gravel path. Our legs were sprinkled with wet.

"You ought to clip back those bushes, ma'am," said the parish priest. "Nothing would give you a cold quicker than wet feet."

"I know that, Father," said my aunt, deferentially, "but they look very pretty on a sunny day; so shaggy and unpretentious."

"On a sunny day!" said the old man. "And when do we get a sunny day in this country, I'd like to know? As far as I can see it's rain, rain, rain."

He shook the bush with petulant strokes of his walking stick, while he was talking, and we knew that his thoughts were back in the days before his ordination, when he wandered along the blistered roads in Rome, and wiped the sweat from his red young face.

He often told us stories about those days, and all his stories had flashes of sunlight in them, that made up for the absence of humor. We thought, involuntarily, of sun pools lying on hot city pavements, between the chill shadows of lime leaves. We thought of barrows of melons and pawpaws and giant vegetable marrows; huge waxy growths of red and yellow. We thought of the young priest from Ireland in his shining black alpaca, laying his hands on them, and smiling to find them warm; for at home they were always chill to the touch, with a mist of moisture on them.

It was extraordinary the way we thought of his youth like that every time we saw him, because it was forty-five years, at the very least, since those days when he knelt to the Pope in Rome, and out of those forty-five years we, ourselves, had only known him for ten; the last ten. And those ten years were the years least likely to make us think of his hot, healthy youth, because during all that time he was delicate and suffering, and the duties of the parish put a great strain on him.

He always looked cold, and although his face was rosy-appled over with broken veins, it nevertheless looked blue and chilly to us as we sat watching him in the bleak concrete church where he went through Mass perfunctorily, and gave out a hard dry sermon, with a blackened silver watch in his hand, and his eye darting from one side of the church to the other, from the back to the front, from the organ stall to the gallery steps, according to wherever a cough or a sneeze escaped from some incautious person. There was always someone coughing, or stifling a cough. He used to say that he would like to preach a sermon some day on avoiding colds; he'd like to tell the ignorant people at the back of the church to close the door quickly when they came in, and not to hold it open for someone halfway down the outside path. There were more colds contracted by false politeness, he explained, than by any other way. He'd like to tell his congregation to cover their mouths when they sneezed. But he knew that a sermon of this kind would not be taken in the spirit in which it was meant, and so he had to content himself with stopping in the middle of a sentence, whenever anyone coughed, and staring at the offender till his stare became a glare. They probably thought that he was annoyed at the interruption, but they might have known, had they any wits awake at all at that hour of the morning, that nothing could interrupt the perfect machinery of his sentences. They ran smoothly in the tracks they had cut for themselves through dogma and doctrine, over forty years before, when he was a careful curate, working under a careful pastor.

It was very remarkable the way Father Gogarty could pause to glare around the church, or even pause for a longer while, to take out his handkerchief, shake it, blow his nose in it for a considerable time, and finally fold it carefully and tuck it back in the pleats of his surplice, before he finished a sentence. And yet he always went on at the exact place where he had stopped, and never repeated as much as a preposition of what he had already said.

Once in a while he dropped hints in his sermons about the damp of the church, hoping perhaps that some confraternity would get up a subscription for a heating apparatus. The confraternity members, however, thought that the cold of the chapel and the draft that came in under the badly hung door and, yes, even the fact that you might get a splinter in your knee any minute from the rotten wood of the kneelers, were all additional earthly endurances that enhanced the beauty of their souls in the eyes of the Lord. The last thing that would have occurred to them would have been the installation of any form of comfort in the concrete church, although there were large subscriptions raised every other year or so, for silk banners with gilt tassels, for brass candelabra, or for yards of confraternity ribbon with fringes and picot edging.

"It's a pity, you know," the old priest used to say, "that the Irish people make no effort to counteract the climate, because it's a most unhealthy climate. It's damp. It's heavy. It is, as I say, very unhealthy to live in."

It may have been his constant talk of health that made us associate him with the pagans of southern Europe, and made us feel a certain sympathy for him, trapped in a land of mist, where most of the days were sunless and where the nights were never without their frost or rain. My aunt often looked out at the sky and sighed.

"It looks like rain," she would say. "Poor Father Gogarty. This kind of weather is very injurious to him."

And when he came to call, the conversation was mainly about galoshes and leaking roofs and the value of wool next to the skin. He was a diabetic. My aunt, of course, had a great sympathy for him, but it would not have exceeded mine, had it not been for the fact that she deliberately exploited his delicacy to gain merit for his calling.

"He's a martyr!" she often said, when we were sitting down to a well-cooked dinner. "Can you imagine having nothing for your meal but a soup plate of cabbage?"

"Or rhubarb," I'd say, because I did feel sorry for the old man.

"Rhubarb is not so bad," my aunt would say, pouring the melted butter over her fish.

"Without sugar?" I would inquire.

"Without sugar?" my aunt would say, looking up. "Are you sure?"

"Of course I'm sure. Diabetics can't have sugar in any form. They can't even have green peas, or beans."

"You don't tell me! I thought they could eat any vegetable they liked as long as it was a vegetable."

And while I was explaining the differences between certain vegetables she would listen carefully, and on these occasions she looked as if she was pleased that I was going to the University and getting such general knowledge.

"Let's not talk about the poor man," she would say at last. "He is a martyr, that is the truth. How the rest of us can expect to reach heaven, is more than I can tell!" And here, she would call back Ellen, the parlormaid, before she retired behind the service screen, to ask her if the cheese soufflé had been sent back to the kitchen. "It hasn't?" she'd say. "Good! I think I could manage a little more. It's so good today," and then, as she scraped the sides of the silver dish, and looked sideways at me to ask if I was quite sure, absolutely sure, that I wouldn't have another spoonful, she would send a message to the kitchen. "My compliment to the cook!" she would cry.

If the old parish priest happened to call, as he sometimes did, after a conversation like that, we would both go out to the garden with him and walk around the sodden paths, urging him to take another head of sea kale, or prizing open the green curls of the cauliflower plants to see if even the smallest head had formed there, that he could have, as a change from what he called the Eternal Cabbage. Father Gogarty was supplied with vegetables from every little plot in the parish, but my aunt tried to keep him supplied with the kinds that were more difficult of culture, and which he would be unlikely to get elsewhere.

On this particular day in September, when he showed such solicitude for our lettuce, the weather was at its dirtiest, and of all places on earth to feel the dismay of rain I think a garden is the worst. The asters alone would depress the most steadfast heart. They were logged to the ground with rain and their shaggy petals of blue and pink and purple trailed dismally in the mud that streaked them all over. As we went slowly round the garden, and printed the path with our footprints, we left in our wake great heaps of vegetable, lettuce here, spinach there, to be collected by the gardener and put into the priest's car.

The gardener shared our sympathy for the old man and when my aunt would be ordering seeds from the catalogue that was sent to her every year from the city, he would often throw in a suggestion for some vegetable that we ourselves did not particularly like.

"What do we want with that?" my aunt would cry, impulsively, but she nearly always checked herself, quickly, before the gardener had time to explain that the old man had a partiality for it. "You are quite right, Mike, I'm glad you reminded me. Put down a large patch of that, too. And I think we could put in more spinach this year. It ran out toward the end of last year."

The gardener was very fond of Father Gogarty, and when the old man came they always had a chat.

"We must keep the old machine going, Mike. Isn't that right?" Father Gogarty would say.

"That's right, Father," Mike used to say. "Mind your health. It's the only thing that will stand to you at the finish."

"Perhaps you'd better throw in a few more of those cabbages," Father Gogarty would say. "And, by the way! while I think of it, I have been trying to keep it in my mind for a long time, to ask you a question, Mike!"

"Certainly, Father. Anything at all I can tell you."

"It's about lettuce. I wonder, Mike, is there any way of keeping lettuce fresh? My housekeeper says it should be kept airtight, but it gets all dried up, I notice, if you do that. I heard other people say they put it in water, but when that is done, I find, it gets yellow and flabby. I thought maybe that you might know of some knack for keeping it fresh. Do you now?"

"I can't say I do, Father, but why do you bother trying to keep it, can't you always get a bit fresh from here any time you want? What is the need in trying to preserve it? There's always plenty here."

Mike would speak from his own bounty, but he would look over the priest's shoulder as he spoke, and talk loudly for my aunt to hear. On these occasions she would nod her approval.

"You're working for a kind woman, Mike. There aren't many like her going the way nowadays. She spoils us all. She spoils us all." The old man sighed. "I suppose it isn't right for me to let her spoil me like this. Eh, Mike?"

"Ah! Why wouldn't you let her spoil you, Father? She loves giving you the few poor vegetables!"

"She does, indeed. She does. I know that, Mike. I can see that. Isn't it a grand thing the way the Irish women are so good to the clergy?"

"Why wouldn't they be, Father? Where would we be only for the priests?"

"I suppose you're right, Mike, but sometimes I say to myself that I shouldn't be taking such care of myself, an old man like me. 'I'll sit down and eat a bit of steak tonight,' I say to myself, sometimes— 'What harm if it kills me, amn't I near the end, anyway!' But then I say to myself that it's everyone's duty to guard the bit of life that's left in him, no matter what happens, and to keep it from giving out till the very last minute."

"You've no need to talk of dying, Father. I never saw you looking better."

"None of your flattery now, Mike," he'd say, to round off the conversation, turning out of the greenhouse to where my aunt and I would be waiting for him. My aunt felt that the few words the priest had with any of the men or women on the place was, in some way, a part of his priestly duty, and she never liked to interrupt.

"Let him have a few words with Mike," she would say to me, and she would busy herself until he came out of the greenhouse, by shaking the clay off the lettuce heads, or flicking slugs off with her long forefinger.

The end of the conversations with Mike, all of which were of a remarkable similarity, took place halfway in and halfway out of the glasshouse.

"It's up to all of us to keep going up to the very last minute, isn't that right, Mike?"

"That's right, Father. We should try to guard the bit of health we have. I've always heard that said."

"Is that so? I'm glad to hear that now, Mike. I must remember that, now."

Yes, the conversations were all alike, almost word for word alike upon every visit he made. But on this particular day that I mention, the day of rain and draggled fuchsias, Father Gogarty stopped and turned back suddenly to Mike, who was picking up a watering can and going back into the greenhouse.

"Aren't you from somewhere around Mullingar, Mike?" he said.

"I'm from three miles the other side, Father."

"I thought that, mind you! Did you know a young farmer there by the name of Molloy?"

"I did, Father. I knew him well, Father."

"I hear he's dead, the poor fellow," said Father Gogarty.

"I'm sorry to hear that now," said Mike. "He was a fine strong fellow, if I remember rightly."

"A big, broad-shouldered fellow?" said the priest.

"Yes," said Mike. "A big, broad-shouldered fellow is right."

"Reddish hair?"

"Red hair would be right."

"About twenty-five years of age?"

"That's him," said Mike.

"Yes, that would be him, all right," said Father Gogarty. "Well, he's dead."

"Is that so?" said Mike, and he left the watering can on the ground. "It just shows you can never tell the day nor the hour. Isn't that so, Father?"

Mike shook his head. Father Gogarty came out of the greenhouse and joined us on the wet gravel.

"I heard you talking to Mike, Father," said my aunt sympathetically. "I heard you talking about some young man who died. I hope he wasn't a relative of yours?"

"No," said Father Gogarty. "No, but it was a very sad case." He shook his head dolefully, and then he became more cheerful. "Do you know!" he said, impulsively, "I'm a lucky man that it's not me that is under the sod this minute, instead of him."

"God between us and all harm!" said my aunt. "Tell us about it, quick."

"I suppose you often heard me speak of my niece Lottie?" said Father Gogarty. "She's my sister's daughter, you know, and she comes to see me once in a while. Every six months or so. She's a nurse up in Dublin. Well, anyway, to tell you about the young fellow that's dead. Lottie got engaged a few weeks back to this young fellow from Mullingar. They were planning on getting married next month."

"Oh, how tragic!" said my aunt.

"Wait till you hear!" said the priest, looking back to make sure that Mike was coming after us with the basket of vegetables to put in the car. "As I was saying, anyhow," he continued, "they were planning on getting married next month, and nothing would do Lottie but that I'd see him before they were married. She wrote to say she was bringing him down. I suppose she had an eye to the wedding present, too, you know, but, however it was anyway, I was expecting them last Thursday, and I told my housekeeper to fix up a bit of dinner for them, to get a bit of meat and the like, as well as the dirty old cabbage and rhubarb that I have to eat. I told her to think up a bit of a sweet for them, too. She's a good woman, this housekeeper of mine, and she is a great cook; not that her cooking gets any great strain put on it with me in the state of health I'm in! But anyway, she put a nice dinner together. The smell of it nearly drove me out of the house. And when I saw her throwing it out in the pigs' bucket next morning, I could have cried. I could. That's a fact."

"Didn't they come?"

"They came all right, but wait till you hear. It appears he had a cold on him for a day or two past, and coming down in the car he must have got a chill, because the fellow wasn't able to speak when they drew up to the door. The car was a ramshackle affair. You wouldn't wonder at what would happen to anyone in it. I wouldn't ride down the drive in it, much less the journey they had made. The niece was very upset and she was fussing over him like as if they were married for fifteen years. Tea, she wanted for him, if you please; right away.

"'Don't mind about dinner,' she said. 'He couldn't look at a bit of food.' Pillows, she wanted for him, if you please. 'Get him a pillow so, if you haven't any cushions!' she said to the housekeeper, pushing her out of the way and going over to the sideboard and opening it wide. 'Is there a drop of brandy here?' she said. 'Or where will I look for it? I want to rub it on his chest.' I was pretty well sick of the fussing by this time, ma'am, as you can imagine, and I gave it as my opinion that the best thing she could do would be to take him back to Dublin as quick as ever she could, where he could be given the proper attention.

" 'But the drive back?' said Lottie, and I saw in a flash what was in the back of her mind.

" 'The harm is done now,' I said, 'another hour or so won't make any difference. A strange bed might be the death of him. Wrap him up warm,' I said. 'I'll lend you my overcoat.' It was my big frieze coat, ma'am, you know the one? It was a good warm coat. But Lottie was fidgeting about. She didn't know what was best to do, she said. I was getting pretty uneasy by this time, I need not tell you. What on earth would I have done if they insisted on staying? The whole house would have been upset. There's only one hot jar. Where would I get blankets enough to cover a big fellow like that? There's only the one woman to do everything, and she has her hands full looking after me. I couldn't stand the excitement. There would be running up and down the stairs all the night. There'd be noise. There'd be talking till all hours. The doctor would be there. The doctor would have to have a meal. Oh, I could see it all! I could see it all! I have to be careful at my age, you know. I have to have everything regular. I have to have quiet. 'If you know what is right,' I said to Lottie, 'you'll take that man right back where he came from, and get good medical care for him,' and as I was saying it, I was thinking to myself that if anyone knew what was right and what was wrong it ought to be her, with her hospital training. And sure enough, there were no flies on her. 'I'll tell you what I'll do,' she said, 'I'll take his temperature, and if he has no temperature I'll take him back to the city and telephone to the hospital. If he has a temperature, of course, it would be madness to undertake the journey back. I suppose the doctor here is passable?' She was pulling out the drawers of the desk while she was talking, looking for the thermometer, I suppose. 'Where do you keep the thermometer?' she said, looking round at me.

" 'I haven't one,' I said, but she wasn't listening to me. 'His forehead is very hot, isn't it?' she said. 'Why wouldn't it be,' said I, 'with your hand on it?' And the poor fellow himself didn't see the joke, any more than her, he was so sick. 'Where did you say the thermom-

eter was?' she said again. 'I said I haven't got such a thing,' said I,
and she was so vexed she could hardly speak. 'Every house should
have a thermometer,' she said, 'it's a downright shame not to have
one.' But she began to gather up rugs and pillows while she was
giving out to me. 'As long as you haven't one, I suppose I'd better
not waste any more time but start getting him back to the city.' She
went over to the poor fellow. 'Do you feel able for the journey
back?' she asked, feeling his pulse and frowning.

" 'I'm all right,' said he. He was a nice lad, not wanting to cause
any commotion, and different from her altogether.

" 'We'll come down another day, Father,' said Lottie. 'I hope
you hadn't made a lot of preparations for us?'

" 'I'll make greater preparations next time,' I said, just in order
to cheer the poor fellow she was wrapping up with rugs and blankets in the back of the car. I wanted to cheer him up because I had
a kind of a feeling that he was worse than she thought he was.
'I'll send you down a thermometer,' she shouted back at me, as they
went down the drive. 'Everyone should keep a thermometer.' "

"That was true for her," my aunt interposed impulsively at this
point, and I could see she was wondering if we had a second one in
the house that she could give him.

"I know it was true for her, ma'am. All I can say is I hope she
won't send me one though. You don't think that a man like me
would be without such a necessary thing as a thermometer, do you?"
He looked at us sternly.

"You had one all the time?" my aunt asked, falteringly.

"Three!" he said. "I had three of them, no less than three, but I
wasn't going to let on to her that I had." His face was crisscrossed
with lines of aged cunning. "Didn't I know by the feel of the fellow's
hand that he had a temperature, but I wasn't going to let myself in
for having him laid up in the presbytery for a couple of weeks, as he
would have been, you know, with pneumonia."

"Pneumonia?"

"That's right, ma'am. He had pneumonia. Double pneumonia,
I should say. He was dead the following evening. I was very sorry
for the poor fellow. He was a nice lad. I was extremely sorry for
him. I can't say that I was so sorry for my niece. It was a very in-
considerate thing, I think you will agree, ma'am, to come along and

visit anyone and bring a man that wasn't able to stand on his feet with a cold? People nowadays have no consideration at all; that's the long and the short of it; no consideration. I sent down to the chemist's and got him to send up a bottle of strong disinfectant to sprinkle on the carpets after they went out. You can't afford to take risks. I consider I am a very lucky man to be alive today, a man in my state of health would have been gone in the twinkling of an eye if I was burthened with a young fellow like that in the house, for maybe a month. He might even have died there in any case, even if he didn't have the journey back, and then think of the fuss! I'd be in the grave along with him. There is no doubt in my mind whatsoever on that score." He stood up. "Here is Mike with the vegetables," he said. "Put the lettuce on the front seat, Mike, I don't want it to get crushed. 'Eat plenty of lettuce,' the doctor says to me at every visit." He shook hands with us. "I'm getting too old to be gadding about in a car," he said, smiling out the car window at us, before he swung the car around and went off down the drive.

"I'll go for a walk," I said to my aunt. "I'll be back in time for dinner." I thought the least said the better.

And when I came back from my walk, I had indeed forgotten all about the incident. The evening had been very sweet and scented after the recent rain. You'd forget anything walking along the roads and hearing the heavy drops fall from the trees on to the dead leaves in the wood, while the sky over your head was bright and blue and cloudless. And when I came back I was hungry. I was looking forward to my dinner. When Ellen came in with a bowl of salad I hoped my aunt would not take too big a helping because I felt I could eat the whole bowlful. But what do you think? Before the girl had time to set the bowl before us, my aunt snapped at her and rapped the table with her wrist.

"Take away that lettuce," she said. "We don't want any tonight."

I was going to protest when I caught her eye and held my tongue. We didn't mention that story of the big red-haired farmer, either then, or since, but isn't it a funny thing, I have been on better terms with my aunt since that day. We get on better. And we have less fights about books and politics and one thing and another.

A Happy Death

"ARE you up there, Mother?" The child's thin voice shrilled up the dark stairs, as she stood at the bottom and looked upward, her small white face tilted back on her thin neck.

"What do you want?"

The mother came to the banister rail on the landing overhead, and leaned across it. It was the custom of the household to eliminate footsteps whenever possible by carrying on conversations from room to room, and even, as in this case, from one landing to another, but the lodger in the lower front room, who was understood to be connected with the stage, had a cold in the head and had not gone out to the theater that day, and it was in deference to the unusual presence by daytime of a stranger in the house that the woman came out to lean over the banister.

"What are you shouting for?" she demanded. "What do you want?"

At the response, however unsatisfactory, from the woman above, the child straightened its neck with relief, but a minute later some urgency in what she had to say to her mother made her strain her face upward again.

"Are you coming down, Mother?" she repeated, in a whimpering voice that seemed to expect a short answer.

"What do you want me for, might I ask?" demanded the mother, uncompromisingly. "Hurry up! I can't stand here all day with my two hands idle down by my sides."

The child was reluctant to give the reason for her request. She thought desperately for a minute, trying to find something to say that would bring the woman downstairs. She had apparently no faith in the efficacy of the truth, but as the woman on the upper landing shrugged her shoulders and made a move to go back into the room she had been dusting, the child was forced, against her judgment, to make what use she could of the truth, weak as it was.

"He's bad, Mother," she said. "He's coughing and moaning."

There was no need to mention a name it seemed. There was only one man in the family, and the lodgers were all women. A pronoun identified him at any time. He was rarely called Father by any of the children, which was hardly surprising since he had less authority in the house than any of them. As for their mother, it was years since she had called him by his Christian name, and there would appear to be something unseemly now in her doing so. Indeed, it was such a far cry from the time she had called him Robert that it hardly seemed possible to the children that Robert and he could ever be the same person. Not that they had ever heard much about Robert, either, but judging by the few fragments of the past they had pieced together from occasional words their mother had let fall, it seemed to them that Robert must have been the kind of young man with whom they themselves would have been proud to have been seen out walking in the park. He seemed to be the immortally romantic kind of young man who could never grow old. He certainly could never have become the hollow-faced nonentity that stole apologetically in and out of the house, and ate his meals in the darkest corner of the kitchen between the sink and the yard door. Why! Robert was their ideal young man. And to Mary, the oldest girl, who had a crippled back, due to a spinal injury in her childhood, Robert was the dominant figure in the long romances she wove as she sat sewing all day. Mary was apprenticed to a dressmaker, being unfit for anything more strenuous. To the youngest child, Nonny, who was now calling up the stairs to her mother, it was doubtful if the name Robert meant anything at all, for Ella had long given up even the most casual remarks about the past by the time Nonny was born.

Nonny was at this time eleven years old. And, this morning, with her small white face, startlingly white in the dark hallway, she looked less than eleven, as she stared anxiously up the stairs, at a

loss to know what to do. At last she stood up uncertainly and went
up a few steps of the stairs.

She could hear the woman in the room above. She could hear
the sound of the sweeping brush knocking against the wainscoting
and against the legs of the bed.

"Please come down, Ma," she pleaded. "He's sick. He's bad. He's
sitting in the kitchen moaning."

The woman came out to the landing again, but her intention was
only to pacify the child.

"Did you ever see him any other way?" she said.

The child, whose eyes had lit with a flicker of hope, said nothing
at this, but after staring helplessly at the stairs, her teeth bit slowly
into her lower lip, and sitting down abruptly on the stairs, she
broke into silent, helpless tears.

The woman looked down at her impatiently and frowned. She
resented the implication of sympathy with the man in the kitchen.
She resented any sympathy with him, from any of the children. She
always fought her corner with them viciously.

"It's easy for him to sit around and complain. Look at me! My
back is broken with trying to keep this ramshackle house in some
kind of order. I declare to heaven I seldom or never see the daylight;
stuck indoors from one end of the day to the other, with a sweeping
brush in one hand, and a mop in the other. Did I ever think I'd
live to see the day that I'd be sunk to this level? I that was never
called on to soil my hands in my mother's house, and had nothing
to do when I wanted a new hat or a pair of gloves but walk out to
the shop and put my hand in the till!"

It was an old song. The children knew it by heart. They had
heard it so often they never doubted the truth of it, and before they
were of an age to form a judgment, the poison of it had entered
their hearts. But they got sick of it sometimes. Yet, all the same,
they despised their father when he took Ella's part.

"That's what ruined your mother," he said. "She had too much
money, and not enough to do with it. She had nothing to do but
walk out into the shop and put her hand in the till and take out all
the money she wanted."

Indeed, they were never quite clear what the trouble was between
their parents. Their mother's complaints, and their father's justifica-

tion of her, were expressed in such similar words they missed the distinguishing emotion that underlay the words.

On this day, as Nonny sat on the stairs, the tears streaming down her face and her satchel strapped across her thin little back, the mother was more than usually irritated. She came out again to the head of the stairs.

"Why aren't you gone to school?" she demanded. "Do you know the time? Get up out of that and get out of my sight."

As she spoke, however, a door opened in the lower hall, and the lodger in the front room came out. She did not at once see the child crouched on the steps of the stairs, but she stared down the dark passage to the kitchen from which at the moment there came a low moan. The woman on the upper landing drew back hurriedly to avoid being seen. The child knew without looking up that her mother was standing back out of sight, but that she was listening intently to all that went on below, her features hard and unrelenting, her hands tightened irritably around the sweeping brush, and her bitter expression heightened by the uncompromising way in which her hair was tied up in an old duster. Out between the banister rails the child could see the other woman, the lower-front lodger. She peered out at her. And a look of cunning came into her face. Her foxy little eyes took in the painted cheeks, and dyed hair, and the big breasts heaving inside a tight red silk blouse, as the muscles of a fine mare ripple under the silk skin. She saw the gaudy turquoise jewelry that dangled from the woman's ears and crusted her fingers and throat. And she sensed their purpose unerringly; they were designed to give pleasure. She longed to have this warm, big-breasted woman go in to her father.

She stirred on the stairs but the woman did not notice her. She moved her foot. The woman looked as if she was about to go back into her room and shut the door. The child coughed, and then, overcome by consciousness of her secret motives she was seized by a fit of timorous shivering and could not raise her head to see if she had been noticed. But the lodger heard her. Putting up her hand hastily to the palpitating red silk blouse she gave a startled exclamation.

"Nonny! How you startled me, child. Why are you sitting there in the dark? Why aren't you at school?" Then, looking at her more intently with the forced stare of the shortsighted, she spoke more sharply. "Was it you I heard moaning?" she said.

"No," said Nonny, conscious of the unseen listener; afraid to say more.

"Who was it so?" said the woman. Then getting no answer she looked down the dark passage again. "Was it your father?" she asked.

The child nodded dumbly, hoping the woman overhead could not see her. But the lodger's next question betrayed her.

"What's the matter with him?" she asked. "Is there anyone with him? Is he sick?" Lifting her head she listened for a minute. "There he is again!" she said. "Is there no one to do anything for him?" She started as if she would make her way down to the kitchen, and although the child longed to let her go, fear of the woman overhead was uppermost in her, and she knew she must not let the lodger into the kitchen. She thought hard and then, as the woman took another step forward, inspired with a sudden duplicity, the child spoke again shrilly.

"It's all right," she said, shrill and loud. "My mother is coming down to him."

"Oh!" said the lodger, and then she looked irritably at the child. "Why didn't you say that sooner?" she said. She felt the wastage of her sympathy. She felt thwarted in her desire to be of use. But the child did not heed her. She sat on the stairs, hard and tight and triumphant, waiting to hear her mother descend. She had triumphed over her. She had forced her to come down against her will. Already she could tell from the sounds above that her mother was gathering her cleaning utensils together to bring them down with her. "I may as well go back to my room," said the lodger, ungraciously. She patted her hair absently. "Let me know if I can do anything," she said.

The child sat up. She must detain the woman, or her plan would fail.

"He's calling you, Mother," she said, urgently, calling up the stairs again.

The lodger turned around again.

"You've better ears than I have," she said, and she listened again. But the small delay had fulfilled its purpose.

"I'm coming," said the mother sourly, and she began to come

down the stairs.

The lodger stepped forward eagerly. She wanted to get a look into that kitchen. None of the lodgers had ever put their foot in it, and a great deal of curiosity about it was shown from time to time in the gossip on the different landings.

"Can I be of any assistance?" she cried.

Ella's face was expressionless, but she was torn between resentment at the other woman's interference, and a consciousness of the necessity to be civil.

"No, thank you," she said. "He's all right."

"But I heard him moaning," said the woman.

Ella stepped over the child huddled on the bottom step.

"He thinks he's worse than he is," she said, and then, as if to dismiss the stranger, she turned back to the child. "What are you doing there?" she said in a harsh, loud voice. "You'll be late for school!"

She caught the child by the strap of the satchel and lifted her to her feet and pushed her forward. In the narrow hall the woman from the lower front room felt that she was blocking the child's way. She saw no course but to go back to her own room. The child, however, suddenly realizing the inadvisability of being left alone with her mother, held the flapping satchel to her side, and darted up the hallway past the lodger. She had got what she wanted. She had brought her mother downstairs. There was a defiant triumph in the way she shut the hall door after her with a loud clap.

The lodger turned in to the open doorway of the lower front room.

"You know where I'm to be found if you want me," she said, calling back over her shoulder.

"I won't want anyone," said Ella, tartly. "He's not as bad as he'd have people think!"

Beyond an occasional mention like this, she made a point of never talking about her husband to the lodgers; never telling them her affairs. She walked down the hallway, and as she did, the man in the kitchen was seized by another violent fit of coughing, which, however, he seemed to be trying to suppress, as he heard the footsteps outside in the passage.

Ella, however, after a secretive look about her to see that the child had really gone to school, and that the front-room lodger had closed her door tightly, walked quickly past the closed door of the kitchen and went and stood at the back door. She had her own plans. She knew her own business, she told herself savagely, and she looked around the yard to find something to occupy her. She was determined not to go into the kitchen. She thought with irritation of the work she had been doing when Nonny interrupted her. If Nonny had not been such a busybody she would have had the top of the house cleaned by this time. Could she go up again, she wondered, now that Nonny was gone? She was inclined to turn and go up again when she remembered the woman in the front room. Ella jerked her body irritably. There was another busybody! There was another person poking her nose into what didn't concern her! Why couldn't they leave her alone? If she went back upstairs, and he continued to cough and moan, that woman would be out in the passage again wanting to know what was wrong. Ella turned back to the yard door. She might put out of her head all idea of going back upstairs. She looked around her to find something to do, to use up the nervous energy that was consuming her. Suddenly she started into activity. She'd clean out the yard! A vision rose up before her of the yard as she had kept it in the first year of her marriage. Robert used to say that he didn't miss a garden, she kept the yard so nice. She used to whitewash the walls every Saturday, and she had butter boxes painted green, and filled with red geraniums. But it wasn't long before she got sense. It wasn't long before she came to the end of such foolishness. Still there was no need to have the place like a pigsty. She looked around at the walls on which there was not a vestige of lime now, but which were covered with a powdery green lichen, and she looked at the ground where the same unhealthy green growth covered the sunken flagstones, making them slippery and malodorous. And everywhere the refuse of years was strewn: rusted canisters, empty boxes, old bottles, and articles of broken crockery.

She could get rid of some of the rubbish anyway. That was one thing she could do. She rolled up her sleeves. She could clean out the drain; it was choked up, and lately the water never went down completely so that there was always a stagnant pool lying over the grating like a disk of discolored glass. She caught up a piece of rusty wire and began to tackle the drain. She began to work with a furious energy and as she did so, it seemed to her that in a little while the yard would be again white and sweet-smelling as it was years ago, and that nothing would be lacking but the green-painted boxes and the red geraniums. And they could be easily got. Robert would get them.

At the thought of him, however, her depression returned, and hearing him cough again at the same moment she frowned. Then she remembered her secret plans, and obstinately shutting her ears, she began to probe the drain with the rusty wire. As long as the lodgers would leave her alone! She dreaded to hear the woman in the front room coming out again to the hall to listen. She dreaded to have her come along again with her interfering offers of help. Why couldn't she see that her help wasn't wanted? Had she ever been asked to help? Had she ever been given any encouragement?

Ella pulled up the wire and with it there came up a clot of green slime that gave out a foul stench.

She never encouraged the lodgers. She never told them her troubles. She never told anyone her troubles, but her pride in her own reticence was spoiled for her by a guilty feeling that if she had concealed her resentment from strangers she had vented it all the more fiercely on the poor wretch himself, and although she defended her conduct on the grounds of loyalty, in the depths of her mind she was uneasy. And it did not make things any better to think that he took all her jibes in silence. As a matter of fact, that was what made her most bitter; his silence.

"I suppose he keeps his complaints for the ears of his friends down at the Library," she said to the children time and again. "I suppose he makes himself out to be a great martyr when he's talking to them."

The children said nothing on those occasions. It was true their father must have a great many friends among the subscribers to the Library where he worked, because he was always bringing home presents he got from them, sweets and cake, and pots of honey or jam.

"He makes out he's to be pitied, I suppose," Ella would say, as she took up the things he had brought, having waited until he had gone to bed before she as much as looked at them in case it might give him any satisfaction to see her do so. And then she would let the children eat as much as they wanted of them without stopping them, as if she hoped they would sicken themselves and that there would be a scene over them next day. As a matter of fact, whether it was a coincidence or not, it seemed as if he never brought home anything without there being dissension over it.

"I wish people would keep their rubbish to themselves," she'd say triumphantly, when one of the children would get sick, or when the floor would be messed with crumbs, or when a wasp would come into the kitchen to annoy them, drawn by a sticky jam jar.

On those occasions he used to rouse himself to defend the donors.

"They sent them out of kindness!" he'd say.

"Kindness?" Ella would curl her lip contemptuously. "Pity would be more like it! I suppose you tell them how badly treated you are!"

He would make no answer to this and so she had to fall back on another familiar jibe.

"I'm glad to see you're ashamed," she would say.

But in her heart she knew that she was making false accusations against him, and that if he talked about her to strangers it would only be to tell them about the old days, about how pretty she used to be when she was a girl, and about how they had eloped together in spite of her parents, and in spite of their having no money, in spite of how young they were—she was only nineteen that summer, and he was only twenty.

Still the thought of his loyalty to their outworn romance did not soften her, and she told herself that it was easy for him to talk about those days, down at the Library, where there was no one to see how the romance had turned out, where there was no one to see the drudge he had made her, and the way she had gone to pieces. She'd like to tell people about the old days, too, but she had to hold her tongue, for who'd believe now that she was ever young, or that she ever had soft hands and fine skin. Sometimes she'd like to tell those painted old actresses that rented her rooms, that she had more beaus than any girl in the town while her hair was still down her back. But they wouldn't believe her. That made her hold her tongue. They'd only ask themselves why she married a broken-down wreck like the man in the kitchen if she had such a great choice.

They wouldn't know how good-looking he was when he was young, any more than she could have known then how much he'd change.

That was what galled her most. It wasn't the fact that she was worn out and had lost her looks; she could have put up with that, but it hurt her sense of pride that he should have lost his own good looks, and grown into such a poor shriveled wretch of a man. Who'd ever have thought it? And yet, she supposed, there were some girls who would have looked ahead, who would have foreseen how things would turn out. Why! her own mother had been able to see clearly what would happen. That was why her mother had been so dead set against the marriage. Her mother had seen what she was too blind to see, that the very things that attracted her to him were the things that would have made another girl cautious. She loved his white skin that was as fine as a girl's. How did she know it would get sickly and yellow? She loved the way the blue veins showed in his white hands. How was she to know that was a sign of delicacy? And one summer, when he was swimming in the river outside the town she had come upon the river bank suddenly and seen his white body, hairless and smooth, flashing through the heavy river water. How was she to know that hair on a man's body was a sign of strength, and that only a foolish, ignorant girl would disgust to it. She knew nothing, it seemed, in those days. And she was so obstinate. She wouldn't look at any other fellow after she met Robert. They all looked so coarse. There was her third cousin, Mat, and her mother thought he would be a good match for her, but she couldn't bear the thought of him after Robert. She hated his thick, coarse skin, and his black hair that always smelled of stale pomades.

"He's dirty!" she said to her mother. "He has warts all over his hands."

"Warts aren't the worst things in the world," her mother said. "Warts are a sign of strength. And anyway you could get them off with caustic."

The thought of treating Mat's warts made her sick in the pit of her stomach. The thought of touching his thick, oily skin at all, made her shudder. But her mother was right. There were worse things than warts. And as for strength! She met Mat a few years ago, and he was as strong as ever, although he was four years older than her. He was like a bull. Such health! Such a red face! Such good humor! He had grown into a fine man. And wasn't it right for a man to be strong? Wasn't it natural for men to have coarse skin and strong hair? They had to be rough to work the way they did. Anyone but her would have known that Robert wasn't made for hard work. Fine skin and soft hair were only for women. Warts indeed! How particular she had been. Why! the welts on her own hands sometimes, after scrubbing down the whole house, were just as bad as warts any day. But there again she didn't mind that. All she blamed him for was for the way he had broken down himself. She had been so proud of him. She would have worn herself to the bone working for him if he had kept his looks, and stayed the way he was long ago when she used to steal out of the house and meet him in the Long Meadow back of the churchyard. He always looked so much cleaner than other men. He wore white shirts and white collars, and they were always dazzlingly white. And his clothes were always brushed and pressed, with creases in them as sharp as the blade of a knife. And his shoes were always shining. You could see yourself in his shoes. She'd gladly have worn herself out if he had kept up his appearance. She'd have broken her back polishing his shoes. She'd have worn her fingers to the bone to keep him in white collars and shirts.

But you can't keep the color in shirts forever, and a shirt never looks the same after it's patched. And shoes won't give the same shine when the leather is cracked. And as for brushing his clothes! It came to a point where she used to hide the clothesbrush.

"They're worn enough," she'd say to him, "without you brushing the threads asunder!"

Long ago when they were making their plans for running away in the evenings in the Long Meadow, they used to count on the fact that they had plenty of clothes anyway.

"They won't wear out for a good while," Robert used to say. "We have enough clothes to keep us going for a long time."

But it was surprising how quickly his clothes wore out. Before they were a year married every suit he had was threadbare. But he wore most of them out sitting about on the benches of the registry offices looking for work. And when he got an odd job now and again it seemed as if you could see the clothes wearing away with the strain. The elbows would get rubbed, the fabric thin, and the back of the trousers would begin to shine, and in the winter the coat would get dragged out of shape with the way he had to pull up the collar against the cold. Clothes didn't last long when you put them to the test. She could see now how unreasonable she used to be about the rough clothes Mat used to wear.

"I can't wear clothes as fancy as the fine gentlemen in the town who sit about reading poetry all day," Mat said once, giving a dig at Robert.

"Robert isn't reading poetry," said her mother. "He's studying." Her mother was set against Robert, but when she was talking to Mat she never let on to be against him. It was part of her mother's plan to make all Ella's suitors appear to be worth nothing in their own eyes, but worth a great deal in the eyes of each other. But Ella wouldn't let the remark pass. She was determined to contradict it, partly because she wouldn't give in to her mother, and partly because she wanted to annoy Mat.

"It is poetry!" she said. "He reads nothing but poetry!"

She was proud of the fact that Robert read poetry. That was another thing she could laugh at now. She used to like to see him with a book of poetry in his pocket, or rather she used to like the rest of the people in the town to see him. She didn't like him to read it to her though, and he was always wanting to read it aloud. She wanted to talk or to tease him. Once in a while she liked to look into the books and see how strange they were, for the more incomprehensible the poems were to her the prouder she felt of him and the more confidently she could boast of him to others.

"What good is poetry to anyone, I'd like to know?" her mother said, and to this she always made the one reply.

"Don't show your ignorance, Mother," she used to say.

And then, too, although she was impatient with him for reading sometimes when they were out in the meadow, she knew that after he had read a few poems in the book he was always more loving to her, and she felt too that it was because he read poetry that he could say such flattering things about her hair and her eyes and her lips. Other men were so tongue-tied. You'd catch them looking at you. That was the only way you'd know what they thought of you. And even then it was your bosom or your legs they'd look at, but Robert was always praising little out-of-the-way things about her, like her ears or her fingernails. He loved her ears. He'd talk about her ears sometimes for ten minutes. And he said her fingernails were like shells. What other man would ever say a thing like that? Shells! It was the poetry put such things into his head. It was the poetry made him different from other men. She had known that then, but to her cost she had known it better later on. More than his compliments came out of the poetry books; all his nonsense came out of them as well. She wasn't long about telling him so, either. And in the end he admitted she was right. The day she gathered up all the old books and threw them into the fire he said nothing for a minute, and then he said she had done right.

"You're right, Ella," he said. "They were the cause of my undoing. A man can't expect to walk with his face turned up to the sky without losing his foothold on the ground. You must keep your eyes on the ground."

"Oh, that's more of your talk!" she said, but she was glad she had forced him to give in to her.

He gave in to her in most things, and if he protested at all it was only a feeble protest.

"You used to like to have me read to you," he said one day.

"I never liked it!" she said, in a fit of temper. "I only let on to like it!"

But she regretted saying that when she saw the look on his face. She wasn't long in learning that he could take any stings she gave him about the poverty and degradation into which they had fallen, but he could not bear her to say anything that spoiled the past. She took back her words that day.

"I didn't mean what I said," she muttered grudgingly, but swallowing her words so that she couldn't be sure if he heard her or not. "I've more to do now than listening to poetry, with those children to get ready for school."

That was the first quarrel they had.

"What can I do?" he said. "What do you want me to do? I'm doing my best." He had got a job as an assistant in a lending library at this time, but the salary was small. "I give you every penny I earn!"

That was true. But it wasn't enough.

"I don't know why it isn't!" he said. "There are bigger families than this living on less!"

"And how are they living!" she flashed out at him, and she drew his attention to his clothes. "I want you to look respectable," she said, "like you used to look at home. If you'd only do as I say."

"What do you want?" he asked again.

"Why do you keep asking that?" she said. "You know what I want! I want to let the front room and add a bit of money to the house."

But it was two years before he gave in to let her take lodgers; not that he could be said to give in, even then, but she took things into her own hands and let the room.

"It's for you I'm doing it," she said. "The first money we can spare I'm going to buy you a new suit, the one on your back is falling to pieces. It's no wonder you got a hint about them cutting down the staff at the Library! They saw the state of your clothes. They wouldn't want to have a shabby person giving out the books. It wouldn't look well. People are particular about things like that!"

"That's not why they gave me the hint," he said. "But what's the use of them having signs up all over the place asking for silence, if I keep coughing all the time? I got a bad fit of coughing this morning."

"Oh, don't start complaining," she said. "If you had a decent overcoat, you'd get rid of your cough." She thought for a minute. "While we're letting one room we might as well let two," she said. "The children could all sleep together, and we could let the middle room as well. Then I could buy you a new overcoat. That would get rid of the cough, you'd find. Never fear! It's not the cough that they don't like; it's your shabby appearance."

They didn't get the overcoat. The day the rent was paid on the rooms, two of the children got the measles and from that day on through the whole winter, there wasn't a single day without some new expense.

"Now what would we do without the rent?" she said, triumphantly, at the end of every week when she laid the household bills beside his salary, and went over to a tin box on the dresser and took out her own money.

Although the money all went to meet the bills, still she didn't forget the clothes for him. She was bent on getting them.

"What's the use," she said one day, "of having a parlor and a

dining room? We never go into the parlor." Her eyes were deep
with calculation. "The parlor would make a grand bedroom, only
some people don't like sleeping downstairs."

He didn't see what she was aiming at, and he joined in the conversation on its face value.

"Delicate people wouldn't mind," he said. "Some people are
not allowed to climb a stairs."

"The very thing!" she said. "I'll put an advertisement in the
paper, saying there's a room suitable for an invalid." She made it
seem as if it was his idea, and he wasn't able to protest. As it turned
out they got a better rent for the parlor than for any of the bed-
rooms.

"Who'd ever have thought it!" she said, as she took down the tin
box and counted the money in it. "I'll get you two new suits," she
said, "as well as the overcoat. The mistake most people make is in
not getting enough clothes at the one time. If you have enough
clothes you can be easy on them, and wear them turn about." She
had been very excited and animated, but he was hardly listening.

"I don't think the new clothes will make any difference," he said
morosely.

"Oh, you make me sick," she said impatiently.

Nevertheless, when she brought home the new suits, her heart
missed its first beat. He didn't look like he used to look at home.
There was some change. She couldn't say just what it was, but there
was a change. What harm!—she said to herself—it'll take time to
bring him back to what he was. I'll get him some new shirts and new
collars. She looked at his feet. I'll get him new shoes. She looked at his
hair—I'll get him some brilliantine for his hair, she said, and then
her eyes brightened—I'll get him a gold tiepin! she said. The thought
of the gold tiepin caused her mind to spin around in furious excitement. She was determined to make him again what he was when they
were courting. "We could let the other room," she said. "We could
eat in the kitchen. It would save my feet, too. I'm worn out carrying
heavy trays backward and forward."

She bought Robert the new collars and the new shoes. She bought
the brilliantine and she bought the gold tiepin, and the morning
he was going out in the new clothes, she was unusually excited.

"There's a lovely color in your cheeks, Ellie," he said.

She ran over to the mirror and laughed happily at her reflection, but when she turned around she noticed how pale he was. Her heart misgave her again, but she pushed him toward the door with affected good humor.

"You'll see! There'll be no more hints about cutting down the staff," she said. "That's the way you looked when you were hired. I don't blame them for getting uneasy. You were looking terribly shabby lately."

She watched him out of sight, and that day she felt that perhaps the bad times they had gone through were over, and that things would take up again, and be like she thought they would be before she was married.

The minute he walked in the door that evening, however, she knew something was wrong. When you got down it wasn't as easy as all that to get up again.

"Well?" she said, and her face darkened, and all the light that had shone in her eyes that morning died out.

He stood in the doorway and looked at her in a strange way.

"I knew it wasn't the clothes," he said.

"What do you mean?" she cried. Why couldn't he speak out plainly?

"It was the coughing," he said, and then, as if to convince her, he was shaken with a hard, dry cough. "They said they were sorry, but they couldn't have me disturbing the people who were trying to read."

She stared at him, and he stared back at her helplessly. Then, before she said anything, he recovered himself and put up a hand to his necktie.

"Where did you buy the tiepin?" he asked. "Would they take it back and refund the money?"

At this some of her old fire had come back.

"Leave that pin where it is!" she cried, and she slapped his hand down from his neck just as she'd slap one of the children's hands. He stared at her. All at once he felt like one of the children. He felt that her authority over him was going to grow into something enormous and unnatural that would shame his manhood. He was confused and weary, but yet he felt that he must defend himself against this wrongful authority of a woman over a man. And al--

though he couldn't collect himself for a minute or two he knew that he had a weapon against her. What was it? He tried to concentrate and then suddenly he remembered.

"You needn't worry about the money," he said. "I'll still be bringing in my share."

He spoke defiantly but she didn't seem to heed his words. It wasn't the money she had minded. She had forgotten about the money. It was the humiliation of their not wanting him any more at the Library. She had been so proud of him when he first got the job there. She used to pass by at night when the windows were lighted just to see him, sitting at his desk in his white collar giving out the books and stamping the date on the flyleaves. And although she had had to give that up when she had the lodgers on her hands, it was only that morning she had been thinking that she'd try and walk down before closing time and see him in his new suit. She had been thinking of it all day. She'd like to have caught a glimpse of the tiepin. She'd like to see if it attracted any attention.

And now they didn't want him there any more!

She couldn't believe it. A nervousness overtook her suddenly. Was there anything wrong with the clothes? Were the sleeves too short? Why were his wrists sticking out like that?—and how thin they were!

There was nothing wrong with the clothes, however, and she was forced to take heed of the way his frame had shrunk. He had changed. Yes, he had changed, and it wasn't the money she was thinking of at all but of this change, when he spoke. Yet she looked up at him.

"If you're not wanted at the Library, where will you get the money?" she asked, dully, because she wasn't interested in this aspect of the thing, but as she looked at him she felt frightened, because she saw that he himself was frightened of telling her where he was going to get it. "Where will you get it?" she asked again, more urgently.

"At the Library," he said.

"I thought you said . . . ?" She stared at him stupidly.

He swallowed hard and moved back from her.

"They said they didn't like letting me go—"

"Well?"

"They said they didn't like letting me go, but that there were people complaining about my coughing."

"Well?"

"—so they said that I'd have to leave the Reading Room."

"Well?"

He simply couldn't go on. He began to cough again.

"They said they could give me another job if I had no objections to it—a job where I wouldn't disturb people."

"In the office?" she asked quietly.

"No."

"Well, where?" There was fear in her eyes and before that look of fear his voice failed and he was hardly audible.

"The porter is leaving at the end of the week," he said. "They thought maybe . . . in these hard times . . . temporarily, you know . . . till something better turns up . . . that some money would be better than none."

He allowed the words to fall from his lips, nervously, unnecessarily, because her silence upset him. Why was she so silent? He had expected abuse.

But she was stunned; stupefied. A porter! A kind of janitor as like as not! Suddenly she burst out crying, and through her fit of tears her anger could only break out erratically.

"A porter! How dare they make such an offer! How dare they! How dare they!" She sat down weakly on the edge of a chair. He stayed on his feet, looking down at her. He was somewhat confused. It appeared that she was not annoyed with him; that all her anger was directed against the people at the Library. But one thing was clear. He was not going to suffer a storm of abuse anyway, and with this thought he felt relieved, and as the phlegm that he had been trying to keep back rose again in his throat he was about to give himself the further physical relief of coughing when he was suddenly seized with a feeling of fear. She wasn't going to let him take the new job. That was her idea. He summoned all his strength once more. He'd have to take it. He'd have to keep his independence. He'd have to pull his weight in the house.

And so before he was overcome by the returning fit of coughing, he managed to summon breath enough for one exclamation.

"I'm going to take the job," he said chokingly. And then the coughing started and he had to sit down.

That day had been the beginning of all their misery. That was when the real trouble had started between them. It was not until that day that the irreparable bitterness had come into every word they said to each other.

He persisted in taking the job. The new clothes were laid aside, and the tiepin was stuck on the wallpaper over the mirror. He wore his old clothes frankly after that, and without even the disguise of darns or patches. There was no longer even an effort to keep them brushed or clean. He wore the new shoes, because after a bit his feet came out through the old ones. But the rest of the clothes were put away in a cupboard.

"They would only attract attention to you," she said. "They would only draw people's attention to the fact that you were lowering yourself below your station!"

Her bitterness knew no bounds. Every hour that he was in the house she upbraided him, and where before she had regarded the money from the lodgers as an addition to their joint money, now she regarded it as the sole support of the family, and sneered at the small sum that he laid on the table every Saturday.

"Is this for your keep?" she used to ask, and throw it contemptuously to one side. And at other times, when they were eating their meals, she would laugh bitterly as she filled his plate.

"You get good value for your money," she said.

Sometimes she called him The Boarder.

"There's more profit on lodgers than boarders," she'd say.

Things went from bad to worse. He got more and more shabby-looking, and as well as that he seemed to shrink and grow smaller and meaner-looking every day. The more sickly and ill he became, the more bitter she grew toward him.

One day, when he left his few shillings down on the table she snarled at him.

"Why don't you keep it?" she said, throwing back the money to him. "Keep it and buy lozenges with it; not that you get much for that!"

He seldom protested against this treatment, and when the children appeared occasionally to take his side he always discouraged them. "Your mother is tired, girls," he used to say. "Don't let her see you are going against her. She has a lot to put up with, and she wasn't used to hardship."

When he said that Ella wasn't used to hardship, Robert's eyes would sometimes seem dim with a recollection, and he would not listen to them any more, but sit there in a corner of the squalid kitchen staring out the window where a few bits of green fern in a pot on the sagging windowsill had power to draw his heart back into the past, and dissolved in their essence dreams and memories of the Long Meadow back of the churchyard in the old town where he was born. And when he came up again from the depths of these memories he was brighter and more cheerful-looking, and the girls felt reassured enough to resume their plans for their own enjoyment. They felt they could forget him with impunity, and they crushed against each other, and jostled each other for preference of place in front of the dirty mirror mottled with splashes that hung over the sink, as they powdered their faces and combed their hair before going out for the evening.

"None of you have hair like your mother," he said, sometimes on those occasions, and he would start to describe how Ella's hair had been, how bright, how glossy, and how it curled around her forehead if the weather was damp. But they didn't want to hear.

"There's not one of you like her," he said sadly, and Dolly, the second-youngest, tittered.

"It's a good thing we're not," she whispered under her breath, because they couldn't see back into the past when Ella was young and decked out for love. But Mary shuddered. She was, in fact, somewhat like her mother, and she trembled in her secret soul at the thought that if her mother was once beautiful and yet got like she was now, then she, Mary, might some day get like her mother.

"Let's hurry!" she'd say, anxious to be out in the impersonal streets. Being the most sensitive of them all to her father's suffering, she was nevertheless least able to bear the sight of it, just as, most sensitive to the strain between her parents, she was least able to stand it, and rushed out of the house as often as she could.

"Goodbye, Father, goodbye!" They would soon be gone, leaving him in the dark kitchen, knowing that his wife would not stop working and scrubbing until he was out of it. She would not stop to please him. She would not give him the satisfaction of seeing her sit down for a few minutes to rest. He began to go to bed earlier and earlier until soon it was only a question of taking his meal and standing up from it to go to bed. When he was out of the way, he thought, she might sit down and eat, or rest herself by the fire.

One Saturday the strain was too much for Mary. After her mother had made some contemptuous remark about the weekly money that he obstinately left on the table every week, she burst out before him.

"Why are you always picking at him, Mother? What do you want him to do? Kill himself? He can't earn any more than he does. He shouldn't be working at all! He's not fit for it."

The mother stared at her.

"Keep out of what doesn't concern you," she said angrily. But after a minute she softened. "I'm not making him work," she said. "I'm against it. I was always against it from the start. Isn't that the cause of all our misery?" She was speaking to Mary, but out of the corner of her eye she tried to see the effect of her words on the man. "I want him to stay at home. I want him to give up that humiliating job. What he earns isn't as much as what I get for one room!"

Mary was surprised. She looked at her father.

"Why don't you do what Mother says?" she asked.

But Robert shook his head. "You don't understand," he said.

"There you are!" Ella went out of the room impatiently.

But if Mary didn't understand, Ella herself understood less. The only difference between herself and Mary was that Mary honestly tried to understand, but she had shut her mind against him long ago and never tried to see his point of view. She saw her own only, all the time, day after day, and when he got fits of coughing, or an attack of the cramping pains across his chest that he got lately, her own viewpoint only narrowed down the more.

"I don't know what notions you have in the back of your head," she said to him, "but let me tell you this! You're keeping me back. People won't take rooms everywhere and anywhere, and when they hear my husband is a janitor they think the place isn't class enough for them. And when they see you going in and out, in your dirty old clothes, coughing and spitting, that turns them more against the place; whereas if you were to give up that job and stay at home and wear your good suits, and put on clean collars it would make the place look respectable. You could help me out, too. There's many a thing you could do. You could order the provisions. It would look well to see you going into the shops. And you could be seen about the place. That counts for a lot. It gives a place a respectable appearance to see a well-dressed man taking his ease in the middle of the day. It would let people see we weren't lost for their last penny. It would let them see we were independent, and that if the price didn't suit them they could go elsewhere. As it is they think because my husband is a janitor I ought to be glad to take whatever they like to offer me!"

A frown settled on her face as she thought of past scenes of haggling over the price of the rent, but it lifted suddenly as she let her mind fly forward to a vision of things as they would be if she had her way.

"I'd like to see you with a clean collar on you every day," she said, "and your good suit, and your tiepin, sitting on the bench outside the front of the house. That would give a good appearance to the place."

She paused to picture him sitting on the bench, and then as if the picture was not complete she bit her lip and seemed to be thinking. After a minute she looked up eagerly.

"You could have a carnation in your buttonhole," she said.

She was carried away with her idea.

From that day forward she never stopped appealing to him, but gradually the appeals grew sour, and took the form of complaints. He, however, remained consistent in his resistance to her. He resisted her all the time. And the weaker his power to express it, the stronger his resistance seemed to grow, until sometimes as he sat by the fire it shone at the back of his eyes in a wild light. He was steadfast in his determination to keep his job. She was steadfast in her determination to make him give it up. But although they were equal in obstinacy and will power, she had an advantage over him in his own decreasing strength. He'd never endure the hardship. His cough was worse week after week.

And so, as she went about the kitchen, she used to watch him out of the corner of her eye. He thought he was going to best her, but she knew that she'd triumph in the end. And when the children worried about his cough, and came to her, and tried to make her get a doctor for him, she smiled in a curious way and gave them evasive answers. For the cough was her friend. It would accomplish what she had failed to do; it would force him to give up.

And when that day came she would triumph. Then she would have him where she wanted him. She'd see to it then that he got out of those shabby old clothes, and put on his good suits. She'd shake out the suits, and press them, and she'd put a great gloss on his collars, and as for shoes, she'd get him two new pairs at least, as well as a couple of pairs of socks. She'd get black lisle socks with colored clocks embroidered on the ankles. And as for his cough! That didn't worry her. She'd cure that in a few weeks. When he had nothing to do but sit out in the sun and take his ease the cough would soon be gone. There would soon be a change in him. He would soon get back some of his looks.

She straightened her back. The yard didn't look much better, but she had made some improvement in it.

Just then there was another fit of coughing in the kitchen, and after it had died down again she heard a distinct moan. Several times before she had fancied she heard moaning, but she had been able to persuade herself that she was mistaken because she had been making a good deal of noise herself in the yard. But now as she stood idle to rest her aching back she heard it clearly. If only the lodgers didn't hear it! If they heard it they would be likely to come down. They were so curious and interfering. And if they did it would spoil everything. She had her own arrangements. Doggedly she stood in the yard and listened to the sounds inside the small window that opened on the yard from the kitchen. She felt that as long as there was no interference with her plans she would soon come to the end of her struggle with him. She was near the end of it now, she felt, and with this thought she permitted herself to move nearer to the kitchen window and listen. But when she was listening deliberately there was no sound. Then, as she was moving away with annoyance, the man in the kitchen was seized with a most violent attack of coughing that was only interrupted by moans and gasps that seemed to be as involuntary as the coughing. The woman leaned forward. He was bad. He was worse than ever he was. A sudden wild elation took possession of her. At this rate he wouldn't be able to go to work today. This was the beginning of the end. What time was it? She strained her head backward to try to see the time by the church clock that could be seen in the distance between the city roofs. Ten o'clock. Could it be that late? Why! he should have been gone long ago! She listened. Her elation grew. Morning after morning he had been getting later and later, but he had never been as late as this! How she had hoped time and again that they would discharge him! Seemingly, however, they were prepared to stand anything from him. They pitied him, she supposed, and her resentment burned more bitterly at the thought that he should make himself the object of pity, of charity. Then, as the clock began to strike, exultantly she listened to the chimes, pealing out loudly over her head. He must not be going to go out at all today. Exultantly she wiped her hands on the sides of her dirty dress. Her day had come. He was defeated at last. Now she had him where she wanted him. She would not be humiliated any longer by having people know that her husband was a janitor. He would be a gentleman again; that was why she had married him. He had been such a gentleman.

She sat down on an upturned box in the yard. She felt weak all of a sudden, but it was a gratifying weakness; bearable, and endurable, after a long, hard fight in which victory, although certain, had been a long time deferred. After a few minutes the tiredness from the heavy work in the yard began to stream away from her, and with it there seemed to stream away the unhappiness that had lain on her now for so many years. Suddenly she felt that all was going to be well. She looked around at the squalid yard and up at the loose bricks of the house, that needed to be pointed with cement, and then she looked at the windows of her house, where, in their early years of occupation, neat curtains of white frilled muslin had made all the windows alike, but where now the different occupants of the different rooms had hung their own different curtains. A tenement! That's what it was. But all that would be changed. She would get a better-class lodger. She might try giving board as well as lodgings. There was more money to be made that way, and it was more respectable. Things would be easier now that she would have Robert at home with her. Before he put on his good clothes in the beginning of the day he could do odd jobs for her about the house. They would coin money. Things would improve. And there wouldn't be as many expenses as there were long ago. The girls were all left school except Nonny. Mary's apprenticeship to the dress-maker would be at an end in two months' time. She could ask for a salary any day after that, or set up on her own. She was as good as any dressmaker already. And Dolly was no worry. Dolly's salary at the factory was more than Robert ever earned, even in the good days when he was in the Reading Room. Then, too, Dolly was as good as married. And Nonny? Ella's worn face brightened even more. She had not done too well for the girls. But there was still time to do something for Nonny. It would be nice to send her to classes and get her made into a typist. Typists were respectable. They didn't get tired and drawn-looking. And she could keep her hair nice, and her hands would be soft and not pricked all over with needles like Mary's, or dyed with chemicals like Dolly's.

Ella looked down at her own hands. If Robert was at home all the time she'd have more heart to keep herself clean. There and then she pulled a hairpin out of her untidy knot of hair, and began to pick the hard, black dirt from under her nails. She put up her hand to her hair again. It wouldn't be so coarse if it was washed once in a while. She felt her neck with her fingers. It was dry and rough. But was that any wonder? She only washed her neck when she was going out in the street. You got into dirty habits when you were all alone all day in a dirty, dark house. It would be different if Robert was with her all day. She'd get through her work early, and they might go out for a walk. They used to go out every Sunday when they were first married. She could remember well how proud she was of him. The brightness in her was a hard, defiant brightness. She'd be proud of him again. The suits she'd bought him a few years ago were still as good as new. And they were a better quality than could be got nowadays. As for his appearance, he'd get back his looks in no time after a few days' rest. That was all he needed; rest. He would look older, of course, but he would be distinguished-looking, and that was what counted with people.

She began to visualize how he would look, clean and rested, and dressed in his good suits, but it was the old Robert she kept seeing and not the poor, shrunken wretch in the kitchen. Aware of the obstinacy of her memory, she made a deliberate effort to take his age into consideration, but it was still the same Robert that used to sit on the wall outside his father's house reading poetry and looking down the street to see if she was coming. Her imagination, in trying to give him the benefit of his years, had done little more than the make-up man in the theater does for an actor, who, in the course of a play, has to take the part of a young man in one scene, and in a later scene has to portray the part of the same man advanced in years. That is to say she imagined Robert with a dusting of gray powder on his hair and about his temples; a few wrinkles on his face no deeper than theatrical wrinkles made with red chalk, and a slight stoop; but under the powder the hair was crisp with youth and life, under the wrinkles the blood ran red and rich, and the limbs that simulated a stoop were free and limber. The Robert she called up before her eyes was a Robert decorated rather than blemished by the marks of age.

She drew a deep breath. Things had been bad but they were going to turn out right in the end. Now that the struggle was over she was prepared to acknowledge that she had been bitter, but not without cause. An intolerable burthen had lain on her for so many long dark years. And although behind her was the dark, decaying house, with its damp, slimy yard, its ramshackle windows and its broken doorway through which there came out, even at that moment, the stench of conflicting food smells as the lodgers in their different rooms prepared their various and inferior foods, nevertheless it seemed to her that these things were nothing, mere details, or external manifestations of a nameless, obscure trouble that had lain over her ever since she was married. A nameless, obscure obstacle had been set in the way of her fulfillment of those bright dreams that had glanced back and forth in her pathway so convincingly and alluringly when she was a girl, contemptuously swinging her foot under the table while her mother abused Robert and said he was good for nothing. Perhaps it had been some fear that her mother was right, and that she was wrong, that had lain on her all those years? And Robert himself seemed to have taken her mother's side. He seemed readiest of all to agree that he was worthless and that she had thrown herself away on him. Why had he not helped her to keep up a show? He had given in so early to other people's opinion of him. He had not put up any fight. He didn't care if he put her in the wrong with her people. But now wasn't she glad she had not given in to him! She had held out all the time. She had fought. And now she had won. In her limited experience and knowledge she knew little of the abstract differences of the sexes, but from some dim memory of a National-school primer she had an idea that women were the upholders of spiritual values and she felt that in all those weary years she had been championing a cause. People might have blamed her for her methods, but they didn't understand. She had had her plans. She had known what she was about. And now her reward had come. Even Robert would have to see that she had been acting for the best. She had been making a way for them both out of the dark forest in which they had been imprisoned, and together now they would flash out into the open glade. That it would be like the green glades of their early youth she did not for a moment doubt.

She stood up. As her tiredness and misery had given way to excitement and exultation, so these emotions had in turn given way to an infinite feeling of peace. She moved toward the back door that led into the house. She would tell him her plans.

But as she entered the mean hallway, her nostrils were assailed by imprisoned odors of the stale past, and she heard him move his feet on the broken cement floor of the kitchen. And immediately her spirits were dampened. She felt tongue-tied. The habits of years were not to be broken so easily. How would she begin? What would she say? For she would now have to deal with the real Robert; the bodily Robert, and whereas it had seemed in her mind, as long ago it had seemed in her heart, that they were one person, indissoluble in intimacy, who could say or do whatever they liked to each other, she had no sooner heard him cough and scrape his foot on the floor than she was aware again that two people never are one, and that they were, as they always were, and always would be, two separate beings, ever at variance in their innermost core, ever liable to react upon each other with unpredictable results. She was uneasy. She had lost her surety before she had crossed the threshold.

And when she heard him call her name in a strange voice as if trying to penetrate some incredible distance between them while she was actually within a few yards of him, with her hand on the kitchen door, all her old irritation came back.

"I'm here," she said. "There's no need to shout." She went into the house.

"Didn't you hear me moaning?" he asked feebly and without

accusation. Her antagonism gathered.

"Are you ever doing anything else?" she asked. The bright flock of hopeful thoughts had taken flight again.

He was dressed for work, and the coarse ugly clothes put a barrier between them instantly. But he, who for many, many years had been so sensitive to the strain between them, seemed unaware of it now. He put out his hand, and it seemed as if he was unconscious, too, of all the other barriers that the years had erected between them. Before she had time to draw it away, he had taken her hand in his.

At the feel of the hard, coarsened hand when it caught hers, Ella drew back roughly and attempted to release her own hand. But Robert only held it tighter, and in his eyes there was a strange expression, and he looked at her in a curious way, almost, she thought, as if it were twenty years back and she was standing in front of him in the Long Meadow. He seemed to ignore or not any longer to see her worn face, and when she tried again to pull her hand away, he seemed not to understand the rough gesture, or to think of it as the capricious withdrawal of bashfulness.

"Don't draw away from me," he said. "I have something to say to you. All morning I was calling you. I have been wanting you to come in to me."

She was disconcerted. This was the style and appearance of the man she had lived with in misery for the last twenty years, but it was the voice and manner of the young man who used to read poetry to her long ago. As a few minutes before in the yard, once again she got the astonishing sensation that she had made her way out of the depth of a forest in which she had strayed for a long time. Over her head the trees were laced together less tightly. Through chinks in the leaves the light was breaking in ever brighter clearings. But whereas in the yard, she had thought she would have to explain all this to Robert, it appeared now that he too had broken his way through to the light. She put her hand to her heart. It was too sudden. It had all come about too unexpectedly. They had flashed out into the glade too fast. She was dazzled.

And so she tried to draw back and take refuge in the habits of the past.

"I heard you!" she said. "And so, I suppose, did everyone in the house! What the lodgers think, I don't know! It's a wonder they stay in the place at all. And as for coming in to you—you know as well as I do that I can't be running in and out every minute for nothing. I have things to do! I wasn't out in the yard for my own pleasure, I assure you!" The flood of words, once released, poured out in a bitter stream. Then as she saw him staring at her, she faltered. "Anyway!" she said, defensively, "I didn't know whether you were calling or coughing!"

Still he stared at her, but his eyes were gentler.

"Would it have been such trouble to come to the door and find out?" he asked. And she was put into confusion, both by his glance and by the fact that he had never before, in all the years, made any protest against her, even a gentle protest like this one.

"Every step counts," she said doggedly.

She persisted in hanging back in the sheltering darkness of former habits. But when she looked at him she saw with a start that he had already flashed out far into the glade. His eyes shone. And in spite of the way the fits of coughing had stooped his shoulders of late, his head was high.

"Every minute counts, too," he said. And this time he put out his hand and took hers, and she let it remain with him, and further than that, looking at him and feeling her hand in his, she ventured a fearful step forward with him into the brightness.

"Are you not going to work?" she said.

He looked at her steadily.

"You've always looked forward to the day I'd have to stay at home, haven't you?" he asked.

So he was going to stay at home! Without further hesitation she rushed into the light.

"You're not going?" she cried. "You've got sense at last!" She drew back for an instant with a vain regret. "If only you'd given it up long ago, as I asked you," but her joy was too headlong to be impeded. Her heart exulted even as she spoke. "You were killing yourself down there! And for what? As I often told you, I get more for one room than you earn in a week." She paused. "At least I would if I had the right kind of people in the house, as I could if the rooms had a bit of decent paper on the walls and a few sticks of furniture in them." She sprang to her feet. "I'll go up and look at the front room this minute and see the condition of the walls. Even a dab of distemper would work wonders with it. And we could give the woodwork a coat of white paint. Better-class people like white paint. They see the worth of keeping it clean. I'd never have put on that ugly mahogany paint if it wasn't for the poor type of people I had to take. I knew they weren't likely to go to the trouble of keeping white paint clean." She was silent for a minute, and her mind was busy making calculations. "New curtains wouldn't cost much," she said. "And we could get a few pieces of furniture out of the money in the tin box." She ran over to the dresser and took it down, but instead of opening it herself, as she always did, she thrust it into his hands. "How much is in it?" she cried, taking him into partnership, her mind leaping away to make other plans. "If we got thirty shillings for the front room," she said, "I'd give notice to quit to the woman in the middle room and we'd do it up, too." She looked at him as she spoke, but unseeingly. "We might be able to do it ourselves, indeed, and then it would only cost us the price of the paint. I often thought that if I had help I'd never need to get a paperhanger; I could do it as good myself; so now, with you at home, to help me, I might manage to do it." She had been talking in a headlong fashion, but suddenly she felt weak from the fever of her excitement. She went over and sat down on a chair at the other side of the table, opposite the man. As she did so her eyes rested on him with more attention as he sat with the tin box in his hands. The tin box was unopened.

"You didn't open the box?" she said, in some surprise, but rushing ahead to interpret his motives for herself without waiting for a reply. "I know it's hard to think of spending the money," she said, "but we can look on it as an investment." She sighed happily. "That box won't hold all the money I'll make now that you're going to stay at home and be a help instead of a hindrance."

To all that she said, however, the man opposite made no reply, and when he said nothing at this last remark, which she felt to be very gracious and generous, she looked sharply at him. To her astonishment there were large tears glistening in his eyes, and a heavy tear was making its way slowly down his coarse cheek, running irregularly between the stubbles of his unshaven face.

"What's the matter with you?" she cried, starting up anxiously.

"I don't feel well!" he said weakly.

"Oh, is that all?" She leaned back with some relief. "I wouldn't mind that. A few days at home will set you up again as good as ever."

But the heavy tears continued to roll down his face.

"I'll be more of a hindrance than ever now!" he said, and then when he conquered a fit of coughing he looked across at her. "How could I be any help papering the rooms?" he said passionately. "How could I help you at anything? I'm fit for nothing now."

The woman pressed her lips together. So this was the way he was going to act. She stood up and glared across at him, about to give him a cutting answer, but what she saw in his face silenced her. He looked bad. There was no mistake about it. But still, her first impulse was one of resentment. To think that he might die now just at the moment of her triumph! But a minute later her heart began to ache and she recollected that when this wretched creature died, there died also the young man with the fair hair who used to sit on the wall reading poetry, and furthermore there died also the fine man in the new suit, with a gold tiepin in his cravat and a carnation in his buttonhole that she counted on having the lodgers see sitting on a bench outside the house. She ran over to him impulsively.

"Don't talk nonsense," she said. "You had yourself worn out, but now things will be different." As she spoke she brightened, and patting him on the shoulder she tried to brighten him up too. "Why don't you change your clothes," she said, "and go out and sit in the sun? I'll make a cup of hot soup for you." She darted over to the cupboard to get a saucepan.

The man did not stir.

"Why don't you do as I say?" she said. "This kitchen is no place to sit."

For the first time in years she seemed to see its filth and squalor, and leaving down the saucepan she ran about straightening the chairs, snatching up the rags and rubbish that littered them, and finally taking up a twig she began to sweep an accumulation of dirt and crumbs into the corner under the sink. This furious activity absorbed her entirely for a few minutes. Then she turned around.

"You couldn't find a healthier spot in the world than that bench outside the house. I can't understand why you don't go out and sit there."

"Let me sit where I am for a while," said the man wearily.

She laid down the sweeping brush, only half convinced that he was unwilling to comply with her. Then she gave in to him.

"Well, you can sit out there tomorrow," she said. "And it will give me time to have your suit aired and pressed. But you'd better not sit here. I'll help you into your room." She went to catch him by the arm. But he shrank from being touched.

"I'd like to stay where I am for a while," he said pathetically, and then he got such an attack of coughing there was nothing to do but to go back to what she had been doing until he got over it. The coughing sounded bad. It distressed her to hear it. He seemed worse, all right.

When he stopped coughing he tried to speak but she couldn't hear what he was saying. She went over to him and bent down her ear to him.

"I like to be here where I can watch you," he said.

She was disconcerted. She laughed uneasily.

"Oh, go on out of that!" she said roughly, but it was a roughness he knew of old, a roughness of embarrassment, a righteous unwillingness to give in to the pleasurable vanity roused by his words. "I'll have a drop of soup for you in a few minutes," she said. "Wait till you see! You'll be a new man after it."

It took some time to make the soup, because in her excitement she tried to do several things at the one time, only thinking to run over and stir the soup when it boiled over and there was a smell of burning. She dragged the ragged net curtains from the window and threw them into a basin of water. She snatched down the mirror that was over the sink and began to wipe off the fly-blows that covered it like a pock. And when the soup was ready at last he could only swallow a few mouthfuls.

"What harm!" she cried. "It will be all the thicker for leaving it on the fire. You can have it later on."

Later on, however, he was less inclined for it than before, and although she patiently held the spoon to his mouth and coaxed him to take more of the six or seven spoonfuls that she put to his lips, he swallowed only a few drops, for the rest ran down on his chin and slobbered his clothes.

At last he protested against the effort of trying to take it.

She looked at the clock.

"But you must eat something," she said. "You've been sitting there all day without a morsel inside your lips!" A frown of worry gathered on her forehead. "What will I do with you?" she asked, but more to herself than to him, for although he kept his eyes fixed on her, watching all her movements, she was beginning to have a curious feeling of being alone. There was certainly no use in expecting any cooperation from him. She wished the girls were home. The day had flown and yet it would be a long time still till they got back from work. Nonny would soon be back from school, but what use was Nonny? She'd be peevish and tired and crying for her dinner.

There was a sound in the passage. That was probably Nonny now and nothing ready for her to eat. Even the soup was boiled away. Well! she would have to wait. Ella went out and banged the kitchen door shut.

It was not Nonny, however, but merely a door that slammed in a draft. The child did not come in for ten minutes afterward.

The instant she opened the hall door, however, Nonny was aware that some change had come over the house, although she did not know what it was. There was the same dark hallway, and the same damp smell came out from the walls. There was the same cold, empty sound as she ran down the bare cement passage. Yet something had lightened and brightened in the atmosphere. She pushed open the door of the kitchen, but as she did so her mother shot out a hand and pushed her back into the passageway.

"Go easy!" cried the mother crossly. "Your father is asleep. What's the meaning of making such a noise? Can't you walk gently? Have you no respect for people's nerves?"

The child stopped up in astonishment. This was something new! Her mother had never before greeted her in this manner. Then recalling that her mother had said something about her father, her face took a scared look.

"Where is he?" she asked.

"He's in the kitchen," the mother said. "You can go in if you go quietly."

The child went in fearfully on tiptoe, not knowing what to expect, but her father was still sitting where he sat that morning, only now his feet were lifted on to a stool and there was a blanket thrown over them. There was also a pillow behind his back.

She looked expectantly at him, but when she saw that he was not going to speak to her she stared at him curiously. The woman gave her a push at last, and after that she stole about the kitchen getting herself some bread and butter. When she had cut and buttered two or three uncouth and crooked slices of bread, she crept out again on tiptoe to eat them in the yard. She had not been sent out to the yard, but all the time she had been in the kitchen she had felt her mother watching her, and this had made her nervous and uncomfortable, and she had knocked into the chairs and clattered the cups on the dresser, and once she had stumbled. Each time she made a noise she felt her mother turn and glare at her although she did not dare look up at her. It would have choked her to eat the bread in the kitchen. It was better out in the yard. She sat down on an upturned box and began to chew the bread and ponder on the change that had come over her mother. It used to be her father that was ordered about and glared at, and it used to be her the mother petted. She sat chewing the bread without relish in the gathering dark in the yard.

The first thing the older girls noticed when they came into the house was the smell of soap and disinfectant, and they saw at once that the passage had been swept. Then, before they went into the kitchen they saw Nonny sitting disconsolately on a box in the yard.

They went to the door of the yard to talk to her and tease her, but when they saw the way the yard had been cleaned up and tidied, they forgot Nonny. What was the meaning of this? They exchanged glances with each other, arching their eyebrows.

Then they smelled the soup. This too was unusual. And all these unusual things prepared them in some way for a change, so that unlike Nonny, when they went into the kitchen they went quietly, and were hardly surprised at all to see their father wrapped up in blankets in the corner.

As if they were in a strange house, the two girls politely refrained from looking around at the freshly scrubbed dresser and the clean curtains, but they were aware of every change, and under their feet they missed the grit and dirt that was always on the floor, and when they went to sit down they were astonished to find the chairs were free of their usual clutter of rubbish.

There was no sign of their supper, however, and their mother, who was always in a fuss at this time getting something hot for them after their day's work, turned around to them with an anxious face and ignored all mention of food.

"How do you think he is looking?" she asked earnestly, and although they had not been told that he was any worse than usual, they felt instantly that he must be bad, from their mother's solicitude for him. And it shocked them to hear her speaking of him to his face as if he neither heeded nor heard.

"He didn't go to work today," said Ella, speaking again without waiting for an answer from them. Then she questioned them anxiously once more. "How do you think he looks?"

Mary drew back, uneasy at talking about him in his presence.

"Don't mind him!" said Ella. "He won't hear you. He's sleepy. He's been like that all afternoon."

Dolly was less sensitive. She stared into the corner.

"He looks bad," she said bluntly. But this did not satisfy Ella.

"Bad!" she said, scathingly. "He's very bad!"

Dolly looked at her mother. She was tired and hungry and her mother exasperated her.

"He's no worse than he has been for months past," she said viciously.

For a moment Ella pondered the words only and her face clouded with worry as she looked distractedly at Robert, then as she became conscious of the mood in which her daughter had spoken her face darkened still more.

"If that's the case," she said, "you might have spoken sooner! You might have drawn my attention to him."

The rebuke was hurled at Dolly, but the bitter glance that went with it included Mary in its wide, reckless orbit. The two girls looked at each other again. Like Nonny they had never before been in disfavor with their mother, but unlike Nonny, they were not misled into a false elation at the change in their mother's attitude to their father. They knew that the habits and instincts of acerbity were unlikely to be stifled at will after twenty years, and that at best they could be but diverted from one direction to another.

They felt that it was they, now, and not their father who stood in the path of their mother's wrath.

Ella herself, however, was unconscious of all except the needs of the invalid. After her few words with Dolly she looked at him critically, but after a few minutes she was able to disregard her daughter's words again and blind herself to his poor appearance.

"He'll be all right in a few days," she said defiantly, and she went over to him and repeated the same words, but in an utterly different tone of voice, half coaxing, half bullying.

"You'll be all right in a couple of days," she said, and she tucked the blanket tighter around him and gave the pillow behind him a jerk.

He said nothing. And his eyes were shut. It gave her a shiver to have him sit so patient and quiet. She caught up the blanket and gave it another and unnecessary shake, and she gave the pillow another and more violent jerk.

He opened his eyes.

All of a sudden looking at his sunken cheeks and his lusterless eyes, she felt that no assurance from herself or from the children would be of any use. He must assure her himself. For the third time she repeated the words, but this time they were in the form of a question.

"You'll be all right in a couple of days, won't you?" she said, and although she stood over him with her arms on her hips in a truculent attitude that seemed to defy him to give her any answer but the one she wanted, into her voice there had crept a whining tone that was new to her.

The man looked up. And for a moment there was a sign of struggle in his face as he tried to summon up enough duplicity for a cheerful answer, but he was already too far gone in weakness to do any more than tell the truth. The truth was the easiest. He had no further energy for subterfuge.

"I don't know," he said. "I feel bad."

"Oh, nonsense," she said impatiently, but she wasn't convinced by her exclamation. She was more convinced by the face of the man in front of her. He was bad. She could see that now. What would she do? She looked around her helplessly for a moment, but the only resort she could find were words; the old ready words that she had used a hundred times. "You'll be as well as ever you were in a few weeks," she said. "And you'll have the best of times. You can lie in bed till the day is well aired, and get up then and put on your best clothes, and go out and sit on the bench in front of the house, and be called in to your meals, with plenty of time to eat them slowly and chew your food. Oh, you'll be all right. Wait till you see. That bench in the front of the house gets all the sun. I don't know how it is, but the sun shines on it from one end of the day to the other. I often wonder that the lodgers don't make more use of it. But, as a matter of fact—" and here she brightened considerably "—as a matter of fact I'm just as well pleased they never got into the habit of sitting on it, because of course you wouldn't want to make free with them when you're sitting out there yourself."

And in the bright picture she drew of him, sitting proud and aloof on the bench in front of the house, she forgot the dismal picture he presented huddled in the chair, with his dull eyes fixed on her. "You'll be all right in a couple of days," she said. "After all, you have something to look forward to now. It would be a different matter if you were going back to that old Library! Yes! You have something to look forward to now, Robert!"

But the truth that had stolen into the small citadel of Robert's soul, taking advantage of the weakness of his body, had taken possession of it now for the rest of its earthly sojourn.

"It's not much to look forward to, Ella," he said, and he looked up at her. "I thought I'd come to a better end than this! I thought we'd make more of our lives than this!" and in spite of the weakness that hung like lead on his arms he struggled to put out a hand from under the coverings and make a gesture to include the house.

"What do you mean?" She was frightened.

"It's not much to live for!" said Robert. "The thought of spending the end of your days sitting in front of a lodginghouse. Do you remember what we planned? Do you remember how we wanted to be together always, just you and I, without anyone else? Do you remember the way we used to be so mad when your young sister, Daisy, hung on to us, and wanted to come for a walk with us, and we couldn't get rid of her? And now," his voice weakened, and he had to stop to draw a long breath, "now look at the way things turned out! Look what happened!" He made a disparaging gesture. "That's what we planned," he said. "And look what happened!"

"What happened?" she asked in a whisper. She truly did not know.

He seemed to get weaker every minute, but with a great effort he concentrated his forces for an answer, but he could only manage at first to give utterance to it in fragments.

"Strangers," he said, and he drew a long breath. "Strangers everywhere." He began to cough. She wanted to hear what he had to say, although it was so painful to watch him she was ready to forego her curiosity, but when she tried to interrupt him rather than see him laboring to talk, he put up his hand to make her listen to him. "We wanted to be together; we wanted to be alone. That's why we left home. And now we are finishing our days in the middle of strangers. This house is full of strangers; strangers; strangers. Strangers in every room in the house. I'm so ashamed! To think we should come to this end."

His voice was stronger toward the end of what he was saying, but he stopped speaking suddenly and sat silent again, and this time it seemed that it was words that had failed him, and not his voice.

In the silence the two girls who after the first few minutes of curiosity had begun, like Nonny, to look around and prepare some sort of food for themselves, began now to whisper to each other. Dolly took up the father's words.

"I told you," she said, turning to Mary. "I often said it was degrading to keep lodgers. I am always afraid they'll find out at the factory that we keep a lodginghouse. They'd look down on me so much!"

But before she had finished speaking the man in the corner caught the sound of the voice. He raised his head and strained to lift himself higher in the chair, but it seemed that he could not see well because he suddenly broke out again in a passionate complaint, and his anger gave a spasm of strength to his voice.

"Even here we are not alone," he cried. "I hear people talking over there in the far corner. Who are they? Why must there be strangers everywhere? Why must they be in here?"

The girls were startled.

"He's delirious," said Dolly, under her breath. "He doesn't know who we are!" and she turned around as if she would go over to him. But Mary suddenly caught her by the sleeve and held her back.

"He knows who we are all right," she said, "but he doesn't want us here." But she herself made no move to go out either, for to stay where she was seemed less conspicuous, and Dolly, who hardly comprehended her, just stood where she was also, staring at the sick man, a pot of tea in one hand and a cup in the other. But Nonny who, under cover of the older girls, had stolen back into the kitchen, and who had been listening to the last few words that had passed between her sisters, caught at their skirts in fright, unable to understand what was wrong. She had known all day that something was wrong and had hoped to find out when the other girls came home, but although she had caught every word that was uttered, the words themselves were incomprehensible to her.

"Who doesn't want us?" she cried, dragging urgently at Mary's skirt and then at Dolly's, and getting no satisfaction from them, she was just beginning to cry when suddenly their mother created a diversion. For Ella had suddenly flung herself on her knees in front of the sick man.

"Why didn't you tell me you felt like that?" she cried, in a bitter reproach. "Why didn't you tell me? I thought you wanted us to make money. You used to say we'd make our fortune in the city. I only tried to help." She threw up her hands. "Why didn't you tell me how you felt!" she cried again, and then she put her hand to her forehead distractedly. She was bewildered. They had wanted to make money, hadn't they? That was why they had come to the city, wasn't it? She tried to recall the long talks they used to have in the days before they ran away from home. But it was all so long ago. She couldn't remember. Yet surely they had been determined to make money. Wasn't that what all normal people wanted to do—to make money, and rise in the world?

But he was muttering something different.

"The two of us," he said. "Just the two of us; that's what we wanted; to go away together, and not have your mother all the time nagging at us!" His face had brightened somewhat as he spoke of the long-gone days when they had made the plans that never fruited, and it was almost as if it was of the future he spoke and not of the past. "The two of us," he said, "the two of us." And he began to smile. But suddenly his glance got dark again and he tried to see across the room into the corner where the girls were whispering together. "And now," he cried with a loud bitter voice, "now I'm going to die in a house full of strangers."

The girls looked at each other again. Then Dolly plucked her mother by the sleeve.

"Tell him it's only us," she said.

But her mother swung around.

"Don't bother me," she said. "I'll tell him nothing. What are you doing in here anyway? Get out of the room. Can't you see you're irritating him?"

In their surprise the girls made no protest but moved to the door, and as they went they heard their mother speaking to their father again, her voice so excited and strained that her words were hardly coherent.

"Why didn't you tell me, Robert?" she cried. "I didn't know. But we can go away now. We'll get a cottage. We'll go away, and get a little cottage, and be together, Robert! Robert!" She raised her voice as if she would force him to hear her. "Do you hear me?" she cried. "We'll get out of this place. We'll get a cottage, away out in the country, just the two of us; like you wanted." She sprang up and rushed across the kitchen. "There was a cottage advertised in the paper yesterday," she said, and they could hear her searching for the paper. Then they heard her run back to him. "I can't find the paper now," she cried, "but it's somewhere about the place; I'll look it up. That cottage might be the very thing for us. Three rooms; it said in the paper; three rooms, and a garden at the back. Think of it, Robert! You'd like that, wouldn't you?" She was suddenly triumphant again, a person who could not be bested. For a moment things had looked dark; for a moment it had looked as if something had gone wrong with her plans. But now everything would be all right again.

Outside in the passage Dolly and Mary were listening.

"Did you hear that?" said Dolly. "The two of them! And what about us?" Two angry spots of red burned in her cheeks. But Mary looked pale.

"I think Father is delirious," she said. "I think he's forgotten about us." Her eyes opened wide. "I think he doesn't remember we were ever born!"

Dolly only grew more annoyed.

"What about Mother?" she demanded. "She knows we were born! She's not delirious. What does she mean talking about a cottage in the country with three rooms?"

All of a sudden Nonny began to whimper.

"Now see what you've done," said Mary to Dolly. "Hush, Nonny. It's nothing to worry about. Mother and Father are only planning a holiday."

But it was their mother alone who was making plans. She dashed out into the hall just then.

"Where is yesterday's paper?" she cried, angry and querulous, as if one of them had deliberately withheld it from her. She went over to the miscellaneous pile of things that she had gathered together in armfuls and flung in a corner of the hallway, but she was too distracted to know what she was doing. Mary went over to help her and soon found the paper. When she handed it to her mother Ella snatched it up and eagerly searched out a small paragraph in the advertisement columns. Then she ran back to the kitchen with it.

"Look at that," she cried, and pressed it into Robert's hands, but she was too impatient to wait for the tired eyes to focus on it and she caught it up again to read it for him. "I'll read it for you," she cried. "Listen!" And when she had read it she exclaimed on every point of it. "Three rooms!" she cried. "A garden! Think of that, Robert. Just what we want. Just suitable for two people. Just what you wanted: just the two of us."

In the hallway Dolly put an arm around Nonny. She felt suddenly sad, but it was not sadness for herself; it was for Mary and Nonny. After all, she would be getting married soon. She looked down at Nonny. She might be able to have Nonny to live with her. But Mary? What would become of Mary? But Mary was smiling.

Mary was smiling. That was true. Although it was a sad, weak smile, Mary was smiling. Just then they heard their father trying to say something, and their mother evidently could not hear what it was because she came to the door and called them.

"What is he trying to say?" she asked, and she beckoned them to come back into the room.

They listened. Their father spoke again. Dolly couldn't catch what he said, but Mary bent close to him.

"It's too late now," said Robert.

Mary raised her sad eyes. "He said it's too late now, Mother," she said.

"Too late? What does he mean?" Ella stared at Mary. Was she to be defeated after all? She wanted to contradict him, but she had no longer the strength to argue. All she could do was try to make use of Mary for her own purposes. "Tell him he'll be all right in a couple of days," she said. "Tell him the country air will cure him. Tell him about this—" and she pointed to the paper in her hand. "Tell him about the cottage I saw advertised here."

But when Mary bent again to her father he put out his hand, and with a violence unexpected from one in his weak condition he gave her a push and knocked her back against the table.

"Strangers," he said bitterly. "Strangers everywhere."

Mary turned to her mother.

"I think he's delirious, Mother," she said, but even as she spoke she was struck by the expression in her father's eyes as compared with that in her mother's face. Her mother was the one who looked distracted, whereas the father in spite of his rambling talk was looking at her with a fierce and keen expression that seemed to be the result of a conscious antagonism. But such a groundless antagonism was in itself unnatural. "You ought to get the doctor for him, Mother," she said.

Ella, however, was not listening.

"Her mind is wandering too," said Dolly impatiently. "Just listen to her!"

For Ella was sitting down with the paper in her hands, staring at the advertisement for the cottage.

"I'm sure there wouldn't be many people looking for that cottage," she said. "I'm sure they couldn't ask a high rent for it in the heart of the country. I'm sure we could get it." She looked dazed.

"What will we do?" said Mary despairingly.

The man in the corner was muttering louder and louder, and shouting out against the strangers that he seemed now to imagine all around him. He even made efforts to struggle to his feet in order to get at them and put them out of the house.

"We'll have to do something," said Mary, wringing her hands, and she caught her mother by the arm. "Mother! Mother! Listen to me! We ought to get the doctor for Father."

The mother shook off Mary's hand.

"Get me a scissors," she said. "I'll cut this piece out of the paper so that it won't get lost. Someone might tear up the paper on me."

Mary appealed to Dolly.

"Can you make her listen to you?" she said.

Dolly went over and took the paper out of her mother's hands.

"We can talk about the cottage later on," she said, "but you ought to get the doctor for him now."

But it was Nonny who brought things to a head. She was sorely perplexed; the strain had told on her. Sisters were only sisters, but what she wanted was a father or a mother. And now there was this strange talk about her parents going away. Where were they going? And what was to become of her? She looked from one of her parents to the other. Which of them would tell her? The distraught condition of her mother and the bright, alive look in the father's eyes determined her to turn to him, and running over she buried her golden head in the blankets about his knees. Instantly there was tension in the room. Mary started as if to hold her back but she was too late. She could only stare. Robert stopped muttering. It seemed for a minute that he knew the child, so concentratedly did he stare at her, but after a moment they saw it was the concentration of unutterable anger. Gathering up unbelievable strength he put out his thin bony hands and gave the child a violent push backward.

"Who is this child?" he cried. "Take her away. Am I never to have any peace?" And then raising his voice he began to shout. "Strangers!" he cried. "Strangers! Strangers!"

There was dead silence for a moment, and then Nonny began to scream. Opening her mouth to show her small, unformed teeth she screamed and screamed. Ella came to her senses.

"Come here, Nonny," she cried, and she caught the child to her breast. "He doesn't know you, darling," she said appeasingly, and her own tears began to flow down her face.

"We'll have to take matters into our own hands," said Dolly. "Where will I go? What doctor will I get?"

But there was no need to take things into their own hands. Nonny's tears had roused Ella. Her own tears had been the beginning of her capitulation to the force of events. She got to her feet. She was more urgent than any of them now.

"We should have got the doctor hours ago," she said, and she was blaming everyone. "I'll go for the doctor myself," she said. "He wouldn't come quick enough if one of you went for him. But I'll make him come." And snatching her coat she ran toward the door. "I won't get the dispensary doctor," she said. "Robert wouldn't like that. I'll get a private doctor." She halted at the door. "Which is the best doctor to get?" she cried, and then she ran back into the room and threw herself down on her knees again. "I'll get you the best doctor in the city," she said, shaking the man to make him hear. "He'll have you all right inside an hour!"

Mary was strained to breaking point.

"Get some doctor anyway, quick," she said, "or it will be too late."

When the doctor came he said that Robert would have to be taken to hospital. He told the girls and they were hardly surprised, but they dreaded to tell their mother. Yet Ella, when she heard it, took it fairly well and began at once to busy herself with preparations for his removal.

"Get the best ambulance you can get, Doctor," she said, and she kept impressing this injunction on him all the way down the hall as he took his leave.

And when the ambulance came it was she who saw to everything, and made the ambulance men promise not to jolt the stretcher, and even went out into the street with them and sent away the crowd of children that had collected to gape at the spectacle. She did everything, and she would have ridden to the hospital in the ambulance but the regulations forbad such a thing.

"No one is allowed to ride in the ambulance, ma'am," said the stretcher-bearers as they prepared to take their departure.

She had to give in to them of course, but she ran to the front and spoke to the driver.

"Drive carefully," she cried to him, and then, just as they moved away, she remembered something else and she ran along the path beside the moving vehicle. "Take care would you let him be put in a public ward!" she cried. "I want him put in a private room."

And as the attendants did not appear to hear her she turned frantically to her daughters.

"Hurry, girls!" she cried. "You can go quicker than me. Go down to the hospital and be sure he's put into a private ward. And tell the nurses he's to get every attention. Tell them that. Let them know we can pay for it all. Let them know he has people that care about him. That counts for a lot with those nurses." They were standing out in the street, and the girls were ready to go, but she called them back. "Wait a minute," she said. "You'll need money. I want you to give the janitor a tip too. It will let him see that Robert is a person of some importance. He'll be able to let us in and out, you know, on the sly, outside the regular visiting hours." She rummaged in the pocket of her skirt and pulled out several notes and some small coins. "Have you enough, do you think?" she cried, as she pressed the money into their hands. They took the money and turned away, and as they went they heard her calling after them urging them to hurry. Yet they had not reached the end of the street when they heard her running after them. "Come back a minute," she cried, and she was panting from lack of breath. "I forgot to tell you— Find out if there's anything he wants, and if there is get it for him."

"Aren't you going to come to the hospital yourself, Mother?" asked Mary.

"I am of course," said Ella, "but I want to go down to the shops and get him a few things. I'll bring them with me. His nightshirt is a show. I want to get him a new one. I wouldn't want him to be ashamed in front of the nurses. And I'll get him some oranges. Oranges are a great thing to have beside your bed when you're sick."

Robert however was a bit far gone for oranges. And as Dolly remarked to Mary, it didn't make much difference to him whether he was in a private ward or not, although their mother, when she arrived, was most insistent that he be changed. For Robert had been put into a temporary ward until a bed could be vacated in one of the wards proper, and although it was a long airy passage with only another occupant in a bed at the far end, Ella kept after the authorities all next day until he was moved into a proper ward on the first floor.

The girls were embarrassed at the fuss their mother made.

"They'll move him when they get a chance, Mother," said Mary, "and this place is nice and bright." She was thinking of the damp room at the back of the kitchen where he had slept for the last twenty years.

Dolly protested also, and she tried to kill two birds with the one stone, and make her mother see how bad their father was.

"I don't see what it matters where he is at the moment," she said. "I don't think he knows where he is at all. He doesn't take any notice of anything."

"It does matter," said Ella. "We must let the nurses see that we are particular about him." She looked down at the lifeless figure stretched on the spare hospital bed. "He's quiet because he's resting," she said. "That's what he needs; rest. Don't disturb him." She looked around. "I hope there won't be noise here," she said, and the girls were embarrassed again because there was only one other patient in the ward. This patient was a brawny young man, whose leg was tied up in some kind of splint, and whose main object was to get the nurses to sit on the side of his bed and talk to him. He looked good-natured and considerate and they hoped he would not think their mother's remarks were a reflection on him. They whispered together and then Mary drew their mother's attention to him, but Ella, when she turned to look at him, saw only the table beside his bed, for on it there was a plate with a large bunch of purple grapes.

"Grapes!" said Ella. "I should have got Robert some grapes. I heard one time that a person can swallow the pulp of a grape when nothing else will stay in his stomach." She opened her bag and pulled out a five-shilling piece. "There's a shop around the corner," she said. "I saw it when I was coming in here, and they had lovely fruit in the window. Run out and see if you can get some grapes." She looked back at the other bed and her eye fell on a pile of papers and magazines. "Get him some papers too," she said. "He used to like reading the paper."

Mary hesitated. She did not take the coin.

"I have the money you gave me yesterday," she said evasively.

But Dolly spoke out.

"What's the use of spending money foolishly?" she said. "He's too far gone to eat anything. And it's only nonsense to think of him reading, when he doesn't even know where he is!"

"Mind your own business," said her mother sharply. "You ought to be ashamed of yourself," she said, "to talk of saving money at a time like this." She raised her voice and bent over the man in the bed. "Wouldn't I get him anything in the whole world that he wanted?" she cried. "Wouldn't I? Wouldn't I?"

He was moved next day to a ward on the top landing. Ella was more or less satisfied.

"It shows they think something of him," she said, and she looked around her with satisfaction. "You can see this is a good ward by the class of patients in it."

There were five other beds in the ward. In one there was a young man who was still under the influence of an anesthetic. In another there was a small boy with a bad leg. The third bed was occupied by an elderly man who was allowed to get up and move about the ward in his dressing gown.

Ella looked at all these patients and noted the crowded condition of the small enamel tables beside their beds and everything she saw with these other patients she wanted to get for Robert.

"I must get him some apples," she cried, as she saw the old man painstakingly peeling a large red apple while he sat on his bed with his legs dangling.

And when she saw some storybooks on the young boy's table she went home and rooted out two or three mildewed volumes of poetry in old-fashioned bindings with gilt edges that had somehow been saved from the ragman's bag and she brought them up to the hospital.

"When he starts to come round to his senses," she said, "he'll be glad to see them."

Dolly nudged Mary.

"It's a good job there's a screen around the bed at the end so she can't see what's behind it because if she brings in any more stuff to Father it will have to be put under the bed."

She laughed, but Mary could not laugh. She looked down the ward.

"I wonder what's the matter with that patient?" she said. "He must be dying." For the bed at the end of the ward had a large screen around it, and nothing could be seen of the patient, although at visiting hours a thin nervous woman in black came up the ward and noiselessly passed behind it to take up a position of vigilance at the bedside of the patient. Through the joining of the screen this thin black figure could be seen sitting silent and tight-lipped, her fingers ceaselessly moving as she passed the beads of a worn rosary through them with the dexterous movements of a card player slickly dealing out the cards. The woman never seemed to bring anything to the patient behind the screen.

"He's too ill to appreciate anything, I suppose," said Mary.

"She has more sense than Mother," said Dolly. "I suppose she's his wife."

The woman was at that moment passing down the ward, unsmiling and walking noiselessly with her eyes to the ground. The two girls looked after her curiously, but they were recalled to their surroundings by Ella.

"Calf's-foot jelly!" she said in a loud voice, speaking out of a deep reverie. "There's nothing so good for a sick person. I'll get him a jar of calf's-foot jelly."

"For goodness' sake, Mother, don't bring anything else for a while," said Mary. "Wait till he's able to enjoy things."

Dolly nudged her.

"Don't be giving her false hope," she said. "He'll never enjoy anything again." And she looked at the man on the bed, the counterpane motionless under his inert body, and she looked at the littered table beside the bed. "Those grapes will get rotten," she said. "He'll never eat them!"

As a matter of fact after a day or two the grapes began to lose their bloom and the girls ate one or two of the oranges. The magazines began to get crumpled and used-looking and marked with wet rings from the glasses and medicine bottles that the nurses left down on them. As for the poetry books, the nurses put them into the locker under the table because they were only cluttering up the small space of the cubicle.

But still Ella brought in paper bags of fruit and biscuits and sweets. And all the time Robert remained unconscious of her ministrations, or at least as indifferent to them as he had been to her promises of a bench outside the house and a carnation for his lapel. He just lay on his back looking up at the ceiling, and Ella's consolation in the fact that he sometimes nodded his head when she bent down and spoke to him was spoiled somewhat by the fact that he also did it once or twice when no one was speaking to him at all. He divided his time between long periods of complete unconsciousness and moments when he seemed to come to his senses again but only to carry on long incoherent conversations with himself in an undertone.

When he was three days in the hospital there was hardly room to sit beside him in the cubicle with all the things that Ella had brought with her to try and attract his attention.

"Look, Robert," she'd cry, bending over the bed and holding out something for him to see. But Robert could not see.

Finally the nurses got impatient with Ella and spoke irritably to the girls.

"I wish that woman would stop bringing in this rubbish," said one of them one day as she found difficulty in making a place for the thermometer on the top of the crowded table. She turned to Mary. "Can't you make your mother see that he is too far gone to take any notice of these things? What kind of woman is she? Why can't she behave like other visitors? Look around! No one in the ward is treated the way she treats this man. No wonder he doesn't come back to his senses. She has him bothered. She shouldn't be let in here at all!"

Mary was embarrassed. She resented the harshness of the nurse, but she could understand her irritation all the same. Afterward she spoke to Dolly.

"It's true for the nurse," said Dolly. "I wonder why she's behaving like this? I suppose it's remorse for the way she treated him in the past!"

But Mary looked away and the sad look came into her pale thin face and her dark eyes shone with tears.

"It's not as simple as that," she said. "Mother doesn't feel any remorse. If she did she would be more upset. She would probably break her heart. But I don't think she realizes how unkind she has always been to him. I don't think she is aware of the way their lives were wasted away in bitterness. I think it just seems like a bad spell they got into, and that it will pass away and they will come out again into a bright happy time like they used to have long ago. She doesn't blame herself at all. She thinks they were both the victims of misfortune."

Dolly looked at her sister. She didn't fully understand what she was saying. She was staring at her and thinking how different they were. She is more like Father, she thought. I'm more like Mother, and she felt irritated with Mary's subtlety and gentleness.

"I think it's us who were the victims of misfortune," she said. "We've heard nothing but quarreling and fighting since the day we were born." Suddenly she wanted to hurt Mary. "Thank goodness I'm going to be married soon and get away from it all." Then as she looked at the unconscious man in the bed a disturbing thought came into her mind. "If he dies now I suppose I'll have to put back my plans for another six months."

Mary's face quivered and she looked anxiously at the bed. "Mind would he hear you!" she said.

"Don't be silly," said Dolly. "You're as bad as Mother with her grapes and her nonsense. Can't anyone with an eye in their head see that he's unconscious?" but she looked at him anxiously, regretting her words. Then she went over and bent down. "Father!" she said, speaking firmly and authoritatively, and unlike her mother's cringing appeals to him. "Father! Can you hear me?" There was no stir of life on the white face. Dolly straightened up. "It's my belief that he won't come to his senses at all."

Mary nodded her head in agreement. "Poor Mother," she said. "I wish for her sake that he would come around enough to notice all she tried to do for him. If she could have the satisfaction of his seeing all the things she brought him." She brightened. "It would be nice for him too. I'd love him to know how she tried to make up to him for the past. He would think it was like the old days. All the years that have gone between would seem to have been only a bad spell and he would think they had come out of it again with a flash." She caught Dolly's arm eagerly. "Do you remember once in a while he used to talk about the time when they were young, and about how yellow her hair used to be, when she used to walk in the old meadow with him. I often think of that. It was sunny weather. I think that if he could only see all she's doing for him now it would be just like as if that sun had burst out again after a long time, and it wouldn't matter how dark it had been, or how long the darkness had lasted. Nothing would matter as long as that sun shone out again, bright, bright, bright, even for a few minutes." She moved nearer to the bed and she looked down at the man with a sudden dark passionate look in her eyes. "If only he'd open his eyes. If only he'd speak. How happy they both would be!"

But Dolly shrugged her shoulders. She was still suffering from irritation at the thought that she might have to postpone her own plans.

"I don't think they deserve to be happy!" she said bitterly.

"Don't say that," said Mary sharply.

"I will!" said Dolly. "I'm sick of it all." But just then the man in the bed murmured and seemed to be in pain. "Do you think he's suffering?" said Dolly, instantly regretting her bitterness again. "Poor Father! I suppose he deserves it."

"Deserves what?"

"Oh, all you were saying about the sunshine, and all that. I wish for his sake he could see the way she is trying to make up to him. If he did, I suppose he'd die happy." Soft tears came into her eyes, but her softness only lasted a moment. "I can't say our mother deserves much!" she said. "It would serve her right if he died without getting back his senses." She looked angrily at the plate of grapes. Several of the grapes were beginning to rot and around them a fly buzzed. "I'm going to throw them out!" she said and breaking off some of the rotted grapes she caught them up in the palm of her hand with an expression of disgust and looked around for somewhere to throw them. At the far end of the ward there was an open window, and walking across to it she threw them out into the street. "I don't care!" she said, in answer to the unspoken criticism on her sister's face. "I was sick of the sight of them."

When Ella arrived the first thing her eye fell on was the plate of grapes from which the large bunch had been cut. Her face, that was dirty and tired, straightened out, and a light came into her eyes. Her gaze flew to the man in the bed.

"He ate the grapes?" she cried, in delight.

The girls said nothing for a minute. Mary's lips moved. If Dolly were not there she would have told a lie and said he had eaten them, but she felt her sister's eyes upon her, defying her to do so, defying her to give in to such weakness.

Ella read Mary's face. Her eyes grew dull again. She took out a soiled handkerchief and began to wipe her face. There was sweat on it from the strain of climbing the stairs in a hurry.

"Don't cry now, Mother," said Dolly, crossly, and Ella looked meekly at her and put away the handkerchief. Her old obstinacy was broken down. She was getting uncertain about everything. She did everything she was told to do. Now she longed to talk about her disappointment over the grapes, but she was afraid of Dolly. But just then the Sister-in-Charge came into the ward. She was a small red-faced nun, with a kind face, secure and complacent in her own beliefs. Ella turned to her eagerly.

"I thought he ate the grapes," she said, and she sat down despond-ently on the bed, another paper bag of fruit unopened in her hands.

But the Sister had heard the complaints of the nurses. She dis-regarded Ella and spoke in an undertone to the girls.

"I think it would be better if she could be made to understand that he's too far gone for these things. It's only waste of money." She looked at their poor clothes, and Mary blushed. She knew what the nun was thinking.

"We don't mind the money!" she said, defensively.

Ella raised her head. She overheard the last sentence.

"That's right," she said, looking at Mary. "Spare no expense!" She turned and appealed to the Sister. "Is there nothing I can get for him?" she cried. Then she turned and threw herself across the coverlet of the bed. "My poor darling," she cried. "Robert! Robert! Is there nothing I can do for you? Why don't you know me? It's Ellie. It's your own Ellie! Ellie—who'd do anything in the world for you!" But the impassive face had no reply, and she turned back to the others. "If only there was something I could get for him; some-thing to ease him!"

The girls said nothing. They looked at the nun. The nun looked back at them as if she would like to have conferred with them alone, but since this was impractical then, she nodded her head to signify that she could not neglect the opportunity afforded at the moment. She put her arm around Ella.

"You want to do something for your husband, don't you? Well, there is only one thing you can do for him. You can pray that God will give him the grace of a happy death."

Ella drew back from the nun's protective embrace.

"He's not going to die!" she said fiercely.

The nun had entered into a familiar domain. She ignored the

nervous murmuring of the girls, and even a slight stir in the man in the bed.

"We must all die," she said, "sooner or later. It doesn't much matter when we go. But what does matter is the manner in which we die! Will we get the grace to die a happy death, or will we not? And if we are unable, like this poor man, to pray for that grace for ourselves, what more can those who love us do than pray that God will give us the grace we are unable to ask for with our own dying lips?"

The words fell easily from the untroubled lips of the nun, like a lesson long learned, and it echoed in the ears of those around with faint familiar notes heard a hundred times in sermons and mission lectures. Then the nun's voice grew warmer and more personal. She took Ella's hand and pressed it.

"Pray for him, my child," she said. "Pray that God will give him that inestimable thing that surpasses all else in the world—the grace to die a happy death. You can give him no greater thing."

Ella pulled away her hands to wipe her face. The tears had begun to flow again in her eyes. The nun looked around her quickly, and taking up a bunch of the decaying fruit she held it in front of Ella.

"Think of all the Masses that could have been said for the benefit of his soul with the money that was spent on this perishable matter!"

There was a pause. Had the nun's words succeeded? The girls held their breath. In the next bed the old man, who had been putting on his socks, sat still with one sock on and one sock off. The nun herself could be seen silently moving her lips in prayer while under the fold of her habit her fingers ran over the wooden beads of her rosary.

Then Ella suddenly stood up. She swung around to face the girls.

"How long is it since he was at the Sacraments?" she cried.

They all exchanged glances. She had not only comprehended the nun's words, but with her impetuous nature she had already outstripped them in thought. She had turned back to the nun.

"Do you think is there any danger that he would die without recovering consciousness?" she asked, but she didn't wait for an answer. "We should have sent for the priest for him," she said. "We should have done it long ago. Why didn't someone mention the

matter to me?" But when the girls made a stir as if they would do
something about it, she pushed them aside. "I'll attend to this,"
she said. "Some priests are more sympathetic than others. I don't
want him to be upset. Some priests have very poor manners! I'll
get a Franciscan; that's what I'll do. The Franciscans are all lovely
men." Her enthusiasm rose and swelled into a great flood, but suddenly she stopped talking and a look of fright came into her face.
She caught the nun's arm.

It was like the bench in the front of the house, the cottage with
the three rooms, the grapes, the oranges, the books of poetry with
the gold edges. She was ready to dart away at once to get them. But
she stopped, frightened, and caught at the nun by the arm.

"What will I do if he doesn't get back consciousness?" she asked.
"He won't be able to make his confession! He won't be able to talk!"
She was startled. She was terror-stricken.

"He can be anointed," said the sister gently. "He can be given
conditional absolution."

But this wasn't enough for Ella. For days they had been unable
to convince her that he was dying, but in her determination to procure him all the rites of the Church she was reconciled to the fact
that these rites might be the last that she could procure for him.

"Conditional absolution isn't enough," she cried. "He'll have to
come around to his senses." Suddenly she threw herself down on
the bed again. "Robert!" she called, "Robert!" Then she looked
around her wildly. "He'll have to come around!" she cried.
"Couldn't the doctor give him something to bring him around, just
for a few minutes; just for long enough to make an act of contrition?" Then she remembered something else. She straightened up.
"There should be a blessed crucifix placed in front of him so that
his eyes would fall on it if he opened them. Just to look at the
crucifix would save your soul, even if you weren't able to speak.
Did you know that? I always heard that said. Where will we get
one?" she asked, and she began to fumble in her pocket for money
to send the girls out to buy one. The nun put out a hand to calm
her, and detaching the long brass crucifix that dangled from her
belt she proffered it. But Ella pushed it aside. "It should be made of
wood," she said authoritatively, and drawing still further upon this
obscure fund of theological superstition she cried out again. "A

habit!" she cried. "He should have a habit ready. If he only got one arm out in the sleeve of it he'd be saved. The left arm, nearest the heart." She drew out a greasy purse and gave it to Mary. "Get a habit," she ordered, "and a crucifix. I'll stay here and try to bring him around to his senses." A fever of energy had made her cheeks glow, and from the depths of some repository of knowledge and superstition, long undisturbed, she brought up a score of suggestions.

"If we held a lighted candle in front of his eyes, he might open them!" she cried. "If we wet his lips he might speak! Do you think it would be any use to wipe over his face with a cloth wrung out in cold water?"

She was determined to bring him around, if only, as she said, over and over again, if only for one moment.

From that hour there was continual excitement. Ella was in and out of the hospital as often as she could gain admittance, and in the intervals she did not rest but sped all over the city, going from church to church lighting blessed candles and arranging to have Masses said for special intentions. The special intentions were all the same. They were all offered for Robert's return to consciousness. And when she was in the ward there was such confusion that they put a screen around Robert's bed, while the mother of the small boy in the opposite bed made so many complaints about the noise they had to move the boy to another ward.

"What will we do with her at all?" said the nun who had first put the idea of a happy death into her head. For Ella was inconsolable. "After all," said the nun at last, "you haven't such great cause to worry. Your husband led a good life. He was a good man. And he can be given conditional absolution. God is merciful, you know. But what would you do if you were that poor creature?" The nun nodded down toward the end of the ward where, behind the heavy screen, the woman in black was just discernible sitting alert and vigilant beside her husband's bed. "That poor woman has cause to worry," she said. "Her husband is unconscious too like yours, but how different his life has been!"

Ella was barely listening, but the girls looked curiously at the closed screen.

"An atheist!" said the nun in an undertone, and she made the sign of the cross over her breast as inconspicuously as possible, because the woman in black had raised her head and seemed to be looking in their direction. "She can't hear us," said the nun reassuringly as Mary's face reddened. "And even if she did, she wouldn't mind. She's a saint if ever there was one. She doesn't mind who knows her story. It will be a lesson to others. That's what she said to me. And so it will. There he is now, after his life of sin and blasphemy, stretched speechless without the power to utter one syllable in supplication for God's pardon!" The nun shook her head sadly. "That poor woman's life has been a trial to her from the day she married him, but she never lost her faith in God's goodness. She offered up all her sufferings to the Almighty. And she never ceased praying for his return to the Faith. Even now, she has not lost hope, and every hour that she spends by his bedside is occupied in silent prayer for him."

The girls felt uncomfortable at this point, fancying that there was an implied criticism of their mother in the nun's words.

"Is he unconscious too?" asked Dolly.

But the nun shook her head.

"Alas! Not all the time," she said. "How much better it would be if he were!"

Dolly did not understand.

"Whenever he comes to his senses," said the nun sadly, "it is only to utter curses and blasphemies. Fortunately the periods of consciousness are getting fewer. When he was first brought in here it was terrifying to listen to him. The night nurse would not stay on duty alone. She said it was as if there was an Evil Presence in the ward!" The nun shuddered. Then she looked at Ella. "It should console your mother," she said, "to hear about that man. What would she do if she was that man's wife?"

But Ella was not to be consoled by anything. She had set her heart on one thing, and she was determined that Robert would come to his senses.

"If we brought Nonny up to him!" she exclaimed when the girls were trying to make her listen to what the nun had told them about the other man. "He might hear Nonny. He might heed her where he wouldn't heed anyone else. A child's voice is very penetrating."

But Nonny was so timid she could hardly be persuaded to open her mouth, and when they urged her forward to the bedside, she hung back and clutched at Mary's skirt.

"Call him, Nonny!" ordered Ella. "Call him. He'll know your voice. He'll hear you! He'll come back to his senses when you call him. Go on. Call him."

Nonny opened her mouth but she could hardly be heard by those standing beside her. The mother gave her a jerk.

"Who could hear that?" she exclaimed irritably. "Where is your voice? Call him again. What are you afraid of, anyway? Raise your voice. Go on! Call him. Call him again."

But the child was nervous and overconscious and would only utter a few weak cries. Finally Ella sent her home in disgust.

"The priest!" she said. "When the priest comes he'll bring him back," she said. "The priests have wonderful power in their tongues. Wait till the priest comes."

The Franciscan Father, when he came, however, occupied himself more with Ella than with Robert.

"You must not give way to despair," he said. "You must trust in God. God's ways are strange. God's ways are not our ways." Then he became more practical. "There doesn't seem to be any immediate danger," he said, "or I would anoint him, but I'll look in later in the night, to see how he is getting along. At the least sign of danger I can assure you I will exercise my powers." He patted Ella on the shoulder reassuringly.

"You're not going, Father!" cried Ella. She was afraid to let him away. "He might take worse suddenly," she cried, glancing fearfully at Robert.

But the priest had other duties. He explained rapidly to the girls in a low voice.

"I have other sick calls to make," he said. "I must try to be where I am needed. I do not think I am needed here, just yet."

Afterward they all recalled his last words.

"God's ways are wonderful indeed," said the nun.

For just as the priest was bowing his head about to pass down the aisle between Robert's bed and the wall, there was a sudden sound of a chair being pushed back and a woman's voice rose in a sharp exclamation. A minute later the screen by Robert's bed was pushed aside and the woman in the black dress rushed into the cubicle.

For a moment it was as if they did not recognize her, in spite of the familiar black garb and the pale face and the tightly drawn knot of black hair, for instead of the tight-lipped, obstinate countenance that had seemed never to relax for a moment from the effort of outfacing the enemy, on her face, as she stood there, there was such an expression of triumph as amounted almost to beatitude. Then, with a rush, she spoke:

"My prayers have been heard!" she cried, and she began to clasp her hands together and even to laugh in an uncontrollable ecstasy of triumph.

In spite of what they had heard about the man in the other bed, the members of Robert's family could not immediately comprehend what had happened, but instantly the Sister and the nurse sprang up. They understood at once what had happened.

"God be praised," cried the nun, and she too clasped her hands and over her face also there came a look of rapturous happiness. The nurse too was all excitement and curiosity, and forgetting Robert, forgetting Ella, forgetting even the Franciscan, she pushed aside the screen and ran down the ward. The word flew around the hospital. Doors were opened and shut. Other nurses and sisters that Ella and her family had never seen came running into the ward.

Then the nun who had spoken to Ella rushed back and whispered a few words to the priest, who had stood uncertain and awkward during the confusion. He had heard nothing about the other patient. But when the nun whispered to him he was immediately animated and alert.

"Thank God I was here!" he said, and like the rest, forgetting Robert, forgetting Ella, forgetting even to push aside a chair over which he stumbled, he too rushed down to the other end of the ward from which at the same moment there came a long-drawn-out despairing cry.

It was not until they heard this anguished cry that Robert's people comprehended that the man behind the screen had repented his sins and wished to die in the peace of the Church.

At the thought of such a miracle, they, too, were impelled to move out into the center aisle of the ward, and blessing themselves they strove to catch a glimpse of the sinner from whose bed the screens had been hurriedly pushed aside to permit the passage of nurses and nuns going in and out on urgent errands with crucifixes and lighted candles.

The man who had lain prone for so many days had started wildly up from the pillows, and in spite of the hands that strove to hold him down, he was almost standing in the bed, as with the eyes rolling in his head and the sweat breaking from his forehead in beads, he called out for all to hear him.

"Mercy!" he cried, his voice terrifyingly clear and loud. "Mercy! Mercy! Have mercy on me, oh God, miserable sinner that I am! Mercy! Mercy!"

And so intense was the gaze of the wild eyes that were cast upward to the ceiling that it seemed as if the sinner was at that moment gazing into the Face of the Godhead on whose dazzling countenance he was unable to distinguish the attributes of mercy from those of divine wrath.

"I'm lost," he screamed at one moment. "I'm lost. A sinner. A miserable sinner; what hope is there for me?" And at the next moment throwing himself forward as upon the bosom of the Deity, he sought to claim the sinner's right to partake of the bountiful feast of love and pardon prepared for the prodigal sons of God. "Forgive me. I sinned but I repent. Forgive me. I take it all back; all I said against Thee; all I did. I take it back!"

His face was ravished with fear and anguish. And yet it seemed that in spite of the fixity of his gaze into the heavens, his vision of the terror and glory of the Godhead did not blind him to the fact that he still dwelt in his earthly habitation, for putting out his hands he clutched now at the woman in black, now at the nurses, beseeching and imploring now one and now the other to assure him that God would hear his voice, even at this late hour.

At one moment it seemed that he had hope and he mouthed a babble of badly remembered prayer.

"Lord save me, I perish. If I did but touch the hem of Thy garment, save me, I beseech Thee. In the name of the Father and the Son and the Holy Ghost. Who art in Heaven from all Eternity."

And on those occasions, frothing horribly about the corners of the mouth and dripping saliva from his hanging lower lip, he assumed that he was already forgiven and secure, and incoherent, maudlin words of thanks were lost in the pillows into which he sank back exhausted.

But those moments were rare. More often he was in despair, without faith in the efficacy of his last-minute cries upon God's pardon.

"There is no salvation for me," he screamed, clutching and tearing his hair. "I sinned against God and man. There is no mercy for such as me. A blasphemer— Hell is open to receive me!" And then, as if he saw the yawning abyss of damnation, he would start up wildly again in spite of the restraining arms of those around him. "Hell's fire! Hell's fire for all eternity. To burn in hell for all eternity. To burn! To burn!"

And to think that this was the man who had lain with the closed and impassive countenance, defiant of God, contemptuous of prayer, and determined until a few hours ago to torture his wife by his blasphemies.

"A priest!" the poor wretch screamed. "I want to see a priest!" And catching at his wife's hand he tried to drag himself erect. "Don't let me die without the priest," he implored. "For God's sake get me a priest!"

And so tortured was his mind that when the Franciscan made his way to the side of the bed he did not recognize his garb but tried to push him away. And even when he had been made to understand that the priest was there, even then his state of mind fluctuated, for although at one moment he clung to the priest, craving for forgiveness for his sins and even covering the priest's hands with kisses, at other moments, in spite of all that the priest could do, it seemed as if behind his back as he lifted his hands in prayer, the man could see some flickering shadow unseen to anyone else in the room, for on those occasions he could not listen to the priest and had even to be held down in the bed, so violently did he struggle and shake with passions of remorse and fear.

"Hell's fire for all eternity," he cried. "To writhe in agony for all time!"

In the other beds in the ward the patients were sitting up in excitement. All the ward was in a stir, except for Robert, who lay still behind his screen, which was slightly awry after the abrupt departure of the Sister and the nurse.

Suddenly the Sister who had gone hurriedly out of the ward a few moments previously came back carrying in her hand two tall black candlesticks in which burned long wax candles, the flames of which as she moved flowed backward so swiftly that the eye could hardly see the tenuous thread that connected wick with flame. When the Sister was halfway down the floor of the ward she stopped, and beckoning one of the nurses she pointed with her head at Robert's bed.

"Take that screen," she said. "We can get another one later for that patient."

And before Ella could protest the screen had been whisked away and a moment later, although Ella still stared in the direction of the penitent's bed, she could see nothing but the shadows of those behind the screen, chief amongst which was the shadow of the priest with a raised crucifix in his hands. Then the Sister appeared again around the corner of the screen. She came toward Ella, who was standing alone by Robert's bedside. "My daughters had to go," said Ella. "The little one was frightened and they had to take her home. It's too bad. I thought he might hear Nonny. She has a very penetrating voice." But the nun wasn't listening to Ella. Her thoughts were still occupied with the man at the other end of the ward.

"A miracle!" she exclaimed. "That's what it is; a miracle. God works in a mysterious way. How I hope that I may be shown the same mercy when my turn comes. Think of it! A man who lived a life of sin; an enemy of the Church; a blasphemer. Ah yes; it is true indeed; God loves the sinner."

The nun folded her arms in the form of a cross. Then suddenly she uncrossed them again and looked around her. The light in the ward was fading rapidly now, and the visitors to the other patients had all gone. She became aware of the irregularity of Ella's presence.

"I'm afraid it's time for you to go," said the Sister, but she spoke kindly, and as Ella looked back at Robert she nodded her head in understanding.

"Don't lose hope," she said. "God's ways are wonderful. I'm sure your husband will regain consciousness. You'll see. God will not fail to give him a happy death." She pointed back over her shoulder. "You ought to be greatly encouraged," she said, "by this marvelous example."

As she went toward the door, Ella caught a last glimpse of the scene behind the screen at the other end of the ward. The excitement had abated somewhat, and except for the Friar who stood at the end of the bed with his hands joined in prayer, and the candles that fluttered and strained upward, the scene was almost the same as it had been when Ella first became aware of it. The woman in black still sat with stiffly folded hands at the bedside, and the man, exhausted now, lay on his back staring up at the ceiling. But just as Ella turned to give a last look at Robert, the man started up wildly once more, with a terrifying shriek.

"I burn!" he shrieked. "I burn!" And from the sight of his tortured face, Ella turned away quickly and went out into the passage.

She told the girls about it.

"When the last shriek he gave didn't rouse Robert," she said that night when she was talking over the day with the girls, "when that shriek didn't rouse him, he'll die without coming to his senses. Oh, what will I do? What will I do?" And frantically she looked at the clock to see if there was yet time to have another Mass said for him. "If he only came to himself for five minutes," she said. "Five minutes would be enough."

"But even if he doesn't, Mother," said Mary, "you have no need to worry. Poor Father. He'll go straight to Heaven. What did he ever do that was wrong? He never hurt anyone in all his life."

Under her breath, Dolly muttered. "The only one he ever hurt was himself," she said. "He put his purgatory over him here in this world."

Ella wasn't satisfied.

"How do we know what sins he might have on his soul?" she cried, and she threw up her hands and began to wail. "I'll never rest an hour if he dies without recognizing the priest. What does anything matter as long as a person gets a happy death? Isn't it the only thing that counts in this world?"

And it seemed to her that morning would never come until she renewed her vigil at his bedside, where by now instead of the bags of oranges and apples there was an accumulation of crucifixes and blessed candles, holy water and medals, all of which by turns she pressed against his lips and his forehead and his hands in the hope that they would bring him back from the hopeless silence into which he had sunk.

When the next day came at last it passed in the same manner as the day before it. Robert's condition was unchanged. But there was no sign of the man who had occupied the bed at the end of the ward. When Robert's people asked about him the nurse said he had died shortly after Ella had left the hospital the previous night.

"It was an edifying sight," said the nurse. "To think that a man who wouldn't let the Name of God be mentioned in his presence should die clutching on to the priest's hand and crying and screaming like a child. Such an exemplary death! Is there any end to God's mercy? To think that a man like that should be given the grace to die such a death!" Then the nurse remembered Robert's state and she reddened. "Please God your husband will get the same grace," she said, and she glanced at the bed on which they were all accustomed now to seeing the motionless face of Robert. But suddenly as she glanced at him the nurse gave a startled cry and bent closer. Then she turned and caught Ella's arm. "His eyes are open!" she cried, and she rushed over to the bed, but Ella, who reached the bedside almost as quickly as she, pushed her aside with a violent arm.

"The crucifix!" she cried. "Let him see the crucifix!" and snatching it up she held it in front of him, almost pushing it into his face. "Robert!" she cried. "Robert! Look at the cross. Can you see it?" She stared into the open eyes, but there did not seem to be any answering response in them. "Can you see me at all?" she cried. And then, more anxiously still, she shook his arm. "Can you hear me?" she asked. "Can you hear me? I want you to repeat an act of contrition. Can you hear me? Keep your eyes on the crucifix." And while she held it in front of him, she looked around at the girls. "The priest!" she gasped. "What are you thinking about? Get the priest at once!" Then, turning back to the man on the bed, she entreated him to try and hear her. "I want you to repeat this after me, Robert," she said, and she began to enunciate the act of contrition. " 'O my God,' " she said, and waited for him to repeat the words. "Robert! Can you hear me? 'O my God.' Say that after me. 'O my God I am heartily sorry for ever having offended Thee.' Robert! Robert! Repeat it after me. Can't you hear me?" And the last words were almost a wail, because, although the light of recognition had flickered for a moment in his eyes, it had gone out again. She leaned closer over the bed.

"Robert! Don't you know me? It's Ellie; your own Ellie!" But in spite of her appeal it seemed as if there would be no change in the face on the pillow. Then suddenly a faint light flashed in the dark eyes of the dying man, and the lips moved as if they would say something. Ella put her face down to the pillow. Yes, he was saying something, but what it was, she could not hear. She bent still closer until she could feel his breath on her face, and then faint as the breath itself, she caught the word that with great difficulty was formed on the parched lips.

"Ellie!"

That was the word. Ella straightened her aching back with a sob of relief, and as the nurse came hurrying into the ward, followed by the Sister, she turned around to them, her worn face bathed in happiness.

"He has come to his senses," she cried. "He spoke to me." And then, tireless in her determination to achieve her end she bent down over the bed once more.

"Robert darling, you know me? You can hear me? It's your own Ellie. And she wants you to do something for her. She wants you to make an Act of Contrition. Repeat the words after me— 'O my God—' "

The girls crept closer, and the nurse, without saying anything, sat down on the chair beside the bed and took the thin wrist in her hand to feel its pulse. Then she looked at Robert's face.

"He's trying to say something," she said, for although no sound came from the lips, it seemed that the man was making some effort to speak by the way the muscles of the poor worn face had begun to work. They listened.

Then, scarcely audible, a few words struggled from his lips.

"My own Ellie!"

Ellie's face showed some relief, but there was still a certain anxiety in her eyes.

"Yes, yes, your own Ellie," she said impatiently. "But now, Robert, I want you to repeat something after me."

"Just a minute," said the nurse, and taking a spoon and a bottle she went over to the patient and forced something between his lips. "Now!" she said, nodding encouragingly to Ella.

Ella bent over him.

" 'O my God!' " she said. "Repeat that after me. Robert. 'O my God I am heartily sorry for ever having offended Thee.' Repeat that. 'O my God . . .' "

But it seemed as if Robert had slipped back into his world of darkness. His eyes were once more closed and the imperturbable look had settled once more on his ashen face.

"Robert! Robert!" Ella's voice implored him to hear her. The eyes opened again. "Don't slip back on me, Robert," she cried. "You know me, don't you? It's Ellie, Ellie!" she cried.

Then the dying man spoke again.

"Ellie!" he said. "Ellie!"

Although showing signs of exhaustion, Ella wasted no time.

"Repeat this after me," she cried. " 'O my God I detest all my sins,' " she said, and then, confused, she began to forget the wording of the prayer. " 'I am heartily sorry,' she said. " 'Never more to offend Thee.' " But now she was not looking at the silent lips, she was turning in despair to the Sister and the nurses. "What is keeping the priest?" she cried. "Why doesn't he come? This may be our only chance. He may slip back altogether after this!" She was distracted, and on the point of collapse.

But just then the priest appeared at the door. Under a white cloth he had the Sacrament for the dying.

"God is good," he said, by way of salutation to those around the bed, as they knelt down before the Presence he brought with him. Before he moved over to the bed, the priest stopped to whisper to the Sister. "If he wants to make his confession," he said, "I'd like you to draw back from the bedside. Just a few paces; that will be all that will be necessary."

Without waiting for any more those around the bed withdrew.

"The goodness of God!" cried the nun. "Two such miracles in the one day." And turning she took Ella's hand in hers. "God has heard your prayers!" she said. "You have a lot to be thankful for. I must admit there were times when I thought your husband would never regain consciousness."

Just then the priest, who had bent over the man in the bed, straightened up and looked back over his shoulder. He appeared to be in some difficulty. The nurse stood up and went over to him.

"Do you want something, Father?" she asked, and she prepared to hand him first the crucifix and then the holy water.

But the priest wanted Ella.

"I think he wants to say something to you," he said. "He keeps calling your name. It might be better if you remained within his range of vision."

Ella bent over the bed again.

"Ellie!" said the man in the bed, and he stared up into her eyes, and now to her joy they seemed once again to be clear and lucid and to shine with all the brightness of consciousness. "Ellie. My own darling girl," he said, and like the man that had died at the other end of the ward he struggled to raise himself on the pillows.

"He's near the end!" said the nurse to Mary, and she hastened to support him, but Robert pushed her aside. The nurse motioned to Ella then, and Ella put her arms around him and held him up. He turned his head and looked at her, and it seemed that he saw nothing else.

"Just the two of us!" he said, and he put up his hand and stroked her hair with a perfectly normal gesture. The onlookers exchanged glances of satisfaction but a minute afterward they were in doubt again, because although every minute he spoke more clearly, the words he uttered were almost inexplicable to them. "Your lovely golden hair," he said, and taken aback, they all looked at Ella's gray hair on which his hand had rested.

Ella continued to support him, but she turned frantically to the priest.

"What will I do?" she said. "Will I repeat the prayers?" The priest nodded his head. " 'O my God,' " said Ella. "Can you hear that, Robert? 'I am heartily sorry.' Can you hear that?" And this time Robert seemed to hear.

"Sorry?" he said after her, questioningly. Then he closed his eyes for a moment again, but when he opened them they were filled with a rapturous light, astonishing to behold in a face etched with the lines of an almost lifelong sadness and weariness.

"Yes, yes," said Ella eagerly, repeating the line that seemed to have caught his attention, while the priest nodded his acquiescence. " 'I am heartily sorry,' " she said, speaking slowly and distinctly.

Robert put out his hands and eagerly caught at her hands.

"Sorry?" he said again weakly, then his voice grew suddenly strong and vibrant. "There's nothing to be sorry about, my darling," he said. "We were unfortunate, that was all. It wasn't your fault. I wasn't much good. That was the trouble. I should never have taken you away from your comfortable home. I'm the one who should be sorry, not you." Then he raised himself higher in the bed, and some of the lines of hardship seemed to vanish from his face, and an arrogance that was like the arrogance of youth came back into his voice. "But I'm not sorry," he said. "You were all I wanted in the whole world. When I had you I had everything. Even when you spoke harshly to me, I knew it was because you were tired. I knew that I had failed you, and I always forgave you." He pressed her hand tighter. "Don't talk about being sorry," he said again, urgently searching her face for the effect of his words. "There's nothing to be sorry about. You always made me happy, just by being near me. Just to look at you made my heart brighter. Always. Always. It was always like that." He sighed then with a long peaceful sigh, and seeing that he had relaxed the nurse motioned Ella to lower him again on to the pillow. Back on the pillow he closed his eyes, then, but he closed them deliberately and not from fatigue, for a smile played over his face and showed that he was yielding to some happy thought. "The meadow," he said then, in a soft voice little more than a sighing breath. "Do you remember the meadow? How happy we were walking along the headland holding each other's hands." The smile grew deeper and sweeter. "You could never understand why we had to keep to the headland. You used to want to walk in the high grass. 'I'd love to wade through it like water.' You said that one day. Do you remember? You wanted to wade through and pick the clover that sweetened the air with its warm scent, and when I told you it would spoil the harvest, you wanted to trample it all down. You were so willful! So willful, my darling. That was what I loved best in you; your willfulness." Suddenly his voice grew stronger and there was a harsh note in it. "Your mother knew you were willful. That was why she was afraid to speak out against me. That was why she didn't do any more than throw out hints about my health. My health was all right then. It would have been all right if she had let us alone and let us stay where we were happy. We could have got a little cottage outside the town, with a small piece of land. That was what I always wanted." His voice was all harshness now. And suddenly he struggled to sit up in bed again. "I don't like that woman," he said.

Ella, who had been listening with suppressed sobs of remorse and joy, suddenly stopped sobbing. Her mother had been dead for years.

"I don't like her," said the man at the top of his voice. "I won't be humiliated by her. I'll take you away. I will!" He turned suddenly and his face was fierce. "Will you come with me?" he cried. "I'll make you happy. Trust me! Trust me, Ellie." The fierceness that flared up so suddenly died out all at once. "Trust me, Ellie," he said in a soft sweet voice, the voice of a young lover. "I'll make you happy. I promise I will. I know I can do it. We'll go away from here where we'll be alone; just the two of us. Just the two of us. You and I."

He closed his eyes again then, and Ella, who since the first mention of her mother had been sitting with a dazed look on her face, unable to comprehend what had happened, turned around with a vacant look at the priest. The priest moved over to the bedside.

"Perhaps after all it might be well for you to stand aside," he said, "where he wouldn't see you, and then I might be able to gain his attention." But when the priest came within his range of vision Robert's face changed. It grew dark again, and his eyes took on again the wild unnatural glitter.

"There's someone coming!" he shouted, warningly. "I think it's your sister Daisy. She'll want to come with us! And we don't want her, do we? It's so much nicer alone, just the two of us. Let's hide, Ellie. Let's hide, sweetheart. Let's get behind that tree over there!" Dragging his hand free from Ella he began to point wildly.

The priest shook his head, and moved back to the footrail of the bed where he began to confer earnestly with the nurse and the Sister. Ella sat still, stunned into silence. Dolly coughed nervously. She felt embarrassed at the incongruous intimacy of her father's outburst, even in delirium. She turned to Mary in her discomfort. But Mary was smiling strangely, and staring at her father with a secretive smile that was like a smile of complicity. Dolly was aware again, as she had been a few days earlier, of a great difference between herself and her sister. Mary was like the dying man. She was more like her mother. She looked at her sister's face and then at the face of her father, but as she looked at him Robert began to move his lips again.

"Just the two of us!" he said, the look of rapturous happiness returning to his face.

And something about that rapturous look caused the nurse to start suddenly to her feet and make a sign to the priest. The priest, after one startled glance at Robert, without waiting to stir from where he stood, raised his hand in the blessing of conditional absolution. The nurse put her arm quickly around Ella's shoulders to lead her away.

Ella looked up at the priest's raised hand, and then, not comprehending what was happening, she glanced feverishly at Robert. But the serene smile that had taken the place of the rapture of a moment before deceived her, and she did not recognize in it the serenity of death, until her daughters, both together, put their arms about her and began to reassure her.

"Never mind, Mother. Never mind! He led a good life. He never did anyone any harm."

Then Ella comprehended. Throwing up her arms she began to scream.

And as she was led out of the ward a few minutes later, she was still screaming and sobbing, and it was utterly incomprehensible to her that God had not heard her prayers, and had not vouchsafed to her husband the grace of a happy death.